THAT'S WHAT I LIKE
(About the South)

THAT'S WHAT I LIKE
(About the South)

And Other New Southern Stories for the Nineties

Edited by
George Garrett
and
Paul Ruffin

University of South Carolina Press

Copyright © 1993 University of South Carolina

Published in Columbia, South Carolina, by the
University of South Carolina Press

Manufactured in the United States of America

Library of Congress Cataloging-in-Publication Data

That's what I like (about the South) and other new southern stories
    for the nineties / edited by George Garrett and Paul Ruffin.
        p.   cm.
    Includes bibliographical references.
    ISBN 0–87249–863–8 (hard : alk. paper).—ISBN 0–87249–864–6
(pbk. : alk. paper)
    1. Short stories, American—Southern States.   2. American
fiction—20th century.   3. Southern States—Fiction.   I. Garrett,
George P., 1929–   .   II. Ruffin, Paul.
PS551.T48   1993
813'.0108975—dc20   92–43168

CONTENTS

EDITORS' NOTE

We don't plan to waste a lot of space here, space that ought to be used for fiction. And we have an introduction, and a very good one, too, by Fred Chappell, who says the literary things that do need saying. So all we want to do is to tell you a little about how this book came to be in the first place.

We had been thinking about it—the subject, not the book—for a good while. Seemed to us and to others that the usual places and sources for contemporary Southern writing did not begin to show the variety of what our writers are doing. It seemed to us (and still does) that what didn't fit in with the definitions and generalizations of some prominent critics and editors—usually old-fashioned, shrugging, weary definitions—ended up being left out. It seemed to us that Southern writing is alive and kicking and going off in all kinds of directions as this old century staggers to its end. We decided to do something about it if we could; and we began, between us, to solicit all kinds of writers, just about every Southern writer you or we ever heard of, planning at that point to bring out a special issue of *The Texas Review* and, later, if it could be done, a larger gathering of material.

Well, you know how it goes. Some writers weren't interested. Some writers were interested but had nothing available to submit. We were, after all, looking for *original* material, if possible. All of the stories from *The Texas Review* were, of course, original to that publication, and most of the other stories in this anthology are original to it. However, we were interested in people, the writers, and *their* choices of what they wished to be represented by. In some cases, after due consideration, a writer wanted to submit a story that had already been published somewhere or other. That was fine by us.

Even while we were busy putting together the special issue of *The Texas Review*, George Garrett was also working with *Chronicles* magazine (March 1991) to put together a feature on Southern writing and writers. It was there that we first encountered Fred Chappell's "Ancestors." Of course, Fred was already signed on to do our Introduction, and he had his modest doubts about including the story also. We didn't have any doubts. We considered the story absolutely indispensable to and for this collection, so we ignored Fred's protestations. Also from that same issue of *Chronicles* comes our Afterword by Madison Smartt Bell.

Here, then, we have stories, stories of all kinds by all kinds of Southern writers, some of the honored old-timers and a lot of newer names and faces—some of them, we would guess, brand new to a lot of readers. You will notice that any number of fairly well-known Southern writers are missing from the lineup. It would take three or four volumes this size to include all the deserving story writers in the South these days. That, in itself, says something. Meanwhile we offer here a broad sampling from the best of contemporary Southern short-story writers. They come from all over, from Virginia to Texas, and they write about the whole wide world. The unity of the collection is more than purely regional. It is the unity of excellence, living proof that in this final decade of the century, Southern writing and Southern writers are doing well, working with a creative energy which is undiminished and, indeed, thriving.

George Garrett
Paul Ruffin

ACKNOWLEDGMENTS

Most of the stories were written for this anthology (and its earlier version—*Contemporary Southern Short Fiction: A Sampler, The Texas Review*, 1990).

The following are reprinted by permission of the authors: "Ancestors," © 1991 by Fred Chappell, first appeared in *Chronicles*; "The Hungarian Countess," © 1990 by Kelly Cherry, first appeared in *My Life and Dr. Joyce Brothers* (Algonquin Books); "The Field of Lost Shoes," © 1991 by Alyson Hagy, first appeared in *Hardware River* (Poseidon Press); "Out of the Blue," © 1989 by Beverly Lowry, first appeared in *Southwest Review*; "Weeds," © 1990 by Bobbie Ann Mason, first appeared in *Boston Globe Magazine*; "Distance," © 1990 by Eve Shelnutt, appeared in *Western Humanities Review* and *Manoa*; "Time and Tide in the Southern Short Story," © 1991 by Madison Smartt Bell, first appeared in *Chronicles*.

THAT'S WHAT I LIKE
(About the South)

INTRODUCTION

The Good Songs Behind Us:
Southern Fiction of the 1990s
Fred Chappell

When Scarlet tells us that tomorrow is another day, she gives
utterance to a sentiment that Southerners, male and female, black and
white, feel deeply. The past may be something to cherish or to jettison,
to remember or to forget, but it is most of all something to get over, a
trauma in need of healing. Tomorrow is a situation that must be made
up anew, even though the materials from which it shall be stitched
together are faded and patched and sad and tattered. The individual
recognizes an obligation to transform the history, personal or local or
cultural, that he or she is burdened with. That is why the characters
in Southern fiction can be so loudly violent or so dreamily passive, why
they keep digging at the roots of situations; they are trying to hammer
the circumstances of the past into a future that transcends these
circumstances. When they are overcome by the enormity of the task,
they may retreat into themselves and dream dreams and swoon with
visions. Or they may attempt, in some overwhelming bafflement of
emotion, to lay forcible hands upon events and wrench them into a
pattern that gives expression to a personal destiny.

In Madison Jones's "Rage," Herman Coker tries to make the community believe that he is responsible for a series of murders. His actions
were "predictable," the author tells us,

and understandable too, up to a point. He had grown up in a black slum in Birmingham, in a two-room tenement apartment that . . . a farmer wouldn't keep his hogs in. There were six children and the mother but no father that Herman could remember. Until she died when Herman was seventeen his mother worked as cook and maid for a white woman, a job that made her travel twenty miles by bus back and forth every day except Sunday. Herman saw the white woman two or three times and later, after he learned to hate, remembered her with hatred both for his mother's toil and for the ugliness of that wrinkled old white face.

For Herman Coker this wrinkled ugly white face is the face of history; the murders that he mendaciously confesses to are the ones in his heart, his revenge upon history. This part of Herman's story ends in a darkly comic anticlimax, the way stories about quixotic quests generally do. Herman is punished for a crime that the story has made seem a by-product of his fury against the past.

It is difficult to wreak vengeance upon history because it is difficult to define that history. We cannot trust others to report the historical facts for us because they have no better vantage point upon it than we do. History is pervasive; certain poets—Robert Penn Warren, James Applewhite, Robert Morgan, Donald Davidson, and Allen Tate—have posited the thesis that history is mystically but nevertheless physically present in the Southern landscape, in the soil itself. Some Southern fiction writers have made much of this notion; for William Faulkner and James Dickey, for James Still and Wendell Berry and Andrew Lytle, the chthonic forces of the very earth hold obscure but powerful sway over the motives of their characters. These characters tread upon their personal history, they are immersed in it, they breathe it. And yet the lineaments of this history are ambiguous and shifting; the power of history over the characters is undeniable, even though the sources of this power are not easily located.

In "About Loving Women," Ellen Douglas employs memory as a trope for history, and her description of a singular kind of memory may serve as a description of the way history works powerfully but almost invisibly behind and inside Southern fiction:

> You know how there are some memories you're sure belong to you—
> because you've never shared them—like standing by the basin when you
> were three and watching the old lady who was live-in housekeeper the

year your mother broke her pelvis and had to stay in traction for two months. You're leaning against the basin. Your head comes up just high enough so you can rest your chin on the cool smooth curving surface. You're looking up and she (the old lady) opens her mouth and *takes out her teeth*. And then, while you're watching (you can't believe it's happening—she never says a word the whole time and seems not to know you're there), she dips her toothbrush in a can of powder and brushes the fronts and sides and corners and then she rinses them off and *puts them back in her mouth*. How is such a thing possible? Does anyone know about this weird and scary, this magical skill of hers? You believe without even thinking about it . . . that no one is supposed to know.

"You believe without even thinking about it": the phrase limns a Southerner's position in regard to history. The Southerner believes even when rationality says that the belief is impossible. The details here are accurate, surely; this must have been just exactly how it happened when the old lady scrubbed her dental plates. Yet the details are too real; the focus is in extreme close-up, and the objects and actions are magnified in scale and intensity because of the child's angle of vision and her gullibility about experience. The child believes that the event, being magical, must be kept secret. "Something awful may happen if you tell."

I should be unhappy to think that I have done "About Loving Women" an injury by turning the author's paragraph toward the direction of allegory. Ellen Douglas probably had little ambition to philosophize about history and the Southern writer when she set down these keenly sensitive sentences. Even so, one of her themes is the nature of memory and the effects that the past manages to work upon the present. At the end of "About Loving Women" Charles, the narrator, says to his friend in speaking about the loss of a woman: "And you and I, Henry—we can't go back to being the ones we were before she came."

The Southern writer is entranced by Southern cultural history because it is the only story there is. *Once upon a time things were the way they were supposed to be. Then something happened. Since that point, things have never been the same.* Since that point, since that single enormous event occurred, we are not the same people we were before, and our children will have to be different from all the children who lived before our time. Not even the land is the same as it was before, and it records the evidence of that change and our subsequent sorrowful history. We inhabit a fallen world where blind ignorance has replaced our early succulent innocence. The Southerner's history, whether cultural or personal, contains but one large controlling incident: betrayal.

The most dramatic treatment of this theme in Southern short fiction is Faulkner's "A Rose for Emily." That tale is not present in this volume except for the traces it leaves in other stories; it belongs to an earlier era than this book encompasses. But I do not know that its central allegorical intention has been thoroughly remarked. Miss Emily embodies a South who takes her own justice upon the Northerner who has betrayed and attempted to desert her; yet their union is indissoluble even though the death of one of the parties is required to sustain this union. Faulkner's view of our history, that the South so loved America that she was willing to tear it apart in order to keep it inviolate, is debatable—but it is his view.

In Jill McCorkle's "Final Vinyl Days," the terms are sharply reduced from those that Faulkner employed, but the old tale of betrayal, estrangement, and the uncertain future is still recognizable. McCorkle's no-longer-young narrator still keeps his college-kid job as a salesman at a record store so that he can stay close to the music he admires. But he is having trouble with his philistine employer. "I told him he was getting too far away from the old stuff, the good stuff, but he insisted *we go with the flow.* He didn't want me monopolizing the sound system with too much of the old stuff; he said Neil Young made his skin crawl." In the narrator's eyes no one has remained faithful to the first promise of rock and roll—not the aging audience, not the performers, and especially not the industry with its continually changing technologies. "I had no choice but to give into CDs. And yeah, they sound great, that's true. It's just the principle of the thing, your hand forced to change."

That may be the Southerner's credo, whether he consciously subscribes to it or not. The old ways may not have been better than the new ones—indeed, they may have been worse—yet they were the *necessary* ways. The way the world used to be was the way it had to be, but our present world has been arbitrarily and irrationally flung together. When things were worse, we had that fact for a certainty; now that they are better—easier, at least, and more comfortable—we can't say what we've got, except puzzlement, disillusionment, and the urge to mend what is unmendable. McCorkle's record salesman states it memorably: "And now I've come to this: Final Vinyl Days, the end of an era. Perfectly round black vinyl discs, their jackets faded, sit on the small table before my checkout and await extinction. I stare across the street, the black asphalt made shiny by the drizzling rain, the traffic light blinking red and green puddles in the gray light where a mammoth parking deck is under construction. There I see the lights of the store we compete with, Record City, and I can't help but wonder when they'll change their name: CD Metropolis."

It is tempting to think it is a continuous awareness of history that makes the Southerner so avid for symbolism. The world in present time is a sort of palimpsest, an overlay of images upon past time. This palimpsest only partially obscures what came before it, and it comments ironically—even sardonically—on those parts of the past that it lets show through. For almost every situation a Southern writer portrays in present time, there is a spoken or unspoken contrast with a past situation. The writer may be warmly hospitable toward strangers, but Southerners will remain wary of them: not because they came from a different place than his own, but because they inhabit a different era.

Mary Lee Settle's "Dogs" takes this theme as its subject and treats it about as straightforwardly as fiction can treat a theme. The city of Norfolk, Virginia, as she portrays it is literally a palimpsest, images of past and present in the same frame but still separate, each of them a commentary upon the other. Norfolk as we find it in the old photographs still looks, Settle tells us, "like raw and naked farmland with spindly trees defining the new roads. Now the trees almost meet over the streets. The huge solid houses have aged into brick and stone monuments to a past when everyone was 'well-off' and life was supposed to be more stable." This landscape embodies the idea of a past a Southerner recognizes, even when he knows the idea to be incomplete, or even false, as Settle's narrator admits: "I don't believe it was [more stable], because a residue of the times remains and can be read like books about Southern stereotypes, when relatives lived together and got on each other's nerves, old women developed strange habits, men committed suicide when they lost their money or their minds, and plain people were no kin."

This latter sentence gives us the facts of the case with such force and dark knowledge that we can hardly doubt them. Yet facts can be brought into line with ideas by means coolly insouciant, casually ironic: "The whole district is now on the Historic Register, and nobody can put up a fence or a garage without the approval of a committee appointed by the city council."

The calm acceptance of the ironies implicit in that gesture—listing the whole district in the Historic Register—ought to give pause to those who so forwardly accuse Southerners of ancestor worship. Yes, the charge is broadly true, but it is ignorantly made. A Southerner will revere his forebears not because they were smarter, braver, or more virtuous than he believes himself to be, but because they inscribed with their lives the History that he sees as a counterpart of Nature; it is almost as large as Nature in his thinking and, as we have remarked, not entirely separate from it. Our ancestors did not simply die; they died in the cause of the past, in the service of the History that they lived in order deliberately to create. Professor Marlowe, the narrator of Alyson Hagy's "The Field of Lost Shoes," has it explained to him: "An old claw hammer banjo player I once knew had put it like this: *My dead daddy played best and his daddy played better before him, I done lost the good songs behind me.*"

"The Field of Lost Shoes" tells again the story of past betrayal, present disillusionment, and a bleak future. Marlowe's former lover desires to stoke up the old relationship again, even though she is still married and now in the company of her young son. But Marlowe turns his back on the opportunity, though with deep regret: "I wanted to hold her. I wanted to make love to her for a hundred dark and separate nights. But the truth was there beneath the light, powdery makeup that had softened on her cheeks. My Ellen was old—not so much in body as in heart." Marlowe knows that the past cannot be recaptured, that both he and Ellen must make do with a future in which their shared past will be always present but always powerless.

The story is set against the background of the Civil War battle of New Market, perhaps the most valiant and heartbreaking military encounter in Southern history. The former lovers meet at the tourist center of the battle site: "Ellen seemed to think it would be the perfect place for me—for us—because I was a historian, just like her husband." The site is tended by an old gentleman for whom the past holds a greater degree of reality than the present. When he notices Marlowe's car license plate, he does not identify the professor by present place or in past time: "I noticed you were from Tennessee," he says. "The Volunteer State. Bloody Murphreesboro."

When Marlowe refuses to resume his former relationship with Ellen, they quarrel and she retreats from him. But his immediate thought is of the site attendant: "I thought first of the old man with the broom, wondering what he would think of such behavior. He would probably find us profane—whispering and shouting about love in a hall full of valor and death."

Hagy implies that our mature lives are products of civil wars. We have fought for our lonely independence against our parents, our children, our spouses, our lovers. The legacies of our histories, personal and cultural, have insured that we shall again rebel most fiercely against these same histories. The South with its love of tradition, with its reverence for the old order (the same one that Katherine Anne Porter so mercilessly exposed), is also the most fruitful seedbed of revolution. The Civil War began in the South as a conservative movement; the civil rights struggle too began in the South, and its later betrayal by radicals like Stokeley Carmichael and David Duke makes that struggle look like another kind of conservative movement. In the strictest sense of the term, the civil rights movement was conservative, since its immediate aim was to preserve individual freedom and dignity from legalistic and bureaucratic oppression. Perhaps it has always been a duty of conservative politics to protect opportunities for liberal thought and spirit.

At any rate, there is a particularly close relationship between Southern cultural history and individual Southern lives that the literature has always been at pains to remark and ponder. Professor Marlowe takes Ellen's son Timmy on a walking tour of the New Market battlefield, the place where victory had seemed impossible, but where the South had triumphed. "The Confederates had been outnumbered and outgunned. Lee was across the mountains. Stonewall Jackson was dead. But the Yankees had been turned back, the farmers left free to cultivate their wheat and corn." As they walk along, Marlowe tells Timmy the story, and the lad asks him if he would have been scared if he had been in the battle. The man admits that he would have been afraid to die. The boy is sure of his own courage—"I wouldn't be scared"—and a moment later pulls himself "onto the orchard fence, aiming his fingers toward Yankee territory."

Marlowe does not for an instant doubt Timmy's avowal of bravery; it was "the perfect courage of boys" that bought the victory at New Market. But he knows too that courage prevails only in the storm of battle and that victory does not endure:

> And I wished I could explain everything to him—his mother, my broken feelings, myself. . . . I wished hard for the impossible: that I could tell him about the inevitable douse of failure and the struggle to capture even one inch of our lives. But I didn't. Given the burdens of my age and the buoyancy of his, I could only follow his launch into the fife melody of a lie, watch him run with its simple purity across that field, gold and green and now untrodden, barely led by the twin barrels of our long, misshapen shadows.

I have not desired to advance any new thesis here. Southern literature is now almost as legendary a part of Southern history as the battles and the politics. Its salient qualities have been closely described: "The defining characteristics of Southern fiction: deep involvement in place, family bonds, celebration of eccentricity, a strong narrative voice, themes of racial guilt and human endurance, local tradition, a sense of impending loss, a pervasive sense of humor in the face of tragedy, an inability to leave the past behind." There is enough strength in these materials to establish Southern literature, in American terms at least, as king of the mountain.

But the Southern writer is likely to be set upon by some imp of the perverse so that he or she wishes to rebel against tradition. He may look upon the opulent mansion of Southern fiction and feel a nettlesome impulse to set this house on fire. There may be a problem for a writer in being too well endowed with a literary culture, so that the urge to work against it, even to fleer at it, is irresistible.

Prominent among the literary dissenters would be such authors as Calder Willingham, Madison Smartt Bell, Harry Crews, Dabney Stuart, Lewis Nordan, Kelly Cherry, and Barry Hannah. In fact, a Southern writer would have to be a bit obtuse not to feel that the modernist legacy of Faulkner, Tennessee Williams, and the Fugitives was in some respects onerous. A contemporary author may well decide—it will have to be a deliberate intellectual decision—that the "irredeemable blood guilt" which so perturbed Faulkner no longer exists, that the nearly mortal wound delivered by our Civil War has been annealed, and that the old themes tried and true are gone with the wound. Perhaps it will seem that our familiar transgressions—racial injustice, chauvinism, orgiastic violence, and so forth—have become trite and that even our gossip has lost its savor; maybe it is time to move on to other vices, other rumors.

So it is that readers can confidently look forward to such forthcoming literary experiments as George Garrett's novel about Florida dog-racing, *The Sand and the Furry;* Alan Cheuse's historical tale about a medieval monk's struggle with melancholy, *The Sad Bede;* and R. H. W. Dillard's touching portrait of the Romantic Comedian, *A Straight Man Named Desirée.* Works like these are as certainly in our future as kudzu.

Because the rebel impulse will not give the Southerner, and even the well-respected Southern author, peace. A well-established part of Southern literary tradition is that it not only tolerates but warmly invites parody and even self-parody. Sometimes it is impossible to distinguish between seriously intended work and blague. Faulkner's story "Afternoon of a Cow" was first published under a pseudonym as a parody of William Faulkner, but then became an integral, and irreplaceable, part of a serious work, *The Hamlet.* Harry Crews and Barry Hannah and Lewis Nordan carry on that particular tradition of Faulkner's.

And so does R. H. W. Dillard with his story "That's What I Like (About the South)." Here is a work so well versed in Southern literature and in the tradition of Southern self-parody that it has ventured to include even the parodies among the targets of its satire. Dillard's story is an attempt to be the last word about Southern literary self-consciousness. But no matter how successful "That's What I Like" is as a story, it will fail in its ambition to be the last word. Southerners never stop talking—especially about themselves. The "puny inexhaustible voice" that Faulkner prophesied will continue even until the end of time has an unmistakable Southern accent.

Richard Bausch

BILLBOARD

Around the time all hell starts breaking loose with Eddie and you
know who, I keep getting this dream where I'm on a big billboard with
a cigarette in my fingers, and it says "Alive with pleasure." Big letters
six feet tall. My face ten times bigger than that. Handsome as shit. I
go by this thing on my way to Betty's. I'm flying, doubled up on this
motor scooter, a tiny little mother that makes a squeak like an un-
oiled wagon or something. I'm heading over to see her, even knowing
the whole thing and living absofuckinglutely in the middle of it. And
there it is, bigger than shit. This billboard. Me. Looking good. Looking
like Hollywood.

I'm roiling around in broken glass under my skin, right? But it's like,
you know, Betty's waiting for me and I'm going to bring her over there
and park and wait for her to look up and notice something. Hey,
Betty—look who's alive with pleasure. Only in the dream I can't find
her house. It's gone. So I'm driving all over Fauquier, and then I know
all over again that she's gone off with my own goddamn brother and
the rest of the dream I'm looking for both of them even knowing I'm
asleep, like it might be fun to kill them both in there where it doesn't
matter, and you can wake up.

You figure it means something I'm on a fucking scooter?

I'm given another opinion, of course. From Jane that works with me
in the stereo department. "Everything means something," she says,
very importantly.

We've been doing a lot of this kind of talking. I don't think it means anything in particular. Right?

I'm thinking, Fucking Eddie and that convertible Olds. My own little kid brother.

And it took my mother telling me. "Larry," she says, "you got something else you want to do tonight?"

Like that.

"What're you getting at?" I say, though I guess I know.

"Eddie's out with Betty. They headed north, son. Getting married."

"Eddie?" I say. "Betty?"

And she nods like it's news they're dead.

Well, they might as well be. The two of them traipsing all over New York and her wearing clothes I bought her, since I'm the one with the job. Clothes I bought her and listening to tapes I made for her. And down here I have this dream, running around on a scooter. My face on a billboard.

"You know what I think it means?" Jane says. "I think it means you got a big head."

"Jesus Christ, Jane."

"Well, there it is. It's just your head in the picture, right?"

"I don't know why I tell you anything," I say. But it's fairly good-natured.

"Well, it is your head, right? Big as a house?"

"It's my face."

"Well, your face is on your head."

"It's a picture. Like the one on Interstate 29."

"That's Jeff Bridges, id'n it?"

"This is a dream," I say.

"No, the real one. Id'n that Jeff Bridges?"

You figure Jane's just trying to work me a little?

Of course, talking to Jane is always like trying to give complicated instructions to a foreigner.

"I know what it means," she says. "You're not as big as you wish you were. That's why you're on the scooter."

"No," I say. "I owned a scooter last year."

"You never rode it," she says, sings. When she thinks she's got me, she sings her sentences.

"It doesn't matter whether I rode it or not," I say.

Jane's tall. Smart. Skinny and not much up top. You get the feeling if she melted she'd go on a long, long time. A river of Jane. Everywhere I go at work, there she is.

"I don't think your dream means anything," she says.

"You said before you thought everything means something."

"Only if you want it to."

"Bullshit," I say.

"That could mean something," she says.

"A repeated dream means something."

"You're mad at Eddie."

"Raging," I say.

"He fell in love," she says. "Poor guy."

"He snuck around behind my back," I say.

"I think it's like in the movies," she says. "All romantic and sweet, like it should have music playing behind it."

"Shut up, Jane," I say.

"Did you love her?" she says.

"She was engaged to me," I say.

"Yes, but did you love her."

"I don't know what love means," I say. It's what I used to say to Betty. "I was going to marry her."

"But is that what you used to tell Betty?" she says.

Sometimes I wonder what goes through Jane's mind when I'm quiet, like is it my thoughts.

"Well?" she says.

"Lay off me," I say.

"Tell me what you used to tell Betty."

I tell her I'm not in the habit of giving reports like that about my love life.

"I bet Eddie said something a little more definite than he doesn't know what love means."

"All right," I say. I used to tell her, "Go, go, go, don't stop, don't stop, do it."

"Fiction," she sings. "I hear fiction."

This goes on all day in the store. Nobody comes in. Mr. Calhoun is going to go bust. "Put up a billboard," I tell him. "You have to advertize."

"I heard that," Jane sings.

In the stockroom there's some boxes to break up, so I break them up. I wreck them. Boom. Boom, with a hatchet from the hardware section. Splitting Eddie's skull. Splitting Betty's. Boom, little brother. Boom, Betty-bye.

"I heard you back there," Jane says.

"I wasn't striving for quiet," I say.

"Tell me more about your dream."

There's nothing else to tell. So I say that.

"You never find her house, right?"

"Right," I say.

"Want to go find it tonight?"

"Why," I say. "I know where it is."

"Maybe it'll help," she says.

No. I know there's no one there to meet us, no one to see me pull up with long Jane in the car. Another girl. Betty's house is empty. And the next thing I do is walk over to the hardware section for a gas can.

"You're asking for it," Jane says, behind me. Singing again.

"Look," I say. "Go find somebody else to bother."

"I'm the voice of your conscience," she says.

"Fuck off," I say.

"Okay," she sings.

But then when it's closing time she's all hot to come with me. I tell her no.

"I know what you're going to do, Larry."

And she does. I can see that much. I may not know when my fiancée is getting set to run off with my brother, but I can see when somebody's figured out my plans. "What'll you do if I don't take you?" I say.

"It would be a real crisis of conscience for me," she says.

I don't have any desire to listen to more of this kind of talk, so I take her with me and we drive to the Gulf station and fill the can up. I think I might tie her up somewhere and let her spend the night worrying about the creatures in the wild, how scared she is of snakes. But it feels almost ordinary with her sitting there on the passenger side, waiting for me to get back in. She smiles like it's perfectly normal to go out in the woods and burn a house down with everyfuckingthing in it. We head on out to Betty's house. This little cottage out past the graveyard behind the Safeway. Betty's own house. The gas is smelling the inside of the car up. Jane opens her window and sticks her head out.

"You know, this is against the law," she says.

"I'm stunned and disappointed," I say.

"I can't hear you," she says. "The wind."

"I said I know it's against the law."

"Sorry."

You figure there's something intentional about how she can't hear me?

We get to the turnoff to Betty's little house. There's the billboard. We look at it.

"Jeff Bridges," she says.

"It doesn't say so."

"Well, it ain't you, Larry."

"I didn't say it was."

She stares at it. "He doesn't look like a smoker."

"He's just somebody in a picture," I say.

"Hey, Larry," she says, "you remember when you went off to join the Air Force?"

"No," I say. "It slipped my mind until you mentioned it. Was I ever in the Air Force?"

"You remember how you kissed Betty and then shook hands with little Eddie, how old was he?"

"Fourteen," I say, remembering how sick he got after his sixteenth birthday, seeing myself shaking his fourteen-year-old hand and then being there, like I'm dreaming it. I've got power to see the future, and knowing he's going to be sicker than shit in two years makes me smile.

"Think of it," Jane says. "Time just flies."

"What about it?" I say.

"Well, you're not as hurt as you are mad. I think you'd be more hurt if you really loved Betty."

This is the kind of thing she's just as likely to say. I was crazed about Betty. Nobody ever saw anything like her, and she belonged to me.

When I was with her, I was big as that face on the son-of-a-bitching billboard.

I pull into the road toward her house. I'm going to burn it to the ground no matter what. I don't have the slightest trouble finding it.

"Okay," I say.

"I was going to tell you something else about when you joined the Air Force."

"I don't want to hear it," I say.

"He looked up to you," she says. "You were big as any hero to him. He told me. I did too, of course."

I get out of the car and then reach into the back seat for the gas can. The house is back in the trees.

"Larry," she says. "Wait for me."

I don't stop. She's coming along behind me, and then she's next to me. "Maybe we can run away after this," she says.

And I'm not sure I hear her right. When I stop, she stops.

"They'll be after you," she says, and she looks down.

"How're they going to know?" I say.

"I'll tell them?" She smiles.

"Wait a minute," I say. "Let me sit down so I can get it straight. You want us to run away together or you'll tell on me?"

"I know it's ridiculous," she says.

I walk on back to the car and put the can in the trunk, with this goddamn ache, like I knew I'd probably never go through with it, anyway. And—but, see—I'm totally at a loss, too. Totally thwarted, which is one of her words. It comes to me that I might tie her to a tree and let the ants crawl, I confess it. Let the ants thwart her around a little bit. But I don't, of course. I'm not half as bad when it's something other than wood and nails.

So we ride without a word back to town and she asks me will I take her home. I do. She asks me in.

"No," I say.

"We've had some kind of breakthrough," she says. "What do you think?"

"I think I'll get drunk," I say.

And she says, "I guess this means we're not running away."

"I wouldn't think so," I say.

"I like the romance of it, I must admit," she says.

Her mother's already waiting in the open doorway of the house.

"Time to go," I tell her.

"I don't suppose you want to kiss me," she says.

And I say, "No."

"Ever?" she says.

"Why?" I say.

And she says, "You can't be serious."

I don't say anything.

"Wonderful date," she says. "We looked at a billboard. We didn't burn a house down." And in the light from her mother's having put on the floodlamps that border the yard, she looks almost pretty.

"Well?" she says. "I had fun."

"Fun," I say.

"I have fun with you," she says. "Even looking at billboards and not burning houses."

I don't even know what to say.

"I know," she says. "It's ridiculous."

You figure there's any significance to her saying it's ridiculous?

Madison Smartt Bell

HAMMERHEAD

Simsy hunkered on a dune, chewing a tail of her lank gray hair, watching her granddaughter wandering in and out of the last low ripples of the waves on the beach. It was low tide; the surf hit the packed sand slap after muted slap. No moon, but there was enough starlight to catch the white foaming line of each breaker as it came in. Light on her feet, Mary Rose would move into each wave just enough to wet her ankles and then dart back. From where Simsy crouched, the dark slick of every wave seemed to curve up and over the girl, before crashing down harmlessly far away from her.

Simsy hooked a finger through the ring of her coverall's zip and yanked it down. She shrugged out of most of the garment and adjusted herself to piss on the ground. Having scrubbed her fingers with a fistful of sand, she rezipped the coverall, took a package of Drum from one of its many pockets, and rolled herself a cigarette quickly in the dark. The wind was coming up from the south, sweeping through the phone-pole stilts of the long pier fifty yards away, blowing Simsy's hair across her eyes. She shook her head back, licked the edge of the cigarette and put it unlit in her skinny lips. The saucer-shaped lights of the pier had begun to snap out one by one from its farthest end and in the greater darkness the *hush-hush* sound of the waves was deepened.

At Simsy's low whistle, Mary Rose turned out of the surf and came running toward her, bare legs flicking pale against the wet-stained sand. Simsy lifted the duffel bag, a long watermarked green thing Marty had saved from the army, and touched the girl's shoulder with her other hand to guide her along. From the strip of parking behind the dunes came the motor of the gatekeeper's truck, cranking and failing, then revving up high. When they had reached the stilts of the pier, they stopped there and waited until the last sound of the truck had died off down the road. Away through the phone poles the beach took a smooth curve off to the sound, and though a few porch lights still burned, widely separate, almost all of the summer houses were silent and dark. The wind dropped and the ocean became so calm that there was a long glassine silence between the moments when each wave turned itself smoothly under to break.

Mary Rose had wandered over to the next row of stilts and stooped to paddle in the pool left in the depression carved by the suck of water around a pole. Simsy heard the girl catch her breath. The water threading through her fingers sparkled with its own green light. Simsy watched as Mary Rose, entranced, traced lines of foxfire from pole to pole. In the dark of the moon she might have written her own name in the phosphorescence if she had been old enough to know how.

Simsy waited a while. No hurry, hours to dawn. When the girl lost interest in the glow and straightened up, Simsy beckoned and then led her up the slope of the dune to a point behind the gate where the pier's platform was little more than head high, her sneakers crunching and slipping a little in the dry sand. She stopped and hefted the duffel bag and rolled it onto the planks overhead. Mary Rose stretched up her arms to be lifted and Simsy swung her up, pushed her high until she could get hold of the single loose strand of rusting barbwire and pull herself the rest of the way onto the pier. The girl swiveled on her knees and pulled the wire higher so that Simsy could get under it more easily once she herself had shinnied up the pole, gripping it with the soles of her shoes.

Simsy curved her back concave as a cat might do, passing under the wire, and came up standing on her feet. A stone's throw back down the pier, the little bait shop was shuttered and dark, and through the slats of the padlocked gate there gleamed one street lamp still alight over the sand-scattered parking places. Mary Rose rolled back onto her behind and stuck her feet out and looked up. Simsy got the little tennis shoes out of another one of her coverall pockets and hunkered down to give them to the girl. Mary Rose put the shoes on and slowly tied them while Simsy watched. The old gapped planks were splintery, they both knew that. At home or anywhere else, Simsy would talk to Mary Rose as often and easily as she might have to anyone, or to herself, but during these night raids on the pier she usually chose instead to enter into the girl's strange silence. Maybe they would come out of it together when they left the pier one of these nights. But Mary Rose had not spoken a human word since Marty did it to her, and that was over a year ago. She was a year behind starting school because of it. Simsy had weasled it out of Marty himself eventually. Her own daughter Nellie was too weak for it, too drunk and drugged out even to notice there was something the matter with Mary Rose, probably. The only thing that delayed Simsy from cutting Marty up into shark bait was the question of who would take care of the child if she, Simsy, had to go to the pen. To do it she would have to be sure of not getting caught, and she was still putting her mind to this problem when Marty took it off her hands by getting his pig self killed in a motorcycle wreck.

Done with her shoes, Mary Rose jumped up and trotted toward the far end of the pier. Partway, she ran the metal poles of the deadened lamps like a barrel race, ringing them softly with the palm of her hand, and partway she skipped along on one leg or the other, landing herself dead center on each plank. *Step on a crack—break your mother's back.* . . . Simsy walked along behind her, humping the duffel, which gurgled slightly at one end.

They passed over the surf where it licked and slowly pulled back at the poles below them. Then there were only the long slow rollers surging forward and returning a long way down under the cracks between the wide boards of the flooring. It was a very long pier. Toward the end it widened out and ended in a blunted T. Mary Rose tagged the farthest railing and buttonhooked back, circling Simsy, who went on to the end before she set the duffel down. The tide was dead low, the measured rush of the surf against of the beach seemed distant now. So clear as it was, the Milky Way itself looked like a shelf of cloud.

Simsy opened the duffel and took out a flashlight bolted to a heavy battery and flicked the switch. She set it on one of the plank seats that were nailed at intervals to the railing. Its lens was masked with a rag of sheet, which made the light too ambiguous to be very noticeable at a distance. But Mary Rose came back toward it like a moth.

The stubby fiberglass rod was on top of the duffel. Simsy propped it against the rail and then lifted out the heavy plastic bag of water and set it down in the wavery oval of flashlight. Mary Rose crouched down opposite to stare through the clear plastic at the two good-sized mullet and one spot-tail bass swimming inside. The fish bunched head to head at one end of the bag and goobled through the plastic back at Mary Rose, who did up her mouth to mimic their fish-lipped expressions. The fish were fluid, of changeable shape; you wouldn't know if it was really them moving or only the shifting of the water and light trapped in the bag. Simsy dug out a kitchen match and struck it on one of her many zippers and lit the cigarette that had been glued in the corner of her mouth for so long she'd forgotten it. Smoking, she fastened the rig to the pole, knotting the blue nylon line. When Mary Rose lost interest in the fish and drifted away, Simsy undid the bands on the bag and drove in her bird-finger to hook one of the mullet through the gill.

Kill you, she said to the fish, in her mind. She refastened the bag and held the mullet high. *You sonofabitch you*— The mullet was wet and slick, alternately stiff and supple in her left hand. From her right unfolded the long serrated blade of her knife. She pushed the point in just behind the fish's rectum and ripped up, then turned the mullet over and parted the new vertical lips with her fingers so the guts slithered out and hung, still attached. The fish moved frantically in her hand. Simsy thrust in one of the outsize hooks behind its head and the other lower in the back, where the barb cut through to the emptied stomach cavity. Having cut the fish a few more times to stimulate bleeding, she swung it out over the top rail and let it drop. No need for a long cast here, and anyway the sharks came closer to the beach at night.

Her cigarette was down to its last twist of paper. She spat it out over the rail and licked a fleck of tobacco from one of her front teeth. For a few more minutes she held the pole, then set its tape-wrapped handle in an improvised holder—two beer cans nailed one above the other to a post. The blue line shifted angles slightly as the bait drifted, the mullet broadcasting its signal of pain and despair through the water just below the surface. The tip of the rod was as thick as a thumb. Simsy reached into a pocket and took a sip from the half-pint of rum she'd been nipping at off and on while waiting for the pier to close.

Mary Rose came back then, and plucked at the coverall's leg and looked up. Simsy dug in the duffel and got out the thermos of cocoa, the cheese and mayo sandwich in a paper sack. Mary Rose sat cross-legged to eat, watching the two fish that still swam in the bag. One eye on the pole, Simsy got out a blanket and folded it into a pallet for the girl. Shifting the flashlight out of her way, she climbed onto the plank seat and put her elbows on the wide top board, which was tilted at an upward angle like a lectern.

The water directly below was invisible, but far out the horizon revealed itself as the curved line where the stars fell into the sea. Simsy sucked on the bottle again and thought of the foxfire underwater, how any underwater movement would illumine a streak of living, glowing things. Tonight it would be like swimming through the stars. She nursed the bottle and waited for a strike that didn't come.

After quite a while she heard a mumble, a cut-off cry behind her. Mary Rose had stretched out on the blanket and was uneasily sleeping there, her limbs all twitching like a dog's will in a dream. Simsy took her shoes off carefully and rearranged the blanket to cover her. Mary Rose snuggled deeper in, sighing herself to a calmer sleep. Simsy looked at the pretty, half-formed profile. A smudge of chocolate at the corner of her mouth. She had a snarl of the strawberry blond hair that had been Marty's only good feature. Simsy herself was as ugly as a toadfish and proud of it, too; still, she hoped the girl might keep her looks as she grew up.

When she got up, she shut off the flashlight so it wouldn't bother Mary Rose. After five or ten minutes, the starlight was more than enough. When she reeled in, she saw something had cleverly stolen her bait. One hook was bare and the mullet head dangled free from the other. She cleaned the rig and pulled the spot-tail out of the bag. *Sonofabitch.* The knife unfolded, the fish jumped in her other hand, *Kill you.* . . . This time there was a hard strike as soon as the rig hit the water. Often that was how they came. Just a little one, Simsy could tell, but well-hooked and madder than hell about it. She let it run just long enough to tire itself. She was not particularly a sportsman. Not sentimental, not a fool, not to be trifled with. . . . All the nots. She was not stoppable. The shark came up out of a wave at last and was cranked up through the empty air like a dead weight swinging at the end of the line.

Just a little hammerhead, not two feet long. Either side of the head curved back more slightly than a hammer's claw, an eye at either extremity. The toothy triangle of mouth was cut into the underside, the dorsal and tail fins wickedly slit. Simsy held it up at the length of the short chain leader and watched it thrash in the starlight. Its skin was prickly, like the fur of a petrified cat. At the end of its tube of flesh, the shark's eye rolled in a white ring of gristle, much more like a human eye than a mullet's. Simsy looked back. *You don't know.* She slapped the shark down on its back and planted her foot on the shank of the hook. *You don't know my mind.* A quick slash opened the hammerhead from tail to gullet. Simsy broke its jaws with a stamp and took back her hook, then impaled the shark on a heavier rig, the new hooks as big as the crook of Mary Rose's arm. *Trade it up.* The hammerhead was still very much alive for whatever that was worth, when she dropped it flailing and bloody back into the water.

Simsy stood tall on the plank seat, her knees bent slightly to meet the high board. The wind had come up and whipped through her chair. With one hand she tested the slow thrum of the rod's tip. There was a last good shot in the pocket friend and she killed it and threw the bottle out high, wide and handsome. It gave back no sound from wherever it fell. Only the waves were still rolling steadily down on the beach, and the wind teasing just at the edge of her ear. Simsy's lips were zipped tight, but in her heart she screamed like a banshee and with the same wild joy. Cutting the hammerhead had opened a rush in her pulse which washed away the horizon's boundary so that the stars and the sea ran together—the stars shining up transparently from the bottom of the ocean. Whenever she chose, she could dive into the water and meet the sharks and destroy them there. If everything was water, she could as easily fly as swim. There were no more distinctions. Ten feet under, the dying hammerhead twisted and finned more weakly at the incoming tide, spreading dark slicks of blood like oil over the water. Below, a big shark angled, reversed, burning a tail of phosphorescence like a comet. It turned upside down and spread its jaws, let the bright constellations of plankton rush over the triple rows of its teeth, and wondered, way back in its tiny brain, if this was what it wanted.

Robert Brickhouse

THE SOCK FACTORY

Cox, an amateur photographer, had long wanted to try his luck around the old hosiery mill across the river. One balmy Saturday in April, after vacuuming the house and babysitting his two young children at the playground sandbox, he decided to drive over there.

He felt a growing excitement, a confident anticipation, as he left behind his tree-lined street, passed the church and the school and crossed the bridge from downtown to the South Side, with his camera resting beside him on the seat of the stationwagon.

The mill neighborhood lay downriver at the far edge of the city. On its old main street, only a few stores remained in business, two decades after the mill had closed. Dilapidated houses, many of them abandoned now, lined the side streets climbing from the river and the railroad. As he drove along the pitted road beside the tracks, Cox could see glittering in the sun the junkyard that filled one side of a nearby hill. At the end of the neighborhood, the mill, its windows shattered, its brick walls dark, loomed over the houses like a ruined palace.

Cox was drawn to such run-down, seedy places to take his photographs. He was proud of his pictures, too; some of his work was really not too bad. A friend at his job, in the budget and planning office of the Department of Mental Health, had recently arranged for a couple of Cox's best black-and-white shots—moody studies around the railroad yard—to be shown at an exhibition at the public library; other such shows and contests were coming up.

He'd driven around the mill neighborhood once or twice before but had never really explored it. He felt safe going there; he was careful to keep a low profile on such expeditions, and the area around the mill, more like a forgotten ghost town than a teeming slum, wasn't known as a high-crime district.

With his Nikon hanging from one shoulder and his camera bag from the other, Cox starting walking. The street was cracked and badly buckling, its gutters filled with dirt and debris. The air carried the muddy smell of the river and, even though the afternoon was warm, wood smoke.

In the shadow of a rock wall, across from a row of boarded store fronts, he stopped to snap an old school bus with white letters across the side announcing JESUS SAVES. This was exactly the sort of picture he was looking for.

Next he shot a panorama of the junkyard shining through the trees. Framed in the distance stood the mill, a good five stories high, its broken windows winking, a silver water tower glinting on its roof.

After walking for a while past houses and a row of stores—a second-hand furniture shop, a hole-in-the-wall market, a taxidermist were among the few still operating—he saw a cinderblock cafe with a torn screen door that formed a sharp pattern of light and dark. Cox took some shots from across the street: KOZY KORNER LUNCHEONETTE was painted in faded letters across the window.

Curious, he crossed over, tugged at the door and entered the gloom. The tight-springed door shut with a bang behind him.

A man and a woman were sitting on stools at the counter, talking to a stoop-shouldered man wearing a dingy white apron. Cox went to the far end, sat and ordered a Coke.

"What you taking pictures of?" asked the counterman as he served the bottle and glass. He had a soft voice and close-cut gray hair, and walked with a limp.

"Anything that catches my eyes," Cox said. "I'm just poking around, headed down to the mill."

The counterman glanced at the man and woman. "I don't see why you'd want to take pictures of that ugly old sock factory."

The woman started laughing, then broke into a violent cough, waving her cigarette. Through a cloud of smoke, Cox saw a garishly lipsticked mouth, a pile of blond hair, a leathery face. She and her companion, a small man in a brown jacket who made Cox think of a rat, were drinking coffee from mugs.

"That's a good one," the woman called to the counterman.

"I'm serious," the counterman said.

"Actually," Cox said, "old buildings make great pictures. In fact, I shot a couple of your place, outside. I hope you don't mind."

"Don't make no difference to me," the man said. He shook his head and began clearing empty bottles from tables.

Cox sipped from his glass and looked around, his gray running shoes hooked under his stool. A bare bulb hung from the ceiling, plaster had fallen from the walls.

He stood, with a hand on his camera. "Mind if I take a picture in here?"

"Help yourself," the counterman said, starting to sweep the floor.

Cox focused on a row of glasses catching the light from the window.

"Hell, honey," the woman said. "You're wasting your film in this dump." She laughed again, looking with raised eyebrows at the man in the apron.

"No, I'm not," Cox said. He suddenly saw that the pair would make a good picture and asked, "Do you mind if I take one of you folks?"

"You don't want to do that," the man in the brown coat said.

"Let him," the woman said, sitting up straight, crossing her legs and tugging her skirt.

The little man ran a hand through black oily hair.

"Come here, Fred," the woman called to the counterman. "You get in here too."

"Not me."

"Come on," she said and waved him over.

The counterman crossed the room in his apron and leaned in, frowning, behind them.

"Good," Cox said and snapped several quick portraits. "These are good." He felt he might really have some great pictures here. "I'll bring you a copy next time I come back."

"If you ever come back," the rat-faced man said.

The woman began coughing again and slapping the counter. Cox took a step backwards and heard something crack like a gunshot. He looked around and saw he'd stepped on the counterman's dustpan and broken the handle. "Oh, God, I'm sorry," he said and offered to pay for it.

"Forget it," the counterman said, taking only some change for the Coke.

"Now you stay out of trouble, honey," the woman said.

Out on the broken sidewalk he heard them all laughing.

Walking with his camera among back alleys and side streets, past beaten-up garbage cans and tall tawny weeds, Cox took more pictures: a leaning picket fence and its snaking shadow; a rusted sign that said SEAFOOD, shaped like a fish; sunlight on a pile of broken glass and cinders. He saw almost no one on the streets; occasionally he glimpsed an old man or woman around a ramshackle house, sweeping a porch or letting out a scrawny cat. Watching over everything was the great brick and glass face of the mill.

Cox sensed good pictures all around him. He couldn't wait to find the ideal shot of the mill, the dream-shot he knew was down in here somewhere. He wondered who lived in such poverty here, in the miserable houses with hardpacked bare yards, "No Trespassing" signs, chained dogs that sometimes barked at him.

In the window of one small tar-papered house, he saw a vase of flowers between white curtains. He studied the scene through his lens, had just shot a picture when he heard a noise behind him.

Turning, Cox saw a blind man tapping along with a cane and stepped into the street to get out of his way. He was about Cox's age, thirty or so, heavy and soft, wearing dark glasses.

As the man shuffled past a fence plastered with old circus posters, clouds shifted and light swept over the scene. Cox snapped a picture. The man stopped at the click of the camera. He listened a moment, then suddenly whipped his cane through the air and walked on.

Soon after, while kneeling in the gutter to photograph a house whose roof had caved in, Cox heard a car speeding down the street. Glancing up, he saw a gray blur, a silver grill like a grinning mouth. A dark-bearded man in a baseball cap leaned out the window on the passenger side and yelled, "Hey!" The car passed so close that Cox could see the cap's insignia: a square black patch with a skull.

Then the car turned around down the street, its rear end sagging.

The front license plate was a Confederate flag. On impulse, Cox took a picture.

As the car screeched past again, the man in the cap lobbed a bottle over the roof. Cox saw it arc through the air and shatter against the curb only a few yards away. "Hey, watch it," he mumbled out loud. He hoped they wouldn't come back to taunt him a third time.

To avoid that possibility, he cut through a vacant lot to another street. River Street, said the leaning sign. Ahead, rising out of the weeds, was the sun-lit back side of the mill. The building was surrounded by a high chain-link fence, its windows jagged and bright. As he walked beside the tracks, looking for a good shot of the towering block-long walls, Cox saw a man sitting on a large white rock. He watched as the man swigged from a bottle in a paper bag. The man had long matted hair, a brown creased neck.

Cox nodded hello.

The man swayed on his rock. "What do you say?" He took another long swig. On the wall of the mill behind him was a white sign that said "Danger Keep Out."

Cox wanted this picture. "Do you mind if I take a shot of you and the mill?"

The man held his bottle between his legs. He was sockless and his shoes didn't have laces.

"Suit yourself, friend."

Cox dropped to one knee.

The man wiped his mouth and stared at the camera. Some pigeons flew from windows near the top of the mill and swooped into the scene, their gray wings catching the sun.

Cox shot several times quickly. "These are good pictures."

The man continued to stare.

"Good pictures," Cox said.

"You're damn right."

"Thanks for letting me take them."

"Hey, buddy."

"What?" Cox said.

"Come here."

Cox came closer.

"Come here."

"I am here."

"Wait a damn minute."

"What is it?"

"I have something important to tell you."

"Well, what is it?"

"Come here."

Cox turned to go.

"Wait!"

Cox kept walking.

"Wait! This is important."

"Well, tell me."

"Come here."

"You can tell me from there."

The man lunged forward. "How 'bout some money for them pictures?"

Cox started walking away again, fast. He felt in his pocket for change, but he'd spent the last of it at the lunch counter.

"Wait a minute! Come here!" The man began to trot after him. "You got to pay for them pictures."

Cox broke into a run as he saw the drunk still staggering up the road after him. He kept running, dodging up side streets, until he was sure he'd lost him for good.

Breathing hard, cradling his camera against his side, he looked up and again saw the mill, squatting a block away. With his eye out for a good angle from which to shoot it, he came to a row of old houses, their gray paint peeling, their yards and rotting porches littered with cast-off furniture, boards, old tires.

In a muddy yard he stopped to photograph a broken doll lying beside two plastic tricycles. A front window of the house was covered with plyboard. A rusty washing machine stood in the mud. Just as he shot, he heard some leaves rattle and saw what at first he thought was a squirrel. But as it dove under the porch, he recognized the tail of a rat.

Cox walked between two of the houses and into a shadowy alley. Brick walls of warehouses lined one side, leading down to the mill.

Two children were there in the alley, playing in puddles. One was a girl about five, the other a boy hardly more than a baby, the same ages as his kids almost. Their shorts, torn shirts, and faces were streaked with dirt.

This was the shot he had come for, the perfect scene he was always seeking: the mill in the background, the puddles reflecting gray light, these poor kids with their dirt-smeared faces.

Cox explained he wanted to photograph the mill and they helped make a good picture.

They went on playing as he moved in closer and lined up his shot. "Do you live around here?" he said, eyeing them through the camera, finding the focus he wanted.

The girl pointed to the back of one of the houses.

Cox checked his light meter. "Is he your brother?"

She nodded. "We're playing this is the ocean."

The boy laughed and stepped into a puddle, soaking his shoes.

"Do you mind if I shoot some while you play?"

The children looked at him wide-eyed.

"If you'll stay just like that, I'm going to take a picture of you and the mill."

He slowly kneeled and focused.

Through his lens he saw them, ragged urchins watching him. In the background gaped the broken face of the mill. Focusing exactly, savoring the shot, he squeezed the shutter release. The children continued to play and look up at him as he took more pictures.

Then a voice behind him: "Who give you permission to be here?"

Cox jumped to his feet. A thin woman in a gray dress was standing at the edge of a yard. Her hair was a coarse brown, her cheeks hollow and rough. It was hard to tell what age she was. She called sharply to the children, "Come here right now."

She said to Cox, "These ain't your children. Who told you you could take their pictures?"

Cox said, "No one. They just made a nice shot with the mill back there."

The children came over to the woman. "Look at you. I told you not to get filthy and wet."

She turned to Cox again. "I saw you snooping around, trespassing right through the yard." The children blinked up at her and then at Cox.

"I'm sorry. I didn't mean to cause any trouble," Cox said.

"What's your name?" she said.

Cox told her, feeling foolish.

"What are you doing here anyway?"

"I told you. I'm just looking for good pictures. I wanted a shot of the mill."

"The sock factory? What do you care about the sock factory? You don't have a right to be back here." She pointed to the children. "Go get in the house."

"Now wait just a minute," Cox said. "This is a public alley. I have a right to be here."

"You don't have a right to come sneaking through my yard. My brother-in-law said he saw you nosing around his house this afternoon too. I think I'm going to call the police about you." She pushed the boy and girl ahead of her and stalked back through the mud to a dim doorway. She yelled over her shoulder, "Somebody ought to teach you a lesson."

Cox walked along the walls of warehouses, stepping over puddles. His soft hands were sweating as he clutched his camera. He saw something scurry across the alley in front of him, then another and another, wiry tails disappearing into the walls.

At a cross street he glanced over his shoulder and saw the woman out there again, watching him. Hands on her hips, she was backlit against the dark mill.

Larry Brown

SLEEP

My wife hears the noises and she wakes me in the night. The dream I've been having is not a good one. There is a huge black cow with long white horns chasing me, its breath right on my neck. I don't know what it means, but I'm frightened when I awake. Her hand is gripping my arm. She is holding her breath, almost.

Sometimes I sleep well and sometimes I don't. My wife hardly ever sleeps at all. Oh, she takes little naps in the daytime, but you can stand back and watch her, and you'll see what she goes through. She moans, and twists, and shakes her head no no no.

Long ago we'd go on picnics, take Sunday drives in the car. Long before that, we parked in cars and moved our hands over each other. Now all we do is try to sleep, seems like.

It's dark in the room, but I can see a little. I move my arm and my elbow makes a tiny pop. I'm thinking coffee, orange juice, two over easy. But I'm a long way away from that. And then I know she's hearing the noises once more.

"They're down there again," she says.

I don't even nod my head. I don't want to get up. It's useless anyway, and I just do it for her, and I never get through doing it. I'm warm under the covers, and the world apart from the two of us under here is cold. I think maybe if I pretend to be asleep, she'll give it up. So I lie quietly for a few moments, breathing in and out. I gave us a new electric blanket for our anniversary. The thermostat clicks on and off, with a small reassuring sound, keeping us warm. I think about hash browns, and toast, and shit on a shingle. I think about cold places I've been in. It's wonderful to do that, and then feel the warm spaces between my toes.

"Get up," she says.

Once I was trapped in a blizzard in Kansas. I was traveling, and a snowstorm came through, and the snow was so furious I drove my car right off the road into a deep ditch. I couldn't even see the highway from where I was, and I foolishly decided to stay in the car, run the heater and wait for help. I had almost a full tank of gas. The snow started covering my vehicle. I had no overshoes, no gloves. All I had was a car coat. The windshield was like the inside of an igloo, except for a small hole where I ran the defroster. I ran out of gas after nine hours of idling. Then the cold closed in. I think about that time, and feel my nice warm pajamas.

"You getting up?" she says.

I'm playing that I'm still asleep, that I haven't heard her wake me. I'm drifting back off, scrambling eggs, warming up the leftover T-bone in the microwave, looking for the sugar bowl and the milk. The dog has the paper in his mouth.

"Did you hear me?" she says.

I hear her. She knows I hear her. I hear her every night, and it never fails to discourage me. Sometimes this getting up and down seems to go on forever. I've even considered separate beds. But so far we've just gone on like we nearly always have.

I suppose there's nothing to do but get up. But if only she knew how bad I don't want to.

"*Louis.* For God's sake. Will you get up?"

Another time I was stationed at a small base on the North Carolina coast. We had to pull guard duty at night. After a four-hour shift, my feet would be blocks of ice. It would take two hours of rubbing them with my socks off, and drinking coffee, to get them back to normal. The wind came off the ocean in the winter, and it cut right through your clothes. I had that once, and now I have this. The thermostat clicks. It's doing its small, steady job, regulating the temperature of two human bodies. What a wonderful invention. I'm mixing batter and pouring it on the griddle. Bacon is sizzling in its own grease, shrinking, turning brown, bubbling all along the edges. What lovely bacon, what pretty pancakes. I'll eat and eat.

"Are you going to get up or not?"

I sigh. I think that if I was her and she was me, I wouldn't make her do this. But I don't know that for a fact. How did we know years ago we'd turn out like this? We sleep about a third of our lives, and look what all we miss. But sometimes the things we see in our sleep are more horrible and magical than anything we can imagine. People come after you and try to kill you, cars go backward down the highway at seventy miles an hour with you inside and you're standing up on the brake. Sometimes you even get a little.

I lie still in the darkness and, without looking around, can see the mound of covers next to me with a gray lump of hair sticking out. She is still, too. I think maybe she's forgotten about the things downstairs. I think maybe if I just keep quiet she'll drift back off to sleep. I try that for a while. The gas heater is throwing the shadow of its grille onto the ceiling and it's leaping around. Through the black window I can see the cold stars in the sky. People are probably getting up somewhere, putting on their housecoats, yawning in their fists, plugging in their Mr. Coffees.

Once I was in the army with a boy from Montana and he got me to go home with him. His parents had a large ranch in the mountains, and they took me in like another son. I'd never seen country like that Big Sky country. Everywhere you looked, all you could see was sky and mountains, and in the winter it snowed. We fed his father's cows out of a truck, throwing hay out in the snow, and boy those cows were glad to get it. They'd come running up as soon as they heard the truck. But I felt sorry for them, having to live outside in the snow and all, like deer. Once in a while we'd find a little calf that had frozen to death, frozen actually to the ground. I would be sad when that happened, thinking about it not ever getting to see the springtime.

I lie still under the covers in my warm bed and wonder what ever became of that boy.

Then she begins. It's always soft, and she never raises her voice. But she's dogcussing me, really putting some venom into it, the same old awful words over and over, until it hurts my ears to hear them. I know she won't stop until I get up, but I hate to feel that cold floor on my feet. She's moved my house shoes again, and I don't want to crawl under the bed looking for them. Spiders are under there, and balls of dust, and maybe even traps set for mice. I don't ever look under there, because I don't want to see what I might.

I tell myself that it's just like diving into cold water, I'll only feel the shock for a second, and that the way to do it is all at once. So I throw the covers back and I stand up. She stops talking to me. I find the flashlight on the stand beside the bed, where I leave it every night. Who needs a broken leg going down the stairs?

It's cold in the hall. I shine the flashlight on the rug, and on my gun cabinet, and for a moment I think I'll go and make coffee in the kitchen, and sit there listening to it brew, and drink a cup of it and smoke a few cigarettes. But it seems an odd time of the night to do a thing like that. The thought passes, and I go down the stairs.

I open the door to the kitchen. Of course there's nothing in there. I shut the door hard so she can hear it. I cross the dining room, lighting my way, looking at her china in the cabinet, at the white tablecloth on the table and the dust on it, and I open the door to the living room. There's nothing in there but furniture, the fireplace, some candy in a dish. I slam the door so she can hear that, too. I'm thinking of all the dreams I could be having right now, uninterrupted. It's too late for Carson, too late for Letterman, too late for Arsenio. They've all gone to bed by now.

I stand downstairs and listen to my house. I cut the light off to hear better. The silence has a noise of its own that it makes. I move to the window and push the curtains aside, but nobody's out there on the streets. It's cold out there. I'm glad I'm in here, and not out there. Still.

I sit in a chair for a little while, tapping the flashlight gently on my knee. I find my cigarettes in the pocket of my robe, and I smoke one. I don't want it, it's just a habit. It kills three or four minutes. And after that, it's been long enough. I find an ashtray with my flashlight, and put out the cigarette. I'm still thinking about that coffee. I even look in the direction of the kitchen. But finally I go ahead and climb the stairs.

I put my hand over the bulb of the flashlight when I get near the bed. I move in my own little circle of light with quiet feet. I keep my hand over it when I move it near her face. I don't want to wake her up if she's asleep. My hand looks red in the light, and my skin looks thin. I don't know how we got so old.

Her eyes are closed. She has her hands folded together, palms flat, like a child with her head resting on them. I don't know what to do with her anymore. Maybe tomorrow night she won't hear the things downstairs. Maybe tomorrow night they'll be up in the attic. It's hard to tell.

I turn the flashlight off and set it back on the table beside the bed. I might need it again before the night's over. I don't want to be up stumbling around in the dark.

"Mama had three kittens," she says, and I listen. Her voice is soft, remarkably clear, like a person reciting a poem. I wait for the rest of it, but it never comes. I'm lucky, this time, I guess.

I sit on the side of the bed. I don't want to get under the covers just yet. I want to hear the house quiet again, and the silence is so loud that it's almost overpowering. Finally I lie down and pull the covers up over my head. The warmth is still there. I move toward her, looking for I don't know what. I think of a trip I took to Alaska a long time ago, when I was a young man. There were sled dogs, and plenty of snow, and polar bears fishing among cakes of ice for seals. I wonder how they can live in that cold water. But I figure it's just what you get used to. I close my eyes, and I wait.

Fred Chappell

ANCESTORS

Harry and Lydie were enduring their third ancestor and finding it a
rum go. Not that they were surprised—the first two ancestors had also
proved to be enervating specimens—and now they regretted the hour
they had joined the Ancestor Program of the Living History Series.
Sitting at dinner, fed up with Wade Wordmore, Harry decided to
return this curious creature to his congressman, Doy Collingwood, at
his local office over in Raleigh, North Carolina.

They were goaded into joining the program by that most destructive
of all human urges: the desire for self-improvement. When, as part of
the celebration of the one-hundred-fiftieth anniversary of the Civil
War, the U.S. Archives and History Division called Harry Beacham
and told him that the records showed he had no less than three
ancestral relatives who had fought in the great conflict and asked if
he'd be interested in meeting these personages, he replied that Yes, of
course, he would love to meet them.

What Southerner wouldn't say that?

It is also in the Southern manner to take the marvels of modern
technology for granted. The crisp impersonal female voice in the
telephone receiver explained that from the merest microscopic section
of bone, computers could dredge out of the past not only the physical
lineaments of the person whom that bone once held perpendicular but
the personality traits too, down to the last little tic and stammer. In
their own house Harry and Lydie could engage with three flesh-and-
blood examples of history come to life. Of course, it really wasn't flesh,

only a sort of protein putty, but it was real blood, right enough. It was pig blood: that was a biochemical necessity.

"Can they talk?" Harry asked and was assured that they spoke, remembered their former lives in sharp detail, and even told jokes—rather faded ones, of course. They also ate, slept, and shaved, were human in every way. "That is the Departmental motto," the voice said. "Engineering Humanity for Historic Purpose."

He asked casually about the cost, and she stated it, and he was pleased but still desired to think just a few days about whether to subscribe to the program.

"That will not be necessary," said the woman's voice. "The arrangements have already been taken care of and your first ancestor is on his way to you. The Archives and History Division of the United States Department of Reality is certain that you will find real satisfaction in your encounters with Living History. Good day, Mr. Butcher."

"Wait a minute," Harry said. "My name is Beacham." But the connection was cut, and when he tried to call back, he was shunted from one office to another and put on hold so often and so long that he gave up in disgust.

So then as far as Harry was concerned, all bets were off. He was a Beacham and no Butcher and proud of it, and if some artificial entity from the Archives Division showed up at his door, he would send the fellow packing.

But he didn't have to do that. Lieutenant Aldershot's papers were in apple-pie order when he presented them with a sharp salute to Lydie. She met him at the front door and was immediately taken with this swarthy brown-eyed man in his butternut uniform and broad-brimmed hat. A battered leather-bound trunk sat on the walk behind him.

"Oh, you must be the ancestor they sent," she said. "Lieutenant Edward Aldershot of the Northern Virginia reporting as ordered, ma'am."

Confused, Lydie colored prettily and looked up and down the lane to see if any of her neighbors here in the Shining Acres development were observing her resplendent visitor. She took the papers he proffered, started to open them, but paused with her fingers on the knotted ribbon and said, "Oh, do come in," and stepped back into the foyer. The lieutenant moved forward briskly, removing his hat just before he stepped over the threshold. "Honey," she called. "Harry, honey. Our ancestor is here."

He came downstairs in no pleasant frame of mind, but then stood silent and wide-eyed before Aldershot, who snapped him a classy respectful salute and declared his name and the name of his army. "I believe the lady will be kind enough to present my papers, sir."

But Harry and Lydie only stood gaping until the lieutenant gestured toward the packet in Lydie's hands. She gave it to Harry, blushing again, and Harry said in a rather stiff tone, trying to hide his astonishment, "Ah yes. Of course. . . . Your papers. . . . Of course."

And for a wonder they were all correct. Here was the letter from History identifying Aldershot and congratulating the Beachams on the opportunity of enjoying his company for three weeks and telling them what a valuable experience they were in for. Then there was Aldershot's birth certificate and a very sketchy outline of his military career and then a family tree in which Harry was relieved to discover not a single Butcher. It was all Beachams and Lawsons and Hollinses and Bredvolds and Aldershots and Harpers as far as the eye could see, all the way to the beginning of the nineteenth century.

"This looks fine," Harry said. "We're glad to have you as one of us."

"I'm proud to hear you say so, sir," the lieutenant said and tore off another healthy salute.

"You don't need to be so formal," Harry told him. "You don't have to salute me or call me sir. We're just friends here."

"That's very kind of you. I'm afraid it may take a little time for me to adjust, sir."

"You'll fit right in," Lydie said. "I'm sure you will."

"Thank you, ma'am," said Aldershot. "I do take tobacco and a little whiskey now and then. I hope you won't mind."

"Oh no. If that's what you did—I mean, if that's what you're used to. Please feel free." A bashful woman, she blushed once more. She had almost said: *If that's what you did when you were alive.* "Harry, you can bring in the lieutenant's trunk, if you don't mind."

The Confederate Officer had too modestly described his pleasures. He did not merely take tobacco, he engorged it, sawing off with his case knife black tarry knuckles of the stuff from a twist he carried in his trousers pocket and chewing belligerently, like a man marching against an opposing brigade. He was a veritable wellpump of tobacco juice, spitting inaccurately not only at the champagne bucket and other utensils the Beachams supplied him as spittoons but at any handy vessel that offered a concavity. The sofa suffered and the rugs, the tablecloths, the lieutenant's bedding and his clothing—his clothing most of all.

In fact, his whole appearance deteriorated rapidly and ruinously. In three days he no longer wore his handsome butternut but had changed into the more familiar uniform of Confederate gray, a uniform which seemed to grow shabbier even as the Beachams gazed upon it. His sprightly black moustache, which Lydie had fancied as complementing his dark eyes perfectly, became first ragged, then shaggy. He would neglect to shave for four days running, and he began to smell of sweat and stale underwear and whiskey.

For he had also understated the power of his thirst. On the first night and always afterward, he never strayed far from the jug and when not actually pouring from it would cast amorous glances in its direction. He drank George Dickel neat or sometimes with sugar water and praised the quality of the bourbon in ardent terms, saying, for example, "If we'd a-had a little more of this at Chancellorsville it would've been a different story." Liquor seemed to affect him little, however; he never lost control of his motor reflexes or slurred his speech.

Yet the quality of his address had changed since that sunny first moment with the Beachams. It was no more *Yes sir* and *No sir* to Harry, but *our friend Harry here* and *Old Buddy* and *Old Hoss*. He still spoke to Lydie as *Ma'am*, but when talking indirectly would refer to her as *our mighty fine little female of the house*. He was never rude or impolite, but his formal manner slipped into an easy camaraderie and then sagged into a careless intimacy. His social graces frayed at about the same rate as his gray uniform, which by the end of the second week was positively tattered.

The lieutenant, though, had not been ordered to the Beacham residence as a dancing master, but as a representative of History which, as the largest division of the Department of Reality, shared much of its parent organization's proud anatomy. And of Living History, Lieutenant Aldershot offered a spectacular cornucopia. The outline of his career that came with him from the government agency barely hinted at the range and length of his fighting experience. He had fought at Vicksburg, Fredericksburg, and Gettysburg; he had survived Shiloh, Antietam, and Richmond; he had been brave at Bull Run, Rich Mountain, Williamsburg, and Cedar Mountain; he had won commendations from Zollicoffer, Beauregard, Johnston, Kirby-Smith, Jackson, and Robert E. Lee. The latter commander he referred to as "General Bobby" and described him as "the finest Southern Gentleman who ever whupped his enemy."

Harry's knowledge of history was by no means as profound as his enthusiasm for it, and he had not found time before Aldershot's arrival to bone up on the battles and campaigns that occurred a century and a half past. Even so, the exploits of the ambeer-spattered and strongly watered lieutenant began to overstretch Harry's credulity. In order to be on all the battlefields he remembered, Aldershot must have spent most of the War on the backs of two dozen swift horses, and to survive the carnage he had witnessed must have kept busy a fretting cohort of guardian angels. Any soldier of such courage, coolness, intelligence, and resourcefulness must have left his name in letters of red blaze in the history books, but Harry could not recall hearing of Aldershot. Of course, it had been some seven years since he had looked at the histories; perhaps he had only forgotten.

For in many ways it was hard to disbelieve the soldier's accounts, he was so particular in detail and so vivid in expression. When telling of some incident that displayed one man's valor or another's timidity, he became brightly animated, and then heated, and would squirm in his chair at the table, sputtering tobacco and gulping bourbon, his eyes wild and bloodshot. He rocked back and forth in the chair as if he were in the saddle, leaping the brushy hurdles at the Battle of Fallen Timber. He broke two chairs that way, and his host supplied him a steel-frame lawn chair brought in from the garage.

He was vivid and particular most of all in his accounts of bloodshed. Although he spoke only plain language, as he averred a soldier should, he so impressed Harry's imagination and Lydie's trepidation that they felt extremely close to the great conflict. In Aldershot's bourbonish sentences they heard the bugles at daybreak, the creak of munitions wagons, the crack of rifles and bellow of cannon, the horses screaming in pain and terror. They saw the fields clouded over with gunsmoke and the hilltop campfires at night and the restless shuffle of pickets on the sunset perimeters. They could smell corn parching and mud waist deep and the stink of latrines and the worse stink of gangrene in the hospital tents.

The lieutenant's accounts of battle went from bloody to chilling to gruesome, and the closeness with which he detailed blows and wounds and killings made the *Iliad* seem vague and pallid. He appeared to take a certain relish in demonstrating on his own body where a minnie ball had gone into a comrade and where it came out and what raw mischief it had caused during its journey. He spoke of shattered teeth and splintered bone and eyes gouged out. When he began to describe the surgeries and amputations, dwelling at great length on the mound of removed body parts at the Fredericksburg field hospital, Lydie pleaded with him to spare her.

"Please," she said. "Perhaps we needn't hear all this part." Her eyes were large and teary in her whitened face and her voice trembled.

"Uh, yes," Harry said. "I think Lydie has a point. Maybe we can skip a few of the gorier details now and then." He too was obviously shaken by what he had heard.

"Well now," Aldershot said, "of course I didn't mean to alarm our mighty fine little female of the house. I hope you'll forgive a plain-spoken soldier, ma'am, one who never learned the orator's art. You're a brave un in my book, for there's many a refined Southern lady who will faint when she hears the true story of things. Especially when I tell how it is to be gutshot."

"Please, Lieutenant," Lydie said. She took three sips of her chardonnay, recovering her composure pretty quickly, but looking with dismay at her plate of stewed pork.

"How about you?" Harry asked. "Were you ever wounded?"

"Me?" Aldershot snorted. "No, not me. I was always one too many for them bluebellies, not that they didn't try plenty hard."

This discussion took place at the end of the second week. At first Aldershot had referred to his ancient opponents as *the enemy* and then changed his term to *the Northern invader*. In the second week, though, it was *bluebellies* every time, and in the third week it was *them goddamn treacherous Yankee bastards,* to which epithet he always appended a parenthetical apology to Lydie: —*saving your presence, ma'am.*

Even that small gesture toward the observance of chivalry seemed to cost him some effort. In the third week the weary Confederate appeared to have aged a decade; his clothes were now only threads and patches, his moustache a scraggly bristle, his eyes discolored and dispirited, and his speech disjoined, exhausted, and crumbling. It was clear that remembering had taken too much out of him, that he had tired himself almost past endurance. He had cut down on his tobacco intake, as if the exercise of a chaw drew off too much strength, and had increased his frequency of whiskey, although this spiritous surplus did not enliven his demeanor.

On the eve of his departure, Lieutenant Aldershot begged off telling of the destruction of Atlanta and gave only the most cursory sketch of the surrender at Appomattox. For the first time in three weeks, he retired early to bed.

Next morning he came down late and took only coffee for his breakfast. He had dragged his leather-bound trunk to the front door and stood with his foot propped on it as he bade the Beachams farewell. Gravely they shook hands. When he spoke to Lydie Aldershot, he held his hat over his heart. "Ma'am, your hospitality has been most generous and not something a plain soldier will forget."

Lydie took his hand; she blushed, feeling that she ought to curtsey but not knowing how.

He looked straight into Harry's eyes. "So long, Old Hoss," he said. "It's been mighty fine for me here."

"We've been honored," Harry said. "Believe me."

Then the government van arrived and the driver came to load Aldershot's trunk and they shook hands once more and the lieutenant departed. As they watched him trudging down the front walk, Harry and Lydie were struck silent by the mournful figure he presented, his shoulders slumped, his head thrust forward, and his step a defeated shuffle. When he mounted to the van cab and rode away without waving or looking back, a feeling of deep sadness descended upon them, so that they stood for a minute or two holding each other for comfort and looking into the bright empty morning.

Finally Harry closed the door and turned away. "I don't know about you," he said, "but I feel tired. Tired in my bones."

"Me too," Lydie said. "And I've got to get this house cleaned up. There's tobacco spit everywhere. Everything in the house is splattered."

"I feel like we just lost the war."

"Well, honey, that's exactly what happened."

"I'll tell you what I'm going to do—if you don't mind, I mean. I'm going to call these government History people and tell them not to send the other ancestors. I'm utterly exhausted. I can't imagine how I'd feel after two more visitors like the lieutenant."

"I think you're right," she said. "Do it now."

Harry got on the telephone and dialed a list of bureaucratic numbers, only to find that each and every one gave off a busy signal for hours on end.

So on Monday morning, at ten-thirty on the dot, Private William Harper presented himself at the front door and handed his papers to Lydie with a shy bow. His was a diffident gray uniform that had seen better days, but it was clean and tidy. He was accompanied by no trunk; only a modest, neatly turned bedroll lay at his feet. "Ma'am, I believe you are expecting me?" he said.

Her first impulse was to send him away immediately, but the van must have departed already since it was nowhere in sight, and, anyway, her second stronger impulse was to invite him into the house and feed him. Lieutenant Aldershot must have been in his early forties—though he had looked to be sixty years old when he departed—but Private Harper could hardly have been out of his teens.

He offered her his papers and gave her what he obviously hoped was a winning smile, but he was so young and clear-eyed and shy and apprehensive that his expression was more frightened than cordial.

Lydie's heart went out to him entirely; she took the packet without looking at it, staring almost tenderly upon Harper with his big bright blue eyes and rosy complexion in which the light fuzz was evidence of an infrequent acquaintance with a razor. He was a slight young man, slender and well-formed and with hands as long-fingered and delicate as a pianist's. He seemed troubled by her stare and shifted restlessly in his boots.

"Ma'am," he asked, "have I come to the right house? Maybe I'm supposed to be somewhere else."

"No," Lydie said. "You come right in. This is the place for you."

"I wouldn't want to be a burden," the private said. "Those government people said that you had invited me to come here. I wouldn't want to impose on you."

"We're glad to have you. Don't worry about a thing."

He looked all about him, wonderstruck. "You belong to a mighty grand place. It's hard for me to get used to the houses and everything that people have."

"We feel lucky," Lydie said. "Lots of people are not so well-off." Then, seeing that he could formulate no reply, she stooped and picked up his bedroll. "Please come in. I was just getting ready to make some fresh coffee. You'd like that, wouldn't you?"

"Yes, ma'am."

In the kitchen Private Harper sat at the table and watched moonily every step and gesture Lydie made. His nervousness was subsiding, but he seemed a long way from being at ease. She took care to smile warmly and speak softly, but it was apparent to her from Harper's worshipful gaze that she had already conquered the young man's heart. When she set the coffee before him with the cream pitcher and sugar bowl alongside, he didn't glance down, looking instead into her face. "Now, Private Harper," she said, "drink your coffee. And would you like something to eat? I can make a sandwich or maybe there's a piece of chocolate cake left. You like chocolate cake, don't you?"

"No ma'am. Just the coffee is all I want to wake me up. I was feeling a little bit tired."

"Of course you are," she said. "You finish your coffee and I'll show you to your room and you can get some sleep."

"You're awful kind, ma'am. I won't say no to that."

When the private was tucked away, Lydie telephoned her spouse at his place of business, Harry's Hot-Hit Vidrents, to tell him the news.

He was not happy. "Oh Lydie," he said. "You were supposed to send him back where he came from. That was our plan."

"I just couldn't," she said. "He's so young. And he was tired out. He's already asleep."

"But we agreed. Don't you remember? We agreed to send him packing."

"Wait till you meet him. Then send him packing. If you can do it, it will be all right with me."

And having met the young man, Harry no more than Lydie could order him away. Harper was so innocent and willing and open-faced that Harry could only feel sympathy for him when he saw what puppy eyes the young man made at his wife. He offered him a drink— Aldershot had overlooked a half bottle of Dickel in a lower cabinet— and was not surprised when the lad refused. "I promised my mother, sir, before I went off to war."

"I see," Harry said, and reflected gravely on the difference between the lieutenant and the private. "But in the army, that must have been a hard promise to keep."

"Oh no, sir. Not when I promised my mother. And to tell the truth, I don't have much taste for liquor."

He did accept a cup of tea, spooning into it as much sugar as would dissolve, and was profusely grateful.

Harry then readied himself with a gin and tonic for another stiff dose of History. "I suppose you must have fought in lots of battles," he said.

Private Harper shook his head sadly. "Only two battles, sir."

"Which were those?"

"Well, I fought at Bethel, sir, and then we were sent down toward Richmond."

"You were at Manassas?" These were place-names that Aldershot had deeply imprinted on the Beacham memory.

"Yes sir."

"And what was that like?"

"Well, sir. . . ." For the first time, Private Harper lifted his eyes and looked directly into Harry's face. His boyish countenance was a study in apologetic confusion as he steadied his teacup on his knee and said, "Well, sir, if you don't mind, I'd rather not talk 'bout that."

"You don't want to talk about Manassas?" Harry asked. Then his surprise disappeared with the force of his realization: Manassas would have been where Private Harper had died.

"I don't like to talk about the war at all, sir."

"I see."

"I know I'm supposed to, but I just can't seem to make myself do it. It opens up old wounds."

"That's all right. I understand."

"No, sir, I don't believe that you do understand. It is too hard for me right now. It opens old wounds."

"That's quite all right. Where are you from originally?"

"Salem, Virginia," Private Harper said. "We had a farm right outside town. I miss that place a great deal."

"I'm sure you do."

"I miss my folks too, sir. Something terrible." And he went on to talk about his life before the war, and his story was so idyllic and engaging that Harry called Lydie from the kitchen to hear it.

The private spoke rhapsodically of such ordinary tasks as planting corn, shoeing horses, repairing wagons, cutting hay, milking cows and so forth; his bright face glowed even friendlier as he spoke of these matters, and as he warmed to his stories his shyness melted and his language became almost lyrical.

He was the only male in a female family, his father having died when Billy was only eleven. He allowed that his mother and three sisters had rather doted on him, but it was obvious to the Beachams that he had no real idea how much they doted. He had not been required to join the army; he had done so only out of a sense of duty and from a fear of the shame he might feel later if he did not join. He had supposed that the colored men attached to the family, Jupiter and Peter—who were not thought of as being slaves—would look after the ladies and take care of the farm. But shortly after Billy went away to war, those two had slipped off and were not heard of again. He had been in the process of applying for permission to return home when the Battle of Manassas befell him.

He seemed to remember mornings fondly, and summer mornings most fondly of all. To wake up to the smell of ham and coffee and biscuits and grits, to look off the front porch into the dew-shiny fields and to see the little creek in the bottom winking with a gleam through the bushes—well, these sights made him feel that Paradise might be something of a letdown when finally at last he disembarked upon that lucent shore. The haze-blue mountains offered deer and partridge, possum and quail, and Billy loved to take his bay mare, Cleopatra, and his father's old long-barreled rifle and hunt on those slopes from morn till midnight.

About that mare he was rapturous. "If I told you how smart Cleo was, and some of the things I've known her to do, you'd think I was straying from the truth," he said. "But I'm not. She really is the best horse in the world, the smartest and the gentlest. Not that she doesn't have a lot of spirit. Why, I believe she has more courage than a bear, but she's as gentle with children as a mammy. And she's the best hunter I know of, bar none."

The Beachams smiled, trying vainly to imagine that Private Harper would deliberately stray from the truth; but it was clear that in regard to his horse his infatuation might fetch him out of the strait path of accuracy without his ever being aware. It seemed that Cleopatra knew where game was to be found up there in the hills and when given her head would unerringly seek out the best cover to shoot deer and fowl of every sort. There never was a horse like her for woodlore. Harry felt his credulity strained when Harper mentioned that she could also sniff out trout in the river and would carry her master to the sweetest fishing holes. And Lydie left unspoken her reservations about Billy's account of Cleo's stamping out a fire and thus saving the Harper farmhouse and barn and the lives of the four of them.

A skeptical expression must have crossed her face, though, because Billy looked at her imploringly and said in the most earnest tone: "Oh, it's true, I assure you it is. You can ask Julie or Annie or my mother. They'll tell you it's gospel truth." Lydie realized then that she must keep her emotions out of her face, that Billy Harper always forgot that his family was sealed away in time past and that he was an orphan in a world of strangers.

He forgot himself so thoroughly when he spoke that his unhappy situation appeared to escape his memory. Yet something was troubling him. As the day went by, he grew restless and his soft volubility began to lapse. Toward the end of the second week, not even questions about Cleopatra could alleviate his distractedness.

On Monday of the third week he spoke his mind. "I know you-all want to hear about the war," he said glumly. "And I know that's what

I'm supposed to be telling you. It's just that I can't bear to open up those wounds again. I guess I'd better try, though, since that's what I'm sent here to do."

"You're not supposed to do anything that you don't want to," Harry said. "We haven't been notified that you are required to talk about the war. In fact, we haven't been notified of anything much. I wish I could get a phone call through to those History folks."

"That's right," Lydie said. "I'm tired of hearing about that ugly old war. I'd much rather hear about your mother and sisters and the farm."

All their reassurances would not lighten Billy's darkened spirits. The more they spoke soothing words, the gloomier he became, and they could see that he was steeling himself to broach the subject and they became anxious about him, for his nervousness increased as his determination grew.

When he began to talk, after supper on his third Wednesday, he was obviously desperate. His hands trembled and he kept his eyes trained on the beige patch of living-room carpet in front of his armchair and he spoke in a low mutter. His sentences were jumbled and hard to understand. He was sweating.

"There were onlookers up on the ridges," he said. "We were down in the bottom fields there at Manassas when McDowell brought his troops around. We could see them up there, the spectators, I mean, and I borrowed Jed's glass and took a look and they were drinking wine and laughing and there were ladies in their carriages, and younguns too, setting off firecrackers. So when I handed him his glass back I said, 'I don't believe it's going to be a fight, not with the high society people looking on; I expect that McDowell and General Bee will parley.' And he said, 'No, it'll be a fight, Billy. Can't neither side back off now, we're in too close to each other. McDowell will have to fight here right outside of Washington because Lincoln hisself might be up there on a hilltop watching.' But I didn't believe him. I never thought we'd fight that day."

He paused and licked his lips and asked for a glass of water. Lydie brought it from the kitchen, ice cubes tingling, and told the private with meaningful tenderness that he did not need to continue his story.

Harper took the glass and sipped, appearing not to hear her words. He kept his eyes downcast and began again. "At nine in the morning it was already warm and we knew we'd be feeling the heat and then with no warning it started up. Sergeant Roper hadn't no more than told us to brace ourselves because there appeared to be more Yankees here than ants in an anthill when we saw gunsmoke off to our left, a little decline there, and heard the shots and in that very first volley Jed fell down with a ball in the middle of his chest, but before he hit the ground he took another one in his shoulder that near about tore his left arm off. I didn't have a least idea any of them was close enough to get a shot at us. I laid down by Jed and took him in my arms but couldn't do nothing and they made me let him lay and start fighting."

His face had been flushed and sweaty but now was sugar-white and drenched. His eyes wore dark circles, and when he raised them for the first time, caught up as he was in his memories, he seemed not to see Lydie or Harry or anything around him. He was sweating so profusely his uniform was darkening—that was what Lydie thought at first, but then she rose to clutch Harry's arm. Blood was dripping from Harper's sleeve over his wrist and onto the rug.

"So I got on one knee to see what I could and brought my rifle up, but I didn't know what to do. I could tell they were all around us because my comrades were firing at them in every direction but I couldn't spot anything, so much smoke and dust. I saw some muzzle blazes on my right and thought I might shoot, but then maybe that was one of our lines over there. I was a pretty good marksman to go a-hunting, but in a battle I couldn't figure where to aim."

His voice had sunk almost to a whisper, and his tunic and the chair he sat in were soaking with blood. Harry remembered that it would be pig blood and not human, but he was horrified all the same—more disturbed, perhaps, than if it had been Harry's own blood. He looked quickly at Lydie and then rushed to her aid. He knew now what Billy Harper had meant when he said that to talk about the war opened old wounds.

He took his wife by the arm and drew her toward the bedroom. She went along without a murmur, her face drawn and blanched. He could feel her whole body trembling. He helped her to lie down and told her to keep still, not to move; he would take care of everything, he said. It was going to be all right.

But when he returned to the living room, Harper was lying face down on the floor. He had tumbled out of his chair and lay motionless in a thick smelly puddle of brownish blood. Harper knelt to examine him and it was obvious that he was gone, literally drained of life.

Harry telephoned for an ambulance and sat down to think about what to tell the medics when they came. Perhaps they wouldn't accept Private Harper; perhaps they wouldn't regard him as a real human being. To whom could he turn for assistance in that case? He knew better than to call Archives and History; the last time he had called those numbers, a recorded voice informed him that they had all been disconnected. Now he was trying to reach, by mail and telephone and fax machine, his congressman, Representative Doy Collingwood, but so far had received no reply.

When the ambulance came, though, the young paramedics understood the situation immediately and seemed to find it routine. The fellow with the blond-red mustache—he looked like a teenager, Harry thought ruefully—only glanced at the inert figure on the rug before asking, "Civil War?"

"Yes," Harry said. "My God, it was awful. My wife is almost hysterical. This is just terrible."

The fellow nodded. "We get them like this all the time. Faulty parts and sloppy workmanship. Sometimes we'll get four calls a week like this."

"Can't something be done?"

"Have you tried to get in touch with Ark and Hist?"

"With whom?"

"The Archives and History Division . . . in Washington," he asked, then saw Harry's expression. "Never mind, I know. Tell you what, though. I'd better have a look to see if your wife is okay. Where is she?"

Harry showed him the bedroom and stood by while he ministered to Lydie. She murmured her gratitude, but kept her eyes closed. The young medic gave her some pills to take and went with Harry back to the living room. "She'll be all right," he said. "Probably have a couple of rough nights."

The driver had already put down a stretcher and rolled Harry's body over onto it. His eyes were open and a dreadful change had come to his face, a change that was more than death and worse, a change that made Private Harper look as if he'd never been human—in this life or any other.

Harry had to look away. "My God," he said.

"Pretty awful, isn't it?" The medic's response was cheerful, matter-of-fact. "Shoddy stuff, these Ark and Hist sims. But there's some good salvage there, more than you'd think by looking at it."

"What did you call him?" Harry asked. "Simms?"

"Sim. It's a nickname. A simulacrum from the Division of Archives and History. Your tax dollars at work, know what I mean? Sign here," he said, handing Harry a clipboard and a pen. "And here," he said turning a page. "And here. And here. And here. And here. And here. And here. And here."

The medic had predicted rough nights for Lydie, but she suffered bad days as well and took to her bed. She kept the shades drawn and the lights down and watched chamber music on the vidcube. Harry gave his shop over to the attentions of two assistants and stayed home with his wife, preparing her scanty meals and consoling her and monitoring the installation of the new carpet and choosing a new chair for the living room. Lydie would probably hate the chocolate-colored wingback he'd bought, but that was all right. She could exchange it when she was up and around.

He planned to stay home with her for a week or two—for as long as it took to make certain that the government was sending to the Beacham household no more sims. Harry pronounced the word with an ugly angry hiss; *sssimsss*. He put as much disgust into the sibilants as his teeth could produce, but there was no satisfaction for him.

He was so infuriated and felt so impotent that he began to wish a new specimen would turn up, just so that he could send it away with a message for the people who had dispatched it. He prepared several speeches in his mind, each more savage than the last, each more heartfelt and more eloquent.

He never got to deliver any of them, even though the expected third visitor did, after all, show, a week later than had been stipulated. But he didn't announce himself, didn't knock at the door and present his papers as Aldershot and Harper had done. He just stood in the front yard with his back turned toward the house and gazed at the houses opposite and at the children riding bicycles and chasing balls along the asphalt lanes of Shining Acres. Often he would look at the sky, at the puffy cloud masses scooting overhead, and he would take off his big gray hat with the floppy brim and shade his eyes with his hand.

This hat was not of Confederate gray but of a lighter, mineral color, nearly the same gray color as the man's clothing. Nor was his attire military; he wore cotton trousers held up by a broad leather belt and a soft woolen shirt with an open collar. When he removed his hat, shining gray locks fell past his ears and the sunlight imparted to this mass of silver a whitish halo effect. He turned around to look at the Beacham house, and Harry saw that he wore a glorious gray beard, clean and bright and patriarchal, and that his eyes were clear and warm.

Even from where Harry stood inside, the man's gaze was remarkable: calm and trusting and unworried and soothing. When he replaced his hat Harry recognized his gesture as easy and graceful, neither sweeping nor constrained. There was a natural ease about his figure that put Harry's mind at rest. He would still send him away, of course he would, but Harry began to soften the speech he had planned to make, to modify its ferocity and to sweeten a little bit its bitterness.

But when had this fellow arrived? How long had he been standing there, observing the world from his casual viewing point, with his little gray knapsack lying carelessly on the lawn? He might have been there for hours; nothing in his manner would ever betray impatience.

Harry opened the door and called to the man. "Hey you," he said. "Hey you, standing in my yard."

The man turned slowly, presenting his whole figure as if he wished to be taken in from crown to shoe-sole, to be examined and measured for what he was as a physical being. "I am Wade Wordmore," he said, and his voice was full of gentle strength. "I have come a great distance, overstepping time and space; I am the visitor who has been sent."

"Yeah, that's right," Harry said. "The government sent you, right? The History people? They sent you to the Beacham residence, right?"

"That is correct in some measure," said Wade Wordmore. "But I believe there is more to it than that."

"Well, go away," Harry said. "We don't want you. We've had enough—" He didn't finish the sentence he had planned to say; he found that he could not look into Wordmore's gaze and say, *We've had enough of you goddamn sims to last us a lifetime.*

Ssssimssss.

"Gladly I go where I am wanted and unwanted," Wordmore said. "The world is my home, in it I am free to loaf and meditate, every particle is as interesting to me as every other particle, the faces of men and women gladden me as I journey."

"I don't mean for you to wander around like a stray dog," Harry said. "I mean, go back where you came from. Go back to the government."

"But what to me are governments?" the gray man replied. "I, Wade Wordmore, American, untrammeled by boundaries, unfixed as to station, and at my ease in all climes and latitudes, answer to no laws save those my perfect nature (for I know I am perfect, how can a man tall and in pure health be not perfect?), and am powerful to overstep any border."

Here was a stumper. Harry had foreseen that Ark and Hist would send another defective simulacrum, but he had not imagined being put in charge of a bona fide grade-A blue ribbon lunatic. It was clear from Wordmore's manner as he stooped to take up his knapsack and sling it on his shoulder that he was willing to stroll out into a century he knew nothing about, utterly careless about what would happen to him for good or ill. And beyond this privileged residential suburb, Wordmore's adventures would be mostly ill; his strange aspect and wild mode of speech would mark him as an easy victim to chicanery and violence alike.

"Oh, for God's sake," Harry said. There was no help for it. "For God's sake, come in the house."

As Wordmore stepped over the threshold, he removed his floppy hat. But this gesture of deference only served to underscore a casual royalty of presence; he entered Harry's house as if he belonged there not as a guest but by right of ownership. "I am most grateful to you, sir, and to everyone else in the house. White or black, Chinaman or Lascar or Hottentot, they are all equal to me and I bid them good day."

"We're fresh out of those. There's no one here but me and my wife Lydie. She's not feeling well and she's not going to be pleased that I let you come in. I'll have some tall explaining to do."

But Lydie stood already in the hall doorway. She had drawn a bright floral wrapper over her nightgown, yet the cheerful colors only caused her face to look paler and her eyes more darkly encircled. She appeared feverish. "Oh Harry," she said softly, wearily.

"Honey—"

"Among the strong I am strongest," Wordmore said in a resonant steady voice that then quieted almost to a whisper: "Among the weak I am gentlest." He tucked his knapsack under his left arm and went to Lydie and took her hand and drew her forward as if he were leading her onto a ballroom floor. He placed her in the new chocolate-colored wingback chair and smiled upon her benevolently and gave her the full benefit of that gray-eyed gaze so enormous with sympathy.

She responded with a tremulous smile and then leaned back and closed her eyes. "I hope you will be nice to us," she said in a voice as small as the throbbing of a faraway cricket. "We've never harmed anybody, Harry and I. We just wanted to know about his ancestors who fought in the Civil War. I guess that wasn't such a good idea."

"You know," Harry said, "I don't recall hearing about any Wordmores in my family. Are you sure you're related to me?"

"Each man is my brother, every woman my sister," Wordmore stated. "To all I belong equally, disregarding none. In every household I am welcome, being full of health and good will and bearing peaceful tidings for all gathered there."

At these words Lydie opened her eyes, then blinked them rapidly several times. Then she gave Harry one of the most reproachful glances one spouse ever turned upon another.

In a moment, though, she closed her eyes again and nestled into the wingback. Harry could see that she was relaxing, her breathing slowed now and regular. Wordmore emitted a powerful physical aura, an almost visible emanation of peaceful healthful ease. Harry wondered if the man might have served as a physician in the War. Certainly his presence was having a salubrious effect upon Lydie, and Harry decided it would be all right to have Wordmore around for a few hours longer. If he was a madman he was harmless.

"Can I offer you a drink?" Harry asked. "We still have some bourbon left over from an earlier ancestor."

"I drink only pure water from the spring gushing forth," Wordmore replied. "My food is ever of the plainest and most wholesome."

"Tap water is all we've got," Harry said.

"I will take what you offer, I am pleased at every hospitality." He turned his attention to Lydie, placing his delicate freckled hand on her forehead. "You will soon be strong again," he told her. "Rest now and remember the summer days of your youth, the cows lowing at the pasture gate and the thrush singing in the thicket and the haywain rolling over the pebbled road with the boys lying in the hay, their arms in friendship disposed around one another."

Lydie smiled ruefully. "I can't remember anything like that," she said. "I grew up in Chicago. It was mostly traffic and street gangs fighting with knives."

"Remember then your mother," Wordmore said. "Remember her loving smile as over your bed she leant, stroking your hair and murmuring a melody sweet and ancient. Remember her in the kitchen as the steam rose around her and the smell of bread baking and the fruits of the season stewed and sugared, their thick juices oozing."

Lydie opened her eyes and sat forward. "Well, actually," she explained, "my parents divorced when I was five and I didn't see much of either of them after that. Only on holidays when one of them might visit at my convent school."

He was not to be discouraged. "Remember the days of Christmas then, when you and your comrade girls, tender and loving, waited for the gladsome step in the foyer—"

"It's all right," Lydie said firmly. "Really. I don't need to remember anything. I feel much better. I really do."

Harry returned with the ice water and looked curiously at the duo. "What's been going on?" he asked. "What are you two talking about?"

"Mr. Wordmore has been curing me of my ills," Lydie said.

The gray man nodded placidly, even a little smugly. "It is a gift that I have, allotted me graciously at my birth, as it was given to you and you, freely offered to all." He sipped his water.

"To me?" Harry asked. "I don't think I've got any healing powers. Business is my line; I own a little video rental shop."

"Business too is good," Wordmore said. "The accountant weary, arranging his figures at end of day, his eye-shade pulled over his furrowed brow and the lamplight golden on the clean-ruled page, and the manager of stores, the keeper of inventories, his bunched iron keys jangling on his manly thigh—"

"Well, it's not quite like that," Harry said. "I can see what you're getting at, though. You think business is okay, the free enterprise system and all."

"All trades and occupations are equal and worthy, the fisherman gathering in his nets fold on fold, and the hog drover with his long staff and his boots caked with fine delicious muck, and the finder of broken sewer pipes and the emptier of privies—"

"Yes, yes," Harry interrupted. "You mean that it's a good thing everybody has a job to do."

Wordmore smiled warmly and took another sip of water, gently shaking the glass to enjoy the jingle of the ice cubes.

"Maybe it's time we thought about making dinner," Harry said. "I'm not a bad cook. I'm sure Lydie would rather stay and talk to you while I rustle up something to eat."

"Oh no!" she exclaimed. "That would never do. I feel fine. I'll go right in and start on it."

"I wish you wouldn't," Harry said. "You ought to be resting."

"Honey," said Lydie with unmistakable determination, "you're going to be the one to stay here and talk to Mr. Wordmore. I don't care how much I have to cook."

"My food is ever of the plainest," Wordmore intoned. "The brown loaf hearty from the oven, its aromas arising, and the cool water from the mountain spring gushed forth—"

"Right," Lydie said. "I think I understand."

They knew pretty well what to expect at dinner, and Wordmore didn't surprise them, drinking sparely and nibbling vegetables and discoursing in voluminous rolling periods upon any subject that was brought up—except that he never managed to light precisely upon the topic at hand, only somewhere in the scattered vicinity. Yet it was soothing to listen to him: his sentences which at first were so warm and sympathetic and filled with humane feeling and calm loving-kindness lost their intimacy after a while. They seemed to become as impersonal and distant as some large sound of nature: the muffled roar of a far-off waterfall or wind in the mountaintop balsams or sea waves lapping at a pebbled beach. His unpausing talk was not irritating because his good will was unmistakable; neither was it boring because the Beachams soon learned not to listen to it for content and took an absent-minded pleasure in the mere sound of it. Harry thought of it as a kind of verbal Muzak and wondered how Wordmore had been perceived by his contemporaries. They must have found him as strange an example of humankind as Harry and Lydie did.

On the other hand they must have got on well with him. He'd make a good neighbor, surely, because he never had a bad word for anyone. He had no bad words at all, not a smidgen of disapproval for anything, as far as they could discern. If potatoes were mentioned, Wordmore would go a long way in praise of potatoes; if it was bunions, they too were champion elements of the universe, indispensable. Housefly or horsefly, rhododendron or rattlesnake, Messiah or mosquito—they all seemed to hold a high place in the gray man's esteem; to him the world was a better place for containing any and all of them.

He went on so placidly in this vein that Harry couldn't resist testing the limits of his benignity. "Tell me, Mr. Wordmore—"

"Among each and every I am familiar, the old and the young call me by my First-Name," Wordmore said. "The children climb on my lap and push their hands into my beard, laughing."

"Sure, all right. Wade. Tell me, Wade, what was the worst thing you ever saw? The most terrible?"

"Equally terrible and awesome in every part is the world, the lightnings that jab the antipodes, the pismire in its—"

"I mean, personally," Harry explained. "What's the worst thing that ever happened to you?"

He fell silent and meditated. His voice when he spoke was heavy and sorrowful. "It was the Great Conflict," he said, "where I ministered to the spirits of the beautiful young men who lay wounded and sick and dying, their chests all bloody-broken and—"

"Harry!" Lydie cried. "I won't listen to this."

"That's all right," Harry said quickly. "We don't need to hear that part, Wade. I was just wondering what kinds of things you might think were wrong. Bad, I mean."

"Bad I will not say, though it was terrible, the young men so fair and handsome that I wished them hale again and whole that we might walk to the meadows together and there show our love, the Divine Nimbus around our bodies playing—"

"Whoa," Harry said. "Wait a minute now."

"Are you gay?" Lydie asked. She leaned forward, her interest warmly aroused. "I didn't think there used to be gay people. In Civil War times, I mean."

"My spirits are buoyant always, with the breeze lifting, my mind happy and at ease, a deep gaiety overtakes my soul when I behold a bullfrog or termite—"

"No, now. She means—well, *gay*," Harry said. "Are you homosexual?"

"To me sex, the Divine Nimbus, every creature exhales and I partake willingly, my soul gladly joining, my body locked in embrace with All, my—"

"All?" Henry and Lydie spoke in unison.

Wordmore nodded. "All, yes, All, sportively I tender my—"

"Does this include the bullfrog and the termite?" Harry asked.

"Yes," Wordmore said without hesitation. "Why should every creature not enjoy my manliness? Whole and hearty I am Wade Wordmore, American, liking the termite equally with the—"

"Wade, my friend," Harry said. "You old-time fellows sure do give us modern people something to think about. I'd like you to meet my congressman and give him the benefit of some of your ideas. Tomorrow I'm going to drive you over to the state capital and introduce you. How would you like that?" He slipped Lydie a happy wink.

"The orators and statesmen are ever my camaradoes," Wordmore said. "I descry them on the high platform, the pennons of America in the wind around them flying, their lungs in-taking the air, and the words outpouring."

"It's a date then," Harry said. "Pack your knapsack for a long stay. I intend for you and him to become fast friends."

But when they arrived in Raleigh the next day and Harry drove around toward Representative Collingwood's headquarters, he found the streets blocked with cars honking and banging fenders and redfaced policemen trying to create some sort of order and pattern. The sidewalks too were jammed with pedestrians, most of them dressed in the uniform of the Army of the Confederate States of America.

Sssimssss.

"My God," Harry said. He could not have imagined that so many people had subscribed to the Ancestor Program, that so many simulacra had been produced. Looking at the people who were obviously not sims, he saw written on their faces weariness, exasperation, sorrow, horror, guilt, and cruel determination—all the feelings he and Lydie had experienced for the past weeks, the feelings he now felt piercingly with Wordmore sitting beside him, babbling on about the Beautiful Traffic Tangles of America.

Finally a channel opened and he rolled forward, to be stopped by a tired-looking policeman.

Harry thumbed his window down, and the officer leaned in.

"May I see who is with you, sir?"

"This is Wade Wordmore," Harry said. "You'd find it hard to understand how glad he is to meet you."

"I am Wade Wordmore," said the graybeard, "and glad of your company, admiring much the constable as he goes his rounds—"

"Well, I'm glad you like company," the policeman said. "You're going to have plenty of it." He turned his bleared gaze on Harry. "We're shifting all the traffic to the football stadium parking lot, sir, and we're asking everyone to escort their ancestors onto the field."

"Is everybody bringing them in?" Harry asked.

"Yes, sir, almost everyone. It seems like everybody ran out of patience at the same time. They've been coming in like this for three days now."

"I can believe it," Harry said. "What is the History Division going to do with them all?"

"There is no longer a History Division," the policeman said. "In fact, we just got word a while ago that the government has shut down the whole Reality Department."

"They shut down Reality? Why did they do that?"

"They took a poll," the policeman replied. "Nobody wanted it."

"Good Lord," Harry said. "What is going to happen?"

"I don't know, sir, but I'm afraid I'll have to ask you to move along."

"Okay, all right," Harry said. He drove on a few feet, then stopped and called back: "I've got an idea. Why don't we ship all these sims north to the Union states? After all, they're the ones who killed them in the first place."

"I'm afraid that those states have the same problem we do," the policeman said. "Please, sir, do move along. There will be someone at the stadium to give you instructions."

"Okay. Thanks." He rolled the window up and edged the car forward.

Wordmore had fallen silent, looking in open-mouthed wonder at all the cars and the Confederate soldiers streaming by and mothers and children white-faced and weeping and dogs barking and policemen signaling and blowing whistles.

"You know," Harry said, "I just never thought about the Yankees wanting to meet *their* ancestors, but of course they would. It's a natural curiosity. I guess it must have seemed like a good idea to bring all this history back to life, but now look. What are we going to do now?" The station wagon in front of him moved, and Harry inched forward.

"The history of the nation I see instantly before me, as on a plain rolling to the mountains majestic, like a river rolling, the beautiful young men in their uniforms with faces scarce fuzzed with beard—"

But Harry was not listening. His hands tightened on the steering wheel till the knuckles went purple and white. "My God," he said. "We've got all our soldiers back again and the Yankees have got theirs back. War is inevitable. I believe we're going to fight the whole Civil War over again. I'll be damned if I don't."

"—the beautiful young men falling in battle amid smoke of cannon and the sky louring over, the mothers weeping at night and the sweethearts weeping—"

"Oh, shut up, Wordmore. I know how terrible it is. It's too horrible to think about." He remembered Lieutenant Aldershot and Private Harper, and a gritty tight wry little smile crossed his face. "Bluebellies," Harry said. "This time we'll show them."

Kelly Cherry

THE HUNGARIAN COUNTESS

While I was in the mental hospital, my brother ran off with a
Hungarian countess. I found this out when I called Connecticut.
Maureen, the woman he had been living with before he came back
from the countess and moved in with Alma, answered the telephone.
"He's in Spain," she said, "with a Hungarian countess." You hear far
stranger things than that when you are a patient on a psych ward, so I
just said, "When's he coming back?" He was the only stateside relative
I had, bad blood though some might call him. "How should I know?"
Maureen said. "He's in *Spain* with a fucking Hungarian *countess.*"

I hung up the telephone and crawled back to bed. I stayed there for
three weeks. It was a semiprivate room. Then I went home because
there had been a blizzard and I had to shovel my sidewalk. Living in
Wisconsin, I devote much of my energy to worrying about snow. Will
it? Should I stay up late to see whether it stops before midnight so if it
does I can get up early to clear it off before I leave for work, since
there's a noon deadline, or will it go on after midnight, in which case
the city will give me until noon of the following day and I can get to
sleep early, except that I will have stayed awake until midnight to
determine this? Excessive worrying was one reason I wound up in the
hospital, and it was the reason I left.

Wisconsin is a state made for worriers. Our hyperbolic legalism is
both a symptom and a cause of the extreme worry that goes on in this

state. We march against U.S. imperialism and big brotherism and send Joe McCarthy to the Senate. We tax people out of sight to support social agencies and then pass a Grandparent Liability Act to make private citizens ineligible for state aid. What do all those inaccessible agencies do? Whom do they serve? Wisconsin is working on these questions right now. It plans to draft a report to the American people as soon as it discovers the answers.

Meanwhile, my brother had come back from Spain. Without the Hungarian countess. A true member of the jet set, she had moved on to Costa Rica. My brother was now with Alma, who had up to this point been best friends with Maureen but who was now Maureen's archenemy. "How was Ibiza?" I asked him on the phone.

"Fine," he said, "but the countess was a teetotaler."

My brother, once arbiter of my life and still at that point bound to me in ways so subtle I had yet to understand them, was dying—to use a short word for a long process. I had consulted with his doctor, also by telephone, who said my brother was about seventy years old internally. I imagined an old man inside a not-so-old man. I imagined a decrepit liver, a withered heart. His insides would have a sheen of green, like time-tarnished bronze. The cause was alcohol, which was what my brother thought flowed in a real man's veins instead of blood. It certainly flowed in his veins, and had been so flowing since his first year in college, at a Baptist institution in Virginia from which each of us was in turn expelled, one for cutting classes, one for taking more credits than was considered healthful for a clean-minded young woman.

"How was the mental hospital?" he asked, in return.

It was the first of December; I hadn't yet unpacked my bag. I had shoveled the sidewalk first thing. The red shovel lifted the snow like a giant mitten. The pale sun gleamed in the sky behind the blue spruce like a fragile Christmas tree ornament.

"Ninotchka," he said, "inasmuch as I'm dying, will you do me a favor?"

He was forty-seven. He had refused the liver scan. If he continued drinking and what he had was only cirrhosis, he could last six months to a year. If it was liver cancer, three months. This was from the doctor, so I accepted it—if it had come from my brother, I wouldn't have known to what extent he was dramatizing the facts: my brother had never allowed himself to feel restricted by the truth.

"Of course," I said, "but if you'd just quit drinking, you could perhaps live for a long, long time and I could do you many more favors."

"But if I gave up drinking and died of liver cancer anyway, I'd resent being a sober corpse. Besides, this is all academic. You know I can't quit."

"You could if you wanted to," I argued. I was not yet knowledgeable about the biochemical basis of alcoholism. "I wish you would have the liver scan done."

"I can't afford the liver scan."

"I'll pay for it."

"Honey, I'm losing weight every day. I have jaundice. My liver's so big it feels like a football, pure pigskin. It's too late." I wanted to cry when I heard this, but I was also rather bored, because I had heard it many times. We always talked about him and his problems. He would ask a pro forma How are you? but the conversation quickly reverted to him. He was the center of the universe. "Besides," he said, "I don't care about living anymore."

"Does Alma know that? Does Babette know that?"

"That's what I called about," he said. "My daughter."

I wished he would just call her Babette. I knew she was his daughter. Whenever he said "my daughter," I was reminded that I had no children.

"What about her?"

"She's here."

She was supposed to be in Athens, Georgia, with her mother. Who was Wife Number Two. (Alma, Maureen, and the countess were girlfriends. Andrea, Janice, and Carlotta were the wives, in that order. These were the main players in a cast of thousands.)

"How did she get there?"

"She hitchhiked." He said this with pride, as if to say: How much she loves me!

But what I thought was, Thirteen years old, hitchhiking from Georgia to Connecticut! Jesus!—though I sensed his need to view this feat as confirmation of his superior parenting. See, he was saying to himself, she prefers me to her mother. He seemed not to understand that because of his drinking he had been an erratic, improvident, sometimes self-pitying and often sarcastic father.

"I wish I could keep her here," he said, "but Alma can't run the risk of having a teen-ager in the house. You know how tenuous her health is."

I didn't like Alma. She had black penciled-on eyebrows that charged at each other over her eyes like two mad bulls, pulled together by a permanent frown. She was stingy. She had turned on Maureen like a vicious dog—according to Maureen, at least. I kept track of all these developments from long distance. It was better than "As the World Turns."

"Send her back to Janice."

"That bitch," he said. "She put out an all-points bulletin, but now that her daughter turns out to be safely here, she doesn't want her back."

"You want me to take her." Light dawned, as I remembered now that he had asked for a favor.

"Do you mind?"

Did I mind? Never! On the contrary, his request made me feel as if I had a purpose in life—and not having a biological purpose in life was another reason I'd wound up in the mental hospital. So I said yes. He didn't tell me that the reason she'd run away from home was that she'd gotten knocked up.

She stood in the middle of the bus station, shivering in a brown coat that had lost its buttons. She was clutching both sides of the coat collar to keep it from falling open. It fell open anyway, over her little hillocky stomach. On the floor next to her was a blue speckled Samsonite suitcase.

She had long brown hair, freckles on her nose, the bone structure of a *Vogue* cover girl, and a hearing aid. She wore her hair long to hide the hearing aid. When you could glimpse it, it looked like a small mushroom growing in the cave of her ear.

"We'll have to get you a parka," I said.

"Did my father tell you I was pregnant?"

I nodded, lying, and picked up the suitcase.

"I'm too far gone to have an abortion," she said defiantly. I think she expected me to take her straight from the bus station to the abortionist.

"Okay," I said. "You still have to have a parka. It gets a lot colder here than it does in Georgia."

"It gets pretty damn cold in Georgia."

I could see she had not been going to her geography class.

After supper, we sat in front of the fire and she attempted to cure me of my lack of sophistication. "My boyfriend's name is Roy," she began. "He's quite mature."

"How mature?"

In her honor, I had lit candles. I had put chrysanthemums in the center of the table in the dining room. Soon I would buy a Christmas tree that would stand shyly in a corner of the sunroom. My little dog sat next to me in the reading chair, but from time to time he darted over to the couch to let Babette pet him.

"Twenty-two," she said.

I thought that was entirely too mature for a thirteen-year-old, but I held my tongue. She was my niece, not "my daughter"—though considering a black night some years ago, she might have been.

"He deals," she said, determined to strike terror in my heart.

"He what?"

"Deals. You know, drugs and stuff. Naturally he's always got lots of money."

"That's nice," I said.

"Yeah," she said. "So I decided to go to bed with him."

"Because he's got lots of money?"

"Because he's mature."

"What does your mother think of all this?"

"She likes him."

"She does?" I found this hard to believe.

"She says she wishes *her* boyfriend was as nice as Roy is."

"I thought they were married."

"Mom just likes people to think they are. She's afraid he'll lose interest in her and leave. She's afraid he'll get interested in me. She said so. She said she thought it was a good idea for me to go out with

Roy because then Eugene would know better than to try anything. She says Roy is protection for both of us."

"I see."

"Do you want to know how I got pregnant?" she asked.

I had naively assumed I already knew how she got pregnant.

"We were watching television. Me and Roy. There was this neat-o movie on where everybody got killed. Like there was this one scene where this girl had her head cut off and she still ran around in a circle like a chicken. Gross." Babette got up and walked around in a circle, holding her neck with both hands, then fell back on the couch. "It was July and awfully hot so we started taking off our clothes. And then we just did it. I turned my hearing aid off since I couldn't see the movie with Roy blocking my view anyway."

"That was sensible," I said.

"And afterward," she went on, after I thought the story had ended, "because it was so hot, Roy went into the kitchen to get a beer and he brought me one, and I had turned my hearing aid back on and was watching television the way I like to, like this." She swiveled around so that she was backward on the couch with her head on the floor and her legs against the wall behind the couch. My dog sprang from the chair and went over to sniff her hair. He began to lick her face.

"You still didn't have any clothes on?" I asked. I wanted to be sure I got the picture right.

"It was *hot*, Aunt Nina. Anyway," she continued, from the floor, "I was watching the end of the movie like this and Roy brought me a beer and I started trying to balance the can on my forehead, just for the hell of it. I don't know if you've ever tried to balance a beer can on your forehead. It requires concentration."

"I'm sure," I murmured.

"Anyway, that's what did it."

"You got pregnant from drinking beer?"

"You're so funny, Aunt Nina," Babette said. "My father always said you have a really good sense of humor."

"Your father exaggerates."

"Well, don't you see? It was because I had my legs up against the wall like this." She righted herself on the couch. There was a baby in that stomach—probably a very dizzy baby. "All that stuff—you know that stuff?"—I nodded to indicate a tentative acquaintance with semen—"all that stuff was running up inside me, because I was upside down. It couldn't leak out the way it always did before. That's how I got pregnant." Her smile disappeared and she looked glum. "If only I hadn't been balancing the beer can on my forehead, I wouldn't have gotten pregnant."

I got up and went into the kitchen for scissors, snipped a burntsienna blossom off the chrysanthemum plant, and tucked it behind her ear, the "good" one. Much depended on how hard she was trying to listen. "You better go to bed," I said. "It was a long trip."

I banked the fading fire, blew out the candles, and led her to the bedroom I'd prepared for her. She asked for a glass of water to put her chrysanthemum in, and I brought her a shallow glass bowl. The blossom floated like a little boat. From her blue-speckled suitcase she extracted a pair of pajamas and put them on. They were white with tiny dogs and cats all over them, and black teardrops representing rain. There was a drawstring around the waist instead of elastic. Her stomach had a soft bloom to it, like the chrysanthemum. "Aunt Nina," she said, "there's something I have to tell you."

"What's that?" I asked, savoring the maternal pleasure that went with having her in my care, though only temporarily. I pulled the covers up around her shoulders.

"Roy said he might come out here," she said. "You know, to visit?"

I enrolled Babette in school. She didn't want to go because, she said, everyone would make fun of her condition, but in a few days, she had girlfriends who dropped in after school to talk about boyfriends. I gathered that they wanted Babette to tell them what it was like to "do it." She would tell them about the beer can but she never really said what it was like to do it. They giggled incessantly, a sound like crystal beads spilling on a floor. If you said, "How are your parents?" they giggled. If you said, "How's school?" they giggled. They spent a lot of time picking out names for the baby.

I took Babette to my gynecologist. He told me she was malnourished. "Make her eat three good meals a day," he advised. "Plenty of milk, protein, vegetables. Where is her mother?"

"Georgia."

"I don't like this," he said, beating a tattoo on his desk blotter with his pencil. Babette was waiting for me in the waiting room. This doctor had helped me to try to get pregnant. He considered that he had an almost uxorious interest in me. "Why isn't she with her mother? Are you sure you can handle this? Are you sure you want to?"

"I don't know," I said. "It's certainly painful to watch someone else being pregnant, but on the other hand, I like having her around the house. I think her mother feels threatened by her because she's so gorgeous."

"I see," he said, wrinkling his forehead. He was a sexy, vigorous man still in his thirties. And open-minded: he'd had a permanent. His dark blond hair rippled in waves like wheat. "Well, make her eat three meals a day. Lots of milk, protein—"

"Vegetables," I said.

Babette's mother called. "Hello, Janice," I said. "I guess you want to know how Babette is doing. She's fine." I didn't say anything about malnutrition. This was a tightrope I was walking—I could wind up with everyone angry at me.

"Listen," Janice said, "it's not my fault she got pregnant. It happens to girls all the time. I did my best."

"I know you did."

"I can't be watching her every minute of the goddamned day."

"I know," I said.

"You just don't know what it's like," she said, "living with a teen-ager."

"I guess I'm about to find out."

"Well," she said, "call me if there are any problems or anything. Good luck."

"Don't you want to talk to her?"

"Not now." She whispered into the phone: "I'm not alone."

"Would Eugene really mind if you talked to your daughter?" I was beginning to think of Eugene as the Monster of the Hemisphere.

"Mind?" She laughed. "He'd kill me. That man," she said, "is a tiger. I have to hold him by the tail."

She hung up. Babette was standing next to me.

"She didn't want to talk to me, did she," Babette said.

"She said she couldn't. Eugene was there."

"That's just an excuse. She didn't want to talk to me."

She ran upstairs and slammed the door to her room.

I was afraid to get too close to Babette—and not only because she was subject to the higher authority of her mother and father and would be leaving at some as yet unspecified point. Her presence in my house seemed to me to be a kind of victory for my brother. A thousand miles away, I was his fourth wife, mothering his child. I had been haunted by an image of the two of us growing old together, a parody of a marriage. I had looked for a husband, hoping to escape that destiny— but for twenty years I never told a man why I was so eager, or why I felt so unfit. My one actual husband, who for sure didn't stick around for long, accused me of caring about my brother more than about him—and that was true if "caring about" meant "being in the Svengalian thrall of." My brother had always been determined to keep me in his control. For many years I misunderstood this as love. That's what he called it, and I wanted to believe that's what it was. I *had* to believe that's what it was, or else, I thought, I would hate him and myself and possibly everybody else. After twenty years I learned to defy my brother and stand up for myself and I no longer felt I needed a husband to separate me from him, but destiny is destiny, and here was his daughter, full of phrases she had adopted from him and with his propensity for self-dramatization, as well as the deep sea-green of his eyes.

When I was in the mental hospital I learned that life is a comedy of errors. Previously I had recognized it as sometimes a comedy, sometimes a tragedy, but I hadn't realized the extensive role error plays. I began to think of my own mistakes less as a message that I had no right to live and more as a series of necessary stitches in the hem of existence, which one way or another we have to fit to ourselves.

My roommate was a farmer's wife named Wanda. She had two small children. When her husband told her he was leaving her for another woman, she tried to kill herself. She still had the suicide note she'd written, and showed it to me with satisfaction. It was the longest thing she'd ever written—to her, a novel. *I have took poison,* the note said, *and now I am going to lay down and go to sleep and when I wake up Ill be with Jesus in heaven and you can marrie Tessie Jo. Please take good care of my babies Billy thats all I ask.* She had been sure her husband would come back when he read that note. Every time *she* read it, she felt sorry for herself, so she was sure Billy would feel sorry for her too, and tell Tessie Jo to go fuck herself, and then he'd come back and be a good husband and father again. When it didn't work out this way, she lost all faith in fiction.

"You should show this note to your doctor," I urged.

"What goes on between a man and his wife," Wanda said, "is a sacred secret."

"Tell that to Tessie Jo," I said.

"Tessie Jo gave my Billy a sinful disease," Wanda said. "And now I have it."

"What kind of disease?" I asked.

"I itch all the time. Down there."

"You *have* to tell your doctor about *that*," I said. "Unless you want to itch forever."

The next night she said to me, "I told the doctor. About my itch."

"And?"

"He gave me something."

"That's good," I said. "Now the itch will go away."

At the end of the week, Wanda said to me, "Nina, you know my itch?"

I said yes, I knew her itch.

"It still itches. It's driving me crazy."

"Well, you came to the right place, Wanda. Are you using that cream the doctor gave you?"

"Every morning and every night, just like he told me," she said. "I rub it all over my chest. But I still itch."

Realizing this called for a professional, I fetched one of the nurses and told her what the problem was and hung around the lounge playing pool until the nurse had come back out of Wanda's room.

Wanda was standing in front of the mirror, brushing her hair.

"Now the itch will go away," I said.

A few days later, I asked her how she felt. "I don't itch anymore," she said. "But when the nurse looked at me, she put a radio up there."

I tried to suggest this was unlikely, but she insisted it was the case.

"You can't tell me I don't hear what I hear," she said. "I get 'A Prairie Home Companion.' I even pick up St. Louis."

Wanda was transferred to Mendota State. I heard later that Billy was adamant about a divorce. He told his lawyer he didn't want his kids being raised by a woman with a radio in her vagina.

Babette never wanted to do homework, but I made her. I said, "I'll do the monthly bills and you do your homework, and when we're both done, I'll make us each a cup of cocoa with a marshmallow in it."

She said she'd prefer grass.

Once I had to send her to her room. I turned off the Christmas tree lights. She came back down in an hour, sneaked up behind me, and put her arms around me and said, "Does Aunt Nina forgive me?"

"I don't like being manipulated, Babette," I said.

She glared at me as if I'd betrayed her by calling her bluff. She held my little dog under her chin and talked baby talk to him. She said she was "practicing."

Maureen called. "Have you talked with your brother lately?" she asked.

"Not lately."

"That son of a bitch."

"He's dying," I said to Maureen. "Doesn't that cancel out some of the hard feelings?"

She thought for a while, as if trying to decide whether it did or not. I could hear the ice cubes clinking in her drink at the other end of the line. Alcohol had been her and my brother's strongest mutual interest. "Has he made a will?" she asked.

"I don't know. Why?"

"Because if he thinks he's going to get any of this furniture back, he's crazy."

"Maureen, he'll be dead. What would he want with a bentwood rocker after he's dead?"

"You never know," she said, darkly.

"Possession is nine-tenths of the law," I said, to comfort her.

"There's Janice. She might try to get her hands on the stuff. And Carlotta." Carlotta was Wife Number Three, a broker by day and playwright by night. "Not to mention Andrea. Or the Hungarian countess."

"The countess is in Costa Rica. What does she want with a bentwood rocker? She's rich."

"And not to mention that completely reprehensible woman he is living with now."

"She's your best friend. Her name is Alma."

"I hope you don't blame me for the breakup," she said. "I had to kick your brother out because he was living with her."

"Absolutely," I said, not questioning her sequential logic.

"She's old enough to be his mother."

I had indeed pointed that out to my brother myself. I'd told him he was too old to be acting out incestuous fantasies. He'd said that inasmuch as he was dying, he'd better act out all his fantasies fast. He'd asked me if he could come live with me (he didn't know this was one of my nightmares). I'd pointed out that that was an incestuous fantasy he'd already acted out. In repartee, our lives move past each other like people on a sidewalk, barely grazing sides but going places. The real conversation takes place intramurally: with ourselves. It goes nowhere. Meanwhile, we are full of facts that nose their way out of our pores no matter how thick-skinned we say we are, germs that crawl to the surface of our bodies and say *I am the true you.*

"So are you," I reminded her. "Old enough."

"He must have an obsession."

"Several," I agreed.

"Did you know," she said, thoughtfully, "that the countess has had two face-lifts?"

"No," I said. "I didn't know that."

"Not one. Two."

"That's interesting," I said.

Maureen had descended into another moody silence.

"How does she look?" I asked.

"Who?"

"The countess."

"How should I know? She's in Costa Rica."

How I liked having Babette in the house, the rooms like cardboard boxes for her self, which she was constantly unwrapping! Even her scowls and tears were welcome, the ribbons and bows on the packages. Oh but the presence of Madonna I could have done without, for like a virgin, like a material girl, Babette went to school wearing lace gloves and a black leather jacket studded with rhinestones over a short skirt skewed by her condition, and when she returned, music, of a sort, billowed in the rooms like veils. One day I put my key in the lock getting ready to yell hello and opened the door to find Babette on the couch with a young man who could only be Roy. I switched off the record player.

We shook hands. He had a kind of fluid good looks, his head flowed into his neck, which flowed into his shoulders, on down to the long, rivery tributaries of his legs and the crepe-soled puddles of his shoes. He had that gently flowing grace some young men have that can be diverted or channeled but not easily dammed, though life may do that to them later.

While we were eating dinner, he told me how he was going to make a quick million in Hollywood. He had a surefire idea for a screenplay. It was perfect for Don Johnson of "Miami Vice" or maybe Mel Gibson. It took place in Afghanistan. It opened with a close-up of the hole in the front end of a rifle, a Kalishnikov rifle. At first the whole screen would be black, and as the camera pulled back, the blackness would take on this round shape and then you'd see you were looking right into the wrong end of a rifle and the camera would just keep pulling back slowly and steadily—I looked at Babette and saw that she was entranced with the sexual poise of his measured description—and you'd see the rifleman, the mountains like skulls with caves for eye sockets, and the tall gumless teeth of the trees, the David Lean blue sky.

From the bedroom, where I slept with my dog in a double bed, I could hear the two of them—the narrow cot sang, the narrow cot shrieked. From time to time loud bursts of laughter floated across the hall like balloons.

Their youth dragged me down like a net, I felt tangled in it, and I could feel myself beginning to drown in memories. We start like on dry land but memories, which are like tears, discrete as they occur but cumulatively one element, rise until we are standing in the middle of an ocean, washed by time. Currents we have unwittingly created ourselves now tug us in unanticipated directions, all of them pointing to the past. In the hospital, I had been amazed to discover that I had never advanced beyond my brother's image (the shadow of which I have since cast off)—my past with him had surrounded me so that even when I'd thought I was moving into the future, it was only the past in new guises. My first reaction was to blame myself for having been so dense, so stupid. I told the doctors—I had quite a few, a brigade of doctors—that I felt ashamed, I was so stupid.

"How can a woman of your accomplishments feel stupid?" they said.

"I don't know," I said. "I know it's stupid."

They didn't even laugh. They just shook their heads. I saw their head-shaking out of the corner of my eye because I couldn't look straight at anyone. I kept hiding my eyes from everyone. I kept my head down and if I had to walk down the corridor I felt my way by sliding against the wall. When I came to a blank space, I knew it was time to make a turn. There was method in my madness.

"What's stupid," they tried to explain, "is going from *it's* stupid to *I'm* stupid."

"That's what I said," I said.

"What is?"

"That I'm stupid. I *know* it's stupid to do that, to go from *it is* to *I am.*"

"Then why do you do it?"

"Because I am."

"But you aren't."

"Then why do I do it?"

"You have to answer that yourself."

"I can't answer it. I don't know the answer. I *told* you I was stupid." I glared at them—they were so stupid!

I made a visor out of my hand to hide my eyes from them. The truth was, my neuroticism on the subject of stupidity—while delightfully, from a psychiatrist's point of view, traceable to sibling rivalry, or perhaps even to a female fear of outdoing the parental figure who set the standard, in this instance my seven-years-older-than-me, father-and-mother-substitute brother—was a red herring, designed to throw doctors off the track of my precipitating anxiety, which was a fear of feeling my lifelong condition of not being loved. It was easier to blame myself for this condition, since that allowed me to imagine I might someday find the means to revise it, than to ascribe it to causes outside my control—such as unhappy parents, a psychopathic brother. I was definitely in hiding: from myself too, as at that point not even I suspected my apparent candor was an illusion, if not a delusion.

They had my medication increased. For three days, none of the doctors came to see me. I began to look where I was going.

Lying in bed, I reviewed my life to the musical accompaniment of bedsprings. I remembered how Babette's father had claimed my bed like a birthright. A great many years later, he told me that I made too much of this. It was as inconsequential an event as a one-night stand, no different from any of the hundreds of nights he'd picked up a woman in a bar and taken her home with him. (But that night he had sworn me to secrecy, saying: If you tell anyone, I'll deny it, I'll say you lied. This is monstrous, he had said the next morning. Yes, I am a terrible person and you have ruined my life by letting me do what I did! he said—and so of course I hated myself and felt sorry for him. And he laughed at my confusion.) For twenty years I had felt like a piece of shit—Darwinian shit, unfit for evolution, selected by nature for genetic extinction. This was not a consequence?

Now "his daughter," who in my opinion should have been playing with dolls, was getting laid, exuberantly at that, across the hall. I couldn't decide whether she was paying for the sins of her father's generation, or reaping the benefits.

In the morning, Roy was gone. Babette was in the kitchen communing with the toaster so far as I could tell. She had her back to me.

"Babette," I said, "where's Roy? Did he leave already?"

She didn't answer me. I thought she was sulking.

"Answer me, Babette," I said.

Then a thought struck me, and I shouted her name. Still no answer. She had her hearing aid turned off.

I put my hands on her shoulders and gently turned her around to face me, so she could read my lips. She was crying—silent, adult tears trickling down her stunningly sculpted, dedicated face.

I told her to turn the hearing aid on.

"He's not coming back," she wailed. "Ever."

"Oh," I said, "he might. He might even make a movie and earn a million bucks. You can't say for sure he won't."

She shook her head. Behind her back, the toast popped up.

"He doesn't want to come back. He says he's too young to be a father. He says it wouldn't be fair to the baby."

"Maybe he's right," I said.

"He doesn't need a million dollars. He's already got money."

"Drug money," I said as if I knew, "can't be banked on. Connections go cold or get killed."

"I want to go home," she said, starting to cry harder. "I want my mother."

But first she developed a fever and chills. I felt her forehead, the tight skin hot under my hand. "I'm going to call the doctor," I said.

She was pissed because vacation had started so she wasn't missing a school day. She turned over on her side, away from me. She had kicked off the covers. She was wearing the it's-raining-cats-and-dogs pajamas, and the pants legs had ridden up to her knees and the top had gotten twisted, exposing her midriff like an undeveloped film.

I called the OB/GYN. "Two aspirin and some rest," he said. "No problem."

I wanted a problem. I wanted to feel needed—too soon she would be gone from me, the amphitheater of her mind filled exclusively with visions of Roy in Hollywood. "That's all?" I asked. "For a pregnant teen-ager?"

"Even pregnant teen-agers," he said, "get uncomplicated colds. Especially when they're from Georgia. Are you feeding her well?"

"Milk," I said. "Protein, vegetables."

I got in the car and drove to the mall to buy presents for her: a pretty maternity dress, a tiny pot of lip gloss, stationery, some items for the baby's layette. The enclosed lobby that sidled along the full length of a dozen stores was carpeted with the thick, spongy smells of perspiration and wool, the tangerine sharpness of manufactured pine-needle aroma (sprayed onto artificial Christmas trees). Dazed shoppers trudged by, lugging bulging bags with ropy handles that banged against their sides, like oxen balancing milk pails. And then all at once, there was the man I had loved more than any other, my most Significant Other, coming toward me with the woman he had prioritized over me. I ducked into Gimbels, grabbing a Chaus blouse and skirt to give legitimacy to my desire for a fitting room where I could sit on a stool until my hands stopped shaking. I slipped on the skirt and blouse. The skirt was a cotton tan trumpet-cut, rather long, and the taupe blouse had a V-neck and loose sleeves that stopped at the elbow. I liked the way I looked in them so I bought them, a Christmas present to myself, thinking Cliff would be sorry if he could see me in this outfit. However, he would never see me in it, because even now I was afraid of how I would behave if I ever ran into him. I might weep, or plead, or stutter some nonsense, or even reflexively flirt, or worst of all, act like everything was fine, thereby colluding with all the women who had preceded *me*, including his mother, in their decision to shield him from the effects of his actions. We are such good little girls, all of us, reluctant to wreck our hopes for the future, no matter how unrealistic they may be, on the shoals of calling men to account for themselves. What they get away with, just because there are so few of them! Think of it: women are waiting in line for the privilege of taking care of broken-down drunks like my brother. Anyone who doesn't think men get away with murder should remember that on "Leave It to Beaver," Beaver's last name was Cleaver. That made him Beaver Cleaver. What does this say about America?

I dumped my packages in the trunk of my car and drove home. It was my birthday—the longest night of the year. I put on my headlights. The snow, plowed and heaped along the sides of the road, glowed like glass at the bus stops where people had walked a smooth path over it, grinding the crystals like a lens. In a beautiful short story by Fred Chappell, the mathematician Feuerbach asks his students, "If a man constructs an equilateral triangle on a sheet of paper, what is in the triangle?" No one raises his hand. "The correct answer," Feuerbach tells them, "is *Snow*. It is snow inside the triangle." The students have yet to learn that their admirably remediable brains are as vulnerable and, from the point of view of many, dispensable, as the dime-store water domes inside which snow may be made to fall on a whim. They have not yet felt the chill in their skulls, the increasing numbness. Probably none of them has ever been a patient on a psychiatric ward.

Getting ready to go inside, I heard voices from the yard next door. Children were constructing a snowman. "Merry Christmas!" I shouted. Three children, two belonging to one family, the third to another. The girls are sisters. Last summer, Cheryl wanted to play Wedding, and made Jason marry her little sister Trish. Every day for a week, Jason and Trish got married. Then they got a divorce.

All three waved at me, their mittened right hands like three red stars in the fast-falling night. A certain tenderness in the night's cold touch told me there'd be more snow by morning—not "the snow that is nothing inside the triangle," but very substantive snow in the elongated rectangle that is my sidewalk. I had just rehired my favorite teen-ager to shovel my sidewalk—he'd been in Japan with his parents, who were on sabbatical.

Whiffs of marijuana greeted me at the door, slinking down the stairs like a genie. I threw the packages into the hall closet and raced upstairs. Babette was lying in bed singing to herself. I recognized the lyrics from "Borderline": "Feels like I'm going to lose my mind / You keep on pushing my love / Over the borderline." She couldn't carry a tune and she was singing at the top of her lungs. She had her eyes closed and her hearing aid was on the dresser.

I crossed the room and removed the cigarette from between her fingers—something I had done that night with her father, only that had been tobacco, thinking *If I weren't here, maybe he would have burned the house down,* thinking *I'm not good for nothing; I'm good for something.* Maybe there was an inherited predisposition among members of the Bryant family to pass out with lighted cigarettes between their fingers, God help us. I should ask Cliff the geneticist. (I should not.) "Hey," she said, her lids snapping up like window shades, "what do you think you're doing?"

"I should be asking you that!" I said. "Who the hell do you think you are? Do you know what you could be doing to the baby?"

"I don't care about the baby!" she screamed. "I don't want it! I don't care about you! You don't care about me—all you care about is this stupid baby! I hate being pregnant, I hate it, I hate it!"

My dog went downstairs to his "House"—the traveling case I kept open for him in the kitchen. He escaped from dissension into it, curling into a small furry ball, but he could barely turn around in it.

He kept his big red rubber ball in there, and a much-beloved tuna fish can. When the world was too much with him, that was where he went to get away from it.

Babette had sat up on the bed when she screamed at me and was still crouched there like a cornered animal, beating on the bed with her fists. She stopped.

I thought, looking at her, that the baby was like a piece of furniture, too big for such a little girl to carry. I picked up the hearing aid from the dresser and sat down on the bed with her and pushed her long hair back over her ears. Sometimes I thought she could have been me—a family resemblance in the chin and cheekbones. She was so frantic for a man's love that she'd sacrificed her childhood—at thirteen, the experienced woman, the little mother, the caretaker. My brother liked to think he'd always taken care of everyone else, but everyone else had always taken care of him, including her. Alcoholism is like a psychosis: it reshapes the world along internal lines. But the world has its own tendency to shift its center of gravity in accordance with perceived need, and so Babette, for example, had innocently conformed to her father's reality. We accommodate our madmen.

I fitted the hearing aid in her ear and smoothed her hair forward again. Her eyes were like a view of the Atlantic from Virginia Beach— she was like a mermaid, she didn't belong in this snowy north country.

"Babette," I said, stroking her hair. "I'm glad you came to stay with me even for this short time. Having you here has made me happy. I can't tell you how happy."

She was picking at a scab on her arm. "Yeah, well," she said. "Just because I have a baby inside me doesn't mean I'm not me anymore."

"Is that what Roy thought?"

"Who knows what Roy thinks. Roy sucks."

"Do you feel good enough to come down for supper?"

"I guess," she said.

My dog crawled out of his house to usher us into his kitchen. He put his front paws out on the floor in front of him, raised his rear end, and stretched from one end of his body to the other, getting all the kinks out. Then he wagged his tail for us. From the kitchen window, I could see the snowman glimmering whitely, a sentry for the neighborhood in the night.

I had hoped Babette would get interested in my fourteen-year-old snow shoveler. He was clearly fascinated by her. He was a toothpick six-and-a-half-feet long, a junior-varsity basketball player, good natured and ultra-normal. His brown face was like a flag for me when I saw it in my yard, it made me renew my allegiance to young people. But Babette had ignored him—she was hopelessly in love with a man who had never existed for her: her father. She thought she would find him in somebody sexy and charming, somebody who could control her the way her father controlled the world. Freedom was not for her—her pubertal hormones had brought her a lust for romance, which is finally the urge to see oneself as a hero or heroine, the focus of the family. What an old theme that was—the glorification of the self through averred powerlessness and servitude.

I turned on the radio. Garrison Keillor's soothing voice filled the room, became the medium in which we ate supper. Milk, protein, vegetables. I thought of Wanda and her short-wave vagina.

Babette was right.

I had begun, in spite of myself, to feel that the baby-to-be was in some sense mine. But it was her baby, and she planned to have it in Georgia. What she didn't know was that I'd also begun, in spite of myself, to feel she was mine too. Especially when something struck us both as funny, and we collapsed into shared laughter, I would suddenly catch my breath and think, *This is just like a family. It is!* We smiled at each other. There were days studded with such pleasures. A goldfinch flew past the kitchen window like a zipper on the blue dress of the sky.

On Christmas morning, Babette opened her presents with gratifying glee. My dog poked his nose into the pile of used wrapping paper, wondering where his present was. I gave him a porcupine that squeaked when he worried it with his teeth, a rawhide bone.

The lights on the tree were like musical notes you could see. The blue ones were the deepest, the left hand. The red ones were middle C. The white and yellow lights were the treble clef.

Babette handed me a small box wrapped in tinfoil. "This one's for you, Aunt Nina," she said.

I jiggled the box next to my ear and smiled at her. I unwrapped it and lifted off the lid. A piece of paper.

I took out the piece of paper and read it.

"I didn't have any money to buy you a present," it said, "so this is just a box full of love. Babette."

And now she was going home—in time to return to her old school after New Year's. She had been a warm day in a cold season, but she was not "my daughter." She was my brother's daughter, though he had not sent her even an empty box.

I am too hard on him he was my brother he gave me my vocabulary my first books Brendan Behan/Céline/*Krapp's Last Tape* said describe a different object every day the brick walk/an alarm clock read my poems read me. When no one knew how to handle me, my parents called him in. I was furious with my limitations terrified of failing to live up to what was expected of me justify our parents' lives make up for the way he had disappointed them life had disappointed them. I tried to be what all of them wanted, was angry at all of them for not letting me be myself, even he wanted me to love him the way Mother didn't I couldn't I don't I won't I don't have to incest is not love.

In the empty house that was like a broken violin string after Babette's departure I washed dishes, watched television. My dog invented a new game: he sat on the couch and pushed his red rubber ball to the edge, let it unsuspectingly sit there for a moment, and then nudged it over the edge. Then he leapt after it as it rolled across the rug. In this way, he played catch with himself. I called Janice to confirm Babette's safe arrival. Maureen called me to say she'd seen Alma and my brother buying cigarettes at the K-Mart. She said he was jaundiced and had an old-man walk and was bald on one side of his head because he had a habit of pulling his hair out when he got drunk. Alma looked like *Frankenstein's Widow*—the bride after fifty years. The countess had sent a postcard, which had come to Maureen's address; evidently, my brother had not told her about his new alliance with Witch Alma. Maureen was sure the wives were gathering and would ride on her soon in a furniture raid. She had moved all my brother's things to the garage and was threatening to have a sale if he didn't pay her soon. She had figured up how much he owed her for meals, cigarettes, booze, general wear and tear on the house, and let's not forget her labor. He had treated her like a servant she said and he would pay through the nose. As she talked I watched my dog. After a while he grew tired of his game and went to sleep on the couch, resting his muzzle on his front paws. He is so doggy—my canine lifesaver, since he rescued me from a black hole of depression, the phenomenon that occurs when a mind collapses under its own weight of despair, setting up such intense negative energy that it completely absorbs itself. What a farce life had been then—a comedy of trial-and-errors. I remembered a night I had called the hospital to see if I could admit myself to the psychiatric ward. I talked with a nurse on the floor. She asked me for my name but I refused to give it to her—I don't know why I wouldn't, maybe I was crazy.

"You have to have a doctor's referral," she said.

This was before I had even one doctor, much less the troopship of psychiatrists I was to acquire in the hospital, or the self-important short shrink who succeeded them. So I said, "I don't have a doctor." I had thought a hospital would be a good place to find a doctor.

"Then you can't be admitted," she said. "You have to be admitted by a doctor."

"This is crazy," I blurted out. I wanted in!

"How dare you talk to me like that!" she said. "If you think you can talk to me like that, you're crazy!"

"That's what I'm trying to tell you!" I yelled. "I'm crazy, so please lock me up!"

"We can't do that without a doctor's referral!"

I listened to the echoes in my room. My voice was bouncing off the walls.

So was I. So was the nurse.

I tried to reason with her calmly. "Suppose I cut my wrists," I said. "Then would you admit me?"

"You're playing games with me. I don't believe you. You're not going to cut your wrists."

"I'm not playing games," I said. "I'm—"

I was going to say "desperate," but she hung up on me. So I went into the bathroom and cut my wrists.

I was surprised it didn't hurt. It only stung a little, so I cut deeper.

It still didn't hurt. I was starting to drip into the sink. Bright red beads on porcelain—a song, almost.

I couldn't do this to my dog. I couldn't do it to my friends; in my depression, I thought their lives might have been nicer without interference from me, but I had too great an awareness of their love and generosity to imagine they would not be overwhelmed by guilt and responsibility, if I killed myself. I couldn't send an SOS this way—it would be manipulative (I felt a residual sympathy for Wanda's husband), and besides, I had too much pride. I decorated the shallow cuts with Band-Aids. To the best of my ability, I would be my own doctor. (A decision I should have stuck to.)

When my brother died, his doctor called me even before Alma did. It was April. The snow had begun to melt—a medley of streams harmonized all over town. Walking to work I skipped over rivulets, like skipping over cracks to keep from breaking my mother's back.

My parents were too ill, too ill and much too frail, to return to the States for his funeral. They had not been back to this country once since leaving it. Maybe I felt a little like a vice president, sent to stand in for the president. ("You die, we fly," Bush's staff joked.) The time zone my brother had now entered was the farthest away, sad to cross. If I had been bored, I also wanted to cry.

I flew from Madison, Wisconsin, to Madison, Connecticut (the airport is actually in New Haven), and checked in at a motel. Because of Alma's heart condition, she couldn't put people up—and there was not only me to contend with, there were Carlotta and Andrea and Janice, and even Maureen, who was not going to pass up the chance to dance at my brother's funeral.

At the funeral home, I awaited the wives. We all got in the day before, because the service was scheduled for the morning, and signed on, as it were, at the funeral home. Andrea was the first to arrive. She glided in on celestial runners, a small blond sled toting forgiveness, ready to "share" her feelings with us. She encouraged me to cry. "You have to let it out," she said; "otherwise it'll just fester." I thought of telling her what festers—forced secrets, rage you have to lie to yourself about in order to protect your faith in someone's love for you. (I even thought about telling her that Christ on the cross accusing his father of forsaking him was the very heart of the passion, without which the story could not live. It was Easter week, and this was on my mind.) She slid on her slender, delicate blades of feet over to Alma, who was all in black, from her dyed hair to her textured hose.

Carlotta came next, swinging her elegant portfolio like a baseball player warming up in the bull pen. "Nina, my dear," she said, "how are you? Such a sad occasion—but rather fun, too, isn't it? Your brother would have enjoyed it." And she was right, he would have. Carlotta's lipstick was the color of a house burgundy. She shook my hand as if I had just agreed to invest money in her mutual fund.

Maureen appeared on the scene next, in silk slacks, a turtleneck sweater, and a raccoon coat. The silver threads among her gold were highlighted with rinse. She crossed the room to give me an exaggerated hug, avoiding Alma but playing to her. "It's so good to see you again," she exclaimed in her gravelly boozer's voice. "You'll have to come to my garage sale while you're here!"

"You have no right to sell his things!" Alma said from across the room.

The funeral director gripped Alma solicitously by her arm and moved her closer to the casket.

In that casket lay the body of my brother, which I had been acquainted with as intimately as had these women, as with the night, though none of them knew that, thank God.

The last time I had seen him alive, on a previous visit here, he had sat at the piano in Alma's house and lightly played a five-note tune. "This is what's in my head," he'd said. "It's been in my head for a year now. I can't make it go away. It's always there."

In profile, hunched over the keyboard, his younger self was visible, as if the past were the present in silhouette; as if, from the right angle, you could make time disappear—a simple matter of perspective. Such forcefulness he had possessed, wit that carried the day!

"Why won't it go away?" he asked, removing his hands from the keys and placing them carefully in his lap.

Was he making this up, writing this scene on the spot? Was this an improvised piece of stage business, or did he truly suffer from a motif that had woven itself through his mind like a thread, until pulling it out would have been dangerous?

I was constantly obliged to deal with questions like that, responding with the expected irony to his statements as if I understood what he was talking about when actually I didn't have any idea how much to believe, what was real and what was a joke. From the time I was two, he had treated me as if he assumed I knew what was what—did he really think I did, or did he enjoy the bind this put me in? I tried to be "the person who understands me." I feel exhausted just remembering how much work it was for me to keep up this pretense.

"It hates me," he said, playing the tune again.

"Why do you say that?" I asked.

"It won't go away. It won't leave me alone."

"Maybe it won't go away because it loves you. It wants you to stay alive and finish it."

He laughed. "You never miss a chance, do you?" he said.

I said, "Because I care about you." And I did. My dear brother, handsome, charming, a verbal acrobat and physically a daredevil—he had been a flying young man on a steel trapeze, out-Plimptoning George Plimpton, skywalking the blazing girders above New York, elbowing death aside. He couldn't be as relentlessly selfish as I sometimes now suspected he was. Could he?

And even if he was, was that a reason to stop caring?

"I wish I knew where it comes from. What it means." The tune.

"Why does it have to mean anything?"

"It's in my mind, isn't it? It must mean something."

"There's a lot in your mind that's pretty meaningless." This time I laughed.

"God love you, Nina," he'd said, pleased, and closed the lid on the keyboard. "I do."

It had been a gray day, the faint diffused sun like a ceiling chandelier with the dimmer turned on. At dinner I noticed that his eyes had sunk back into their sockets like two rabbits going underground or dogs slinking off to their corners to die.

Once, the look in his eyes had been so penetrating that it had been almost a sexual metaphor. Look, I said to myself, how these women had been attracted to it and were still mesmerized, compelled to congregate in its memory.

I felt someone tapping on my shoulder as if I were a door. I turned around to greet Janice. She was carrying a baby. "Here," she said, thrusting it into my arms. "It's all yours."

It was the tiniest baby I had ever seen—humanity in miniature. A round head with fuzz on top, worried little eyebrows, big blue-green eyes, a nose like the tip of a thumb, mouth like a musical whole note, chin like a parenthesis—all of it wriggly, especially the wet, protoplasmic bottom. "There are Pampers in here," Janice said, setting on the floor by my side the large carryall that had been hanging from her shoulder.

Janice was wearing a purple dress with a wet spot on the front like a map of Georgia.

"Where is Babette?" I asked.

"Where do you think?" Janice looked disgusted. "This time she hitchhiked all the way to California."

"The Promised Land," I said.

"Yes, well, I promised I'd kill her if she ever dares to come back after this cute trick. She left *this* with me." She gestured at the baby in my arms.

I could hardly breathe. I was holding what I had wanted most. The baby in my arms was like a liquid that had been poured into a hole in my soul. What I'd hoped for, felt guilty about hoping for, given up hope for—all this was now all at once incarnate, it had shape and substance. I wondered if I was holding it right. The head was in the crook of my left arm, next to my heart, and my right arm supported its bottom and back.

At that point the baby, which had been seemingly engaged in listening to our conversation, began to bawl. The funeral director came over to me and said, "Madam, I will have to ask you to take your baby into the next room."

But Alma was approaching too—and Maureen and Andrea and Carlotta. Like mother hens they flocked around to cluck at the baby chick. Maureen, who had raised five children of her own, put the baby on a table and changed her diaper. It was a girl.

"I can't take care of her," Janice said. She was standing next to me. Her voice came and went in my ear like a tide. "Listen to that racket! Eugene just won't tolerate it."

In Wisconsin, Janice would have been legally responsible for her granddaughter until Babette reached eighteen. As I often have, I thought, to hell with Wisconsin law.

"Are you serious?" I asked.

"I wouldn't have made this trip if I weren't," she said. "You think I'd come all the way up here just to see your brother buried?"

"What's her name?"

"She doesn't have one. Babette couldn't make up her mind. She's Baby Bryant on the birth certificate." She reached into her purse and retrieved the birth certificate, as if she were handing over her puppy's AKC registration papers. "I figured that if I actually showed up with the baby, you wouldn't be able to say no."

Maureen picked the baby up again and transferred her back to my arms. She fell asleep almost instantly.

A baby in my arms.

Had my brother had this outcome in mind all along? Was this his way of making amends to everyone, of "taking care" of everyone—and also possibly his idea of a joke? Would Freud have laughed? Probably not, but so what: none of this mattered to the baby, who was holding my finger in her small-scale fist with such firmness that I figured she was destined to be a flutist. She had the requisite lung power.

Janice had brought a thermos inside which you could fit a bottle. Hot water kept the formula warm on the plane, so the baby could swallow when the plane took off and landed, to pressurize her ears. I gave her the bottle now and took her back with me to Maureen's house for dinner.

While we talked, the baby slept in a cradle Maureen brought down from the attic. I liked Maureen best of the women—I felt more comfortable with her.

She had a house old enough to have been officially designated a historical landmark. The sky through the leaded windowpanes was lavender.

She was holding a Bloody Mary. The drink was like a red rose in her hands. "You'd better see your lawyer as soon as you get back," she said.

"I will." My lawyer would be happy for me—he knew how much I had wanted a child.

"It's very important," she said, "to know the law. Your brother was damn lucky I didn't sue him. But I made sure I'm going to get at least a part of what's coming to me. Five cents on the dollar is better than nothing."

"Oh, Maureen," I said, "you aren't really going to have a garage sale? Who's going to buy that old furniture?"

"Let me show you something."

I followed her outside to the garage. Her car was parked in the driveway. The smoke from the fire we'd been sitting in front of rose from the chimney like a dark wide-winged bird. She raised the garage door and yanked on a string. The overhead light came on.

There was my brother's life, all crammed into one room: not only his furniture, but his books, his paintings—his own and the ones he'd collected—his records, his manuscripts.

"I'm going to sell the records for a nickel apiece," she said. "He always acted like they were so bloody valuable, but my son says they've been superseded by tapes and discs."

Kreisler, Oistrakh, Casals, Landowska, Horowitz, Ashkenazy, Claudio Arrau. Christoff singing Godounov. Heifetz. Glenn Gould. Erica Morini. Myra Hess. So many years of listening, of finding in those performances a touchstone for his own life. Beethoven by the Hungarian Quartet, the Budapest, the Amadeus. Many of these records were irreplaceable. There were even some 78s that had once belonged to my grandfather.

"I'll buy them," I said.

She looked at me suspiciously, as if thinking maybe her son was wrong and they were worth something after all. "What would you want with them?" she asked.

"A remembrance," I said. I was looking at a facsimile edition of *Moby-Dick* that had been given to him by his students the year he taught at a private school in New York. When I was fifteen I had copied the last paragraph of *Moby-Dick* into my spiral notebook. Melville had been one of the writers my brother and I both loved. We differed on many others, but there were some, like Melville and Shakespeare, who had given us a private language, a shorthand—the briefest of allusions could communicate volumes between us.

Dust was settling on his paintings, stacked at the back of the garage, the first paintings of his young adulthood and the troubled, slashing paintings, crowded with anger, black with hate, that he'd done after Janice left him.

His manuscripts were in neat blue boxes. I started to open one and then couldn't—I felt as if I were raiding a tomb.

It was as if this garage were a pyramid; these were my brother's worldly possessions and representations, which were meant to go with him into the next world. There he would re-read the books that had helped to define him. The shades of the great musicians would tremble in the breeze like lyres; the light, thrumming wind would play them as if *they* were their instruments. When he looked on his paintings, he would see again the life he had lived, the colors and mutable forms of the landscapes he had lived it among. His words would have a faint mustiness about them, like a mummy. The bond would crackle like papyrus as he piled up the read pages in the top half of the box.

Suddenly I felt as if I had been lured into a trap—as if the door were about to drop shut, cutting off air. I saw myself as my brother's handmaiden, sealed in death, his property in life and the afterlife. I darted from the garage.

Maureen put her arms around me. "I didn't mean to upset you," she said. "Come have another drink."

In the clouds blowing across the sky, I saw my brother, his face bending over me as if I were a text, the moon his racing boat.

In the motel the baby slept beside me while I lay awake remembering my brother. She woke at two and I fed her some formula I had made up at Maureen's house and kept warm in the thermos. He is dead he is like a record I can't listen to ever again never again irreplaceable.

At the service, the women were scattered among a larger crowd, but when we went to the cemetery, the crowd thinned again. It was a warmish, sunny day. A high wind knocked the leaves around but closer to the ground there was a layer of stillness.

At the far end of the cemetery there was a dark snow-spattered pine glade, but where we stood, spring had come. Somehow the efficient funeral-home director had unobtrusively translated the flowers from the chapel to the gravesite, and the small green slope of the hill was a chorus of color—lilacs, jonquils, shy crocuses, tenacious forget-me-nots, and Easter lilies. The lilies were like church bells, a carol of lilies.

The women were individual songs: Andrea a bit on the shrill side despite her extensive analysis, Carlotta contralto, Alma a dirge, Janice a clear soprano though she sang only for Eugene, Maureen the spear-carrier. I held my baby, my little grace note.

In the bright air we listened to the minister's words roll out, round as marbles. As he said them, a black limousine appeared at the gates, moving slowly toward us like an epiphany. It stopped a few feet away and a chauffeur got out and opened the back door. A veiled figure emerged. She was in sable and high heels. Her gloves were black, disappearing under the coat sleeves. A diamond bracelet circled her left wrist. She wore a hat that tipped over her face like a bird swooping down on a fish. The lace veils shielded her from our gaze as effectively as his helmet protects a beekeeper from bees.

She walked over to us, her high heels sinking on each step into the tender mossy grass. When she reached us, she stood unmoving while the minister finished speaking. I wanted to see what she looked like but the veils were impenetrable. Black dots covered the lace-like moles. No matter how hard I looked, I couldn't see her face.

I nudged Maureen with my elbow. "Did you cable her?" I asked in a low voice.

"Why not?" she whispered back. "I had her address from the postcard. I thought we should have the whole gang here. Serves Alma right."

The minister glanced in our direction. The woman had taken a long-stemmed rose from under her coat, where she had been holding it next to her body. She stepped forward and placed it on the casket. Alma started to go over to take it off but Carlotta held her back. The woman turned and began to walk away.

"I thought you said she had a face-lift," I said to Maureen.

"Two. That's what she told me."

She had covered the distance to the car and was now entering it while the chauffeur held the door for her. The engine started.

We stood on the hill, watching the limo pull away. It went into reverse, turned, and headed back down the road, putting on speed as it nosed out onto the highway on the other side of the wrought-iron gates. The countess was gone for good. We were still stuck in our lives; my brother was stuck in the ground. But for one unforeseen, transfiguring moment, the Hungarian countess had appeared before us like the stranger on the road to Emmaus, and her coming and going had brought us face to face with possibilities we had barely dreamed we could realize.

I nuzzled the baby's neck, her skin as soft as a double-ply tissue. Twenty years ago, even a year ago, I could not have dreamed this day, but that, I now saw, was part of the point. The point is that if you knew something was going to happen, it wouldn't be a miracle.

Alan Cheuse

THE PLAN

#409–222–111
September 24, 1991
"The Walls"
Huntsville, Texas

Mr. George Garrett,
Fiction Editor
The Texas Review
Sam Houston State University
Huntsville, Texas

Dear Mr. Garrett:

I am sending you this story at the suggestion of my writing teacher
Alan Cheuse, who gave us some workshops last year. He said to try
this one on you, the magazine being only a couple of streets away from
where I wrote it and I had nothing to lose. That's the truth. Cheuse
told us that we should never insist on a story being good just because it
really happened. Make it art, he told us, and that will make it real. I
hate to disagree with him, but I have to tell you that this story
actually happened. There's a part where I have to hold back some of
the details, but the rest of it is all true. There is a Ronette—I changed

her name, of course—she is out there and she is dangerous, while I
am back here, locked up again, and no danger to anybody but myself.
Unless this story gives you a pain in the neck. I hope it doesn't.

Sincerely yours,

Johnny Wyatt

The Plan   *by Johnny Wyatt*

Point of view, it is said, can make or break a story, and I wasn't
quite sure at first where to begin this one—or how—until I remembered
the afternoon that I walked into the visitors' room for my first look at
Ronette Walters.

The thick viewing shield between us was smeared on her side with
fingerprints and lipstick, the residue of a thousand visits from suffering
females coming from all over Texas to try and pretend that nothing
much had changed since their men had gone inside, except maybe that
their love for these cons had gotten stronger. If guys like me had raised
their butts off one of these little stools and puckered up on our side of
the shield, you couldn't tell. No stains.

"Thank you for seeing me," Ronette said, her high dry voice
sounding kind of tinny because of the instrument she spoke through.
You couldn't pass spit or sperm between you in these surroundings. It
was our first visit. If we played by the rules we'd graduate to a normal
table and chairs with nothing between us but the air filled with
cigarette smoke and cheap perfume and sweat, sour milk smell from
baby bottles, baby shit—there's always at least a dozen kids in that
room squealing and squawking like chickens—and a couple of dozen
dudes in white, some whispering, some speaking up in angry bursts of
sound as if they'd just found out that an appeal—or love—had just
been denied. Which some of them had.

But on that first meeting it was just the two of us, one on each side
of the shield in that room where the lights seem bright at first and then
seem to get dimmer and dimmer as you eat up the minutes you have

left to you in your visits. It was the perfect setting for a plan like Ronette's to be born in.

"I want us to get to know each other," she said.

I nodded, thinking to myself of all those letters she had written from her college and a letter of recommendation from her professor too. Was this some bullshit trick Doctor Gordon was trying to put over on me? He had discussed this all with me and told me he thought that it was a good idea, that it would look good in my parole file. My head was aching—I was starting to sweat hard, all because I was looking at Ronette and trying to find some resemblance to her cousin. (They say rapists don't have an interest in sex, that it's a crime of overpowerment not desire, and maybe that's all true. But I sure remembered Ronette's cousin quite well, if only because of she was the one that got me put away.)

"How's that college over in Austin?" I said, watching to see what she would do with her eyes. I said to myself, if she looks me in the eye, I will cooperate, if she doesn't, I won't, I'll just blow this off.

Well, she stared me down, getting real business-like and taking out a notebook from her big black fake-leather bag and starting to ask me a lot of questions about family and such.

I told her a few things, some true, some stretched a little. My teacher told me from the start that I had a pretty good imagination, the kind of thing that makes for liars in kids and writers in adults. It was still painful to talk about my sister, her dying so soon after I got locked up, or Daddy and Ma for that matter, though both of them had been gone a long time. Because I couldn't get to see Jo when she went into the hospital for her cancer, that got to me, since she was the only one I ever came to like in this world, even though back when we were home alone at night while the parents were working, some of that bad stuff did happen between us.

You feel that you may have had something to do with her cancer, don't you, Johnny? that son of a bitch Gordon said to me.

Now how could that be? I said to him. You think I have supernatural powers? How could I make a cancer grow in somebody else?

But deep in me I knew what he meant.

But I'm drifting.

Well, Ronette came to visit me a couple more times, and she wrote me letters filled with questions in between visits.

How did you feel, physically, on the day that you saw Louise Munson (this is her first cousin Louise) in the mall parking lot?

How did I feel *physically?*

I wrote back: what do you mean by that question?

She wrote back: I am trying to develop the narrative of the event.

That's the first thing that came to me, that she whatever else she said she was doing, writing her master's thesis or whatever on this particular event between me and her cousin, she was trying to steal my story!

Then the sweat season was upon us. There's a con over in another unit I heard of who is suing the state because of our lack of air. For me I like the sweat. It meant that on her next visit Ronette came wearing a short-sleeve blouse.

"You got nice skin," I told her.

She ignored what I said—that was when I should have started figuring just what a tough bitch she was—and went on asking me questions about my life.

That was when Samson, the weight lifter who lives in the house next to mine, walks into the room to see his queer brother or whatever and stares over at me and then at Ronette.

But he backed off real quick when I gave him the Look.

I didn't hear from Ronette for a couple of weeks, which was unusual. I went about my reading and my writing, which is what I do when the rest of the cons dull their brains on the tube. Lucky for all of us, they listen to the TV sound with headphones, otherwise there would be a couple of murders a week. Or at least one.

Then she writes me a letter and asks to see me for another interview. And showed up looking like hell, her hair all rumpled and dirty and going every which way, and her eyes so red it can only come of crying all night.

"Now what is going on here, sugar?" I said to her.

She lowered herself real close to the table.

"I'm in terrible pain," she said.

God, I fell for that, I went right down to the bottom like a dead weight into Galveston Bay.

"Tell me," I said, reaching for her hand. This was against the rules, of course, but it always depended on who was on duty in the visiting room as to just how strict the rule was carried out. Luck of the draw, some guys you'd see them sitting there with their hands up their girlfriends' skirts if they had the visitor on the right day. Ronette's hand felt cold as steel in winter. She let me keep mine on hers for a minute before she pulled away.

"It's too embarrassing," she said.

"Gol, Ronette, don't let that stop you. Shit, talk about embarrassing, what is my life in here? It's all in a file, and everybody from the screws to the warden know when my shit comes out green or—" I stopped myself, talking as rough as I was, expecting her to be disgusted with me. But she was just staring, staring into my eyes.

"Do you want to hear about it?"

"I do," I said. "You know so much about me, I know next to nothing about you. Except that you are Louise Munson's cousin."

Her eyes sparked up a touch at the mention of Louise's name. But I didn't pay much attention to that. This girl has got trouble in mind, I said to myself, and maybe I can soothe her a little. I just didn't know what kind of trouble she had and what it was going to mean for me.

"I'm in pain," she said at last, in a voice real cracked with the torture of sleepless nights worrying about your life, the kind of affliction that a man in my situation knows real well.

"You tell me," I said, lowering myself toward her as I had seen my doctor, and the social worker, do with me.

Her eyes flitted around the room and then, like a bird that finally finds a branch to settle on, lighted back on me. Here is what she told me:

"I've been working on my thesis?"

"Uh-huh."

"And I have this really good professor from the journalism school? And he's been tremendously helpful?"

"You wrote all about the thesis when you first contacted me," I said. "So what's happened to you? He tell you he didn't like your stuff all that much?"

Her eyes squinched down into tiny little slits with lines radiating out from them that made her look older, much older, than she really was.

"He likes it too much," she said.

"Too much?"

"Too much," she said.

"I get it," I said.

A burst of laughter flared up on the other side of the room where a black dude I saw now and then in the weight room was sitting with his girlfriend or wife or whatever she was and a bunch a teen-age kids. Ronette looked so unhappy it seemed almost a sin that other people were having such a good time. But in this place you laughed when you could, there was so much other shit to get you down.

"So you and this professor. . . ?"

Ronette shook her head.

"He . . . took me out. . . ." She was whispering and I had to lean way forward to hear her, which caught the attention of one of the guards, who took a step over in our direction. It was almost like he was the referee and we were boxers or wrestlers about to go into some kind of clinch. But I ignored him, which is all you can do to keep your head on straight around here.

"Uh-huh?"

Ronette sat back up, not because of the uniformed guard but because of something inside her head that told her that she might be going too far in telling me this. That's what it seemed to me at the time, at least. She looked all of a sudden more like a woman who wanted a cigarette than a woman who had grievance with a man. Or maybe the two kinds of women are one and the same?

"Let's hear the rest of the story then," I said. "You know, confession time, like the Catholics?"

That got a little smile out of her, and she settled back in her chair.

"I have to tell you this," she said. "You remind me a little bit of my brother."

"You get to a certain age," I said, "and you've seen enough people in your life so everybody begins to remind you of somebody."

She made a little laugh, and then seemed sort of embarrassed by me getting that emotion out of her, and she ducked her head down and started going through her notes.

"So, tell me," I said. "Who did that professor remind you of? Your brother? or your daddy?"

Immediately she jerked her head up and stared me right in the eye. How did I feel *physically* when she did that? A little startled, because of the quickness of it, and a little scared, too, though that passed, a fleeting emotion as they say. But my heart jumped just a twitch, I admit that.

"Who did my cousin Louise remind you of?" she said.

"Nobody," I said. "She reminded me of nobody. No one I ever knew. No girl I ever seen. Nobody ever. Yeah, she was one of a kind, your cousin Louise. And hey now, I hate to ask you this, but it's a question been on my mind. I was wondering—"

But Ronette was already on her feet and signaling to the guard that our interview was over.

The first hint of her plan came in a letter about a week after that unfortunate session. She was hurting, she had to admit to me, but there was something that I could do to help her with it. Something that she would explain when she saw me next. To read that letter, and somebody in the warden's office probably did, you would have thought that Ronette was writing about her big frustration, with her out there and me behind bars. God, how many letters a week did the turnkeys see with that story in it? Turned out that it was frustration on her mind, but of another sort.

That day she came back everybody seemed to be feeling it. The weather had turned real hot, Texas hot is what I like to call it, and the visitors room was chock full of wives and girlfriends—and I guess some of the young things daring around in bare sleeves and little bitty skirts was daughters, too, and many a man walked in here leaving behind a babe in diapers who by the time he come out was flouncing around in a miniskirt—though you had to murder somebody to spend that much time here, and little do you know when you are pulling that little trigger or jamming in the knife that you are, if life is time, probably killing a lot of your own life as well. It was hot inside as well as out, and the women were showing their men how much they were missing them—which to a dude in here could translate into how much he was missing out on, that's for sure—and so the men were not all taking this as well as could be expected. You could hear laughter, as always, but now and then a little argument would spark up in one part of the room or another. You'd think this would happen, this kind of frustration, in the colder part of the year when the weather outside wasn't all that good and in here the world was dark and damp and every move you make seems to take a hundred years—piss, tie your shoelace, eat a meal, anything, it all seems like it's in slow motion in winter—but it is when you have a little bit of hope, which seeing your girlfriend's bare shoulder or navel can give to you, that things turn all of a sudden real hopeless. Because you know just how much longer you have to go without her.

I knew how much longer I had to go, without no hope of a particular woman waiting for me on the outside either. There are three kinds of guys in here. The ones that live for getting out. Incarceration to them is like a sickness that they're slow to get over. The other kind is the guy who has nothing waiting for him on the outside, never had anything out there to begin with. This kind of guy buries himself in his own body, like it's a garden or something to cultivate or a machine to work on. Or maybe he studies—there's a dude down the block who reads seven languages, I hear. Then there's a third kind, the zombie. Often he's a little guy who gets banged when he first comes in and never recovers, so whether he gets out in three or stays in and turns gray, he is never really alive either here or out there.

I might have gone back and forth a little myself, but the second Ronette told me her plan I knew where I was putting my butt.

"Say what?" I said, staring her right in the eye.

It was hot, I told you, and little beads of sweat ringed her forehead like a little wreath. On mine too probably, if you could have looked at me. I've seen a lot of things since I've been inside, grown men acting like little girls and black men turning white and white men turning black—and even bad men turning good—but I got to admit that when she said what she said to me I was kind of shocked.

"You want me to do *what?*"

"Kill him," she said.

I glanced around to see if any of the guards was close enough to hear, but the nearest one was busy trying to look up the miniskirt of one of the visiting girlfriends.

"I don't think you ought to talk this way in here," I said.

"Where else can we talk?" And then she leaned closer to me, like she was my lawyer, and reached for my hand, like she was my girlfriend, and told me her plan.

"You mean," I said, "you want me to do in your professor *physically?*" Ronette didn't crack a smile.

"That's right," she said. "I'm going to help you get out of here and in exchange you are going to help me out."

"You're going to help me get out of here?" I spoke in a whisper, the way people in church must talk when they are talking about God. "A lot of good that'll do. I don't even come up for parole for another three years."

Miss Ronette Walters squinted her eyes at me and spoke in a voice cold enough to chill the air around us.

"That's not what I'm talking about."

I started out talking about how point of view is important. And now I got to mention transitions, another important part of telling a story. Without them, changes can seem real abrupt and unbelievable. Though nothing would seem unbelievable about how I made my transition from inside to outside if I only could tell you about it. The problem is, if I told you, people could get hurt, because certain readers of mine—the not so sophisticated ones that my writing teacher always warned me against, the ones who take everything you write literally?— could figure out exactly how it happened, and that is something that I don't want them to know.

So let's just say that Ronette made certain arrangements on the outside and I did certain things on the inside, and about four months later I am stepping out into the autumn night, feeling a little drunk from walking a hundred yards without having to stop at a steel door or a gate or a cement wall. Ronette swings up alongside me in her little Escort—I'll say that much, so you know that I am not making this up, it was an Escort—and we are heading west.

I want to get out of my prison whites real fast so I climb over into the back seat and wriggle out of my whites and into the jeans and shirt she's brought for me, it still being so hot in the season that I didn't need a jacket or such. Except that I was shivering from what I'd just done.

"It's going to be three hours," Ronette said to me from the driver's seat. "You ought to take a nap."

"Three hours to what?" I said, stretching out on the back seat. I was suddenly real tired, like I'd just crawled out of some long tunnel—which is a metaphor, so I hope you don't take it literally—or swum across a bay or run real far in my bare feet in the hot sun.

"Three hours to Austin," she said. "That's the plan. We go to Austin, and then you can go wherever you like."

"You think this is some Jim Thompson novel?" I said, staring up at the lights and shadows playing across the inside of the car roof.

"What's that?" she said.

"Jim Thompson," I said. "He wrote—oh, never mind."

"No never mind about this," she said. "We have a plan."

"Pardon me for speaking so bluntly, but fuck your plan. Just stop the car and let me out."

"If you get out here you'll be back inside the prison by morning."

"You know a lot about that, don't you?"

"Don't be ironic. I did my research. Johnny, we have an agreement. If you don't do your part I swear I'll turn you in right now." Her voice was trembling, and I was thinking, well, she might just turn me in for breaking my word, because for breaking his word—for not going out with her after he laid her once or twice—she was going to try and get me to kill her professor. Trying? She was rolling me along through the dark Texas night on toward Austin to deliver me to do the deed.

"You'll turn me in?" I said. "And how will you explain the fact that you're driving me around in the middle of the night?"

"You talked me into helping you escape, and then you kidnapped me."

"You drove all the way to Huntsville to pick me up and then I kidnapped you?"

"Johnny, we have a plan. You agreed to this."

"If you were behind bars you'd agree to a lot of things if you thought it could get you out."

"We're going to Austin," she said, the car suddenly zooming forward, causing me to look out and see dark fields on either side of us streaming past in the night.

"Take it easy," I said. "I didn't break out just to get killed."

"I'll kill us both," she said, turning half around to look at me.

"Keep your damned eyes on the road!"

"Don't curse at me."

She slowed down the car a little, but not all that much.

"Don't curse at you?" I said. "You're trying to get me in this thing that could get me the Big Injection and you're telling me not to curse?"

"The Big Injection?" Her voice caught a little, there in the dark car, and she made a funny noise in her throat. "Oh, yeah, yeah." She eased up on the gas, though we were still flying along pretty fast. "It's going to be real late when we get to Austin. I've reserved a motel room for us."

"Great," I said, sitting up and staring off into the distance, which was a dark line where the fields met the night sky. You'd think a convicted rapist would give a big cheer to hear about that motel room—*any* man might have, isn't that right?—but I didn't have any great pull toward Ronette *physically*. I just wanted to get out of the car and save my life.

"I have this," she said, reaching down alongside her and then passing back over the seat this little pistol.

"Whoa," I said, taking it from her.

"It's not loaded," she said. "Do you know how to load it?"

"I happen to," I said, feeling the weapon cold and hard in my hand. In the first faint glow of the new day I could see that it was a Smith and Wesson .32 caliber, brand new from the look and smell of it.

"So what is it going to do, killing this man," I said, "when you already told me that he doesn't want to get with you anymore?" In that same growing light that let me see the gun I could take a faint picture of her eyes in the rearview mirror. "It won't make you forget him. Believe me, when you do something like that, you don't forget."

"It won't make me forget him," Ronette said. "But it will convince me that there's no chance of getting back with him again." She reached down again and came up with a box of bullets. "Here. Now here's my plan. It's real easy. He lives alone. It'll be early morning, it's a quiet street way up out of the way, in the hills. I'll wait in the car, and then we'll go wherever you want to go."

I slipped the gun and the shells into the pockets of my jeans, as much of them as would fit, anyway.

"You want to ride off into the sunset with a convicted rapist turned murderer?"

The light was coming up fairly strong now and I could study her face real well when she turned to the side to speak to me.

"I like you, Johnny," she said. "I want to go with you." She did a funny little thing with her eyes, something that I hadn't noticed in any of the interview sessions we'd had. "Why, don't you think I'm as attractive as my cousin Louise?"

"Yeah," I said. "Oh, yeah. You're attractive. Different from her. But attractive. I'm attracted to you, no doubt."

"I'm glad you think so," Ronette said, a little smile on her lips. It scared me. I was the one with the pistol in my pocket and suddenly I was the one who was scared. The thing was, there wasn't the slightest resemblance between her and her cousin Louise, not in her face and not in her build. And for that minute it came to me that maybe she wasn't Louise Munson's cousin at all and that she had made up the whole family story so that she could get into the prison to see me and set me up. And maybe the professor wasn't the professor and maybe he was a boyfriend or who knows why or what he was? Husband, brother, father, or just a stranger she was planning to rob?

It was full day now as we reached the Austin city limits, and you could see clouds that marked where the river cut across just below the center of town.

"You want to rest a while?" she said.

"Ronette, I do," I said, "but there is work we got to do first."

"Good," she said, squinting into the road ahead.

"Yeah, we got to beat the rush hour traffic," I said.

"You've been in Austin before?"

"Nope," I said in a lie. "I just know it's a big town so it's got to have a rush hour. Like Houston has a rush. Like every big town. Which reminds me," I said, trying to change the subject. "I'm going to need some money."

"I was going to give you some," Ronette said. "I can give it to you now." She took a hand off the wheel again and dug into her purse.

"This ain't no payment now," I said, taking some bills from her. "It's a loan."

"Uh-huh," Ronette made a noise. But she wasn't really listening, concentrating as she seemed to be doing on getting us through the downtown and then into the hilly part of town on the west side. I lied to her about not being here before, because a while back when I was a lot younger and Jo was still alive we borrowed a car and drove over here from Houston for one of the Armadillo festivals, and it was the first time I had ever seen or heard of Willie Nelson and it was an afternoon that you say you'll never forget but I guess I had forgotten it because it hadn't come to mind for a long time until Ronette and I drove into the town this morning so many years after that day I came here, so many years too since Jo died.

We were pulling up a long hill and then turning right and rolling along another street.

"How do we know he's home?" I said.

"Oh, he's always home," Ronette said. "He's just getting up now to write."

"That's what he does all day?"

"Most days. He teaches a few classes at night."

"Sounds like a nice life," I said. "Too bad for him it's going to be over in a few minutes."

"Don't joke about it," Ronette said. "Just get ready and do it."

And then she was slowing down and stopping in front of a little white shingled house with a run-down fence in front of it, trees growing all around.

"Go on," she said.

"Wait a minute," I said. "I got to load."

"I like you, Johnny," she said while I was stuffing ammo into this gun. "Where will we go?"

"Oh, Jesus," I said. "Florida," I said. "I got some friends there at a dog track. I could get work there."

"Florida?" she said. "I'll bet I can find work there too."

"Yup," I said, "I bet you could. Bet you can. Bet you will." I tried the door, but it was locked, but before I could say anything she flicked a button up front and the locks went up and I was outside. A sort of hilly rise led off behind the house, thick with trees but not too thick. I went through the gate and up onto the porch. There was an old swing, a kid's red plastic scooter lying on its side. She hadn't said a word about him having kids. Was there a wife too? Inside, maybe? A mocking bird was singing in the tree above the porch, just singing its old head off, like it never heard of the troubles I had in mind.

The horn gave the tiniest toot and I looked around, thinking, Jesus, that was pretty smart! And there was Ronette leaning over from the driver's seat, waving to me, *go on, do it, knock on the door!*

I raised the pistol for her to see, waving to her, *adios, muchacha,* and then I sidestepped off the porch and took off around behind the house. I heard a car door open and that bird and other birds singing as I started humping it through the trees and up the little hill. There was a park on the other side, with some mothers and babies and some old Mexican gentlemen sitting in the shade, and a duck pond right in the middle. I slowed down as I walked past the pond just long enough to toss that pistol into the water, scattering the ducks. In a little drug store a few blocks away I called a taxi, hiding back down behind the magazines until the pharmacist signaled to me that the cab had arrived. I stepped outside and looked around and then rushed into the cab. There was a cop down at the bus station, but it wasn't him I was worried about finding me.

I arrived in Corpus late that afternoon and found a room at a motel downtown. The next morning I took a taxi out to the cemetery. Jo's grave was a holy mess, with weeds growing up all over it, and I spent a long time down on my hands and knees, pulling up weeds and just generally smoothing things over as much as I could without having the proper tools.

I should have tried to get to Mexico after that. There are ways of doing it, just as there are ways of getting out of Huntsville. But I stayed around another day, and bought some flowers and took a cab out to the cemetery again and put these on Jo's little grave. I was sitting there on a bench, remembering those mothers and babies and the old gents sitting in that park in Austin, I don't know exactly why that, and the mocking bird singing in that tree, thinking of how the ducks were all settled on that pond, skimming smooth across the surface when the state police cruiser drove right on up alongside me on the grass.

I was kind of relieved it was over, not that it went on all that long.

"Doctor Gordon figured out my plan now, didn't he?" I said to one of the troopers. "He is one smart son of a bitch." But they didn't say anything to me. I got one long last look at Jo's gravesite as they stuffed me into the back seat of the cruiser. And then we were roaring along out of the cemetery, picking up speed for the long drive back to Huntsville. So you see, here's the climax, the ending, the denouement. How did I feel physically? Now that's a question you might ask.

R. H. W. Dillard

THAT'S WHAT I LIKE
(ABOUT THE SOUTH)

The defining characteristics of Southern fiction:

Roy has gotten thirsty again, and, recognizing that it is after all
another long hot day in another long hot summer, Shirley sighs loudly
for Roy's benefit, continues to streak down the flat two-lane blacktop,
but takes the dusty unpaved right-hand fork just beyond the rattling
explosion of the bridge over Cross Creek. The bright red Bronco slips
sideways for a brief second on the dirt and gravel, straightens out, and
speeds on down the back-country road, raising huge battle flags in the
dust that has just begun to settle down from the last car or truck that
broke the heavy stillness of the summer heat.

Two miles past the fork, three tiny black boys crouch in the shallow
bottom of the ditch by the side of the narrow road with a plastic milk
jug half full of water, making tiny mud buildings for a town that their
plastic cars can visit and that the next rain will destroy like a major
flood. They scarcely glance up at the dusty Bronco roaring by, but their
angry big sister shakes her fist at Shirley from the open window of the
small pink house and then slams it shut as the thick dust billows toward
it. Shirley laughs out loud, reaches over and turns up the volume of
Lyle Lovett on the tape player, and pushes the accelerator even harder
to the floor.

Shirley knows from experience that a Coke Slurpee is just what Roy has in mind, so the Bronco swings right again at the hardtop slate road by the forge and then pulls in abruptly onto the hot pavement of the South Fork 7-Eleven. The red and white SLURPEE banner hangs limp and unmoving in the heat, and Roy wishes out loud that the sun were in Capricorn and the air cold and crisp. But the sun is in Leo, and Roy feels almost faint as Shirley bangs the Bronco door behind them and they wade through the heat toward the 7-Eleven.

Roy leans against Shirley, and he hugs her with his big bare arm, pulls her tight against his side. They make their way together across the shimmering pavement, Shirley in his sweat-stained straw hat, worn jeans, and mirror sunglasses, and Roy, sturdy and small in her carefully pressed jeans and eggshell-blue blouse.

deep involvement in place,

Shirley releases Roy and pushes the glass door open for her, putting his hand flat on her firm, smooth back as he urges her into the cool interior of the 7-Eleven. She smiles up at him and steps quickly into the store. Not for the first time, Shirley notices how sure of herself Roy always seems to be, how she moves steadily and unswervingly past the island of the checkout counter, nods hello to Glenn, who was a cheerleader at Roy and Shirley's high school and who is tugging at her bra under the green and red smock she wears when on duty at the store, and walks without a hitch or falter right by the metal, free-standing candy and snack rack, swerves to the left, loops the island, and ends up right between the ice cream refrigerators and the Slurpee machine.

There is something unsettling to Shirley about Roy's single-mindedness. It is not something he can put his finger on, but it worries him from time to time. He is not sure whether it bothers him because it seems inappropriate to a woman (*his mother, for example, would have stopped dead in her tracks just inside the door and looked nervously around for a long time before she would have taken another step*), or because it is so typical of a woman (*he, for example, always likes to stop and scope a room before deciding which way to move through it; get the lay of the land, so to speak; be aware of alternative routes).* "All of Roy's choices," he thinks, "seem to be made before she makes them."

He stands in the doorway, peering at the shadowy room through his sunglasses, glances at the abbreviated aisles with their bright variety of colors and shapes, the leaning tower of straw hats and gimme caps to his right, his eyes skimming all around the room, but then lighting on the rack of bright magazines just to his left by the island, their covers lit up with the luminescent tanned skin, long legs, and lithe arms of slim women in bathing suits. He moves right to them and picks up the one nearest to him as he always seems to do every time he visits the store. He pulls off his sunglasses, folds and slips them into his work-shirt pocket, and settles himself back on his heels for a good, long look.

Roy pulls a medium-sized paper cup, red and white with Slurpee written on it in blue, from the torpedo rack of cups by the machine. Without hesitating, she places her cup under the spout for the Classic Coca-Cola Slurpees and gently eases the smooth metal handle forward. The icy brown coil spills out and into her waiting cup, and she can almost taste its cold freshness as it spirals to the top.

"Nothing's as refreshing as a cold Coca-Cola on a hot day," she thinks happily to herself as she plucks a spoonstraw from the rack and turns to Glenn behind the counter to pay.

"Roy," Glenn says as she watches Roy pop a plastic top on her cup, and then strip the red spoonstraw and insert its scooped end into the X-slit in the center, "don't you want to buy Shirley a 7-Up or something and answer the Question of the Week?" She winks at Roy and punches the cash register, stuffs Roy's smooth dollar bill into it and fingers out twenty-four cents change, while pointing with her other hand to the question printed on the familiar sign on the counter:

"IF YOU FOUND YOURSELF IN LOVE WITH ANOTHER PER-SON, WOULD YOU TELL YOUR CURRENT LOVER?"

The big round numbers which Glenn has carefully inscribed in magic marker on the slick plastic total board by the question read: "YES 27% NO 73%."

A cold chill runs through Roy's chest as she takes her change, and she stops sucking the pulpy, sweet ice of the Slurpee through her spoonstraw and takes a deep breath. Glenn glances over at Shirley by the magazine rack and looks eagerly for Roy's answer. She is obviously disappointed when Roy says that she wouldn't even consider answering such a question.

"These questions," she says, "are just too silly. I mean, as though somebody would know what they would really do anyway. Or tell 7-Eleven." Roy laughs, but really she is shocked by the number of people, people right around here, people just like her and Shirley, who would lie to their current lovers. She, too, glances over at Shirley, but he is completely lost in a well-thumbed copy of *Swimsuit International* and doesn't notice.

Roy strolls back around the store, mainly to get away from any further inquiries from Glenn, who is tugging uncomfortably at her bra again, probably trying to get Shirley's attention away from his magazine. Roy is looking at a display of refrigerator magnets with American and Confederate flags, little red-white-and-blue signs saying "These colors don't run," and Ninja turtles in odd poses, when she begins to slurp noisily at the bottom of her Slurpee. She peels the plastic top off, extricates her spoonstraw, and slips the top tidily into a waste receptacle marked "FEED ME AND SAVE A TREE."

Roy looks across at Shirley, who has put his magazine back on the rack and is talking to Glenn, laughing about something, and suddenly and unexpectedly Roy feels dizzy again. She looks down at her spoonstraw, and she cannot decide what to do with it. Is she supposed to spoon the rest of her Slurpee out in tiny little dips, or is she supposed to guide the scooped end around the bottom of the cup while she sucks like a mini vacuum cleaner? She is filled with doubt and indecision.

She hears Shirley say he needs a cold drink, and she finds herself walking quickly over to see whether he will vote YES or NO, but he disenfranchises himself by choosing and paying for a chocolate YooHoo in a bottle. She doesn't know whether to be annoyed or relieved, and the whole store begins to seem huge and alien to her, as though she has been translated to another dimension like a character on a "Twilight Zone" rerun but can still see back into the one where she formerly resided.

"You ought to ask people," she hears herself saying too loudly to Glenn as she grabs Shirley's arm and pulls him toward the door, "what they do with these dumb spoonstraws. Now, that might be useful information."

Shirley has put his mirrors back on and is chug-a-lugging the YooHoo as they reach the door. Roy looks back and waves, and Glenn calls out good-bye and starts impressively rearranging herself once again. Roy turns back to the door and notices that, as Shirley holds it for her with his back as the last of the YooHoo disappears, with his straw hat on, he measures exactly six feet, two inches tall against the robber ruler by the door.

"I never even knew how tall Shirley was before," she thinks as the heat folds itself around her in the parking lot, and she does not allow herself to think how many other things about Shirley she does not know.

family bonds,

It is only when they are back in the Bronco that Roy notices two odd things. The first is that Shirley did not buy a Lotto ticket. She knows that there was not a winner at the last drawing, that the jackpot must be eight or nine million, and that Shirley has not yet bought a ticket or surely he would have told her. He always buys the same numbers (1–11–12–22–23–33), and he always shows her the ticket, has her hold it or even kiss it for good luck. She wonders what there was about this visit to the 7-Eleven that was different, that made him forget.

Roy glances over at Shirley, who has cocked his straw hat back on his head and is singing to himself, but the words whip out the open window in the hot wind. She wonders just what is making him so happy, but then she thinks of the other odd thing. She remembers that the whole time she was in the 7-Eleven she never once thought of her Uncle Vivian.

When Roy was a little girl, there was a strange man on all the 7-Eleven ads with such an odd, funny voice that everyone listened to those ads as if they were a regular comedy show and talked about them, too. She remembers her father saying one day that the man on the radio sounded like almost as big a sissy as Vivian. Her mother, Vivian's sister, told her father to just hush, but from that moment on Roy has associated 7-Eleven with Uncle Vivian. And, until today, he has always come to mind whenever she goes in the store.

Uncle Vivian was a musician, a precise, round little man, with close-cropped hair and a shiny cherubic face, who always answered her many questions with "Oh, my dear, no" or "Oh, my dear, yes" with the same inflection, as though both answers were exactly as upsetting and vaguely dangerous. He taught piano and was by reputation a very demanding teacher. He always told stories that kept everyone laughing about his students' failings, how they stooped to folly, calling them always by the same names, Little Miss Muffet and Little Master Bates. Roy's mother would always get red-faced with laughter and tell him to just hush that kind of talk in front of the child. Roy never understood why her mother was so worried; she just knew that she loved Uncle Vivian and admired him and thought studying the piano with him would be the most frightening and wonderful thing in the whole world.

But Roy never got her wish and never even learned to play "Chopsticks" on the piano, because one day Uncle Vivian came home from a vacation to Key West, and everything was suddenly different. Roy still remembers that she was in the living room, drinking buttermilk and playing Parcheesi with her best friend, Dale, who was one of Uncle Vivian's beginning piano students and who was surely, given Dale's miserable progress, Little Master Bates in more than one of Uncle Vivian's tales. Roy had been blocking Dale for a long time, and even Dale's patience was beginning to wear thin, when Uncle Vivian burst through the door, his face burning like a Key West sunset, wearing orange Bermuda shorts and a bright pink and orange Hawaiian shirt unbuttoned almost to his stomach. A gold chain around his neck seemed almost painful against the flame of his fiery skin.

"So red the rose," he cried out to anyone interested in hearing, "no redder than I. Kiddies, I'm home."

Roy still remembers her mother's shocked face, how she almost stepped right in the middle of the Parcheesi board and did, to Dale's relief, scatter all the pieces. Her memory stops short there, probably because she and Dale were encouraged to go play outside, but the image of the new Uncle Vivian still burns in her mind's eye. He continued to dress as he had in Key West, so that Roy had ample opportunity to observe the new diamond earring in his right ear

("Zircon," Uncle Vivian had conspiratorially whispered to her one afternoon in his empty studio). He wore flip-flop sandals and an ankle bracelet with his name engraved on it in curlicues, and he began to come over for dinner much more frequently.

"Oh, my dear," he said at the table one evening to Roy's grimly silent father, "I just don't know where Little Miss Muffet and Young Master Bates have gotten off to. I hope they're not up to anything." He still gave lessons, but the student population had dwindled dramatically, so his comic tales began to be repeats, and then he began to brag about one of his few remaining students, Bonnie.

"Bonnie is so charming and so naughty," he would say, "I just let her make mistake after mistake without correcting her. Though correction is just what she needs." These remarks just weren't funny, and Roy could tell that even her mother was disappointed in Uncle Vivian.

And then, as suddenly as he changed after his trip to Key West, he was gone. Just gone, leaving an empty studio and a dusty piano, an empty apartment. Dining rooms all over town rang with the eager voices of speculation and gossip, but Uncle Vivian had clearly gone on to other voices, other rooms. And then, a few days later, it began to be known that he had not gone alone, that he had taken his favorite pupil, Charles Edward, with him, quite without the boy's family's permission. They had found a note addressed to "Bonnie" in the boy's room, noting the time he should be waiting at the studio with his bag packed.

Roy is startled to discover that the Bronco is pulling up at Shirley's house and that she has been thinking about Uncle Vivian for the whole trip there. The 7-Eleven does, she thinks, in one way or another, still remind her of him. And then she realizes for the very first time that she has never quite trusted anyone as fully as she once trusted Uncle Vivian. When he was arrested in Memphis and Charles Edward was returned home to be sent off to military school, Roy was crushed and very confused, and now she realizes that her injury was greater than she has known.

She flinches when Shirley bangs the Bronco door, and she thinks how strange he looks, standing impatiently on the sidewalk, his straw hat tilted forward now over his nose, his hand on his hip, waiting for her to get out and join him. She shakes her head like a dog coming up from a creek, pushes the door open, and climbs out to Shirley, who is, she knows as her eyes squeeze into a pained squint, standing there like an invisible man in the blinding glare of the sun.

celebration of eccentricity,

Roy pauses on the walk under the tree in the yard to let her eyes adjust, but Shirley's hand on her back urges her on toward the rooming house. Shirley has been living in a room here ever since he graduated from high school. Both he and his parents agreed that life in the trailer had just gotten too cramped for them all.

Roy and Shirley climb the steps and nod to the women on the porch, three of Shirley's fellow roomers swaying back and forth in bentwood rockers in the shade, before passing through the screen door and into the hall.

Roy goes on up the stairs and into Shirley's room while he takes a trip down the hall to the bathroom, and as she sits on the clumsily made bed and looks around the room, her eyes pass over Shirley's things as they have done so often ever since she and Shirley found each other suddenly last summer.

The one genuinely neat part of the room is a set of shelves Shirley has constructed out of boards and cinder blocks along one wall. On the shelves he has placed his collection of books and valuable objects. She notices the little black and white Scotty dogs on magnets, the multicolored sets of dice, the salt and pepper shakers that echo each other in tidy rows.

And the books that seem to have no connection one to the other until Shirley explains his interest in doubles, in things that repeat. The Ed McBain mysteries with Detective Meyer Meyer, the copy of *Catch 22* with a character named Major Major, the copy of *The Last Days of Pompeii* by Edward Lytton Bulwer-Lytton, Lord Lytton, that Shirley bought at the annual AAUW book sale, a paperback copy of a book with the queer title *Poe Poe Poe Poe Poe Poe Poe*, and a little book on the philosophy of James McTaggert Ellis McTaggert. Over the shelves, Shirley has taped on the white wall a picture of his favorite actress Simone Simon that he cut out of a book at the high school library. He has not been able to explain to Roy just why he likes these things so much, but he surely does. Whenever he takes Roy out to eat at the Top of the Catch Restaurant and Lounge, she notices that he always orders "Mahi Mahi, the Fish So Good They Named It Twice."

Usually Roy does not worry about this oddness in Shirley's character. In fact, she finds it interesting and attractive, proof that he is not just another good-looking guy in a battered straw hat. But in the strange mood she has found herself in today, she almost feels another chill come over her in the stifling heat of the room, so much so that she glances at the limp blue curtains at the open window to see if a sudden breeze has come up.

When Shirley appears in the doorway, leaning against the door frame, his hat tilted forward and his lower lip pushed out, instead of running to grab him and tickle him the way she usually does, Roy tells him she's feeling a little queasy and asks him to take her home so that she can take a cool bath, lie down in darkness, and have a little nap before they go out later in the evening.

a strong narrative voice,

Well, you can git up an' mosey long ef you wanter, but I'm gwineter tell dish yer tale ef I hatter r'ar my head back an' shet my eyeballs an' tell it ter myse'f fer ter see ef I done fergit it off'n my min'.

"Are you really Uncle Ben?" the little white boy asked politely, more like a girl in his refinement; all the boyishness had been taken out of him by that mysterious course of discipline that some mothers know how to apply.

She, the young mother, thirty something, suntan smoothly glowing against her severely cut, white linen sundress, was standing by the looming display of brown and white rice boxes that the manager of Phar-Mor had constructed for the Grand Opening celebration. She was watching the little boy and me (in my Uncle Ben costume complete with tufts of cotton hair) very closely, so I knew I had to be very careful what I said.

"I speck dat's so," I remarked, "an' a ole nigger dat oughter been dead long ago, by good rights. A pity—a mighty pity."

The mother's face reddened, and she grasped the boy's hand and spun him abruptly away from me. She marched him quickly down the aisle, but her head was scanning from left to right as though she were looking for someone in authority. I decided it was probably a smart time to take a break, so I put my sample tray with all the little cups of hot rice down by the hot plate on the card table next to the display and started walking toward the employees' lounge at the rear of the store. I was in a hurry, naturally enough, but I did remember to shuffle along with bent back, in character. I may have an attitude, but no sense losing a good job on the first day, even if it does only last three days.

"When you wanter be hard headed," I muttered half to myself and half to any interested onlookers, "an' have yo' own way, you better b'ar in min' de 'oman an' de dinner-pot."

I was nearly back to the prescription counter when I saw Shirley looking at a copy of *Playboy* in the book section. I hadn't seen him since I had gotten home from the summer semester at college, so I decided to see whether he would recognize me in the Uncle Ben get-up. I shuffled up to him and prepared to give him a goose, as though we were still in middle school together when I was the voice at the back door every morning, calling him to shake a leg or we'd be late again. But before I could get in range, his name boomed almost unintelligibly out over the store loudspeaker system, and he jumped, looked around guiltily, put the *Playboy* back on the highest shelf of the magazine rack, and bolted for the prescription counter. He didn't even see me in the rush, just another black boy or shadowy native son standing around, looking for something not to do. I shrugged my shoulders dramatically, spread my pale palms wide, and continued to shuffle my way to the lounge.

At the prescription counter, I saw Shirley and a slim blond woman about our age, talking animatedly. So I sidled alongside to see just what was going on.

"That's my prescription," Shirley was saying to the blond, who was clutching tightly in her hand the little paper bag the pharmacist had given her.

"Then why," she asked, "does it have my name on it?" And she shoved the bag under his nose.

Shirley actually blushed and then said in a tense low voice, "That is my name!"

The blond squinted at him, a mean hard squint, and then she popped the bag open, pulled out a blue and white tube and said with some bitterness, "I suppose you use Monostat regularly."

Shirley blushed again, and this time looked confused and baffled to boot. The blond was by this time as flushed as he was. Just then the loudspeaker boomed out his name again, and he turned to see the pharmacist holding another smaller bag with his name on it.

Shirley looked back and forth from the bag to the blond to the bag and back to the blond, and then he said, with a voice touched with what I felt to be genuine awe, almost a whisper, "We must both have the same name."

I hate to inject the teller in the tale here, but before she could answer, I noticed the little boy was tugging his mother my way around the corner of the vitamin shelves, and I decided it was time for my feet to continue doing their stuff. The mother looked strained and almost in tears, but the little boy was very far from crying. He suddenly broke away from her, seized this old darky's hand, and went skipping along by his side.

I led him in a slow curve back to his mother, handed him over to her, and bowed from the waist, before shuffling through the lounge door and out of sight. I could still hear him whining shrilly to her, but I did not falter for a second. I did not look back.

Ain't dat de way you does in books?

themes of racial guilt and human endurance,

The noise and confusion of the Merchants Association Annual Dixie Days Ball makes Roy almost want to shout it is so loud, but when it falls suddenly silent as the skirling of a bagpipe cuts sharply through the hubbub, she almost wishes the noise would continue. She squeezes Shirley's hand tightly as the piper marches sedately across the center of the dance floor toward the bandstand. He is playing, as he does every year, "Amazing Grace," and everyone is standing at excited attention. His appearance always marks the formal opening of the Ball.

Roy does not share the excitement, however, for a terrible sense of guilt sweeps over her like a cold fog swirling down over the scattered sheep and bare crags of the mountains of Glencoe. The icy notes of the bagpipe stir her Campbell blood to a boil, and her face burns with the guilt of the terrible massacre in that pitch-black early morning of February 13, 1692. No Campbell, Roy thinks, must ever be allowed to forget the burden of that guilt. She knows that everyone in the crowded room must be staring at her, so she releases Shirley's hand and, without explanation, pushes her way head down through the mass of excited couples to the Ladies Room.

Only after she can hear no trace of the piper's laments does Roy venture out of the lavatory and back onto the floor of the ballroom. The band has begun to play, the lights have been lowered, and the dancing has begun. She looks around for Shirley but does not see him where she abandoned him nor on the dance floor. She does see a clump of Shirley's friends over near the punch bowl, so she heads in that direction.

She has not seen Allison, one of Shirley's best friends, since he went away to college on a big minority scholarship, so when she spots him in the group, she goes up to him and gives him a big hug. He is dressed in the striped outfit and little striped hat of someone on a chain gang, and he has even got a chain of black cardboard links trailing between his ankles.

"How are you?" she says. "You're looking so good. What are you doing here in town?"

"You're looking pretty good yourself, Roy," he says, smiling at her, holding her by her shoulders at arm's length. "Haven't you heard?" he continues. "I'm playing Uncle Ben at the new Phar-Mor, yassuh, yassuh."

Roy is as confused as always by Allison and as happy as always to see him, but she remembers that she is looking for Shirley. When she asks Allison if he has seen him, Allison grins, pushes a couple of their friends aside, and points to Shirley, who is hunkering on the floor in his riverboat gambler's costume by the punch table, along with three or four other boys they knew in high school.

"It's a hunkering contest," Allison says. "They're going for the championship by seeing who'll last the longest. And there squats

Shirley," he says, with a sweep of his hand, "a veritable fireplug of strength."

Roy stares down at Shirley's confident, determined face, and realizes that he will spend most of the dance hunkered down, waiting for one or another of his friends to fall over, stiff and groaning. She starts to complain, to pull Shirley up right now and get it over with, when she suddenly has a vision for reasons she cannot explain of Dale, sitting in his Great Aunt Sidney's kitchen, sipping buttermilk out of a thick glass tumbler and solving a complicated chess puzzle, missing the dance of the year to take care of her as he does every Saturday night.

Roy stares at Shirley but doesn't really see him. She hears Allison's witty voice but doesn't really hear him. She knows something very strange is happening in her life, but she doesn't know what it is.

local tradition,

Shirley is still one of the two remaining hunkerers when the lights flicker up and down and the announcement for the formal dances and the arch figure blurs out into the room. Roy is dressed as Julie in *Showboat,* and her crinolines and hoops swish and switch as she decides enough is more than enough and pushes through the few remaining observers to Shirley's side. She plants her small patent-leather pump on Shirley's shoulder and gives him a good shove. He cries foul as he falls over backwards onto the floor, but his opponent, a thin boy that Roy does not know with a face red with raging acne, leaps upward with a bounce and shouts in a high-pitched voice, "All right!"

Shirley lies on the floor in a horizontal squat, moaning, until Roy takes his hand and pulls him erect. He crawls up onto his feet among the catcalls of his jeering friends, He is angry, but he also knows that Roy is right, that Julie cannot be expected to walk through the arch without Gaylord Ravenal at her side. All around the room, couples are forming two long lines that, when the band begins to play "Can't Help Lovin' Dat Man," will begin to snake through the Dixie Days Arch of Love, which is bathed in golden light near the bandstand. The local tradition is that young lovers who pass through it together and in perfect step will be wed within a year. Many is the couple that has stumbled out of step at the last moment as they entered the arch, but Roy has every intention of strolling through the arch with Shirley and of not being even the tiniest bit out of step.

As they take their place in the line behind Billy Joe and Billy Jo, who in high school were voted the cutest couple but who somehow haven't made it through the arch together yet, Shirley winces and stretches his legs and grumbles until he notices a pretty blond young woman dressed as an antebellum belle in a pale-pink hoop skirt, standing right beside them. He blushes suddenly and involuntarily, nods at her, and turns to Roy, who is looking up at him with considerable interest.

"Roy," he says, putting his right hand on Roy's smooth, sturdy back, "I'd like you meet somebody I just met," and he puts his left hand on the blond woman's back, noticing how delicate and frail it is, how aware his hand is of the tracery of her spine and shoulder blades.

"And the funniest thing, the most amazing thing," he continues, nervously and quickly, "is her name."

"Roy," Shirley says, "I'd like you to meet Shirley. Shirley, Roy."

Roy feels Shirley's hand almost tremble against her back, and she looks straight into the other Shirley's pale blue eyes, feeling for a second almost as if she were about to float right over the arch and away, when the lights all go out except for the single gold spotlight, and the band begins to play "Fish gotta swim, birds gotta fly. . . ."

a sense of impending loss,

The line begins to move forward, slowly and rhythmically, and the other Shirley, who is unaccompanied, walks alongside Shirley and Roy, chatting about the dance and the arch. Roy has never seen her before tonight, and she wonders whether this new Shirley is visiting in town or has just moved here or has been here all along like a copperhead, dangerous and silent and unseen. She cannot see her china blue eyes in the dim gold light, but she knows they are focused on Shirley. "Like a smart bomb," she thinks.

The succession of couples moves steadily forward as the music yearns and turns on itself.

Shirley turns abruptly to Roy, tightly squeezes her hand, which until now has been lying limply in the loose coil of his fingers. His eyes are like bright metal in the gold light, and he says to her urgently, "I forgot to get my Lotto ticket. Roy, how could you let me forget my Lotto ticket?"

There is an intensity to his voice that Roy does not like or understand, and his grip seems more like that of a vise than a lover's caress.

"I just know," Shirley is saying to Shirley, "that my numbers are going to come tonight when I don't," he squeezes Roy's hand even tighter and hisses through his teeth, "even have a ticket."

Roy knows that Shirley is nodding sympathetically to Shirley as well as she knows that the heat in her face is caused by the rising of her Campbell blood. The golden blur of the approaching arch seems to her like the dawn that finally rose over bloody Glencoe and the scattered corpses of the MacDonalds. She grits her teeth and pulls her hand from Shirley's hard grip just as Billy Joe and Billy Jo step through the arch together, but also just as she hears her father's voice in her ear.

"Roy," he is saying, "I hate to spoil your evening, darling, but there's been a death in the family."

He pulls her out of the line just as she and Shirley are poised to swing through the arch. Shirley and Shirley step out of line on the other side of the arch and look back at Roy and her hovering father. The line of couples falters behind them, unsure of what to do.

"Who is dead?" Roy says. "Mother's not. . . ."

"No, no, Roy," her father says quickly, "don't worry, darling. It's your Uncle Vivian. We just got the call."

An icy numbness sweeps up over Roy, the arch seems to grow and sway, and the loud mourning of the band reduces to zero db in her deaf ears. Once again, she feels as though she is floating right out of herself as the room grows larger and larger in the silence. And just as she feels herself falling back into her father's arms and swaying toward the floor, she sees Shirley and Shirley, in perfect synchronization, rush toward her through the golden arch.

a pervasive sense of humor in the face of tragedy,

The long night passes from death to morning, and all night long Roy tosses and turns, dreaming fitfully of Uncle Vivian and Shirley and

Shirley, mixed-up dreams of a wolf at the door and the iron baby angel by the cemetery gate, a descent into the maelström of dreams and nightmares, Uncle Vivian's voice, and the voice of the 7-Eleven man, and a sound of voices dying all around.

"Follow me down to one of the dark places," Uncle Vivian says to her, and when she tries to follow him, Shirley and Shirley stand in the arch and laugh with her. Dark laughter. Or are they crying for her? She wakes with a start and finds her mother, her red cheeks streaked white by tears, standing by her bed.

"Roy, we're going to have to take care of the funeral and of each other this week," she sobs. "Your father never did like Uncle Vivian, always called him a sissy. And after . . . and after . . . well, you know, after Vivian left town, things just got worse and worse. It's up to us, Roy. Vivian loved us, and we're the ones who loved him."

Roy sits up in bed and hugs her mother. She is crying, too, now, and throughout the next three days, whether she is sorting through the family linen and silver for the reception after the funeral or helping her mother buy a new dress or keeping peace at the dinner table, she finds herself crying unexpectedly and often.

She has not noticed that the winning Lotto numbers were 2–22–23–33–34–44, so she does not comment on it when Shirley calls her and offers to take her for a ride or something. In fact, she is unable to talk to him and coldly dismisses his offers. He calls again the next day, but the next couple of days he doesn't bother.

The morticians pick up Uncle Vivian at the tri-county airport and lay him out in the mortuary in a bright yellow sport jacket, an open-collared pink shirt, and the gold chain gleaming around his neck. He looks very pale and thin, especially with the rouge on his cheeks and lips. Roy weeps when she sees him, terribly and hard, and then she suddenly stops crying, becomes cool and distant and very clear-headed.

Uncle Vivian's partners, two singers called The Romantic Comedians for whom he played the piano, arrive in town the morning of the funeral, two nondescript bald-headed little men with strange smiles.

"I'm Tweedle," one of them explains to Roy when he discovers she has never seen their act, doesn't even know anything about it. "I play the Man, and Dee, my partner, plays the Woman. You wouldn't believe it, but she looks marvelous in drag. We sing the old songs, the great ones, 'Tea for Two,' 'Miss Otis Regrets,' 'Can't Help Lovin' Dat Man,' 'Let's Call the Whole Thing Off,' you know. And of course we camp them up quite a bit." He tosses his hands in the air in a helpless gesture of mixed sorrow and delight.

"Vivian was such a dear," he continues, and Dee chimes in, "The best pianist we ever had." He sighs, looks down at his hands, and then suddenly cracks his knuckles with a sharp clatter.

At the graveside, despite the oppressive heat and without warning, The Romantic Comedians begin to sing a medley of songs. Dee pulls a long purple feather boa out of his pocket to indicate that he is the Woman, and Roy is surprised by how good their voices are. They sing "After You've Gone" and "Ev'ry Time We Say Good-bye" and "The Man That Got Away" and close with "There Will Never Be Another You" and "Too Late Now." As they are singing, Roy's mother begins to sob uncontrollably again, while her father and the minister both stand in stony, grim silence.

The Romantic Comedians are singing "The Man That Got Away" when Roy looks up, past the solemn boy with the close-cropped hair and the gray sergeant-major's uniform, to find Shirley standing with Shirley at the back of the assembly of family friends among Vivian's former piano students of various ages. Shirley looks hot and uncomfortable in his blue suit, and Shirley looks particularly delicate and almost transparent beside him, her hand perched gently on his sleeve.

Dale is standing beside Roy, and she takes his arm and presses her face into his lapel as the sight of Shirley and the sound of The Romantic Comedians segueing into "There Will Never Be Another You" triggers another bout of tears, just when she has begun to think that she will never cry again. Dale hugs her to him, and the sight of his serious, concerned face when she looks up again causes her to break out laughing. Laughing and laughing and laughing.

an inability to leave the past behind.

The rain, which has been threatening all day, begins in the early afternoon. It washes the dust off the leaves of trees and bushes all over the county and causes windows to be hurriedly closed that had been open throughout the entire heat wave. It settles the dry sod into place on Vivian's grave and washes the petals off the few sprays of flowers still tilting on their wire frames.

Shirley is perched by Shirley's window as though poised for flight while he stands behind her. They are looking out over the wet treetops and watching the rain dance on the sidewalk and the top of the red Bronco parked in the street. He wraps his hands around her waist, and she turns her head up to him for a kiss. He is still amazed at how thin she is, how her breasts seem to come out of nowhere and press into his chest, how hugging her is like embracing air or an image in a mirror. A gust causes a mist of rain to spray through the open window and onto their faces and hair, and just for a second Shirley remembers hugging Roy in this window on a rainy evening last spring and how she seemed so substantial and so permanent. But Shirley presses herself into him with such urgency that he can think of nothing else. He wants her so badly, and when she finishes her prescription, maybe, just maybe she will be his. He wants to shout, but she is kissing him so hard she is taking all his breath away.

Roy is sitting across from Dale at his family's kitchen table. They are drinking cold buttermilk and playing chess. The door is open, and the rain is dancing on the flat painted wood of the back porch and on the rambling rose that winds up the porch pillars. The blooms are bright pink, and the rain makes them dance and nod, but Roy finds herself thinking how a killing frost will one day make the whole plant dry and brittle. Roy has Dale backed into a corner, but she finds her attention wandering. She licks a white rim of buttermilk from her lips and finds herself suddenly wishing she had a Coke Slurpee, wishing that she were at the 7-Eleven with Shirley and that she were making him answer the Question of the Week, making the total rise to 74%. She feels her eyes swimming in tears, and Dale's serious, puzzled face seems far away as though she were looking up at him from deep under water.

"Fish gotta swim," she finds herself singing out loud. And then she repeats it, "Fish gotta swim." And then she starts to cry again, saying to Dale over and over again, "I'm sorry, Dale. I'm sorry. I'm really sorry. I'm so sorry."

Allison is looking out of the window of his sister's small pink house at his little nephews jumping up and down in the rain by the drainage ditch at the side of the road. Water is raging in the ditch, and they are screaming "Flood, flood, flood!" His sister is in town at her job, and he has agreed to watch the boys all afternoon. The rain is washing away from the road the dust that always coats the house and makes his sister often keep the windows closed even on the hottest nights. They are open now, and the rain is splashing in on the floor. Allison does not close them; he can always mop the floors later. He is supposed to be working on his honors paper on the uses of African-American folk tales in Southern literature, but he can't help but watch the boys leaping around the muddy yard.

"'Twouldn't 'stonish me none ef we wuz ter have some fallin' wedder," he says aloud. "'Tiz e'en about ez much ez I kin do fer to keep fum laughin'."

Ellen Douglas

ABOUT LOVING WOMEN

I

It was after the fight, walking home from school, that I remembered what had happened—such a long time ago I can hardly believe I remember it.

You know how there are some memories you're sure belong to you—because you've never shared them—like standing by the basin when you were three and watching the old lady who was live-in housekeeper the year your mother broke her pelvis and had to stay in traction for two months. You're leaning against the basin. Your head comes up just high enough so you can rest your chin on the cool smooth curving surface. You're looking up and she (the old lady) opens her mouth and *takes out her teeth.* And then, while you're watching (you can't believe it's happening—she never says a word the whole time and seems not to know you're there), she dips her toothbrush in a can of powder and brushes the fronts and sides and corners and then she rinses them off and *puts them back in her mouth.* How is such a thing possible? Does anyone else know about this weird and scary, this magical skill of hers? You believe without even thinking about it (can you think at all when you're three?) that no one is supposed to know. Something awful may happen if you tell. You slip away—it still seems to you she hasn't noticed you standing there—and you never, never tell anyone what she can do.

And then there are others, stories you've heard people repeat so often you think what you know may be the memory of someone else's telling—like the time on vacation in Colorado when you fell in the Roaring Forks River and almost drowned and your mother ran downstream and threw herself on a log and wiggled out and grabbed you as you went tumbling by underneath. Is that her memory or yours? Because it's like you feel her terror more than the choking and drowning and banging against rocks that went on with you.

The third kind, the kind you must have tried to lose, is what came back to me the other day, sort of during and sort of after the fight. It's been there all my life, just waiting.

It even seems as if some people look at me in a special way because they remember, too. But they're not sure I do and so they never say. My grandmother looks at me like that—as if we have a secret. She wants to talk to me about it, but she sees it's impossible. I even think sometimes that because of this secret she wants to stand between me and my own life, as if I'm not up to it by myself and she has to protect me, and that makes me feel, no matter how much I love her, like I'm trapped in an elevator between floors or nailed in a packing crate or locked in the trunk of a car. Sometimes Uncle Alan looks at me that way, too, but his eyes are—not pitying, but sad and—I don't know—detached maybe.

I could be imagining things about both of them. They may have forgotten. My grandmother may never have known.

So I got in a fight after school last week.

I fight a lot.

I was small for my age until this past year—shot up last summer between sixteen and seventeen—and I've always had to either fight or be sharp enough to stay out of fights if I didn't want my face rubbed in the dirt. It's great when you're little—I mean littler than the other guy—to turn things around, to make him look like a fool in front of his friends for wanting to fight you, to make him have to laugh it off. And fighting's been okay, too, when I've had to do it, even when I got hurt. I've got a fucking terrible temper, and a point comes when I'm so mad I'll pick up anything handy—a stick or a chain or a tire tool—and no matter how much bigger the other guy is, he better watch out. Goddamn it, they're not gonna push me around, I don't care how big they are, that's what I'd say to myself. I'll kill any fucking bastard thinks he's gonna push me around. And I'd forget everything. Nothing hurt. No matter how hard a guy might hit me, I would barely feel it. And so I'd keep coming back.

And then, too (before I grew), if I could scare somebody who was bigger than me or walk into the gym and know they might be saying to a new kid in the class, Yeah, he's a little bitty honky, but don't mess with him, man, just don't mess with him. . . .

But I'm tall now—six-one. I can jump up and touch the ceiling in the hall at school. Not that I'm invincible; everybody else is taller, too, and in the school I go to, you're always having to prove yourself. Some of these black guys. . . . Last time it happened—cornered behind Renfro's Bicycle Shop—I picked up a broken bicycle chain from the trash heap and. . . . Well, I got out alive.

The way it is, you see, your parents have these convictions about public education and maybe you do, too—I'm not a racist, understand. But I'm the one who gets cornered behind Renfro's or has to walk home late, not knowing who's waiting or where. One time, seventh grade, I got held out the window of the third-floor john by my feet. That's helplessness. I kidded this seventeen-year-old eighth-grader into pulling me back in. As a matter of fact, he was white.

Then, last September, everything changed. The truth is I just completely forgot about being tough or not being tough, about being little or big, about fighting or studying or playing ball, about everything but Roseanne. It was like I turned into another person.

I still want to think and talk mainly about Roseanne and I can't seem to stop or even to want to stop, no matter how bad it hurts. I'm driving along in the car and I'll turn the radio off so I can think about nothing but her. Or walking to school. . . . I walk along and imagine I see her. She has a way of walking, a little bit slew-footed and tomboyish . . . and her legs, just so trim and beautiful (she swims a lot) and brown, and her little ass, as round as apples, and her face and her hair. Her hair is real thick and lots of times she wears it in one of those French braids that look so hard to do, and the wispy curls that didn't get braided in fuzz up around her face like a baby's hair. Her eyebrows are straight across instead of curved and somehow to me that gives her a more serious and honest look. I imagine her coming toward me along the sidewalk, glad to see me, smiling. She has a kind of doubtful smile, as much as to say, Here I am and I like you. Okay?

But mainly, of course, I don't think about what she looks like or how she walks or smiles. Instead, I go over and over in my mind the times we've been together. I feel her breast under my hand and the littleness of her waist and the way her hips swell out in such a neat curve. She's my love, I say to myself, my only, only love.

Not that I hadn't fucked a few girls before her. Well, two, to be exact, and one of them it was only one time and didn't work out too well. But I wasn't a damn virgin just screaming for sex, ready to be made a sucker of. All the same, virgin or not, I will never in my whole life love anybody like I love her. Laugh if you want to. Tell me I'm a kid. Tell me I don't know anything about love. But I never will. I know.

So the fight was about Roseanne.

We'd been going out together since September. I knew I wanted to go out with her the first time I saw her. To begin with, she went out with other people, too, but then later only with me and we got serious. She wasn't a virgin either, she said. She'd been with a guy in Birmingham, where she used to live, and she really cared about him, but that was over and now they were friends, but nothing else, and anyhow it hadn't been like us, she said. She was *really* in love with me.

II

Before I knew who he was, he told a couple of friends of mine at school that he was going to fight me, that he was going to *kill* me, for Christ's sake, and of course they told me. People always tell you things like that. He said something about beating me up with one arm tied behind him—he'd been watching me, he said, and I was so clumsy I stepped on my own feet. Well, sometimes I do miscalculate. When you grow nine inches in a year and your feet go from nine C to twelve D, it takes a while to get everything under control again.

Of course he didn't know anything about me either. He'd just moved to town.

His name is Henry.

What happened was that he—his whole family—followed her over here.

The reason Roseanne's folks moved here in the first place was that the company her dad worked for sent him to open a new plant. And Henry—the one who was so crazy about her, the one she was "just friends with" now—his dad worked for the same company, and six months later when the plant got revved up, he was transferred, too.

These are some questions I don't know the answers to: Had they been writing to each other? Maybe talking on the phone? Did he know about me? Were they really just friends now? Does Roseanne even care about me at all? Would she have left me and gone back to Birmingham and him if she could have?

Anyhow, his first day in school he heard about me. He told somebody that he knew her, that they came from the same town, that they'd been tight (this is the way I heard it) and the other guy said, "Yeah, well, she's Charles's girl now." And he said, "Who's Charles?" And when the guy points me out, he looks at me for a while and then he says, "That clumsy big-footed sucker? I don't believe it." And in about three days it went from there to I could murder him with one hand tied behind me. All without our ever saying hello or fuck you.

Where was Roseanne? She could have settled the whole thing with a word.

She had the flu, that's where she was. Or something. Anyhow she stayed out of school all that week.

Every day on the country music station I hear songs about how you can love two people at the same time, not be able to choose between them. Maybe that's what gave her the flu.

So inside a week it gets to the place where he's said so many things at school I can't let another one pass by. It's not that I was thinking maybe she cared about him instead of me. I didn't. I thought she was sick. And she was. Maybe she was. But at some point you know if you let a guy say one more thing like he'd been saying about me, you're going to be in trouble. You're going to lose it—everything you've fought to prove.

I held back as long as I could and then one day after school I waited for him and he knew I was waiting for him and we went out back of the gym where there's a storage building that cuts off the view of the street—a place where you can fight without anybody seeing you—me and three or four friends of mine and him and a couple of the guys he'd been talking to—he hadn't had time to make any friends yet.

I suppose I was half mad and half sad already. What's he thinking? He must be thinking Roseanne is going back to him. He *must*. All he's got to do, he's thinking, is show me up and humiliate me. And what am I thinking? I'm thinking he's made it pretty clear how tight he and Roseanne were in Birmingham and that he's expecting to move back in. And also I'm thinking that the last two days she wouldn't talk to me when I called her. Once her mama said she was asleep and the other time she said her fever had gone up and she felt too bad to talk. That didn't get it. She could talk, for Christ's sake. She wasn't in a coma.

He came at me without saying a word. I looked at him and my arms felt like they'd gotten almost too heavy to lift, like I didn't want to hit him.

To begin with, he was a good bit smaller than me, five-seven or five-eight, and stocky. But it wasn't that—he looked like he was strong enough and he held his fists and moved like he could handle himself. It was the look on his face. He came at me like he really did mean to kill me, to wipe me off the planet—or anyway, out of his mind—forever. His face had that tight look that makes you know somebody is feeling the prickly beginning of tears in the back of their nose and behind their eyes, and a rock in the bone at the top of their throat.

How do you see pure hatred in somebody's eyes? You read in a story that somebody's eyes "twinkled" or "shone with desire" or "glinted with rage." I never have seen anybody's eyes twinkle or glint. But I knew from his eyes that he hated me. He was keeping his face blank because if he didn't he'd start crying, but he hated me so much he couldn't even blink. He just stared at me like a crazy person and came at me.

I'd had a plan for the fight from the beginning. I've got these long arms now and big hands as well as big feet and I figured I could just hold him off. Make an ass of him by keeping him from hitting me. After everything he'd said about beating me with one arm tied behind him, why not put one hand in my pocket and show him who can fight one-handed? I've already said I've been fighting ever since I was in first grade. The truth is, it hasn't all been just crazy, show-off, or mad fights, or self-defense. I went out for golden gloves one year and picked up a few pointers. I figured I could keep out of his way and teach him not to mess with me.

But it didn't turn out the way I thought it would.

I had my left hand in my pocket and when he came at me the first time I put my right hand against his chest and gave him a shove and said something like, "You want to see who can fight with one hand tied behind him?" and he didn't seem to hear me or feel the shove, he just came in again, flailing, and said, "Roseanne."

"Man, you're tough," I said, "but tough don't necessarily get it."

And he came at me again and that time he got past my arm and hit me pretty good, but you could tell he didn't know how to fight worth a shit. All he knew was to keep coming and flailing, so it wasn't any trouble to stay out of his way.

I hit him a couple of times—now his nose is bleeding and his lip is cut a little bit. So maybe he's ready to quit.

"Look, man," I said, "I'm too big to be fighting you. Let's quit. Okay?" Unfortunately I dropped my guard when I was saying that and he came plowing in and the next thing I know he's kneed me in the balls and I'm doubled up rolling around on the ground.

Jesus Christ! That motherfucker kneed me in the balls. I was goddamn near paralyzed. And then he's all over me, on top of me, straddling me, pounding at my ears and my face like a maniac, and my mouth and eyes are full of dirt, but I'm hurting so bad I hardly even know it.

Somebody dragged him off and said, "Hey, man, you kneed him in the balls." And it took two of them to hold him until I got myself together and stood up, and then they let him go and he came at me again.

I wasn't feeling so cool by now, as you can imagine, and I didn't put my hand back in my pocket after that.

I hit him as hard as I could in the belly and he didn't seem to feel it, just came at me, and said, "Roseanne," one more time and the water began to pour out of his eyes and he was crying and trying to kill me at the same time. He grabbed me by the arm where I was holding him off and for a minute, for Christ's sake, I thought he was going to bite me.

That's when the heaviness in my arms got heavier. My hands were as heavy as bricks and I tasted dirt and blood in my mouth and something was floating into my mind and I dropped my hands and he hit me in the face and in the belly, but he couldn't knock me down. And it was almost like I forgot about him, and instead I was watching one of those stick and mud and rock dams—the kind you build across a creek when you're a kid—and I saw it break up and wash away, and I let him hit me again and then again. And afterwards I just turned around and walked off and old Henry was still coming after me and he got me pretty good in the kidney, but a couple of the guys grabbed him and held him and later they told me they picked up a hose by the outside hydrant there and hosed him down and then he left, too.

III

My Uncle Alan and his girlfriend Betsy came to visit us the year I was five. They came again later, of course, and I'm sure they'd come before, but the memory is from the time when I was five. They spent three weeks with us and all that time she loved me—not like I was her kid—not that kind of grumpy bored love like your mother's, the surface part of something so powerful it scares you, but another kind. Maybe, I think, now that I've started thinking about it, remembering it, maybe it's the kind a woman has for a kid who's not hers, when she wants a kid real bad and doesn't have one and no prospect of having one any time soon.

Because they weren't married, and they didn't get married for two years after that, and she wasn't young—twenty-eight or twenty-nine, probably. I remember later when they finally got married hearing my mother say, "Well, I hope they go on and have a kid. Betsy's getting along, and God knows she's wanted one long enough."

I've asked myself what I was thinking when they were with us that summer. But you can't go back to what you thought and how you thought when you were five and time was just starting to tick and people beginning to be separate from you. You felt and saw and smelled, you felt pain, but if you *thought* the way you did, it gets buried. I see myself and remember myself, but the memories are like this: I'm sitting on the ground under a sycamore tree with long bumpy roots on each side of me and I've built a tiny little house out of curly pieces of bark. My butt is against the rough bumpiness of a root and the ground is dusty and I feel the powdery warm dust under my legs and on my fingers and I smell the air—it must be late summer because the smell is the sharp, sad smell of goldenrod. I've scraped a road in the dust leading to my bark house and I've maneuvered one of those big black carpenter ants onto my road with a stick and I'm trying to get him to go into the house I've built for him, and finally he goes in and I'm really pleased. But then another one of those big ants is crawling on my leg and I squash him with my fingers and afterwards I lick my fingers and taste the formic acid (delicious, like pickles or sour grass) and that's what the memory of being five is like—never of thoughts— or not for me, anyhow.

So I'm walking home after the fight with my arms and hands feeling heavy and my balls hurting and dust and blood in my mouth, and the memory floats up—first her face, Betsy's face, floating up in my mind like a face through water, and then her hair, the smell of her hair like the smell of the rosemary bush by the kitchen door, and colors, lavender and pale green and blue; and she's sitting on the side of my bed telling me a story and knitting and the colors are the skeins of yarn around her—she's making something soft and stripy in those colors—and it's after bedtime and she leans over me and kisses me good-night and I'm pressed against her, feeling the softness of her.

And then it's daytime. I'm out in the yard by the driveway and my Uncle Alan and Betsy are loading the car getting ready to leave and my dad is helping them and I see the suitcases going into the car and a box packed with jelly and pickles she and Mama have been making and Uncle Alan's fly rod and the basket full of yarn and knitting needles. Everything is vanishing into the trunk of the car and then the lid is slammed down and there is nothing of theirs—of hers—left in our house, just as there was nothing of hers before they came. And then she's kneeling down beside me in the grass with her arms around me saying, "Good-bye, Charles. Are you coming to see us next year? Next summer?" I hear her voice, as soft as silk and her long hair is falling around my face and shoulders, smelling like grass and like rosemary and my face is against her and her arms are around me, holding me.

She loves *me, me*. But her clothes and her knitting basket and the blue and lavender yarn are in the trunk of the car and the lid has slammed and she is saying good-bye, as if she can abandon me and I can go back to being the same one I was before she came.

And Uncle Alan is saying good-bye, too, and his hand is on my head and then his hand is under her arm making her stand up and leave me and I look at him and see the sadness on his face, but the other thing, too, that I put down earlier—the detachment or knowledge or whatever it is. And Betsy is crying, and she gets in the car and he pushes the lock button down and shuts the door and shuts her away from me and starts around to the other side.

I go after him and he's huge. I'm hitting him as hard as I can on the legs, reaching up, trying to hit him where I know how bad it hurts, and to climb up his legs so I can hit him in the face and choke him and bite him and kill him.

And then he has put me aside and he's in the car and I feel my father's arms holding me and I'm trying to pull free. I hear his voice very low and deep: Charles! Charles! They'll be back, son. Don't cry. They'll be back. The engine starts and the car begins to roll, slow and then faster, and dust spurts out from behind the wheels and gets in my mouth, and then she's gone.

She's gone, Henry. The blue and green and lavender yarn, the hair that smells like rosemary, the breasts as soft as down. Hit me again, if you want to, but it won't help. Still, she's gone. And you and I, Henry—we can't go back to being the ones we were before she came.

Lolis Eric Elie

SILENT SPACES

The eternal silence
of these infinite spaces
frightens me.
　　—Blaise Pascal

Friday night:

　Marie Beauvalon, kids asleep, ear hooked on the telephone, hears recaps
of daytime television.

　The Reverend Waters, car parked around the corner, wife parked across
town, loins parked—but only for a second—hears devil music.

　Billy Dart, red suit thrown across the chair, one red shoe thrown beneath
the bed, hears only the booming bass of the discotheque he left an hour ago.

Saturday morning:

　Picou stops a tune in the middle. Three boys lean against the piano
and hold their horns like longshoremen holding bag lunches. A fourth
would hold his horn like a bag lunch, but tubas are hard to dangle.

　Picou is determined that these boys will learn to play. To play jazz.
His living room—a tiny chamber of exposed brick walls, hardwood
floors, a fireplace, and a record box—is a conservatory. This band of
uninterested youth, a master class.

　On the mantle, a five-by-eight inch picture of Sidney Bechet smiles
approval. From a wood frame near the kitchen, so does Louis Arm-
strong.

　Picou is a small man, a little taller than five feet, less than 150 pounds. But he believes himself a warrior fighting in an urgent cause. And he believes these boys, though more interested in sports than music, more interested in rhythm and blues than jazz, and much more interested in what is going on outside of his house on Treme Street than what is going on inside of it, will be warriors too. He believes that one day they will mold the frivolity of youth into dedication and appreciation.

The trumpet, he explains to one, *plays the melody. The most important part. You've got to play strong, like you're playing the most important part.*

Clarinet, he tells another, *you play off of what the trumpet player plays. You take what he does and improvise around it.*

Tuba and trombone, in the horn section you're the foundation. The harmony and the rhythm. At all times you have to know where you are in the tune.

Drummer, you sound like you're playing rhythm and blues. This is jazz. Second line music. Play a second line on them drums. Nodding his head for emphasis, he demonstrates:

> *Boom chh.*
> *Boom chh.*
> *Boom chh.*
> *Ba-boom boom Boom!*
> *chh. Boom chh.*
> *Boom chh.*
> *Ba-boom boom Boom!*

I know they can play it. If they want to. If they practice. I know they can play it. I will teach them.

He counts off, "When the Saints Go Marching In." *One, two, one two, three, four.*

The trumpet plays the pick-up notes with all the conviction of a rabbi preaching gospel. The rest join in, but it gets no better. Picou doesn't stop them. *You can't keep stopping them or they will get frustrated. They can play this music if they stick with it. Don't get discouraged.*

The clarinet solos first. Up the scale then down. Every note, then every other note. A long note, a few short ones and out.

Daydreaming, the trumpet player hasn't heard the clarinet stop.

Doesn't know it's his turn. He comes in confused. Plays the first measure of the tune while the band plays the third measure. Down the scale, then up.

Lost, the piano player has stopped playing.

Picou picks up his soprano saxophone and plays with urgency. This is how it is done: he starts with the melody, "Oh when the saints," his notes say, then he adds an embellishment. He plays more. You can tell he's thinking "go marching in," but he doesn't play it just so. Then you know he's thinking "Oh when the saints" again, but he just growls one note, the same note, four times.

Keep it simple. Play the melody and a little blues. Melody and blues. They can feel that. "I want to be, right in that number. Oh, when the saints go marching in."

More solos, all bad, and they take the tune out. *Don't get discouraged. Trombone,* he says, *play the melody.*

What?

Play the melody.

That's not my part.

What did I tell you? Everybody has to know the melody. That's what you solo off of. He says it patiently, but seriously. *Clarinet, what key is this tune in?*

Huh?

That's not a key. What key is the tune in?

Blank look.

That's the other thing. Everybody has to know what key to play in. Look at your music. Trumpet, play the blues scale.

He plays eight notes.

That's not the blues scale, that's the major scale. Play a blues scale.

Silence.

Look at your music, I gave you the blues scale last month. When you play, I don't care if it's "Rudolph the Red-Nosed Reindeer," play the blues scale. That's what you need to play jazz: melody, harmony and blues.

As he starts the tune again, the phone rings.

Cleveland, the bass player, can't make the gig tonight. *I know some young bass players who'd love to play with you. Want their numbers?*

White boys?

Who else? Do you want the numbers?

I'll find somebody.

Suit yourself. What's that noise in the background?

I told you about it. My workshop. I'm teaching kids jazz.

The students have abandoned their lesson. They are playing something else. *The trombone player is singing over a funk beat, "Do me, baby.
Tonight."*

Beauvalon, you sound like a bitch when you sing, the drummer yells at
him.

Your daddy sound' like a bitch, Beauvalon yells back.

Either that's a jazz tune I don't know, or you're wasting your time Picou,
Cleveland says. *These kids don't want to play no jazz.*

They'll want to if we teach them. It's important that we teach them.

It's not important to them that we teach them.

If it's not important to them, then we've wasted our whole lives.

Cleveland chuckles. *Then you've wasted your whole life.*

You're wrong.

Any of those kids ready to play?

I'll find somebody to play the gig.

You want the numbers?

I'll find somebody.

Picou hangs up the phone. *Okay, from the top, Oh When the Saints.*

Mr. Picou, the tuba player says, *my mama told me I have to leave early
so I coul' go to football practice.*

Me too, says another one.

Me too, says a third.

Soon, only the clarinet player is left. Picou teaches him last week's
lesson, and the lesson from the week before that. After half an hour,
Picou offers him a cold drink. The boy sits on the piano bench; Picou
sits on the couch. They talk about music, about football, about school.
Picou tries to get a sense of the boy.

In his mind, Picou tried to mold this boy into a memory of himself.
He tries to remember this boy following jazz bands on Mardi Gras Day,
hearing music that made people dance, made people yell to each other
Eh la bas! and yell to musicians *Play that motherfucker, Red. Play that
godddamn horn!*

He tries to remember this boy remembering the sounds of moments
that weren't recorded, and feelings that weren't transcribed. Sounds

and feelings that can only be recalled through the instruments of musicians who have studied thoroughly the alchemy of turning memory and learning into spontaneous expression.

Picou asks the boy questions. Questions that lead directly to proper responses. Questions that, if answered properly, would lend substance to Picou's fantasies. He prepares to hear these responses, but doesn't. Though he struggles to know, he can't tell if the boy is interested in learning music, or if he just has nowhere else to go.

Saturday night:

Treme Street is a resounding silence. There are street noises. Dogs barking. People talking. Music playing loudly. Yet in these sounds Picou hears only deafening space.

Picou takes his saxophone out of the case. Goes to a corner of his living room. From corners of rooms sounds bounce back. They are heard better. From a corner of this room Picou takes aim at this silence. He blows fat notes, expansive sounds that, if notes had the power, would transform this silent space. He does this, as he does each night, hoping that someone will hear.

Marie Beauvalon, window shut, ear hooked on the telephone, hears only weekend gossip.

The Reverend Waters, car parked around the corner, wife parked across town, loins parked—but only for a second—hears devil music.

Billy Dart, green suit thrown across a chair, one green shoe thrown beneath the bed, hears only the booming bass of the discotheque he left an hour ago.

Percival Everett

THROWING EARTH

Joseph Martin straightened with a cracking in his back and winced, and a sigh of release softened his face. Letting the pitchfork rest against the stall wall, he twisted his torso again but found no sound. He leaned his head and shoulders past the gate and gave a call to his son.

Wes left the water trough he was watching fill and walked across the baked-hard corral toward the barn.

"I want you to finish up in here," Joseph said, stepping out of the stall and stomping his boots free of clinging dung and straw. He watched the boy set to work. "I'm going to take a look at your mother's car."

The boy paused, particles from a pitched load settling. "She ain't here."

Joseph pushed up his hat and raked at the perspiration on his forehead with the back of his hand. "She told me her car was acting up." He looked toward the house. "Where'd she go? She say?"

"I don't know, Daddy."

Joseph looked at the hot day. "When you finish in here, come get me and we'll worm the last of the horses."

The boy nodded and Joseph left him to work.

Joseph went to the house and stopped in the kitchen to pour himself a glass of cold water from the bottle in the refrigerator. He held the glass against his face, looking around for a note that his wife might have left. He thought about replacing the leaky tee-pipe at the top of the water heater, but instead went outside and sat beneath the big cottonwood. He soaked up shade and watched the driveway, the road, the magpies, the jays.

Wes came to the front yard, stood by Joseph, stunned momentarily by the shade. "Ready to do the horses?"

Joseph stood up.

"What were you doing, Daddy?"

"Nothing."

"I got the medicine out."

"Good." Joseph slapped a hand on Wes's shoulder. "Good."

They walked to the small corral beyond the barn.

"Daddy, you think it'd be all right if I went out for the basketball team this year?"

Joseph smiled. "Sure, why not?"

"Just figured I'd ask. I know there's a lot to do around here."

Joseph looked at his son and for the first time actually saw his height. "When did you get tall as me?"

"Taller," Wes said.

Joseph pressed his back against the tiled wall of the shower. More of it struck flesh once; now his shoulder curved over a bit. Dirt and dust followed rivulets down his body, twisted off of his legs and found the drain. He turned off the water and dried himself roughly with a towel stiff from hanging on the line.

While he dressed he listened to his wife downstairs in the kitchen, her footsteps, the clattering of plates and pots settling on the table. She was whistling. The tune annoyed Joseph, but he couldn't help listening closely. He laughed softly at himself, discovering his anger, but the emotion was no surprise. He was only startled by the calm of it all.

He dressed and went down to the table and sat.

Wes said nothing, just tore into his meal, his eyes cast down at his busy plate.

"How's your car?" Joseph asked.

Cora was not ready with an answer. Her voice broke as she searched for words. She landed on, "It did fine today, for a while, but the noise started again."

"The squeaking you described?" he asked, not really offering his attention, but tossing a sidelong glance toward the boy.

"Yes," she said.

He nodded and mumbled that he would tend to it. After a silence he asked, "By the way, where'd you go earlier?"

Her response was ready and clear and it pulled Wes's eyes from his fork to her. "I was at Amy's house, helping her choose wallpaper for her kitchen."

"She doing it herself or having somebody come in?"

"Having somebody come in," Cora said. "And of course I picked up some groceries."

The moon was unrelenting as Joseph stared out the bedroom window. The cornbread globe, just shy of full, sang a glow of restful light, but Joseph was up cursing it. He got up and went to the window and looked down at the bay mare in the pasture. He couldn't climb back into bed. He couldn't lie between the sheets with that woman, have her foot brush his leg, have her hair tickle his shoulders. He pulled on his pants and went down the stairs, outside, and across the yard to the corral. The night was cool and not very dark. He took up a hand of earth and looked at it. He knew that if he threw it as hard and as far as he could, all of it would still fall on his land. He let the dirt sift through his fingers.

The next weeks saw a steady rain which had come late, but had come. The pastures were soft and the horses stayed near the trees. Cora's car was gone more and more. He had seen her car parked in the same place in town several times. Refusing to acknowledge that a blind eye is just as or more vulnerable than one that sees, he went about his work, rising early, falling silent in the evenings. He could see her car in his sleep, through the windshield of his truck, the rain rolling down it, the wipers counting cadence.

Finally one day he greeted her with the same face he had for weeks and told her that he knew. She smiled, a wicked smile, Joseph thought, and his calm faded, his eyes narrowed. His brain spoke to her, telling her to feel his pain, the hurt of the betrayal, telling her to open his shirt and see the gaping wound.

Cora's smile went away and she was afraid.

Joseph did nothing, said nothing. "Wes," he called to his son.

Wes came into the room.

"Come on, let's ride into town."

Wes looked at his parents, one then the other. "Okay."

Joseph did not offer Cora another glance. He followed Wes out the door and through the drizzle to the truck. Dusk was coming on when they stopped at a diner.

Wes waited until they were seated and had ordered before he asked, "What's going on?"

"Your mother and I are having some problems."

"No kidding."

"She's been cheating, Wes."

The boy looked at his father.

"She's been with another man."

Wes shook his head and looked out the window. "I don't believe you. Who?"

"Doesn't matter."

The waitress brought the food.

Wes looked at his chicken-fried steak, moved it with his fork. "So, what's going to happen?"

Joseph shrugged, drank some coffee.

Joseph and Wes came home to a dark house. They said good-night to each other. Joseph went to the room he shared with Cora and found her in bed. He sat on the edge of his side, holding his hands, his elbows resting on his knees. He heard her stir, sit up.

"Joseph, we have to talk about this," she said.

He wanted something to happen, wanted to talk, but he couldn't find the stomach for it. He stood up.

"Don't leave," she said.

He turned to face her and she switched on the bedside lamp.

"I'm not leaving, Cora, not this ranch anyway. And I'm not going to ask you to leave. But I'm not asking you to stay."

"I'm sorry," she said.

"Yeah, well, maybe this will blow over. I don't know." He turned away from her, stopped at the door. "I don't want to know who it was."

"It didn't, doesn't mean anything," she said.

Without looking at her, he said, "Oh, it means something."

"I want you to talk to Wes."

"And tell him what?"

Cora switched off the lamp and lay back down.

Joseph leaned against the wall outside his room and looked at his son's bedroom door. Talk to him? He didn't know what to tell him. He didn't know what to tell himself.

It was hot again. Joseph was just about to climb the ladder and find out what was wrong with the vapor lamp on the barn. His stomach had felt uneasy all morning; now there was a pain in his gut. It had been giving him trouble for a couple weeks, but he had waved it off. He swayed a bit, then passed out.

He came awake to the drawling voice of the doctor from Tennessee who had retired down the road. The obtrusive space between his teeth made him hard to look at. Joseph sat up, having been moved inside the house and to his bed. His wife stood at the foot.

"Just a bug, eh, Doc?" Joseph said.

The doctor shrugged. "I can't say. You need to go in and 'get looked at,' as we say."

"Thank you, Doctor Wills," Cora said.

"Yeah, thanks, Doc," Joseph said, not looking at the man but out the window.

When Cora had led Wills out of the room, Joseph wrapped an arm across his tender middle, but stood up anyway. He went and looked out, saw Wes on the ladder fixing the light. Wes looked back at the house and saw his father in the window. He climbed down and came running to the house.

Wes came into the room and gave Joseph a hug.

"Thanks for fixing the light."

"I knew you wanted it done." He studied his father.

"I'm okay," Joseph said.

Cora appeared in the doorway and Wes ignored her obviously.

Cora sighed and left.

"Don't treat your mother like that," Joseph said.

"Yes, sir."

Joseph rubbed the hair on his son's head roughly. "Since when am I a sir?"

"I don't know."

"Go see what you can do to help your mother while I lie down for a while."

Wes left the room.

Cora made an appointment for Joseph, with the same doctor her father had gone to some months earlier. He drove into the city for the preliminary examination, which was short enough but ended with an invitation to return.

"Didn't they say anything?" Cora asked when he returned.

"What do you care?"

Wes stepped into the kitchen just in time to hear his father's words.

"Just that I have to come back," Joseph said.

"Not even a hunch?"

He shrugged. "Said something about it maybe being an ulcer." He sat at the kitchen table to eat the sandwich she had made him.

"That's what it is," she said. "You hold things in. And you don't eat right, Joseph."

He nodded and looked at his son. "I guess I do," he said, turning his eyes to his wife's.

"That's what it is," she said.

Joseph went out and looked at his horses. Wes followed him.

"How you feeling?" the boy asked.

"Fine. Ulcer."

The boy spat into the dust and covered it with the toe of his boot. "They give you pills?"

"Not yet." He put a foot up on the fence. "Everything's fine, Wes." He coughed into a fist. "You any good at this basketball stuff?"

Wes chuckled. "I'm okay."

"I'm glad you're going to play," Joseph said. "It'll keep you out of trouble."

"Right. That's why I'm playing."

The next visit to the doctor started early, one test, then another. The congenial grins faded into knitted brows. Then he was given an endoscopic examination which fascinated as much as scared him. A lighted tube was passed down his throat and into his stomach. Calipers were fed through the tube to its end, and a bit of tissue was extracted, biopsied by pathologists whom Joseph imagined deep in the basement of the University Hospital, and sent back with a note. The note was not a good sign, Joseph thought.

Joseph sat by the doctor's desk and watched the man light a cigarette and blow out a cloud of blue smoke. "How's the ranch, Joseph?"

"Fine."

"Good bunch of foals this year?"

"I've seen better."

The doctor put out the cigarette he had just lit, looking at it with a bit of disgust. "Joseph, it seems we have a problem."

Joseph nodded.

"We have gastro-intestinal lymphomas."

"We do?"

The doctor cleared his throat. "Infiltrates have embedded themselves in your stomach wall. That's why we thought ulcer at first." He coughed into a closed fist. "It's serious. We're in trouble."

"How much trouble?" Joseph asked.

"Chemotherapy might help, but I can't make any promises."

"Are you telling me we're dying?"

"Yes, I am," the doctor said. "You want it straight, Joseph?"

"Of course."

"I wish I could say something good. My guess, well it's more than a guess, is that treatment will only keep you alive a little longer. But who knows? The body is an amazing thing." He studied Joseph's face. "I'd like you to come back next week and we'll run the tests again." He pulled a yellow pad in front of him and started to jot. "Here's something for the pain."

Joseph took the prescription and stuffed it into his shirt pocket. He stood and shook the doctor's hand.

"You all right?" the doctor asked.

Joseph smiled. "Apparently not."

Joseph considered his wife as he drove his pickup out of the parking lot of the medical center. Cora was no pessimist. She had even refused to buy his anger with her and had stonewalled it almost out of existence. He knew that she believed with every ounce of herself that her husband would step through the front door and tell her that he was all right. He knew she expected this and so he planned to lie. Just an ulcer, he would say, then stand witness to her relief. And she would tell him again that it was because he held things in. At a stoplight in the middle of town he recalled how much he disliked the city, he couldn't see any purpose in living like that. He also failed to see the purpose in telling a lie like the one he had planned, a lie which could not be maintained indefinitely. He would tell Cora the truth and be with her through her acclimation to the circumstances. He would tell and she would sniff a little, straighten her back and say that they would see this through. Then he'd tell her that he was refusing treatment because it would only moderately prolong his life and greatly enhance his suffering, at which point she would fall to the floor crying and cursing him. Truth was he had no idea how it would go, or even if he would have the courage to tell her.

Joseph was thirty-eight, a young man. He was younger with the passing of every block as he left the city behind. He saw some teen-agers on the basketball courts of a middle school. He parked and went to stand by the far goal to watch. An errant pass bounced his way. He stopped the ball and picked it up, held it.

"Mind if I take a shot?" he asked.

They told him to go ahead. He put his hat on the ground and stepped forward, dribbled a couple of times. He threw up a thirty-foot jumper that bounced long off the rim back to him. He walked closer to the basket, bouncing the ball slowly.

"Come on, man, shoot," said one of the boys.

"Why don't you try guarding me?" Joseph said. A breeze pushed at his back.

The boys laughed and the one who had told him to hurry came forward, flashing a smile back at his buddies. He was a tall boy with long arms and fancy basketball shoes. He took a quick swipe at the ball, but Joseph turned his body.

"Make a move, old man."

Joseph gave the kid a head fake and dribbled left. The kid stayed with him, so he spun right on the heel of his boot and put a fall-away jumper.

"Yes," Joseph said as the ball banged around the rim and fell through the hole. "How do you like it, sonny?"

The boys teased their friend. The kid shrugged and shook it off, got the ball and dribbled to the top of the key. He pointed at Joseph and gestured for him to come. Joseph smiled and went to him. The kid tried to drive right, but Joseph stopped him. Joseph feigned a move for the ball and the boy almost lost control of it.

"Okay, old man," the teen-ager said and made a move on his last word, again to the right.

Joseph was caught flat-footed in his heavy cowboy boots and fell a full step behind. Joseph reached out and pushed the kid from behind. The shot went wild and the boy fell and rolled across the blacktop into the grass.

The kid got up. "What's the matter with you, man?" The other boys rallied behind him.

Joseph was confused but angry, and he found himself stepping to the kid. "What's the problem?" He squinted up at the sun. "Are you mad at me?" he asked the boy. The kid looked at him like he was crazy, ready to back away, ready to run, but Joseph wouldn't let him. "You're mad at me. I can see that. You want to hit me, don't you? Don't you?"

"Naw, man, I don't want to hit you. I just want you to go away."

"Come on," Joseph said. He knew what it felt like to be a jerk. He pushed his chin out. "Punch for punch, mid-face. You go first."

"You're crazy," the kid said.

Joseph moved closer. He was just inches from the boy's face, could see him sweating. "Don't be scared."

"I'm not scared."

"Why don't you just go someplace," another boy said.

Joseph silenced the smaller boy with a look and returned his attention to the first kid. He pushed him, two hands flat, but soft, against the chest. "I said for you to hit me."

The boy fell back a step and swallowed hard, his eyes wide open. "Hey, man."

Joseph shoved him again.

The other teen-agers stepped in and stood between them, all unsteady, heaving in deep breaths.

"Go home," the kid said from behind his friends.

"All right, I will, but first I want you to punch me. Hey, I've been an asshole out here. I won't hit you back, I promise. You can't let somebody be such a jerk and get away with it."

"Go on and hit him, John," one of the boys said.

"Yeah," said another.

"I don't want to," the kid said.

"Your pals are here, so I can't very well hit you back, right?" Joseph felt a smile on his face.

The kid squeezed through his friends, and Joseph again thrust out his chin, pointed to it. The boy threw out a weak open-handed tap that Joseph barely felt on his cheek.

"Harder," Joseph said.

Another blow, a little sharper. The boy was trembling, his lips parted and quivering.

"Hit me like a man!"

"Let him have it, John."

"Yeah."

When Joseph came around, he was alone. The sun was almost gone and a light drizzle was falling. His face hurt. The wind blew trash across the blacktop. His brain throbbed. A violent shudder ran through his body as he considered what he had done. He wanted to find the boy he had terrorized and apologize, then he hoped that the punch had been good enough, satisfying for him, hoped that the boy's fear would be short-lived, hoped he would never see him again. Maybe all the boys would get a good laugh out of it, nervous and falsely cocky at first, Joseph imagined, but later a genuine laugh. "John, remember that crazy . . ." he could hear them.

He felt better when he could see the hills scissor-cut again the western sky. It was dark when he rolled into home. The night smelled good. When he entered the house, he found there was little need to tell Cora anything. She looked at his swollen face and tears came. She begged him not to die.

"Okay," he said. He held her for a while there by the door and took deep breaths, thought about things like insurance and debts.

She pulled from him and walked stiffly away.

Joseph went into the bathroom and looked at his face in the mirror, rubbed his jaw.

Wes came in.

"Hey there, cowboy," Joseph said. He could hear Cora crying in the bedroom.

"You okay?"

"Naw, I guess I'm not doing so hot."

"What happened to your jaw?" the boy asked.

"Tried to knock some sense into myself." He looked at Wes's face in the mirror. "Why don't you see about your mother?"

Ben Greer

BLUE HANDS

The fella walked through the door of Duck's Place. He looked
around and then sat on a stool at the counter. He read the menu which
hung on the wall above the grill.

"This is a hot dog joint?"

"Pretty much," Duck said.

"I see you just got hot dogs up there."

"We got country cooking, too."

"What's country cooking?"

Duck glanced at me. I was at the other end of the counter.

"It's Confederate-fried steak, fried chicken, fried ham, fried okra.
Fried stuff," Duck said.

"Why don't you have it up there?"

"Just ain't got round to it yet."

The fella was big. He wore a navy blue suit and blue tie. His shoes
were old and black. I could tell by his accent he was a Yankee.

"You got a kraut dog?"

"A what?"

"A kraut dog. Sauerkraut and a frank and a bun."

"We just sell hot dogs and beer, mister."

"That's what I'm asking for. A kraut dog."

"And country cooking," Duck said. "We got that."

The fella put his hands on the counter. They were big and black
with hair. His little finger was missing on the right one. He wore a gold

ring on the stub. He stuck out the hand with the missing finger. "I'm Joe Panetti."

"Duck Smith."

They shook hands. Joe Panetti looked at me and I went down and shook his hand. I told him my name.

"So, Bobby, what kind of hot dog should I get?"

"I'd get the slaw dog," I said.

"What's it got on it?"

"Slaw and chili and onions."

"And mustard," Duck said.

"Oh, yeah," I said. "It's got lots of mustard."

"All right, gimme two slaw dogs and a Budweiser."

"No beer," Duck said.

"You just said you sold beer."

"I do, but not today. It's Sunday."

"So?"

"You must be from up North," I said.

"Jersey."

"They sell beer up there on Sunday?"

"They sell everything up there on Sunday."

Duck was making the slaw dogs.

"Dev'essere un bel posto," I said.

Joe turned to look at me.

Duck set the slaw dogs on the counter.

"The accent's kinda funny, but you speak it okay. Where'd you learn it?"

"I got a book at the store. I just learned a few words," I said.

"Benissimo."

"Gratia."

"Grazzzie," Joe said. "Make the z real strong."

I tried not to watch him while he ate the hot dogs.

Duck took off his apron. He started turning off the beer signs.

"What I wouldn't give for one of those," Joe said.

"I got some up in my apartment," I said.

"You do?"

"I got a six-pack. Be happy to share it."

Joe wiped his mouth with the back of his hand. His bald head was sweating. "You wouldn't mind?"

"No, sir."

"Don't say 'sir.' I'm just Joe, okay?"

"Got to go, fellas," Duck said.

"They were good," Joe said. "I like the chili."

"Chili's the secret to hot dogs," Duck said.

Joe Panetti got up. I followed him to the door. Just before he pushed it open, he stopped. "Hey, kid, would you do me a favor?"

"Sure."

"Would you walk out first?"

I didn't know if he was kidding or not, but I pulled open the door and walked out and looked up and down the street.

"It's okay," I said.

We got in my car.

On the way to the apartment Joe said he wanted to go by a store.

"I ain't had any Italian food in a week," he said.

"I can make Italian food."

"Oh yeah? What kind?"

"Spaghetti and meatballs."

"You can't make meatballs."

"Yeah, I can. I got Carmine's Italian cookbook. I make spaghetti and meatballs a lot. Want to hear the recipe?"

"That's okay. Pull in here."

Joe said he was going to do some real Italian cooking. He told me to watch the car.

When we got to my place, Joe went in first. He set down the groceries, then saw the posters. I had put up eight or ten. There was Rome and Florence and Naples. I put up every one I could find.

Joe shook his head.

He took the stuff out of the bags and set it on the table. He waved me over.

"Okay, what do you think's missing?" he asked.

I looked at the food. There was no hamburger and no tomatoes and no onions. I thought everything was missing, so I just shrugged.

Joe laughed and pulled off his coat. The pistol hung low over his ribs. The holster was dark with sweat. He saw me glance away.

"Yeah, it's a nine millimeter. I used to carry a .38, but that was in the old days."

He rolled up his sleeves and stuck his tie into his shirt. "Now what I'm making for you is spaghetti carbonara. Northern Italian. No tomatoes. No garlic. E un piatto squisito."

Joe had me break open the eggs and mix them in a bowl. He fried the bacon and boiled the pasta. After the pasta was drained, he told me to put in the eggs. He said the hot pasta would cook them. Then he put in the bacon and the Parmesan cheese and mixed it up.

Before he sat down, he went over and locked the door. He laid the pistol beside his plate.

I got two beers from the refrigerator and sat down and we ate the carbonara.

It was the best Italian thing I had ever eaten.

I put the plates in the sink and looked out the window at Main Street. I could see the white flowers of the dogwoods under the streetlights. There was the Baptist Church and boarded-up stores and the movie theater and the mill.

I got two more beers and gave one to Joe. He had his hands behind his head.

"So, Bobby, how'd you start liking stuff Italian?"

"I saw *The Godfather.*"

"Huh? Oh, the movie, yeah."

"I saw it twenty times."

Joe smiled. He patted his chest. "Thirty-two."

"You saw it thirty-two times?"

"Probably more."

"I love ole Don Corleone."

"I used to know a guy like him. They called him the gentle Don. Un uomo da rispettarsi."

"What happened to him?"

"He made a mistake. In our business, you don't make a mistake. Some punk blew his brains out. Some nobody."

Joe downed his beer. He put his pistol back in the holster and reached for his coat.

I got up.

"You stay here. It's right down the street."

"The Ramada?"

"Little boarding house right behind it."

He shook my hand. "Remember carbonara, kid."

I opened the door and he walked out slowly.

"Hey, Joe. Any way I might see you tomorrow?"

He smiled and pulled his tie out of his shirt. "Maybe. Buona sera."

"Buona sera," I said.

The next afternoon I went home and scrubbed my hands hard. It helped a little, but they were still blue. I knew they would stay blue for a long time. This week my shift was in the dye room.

Around six o'clock, I started to go over to the boarding house, but I thought it might be forward, so I just went back to Duck's.

These two fellas came in about an hour later. They were young. They wore white suits and white shoes, and both of them had gold chains around their necks. One of them wore sunglasses. He stuck his hands in his pockets and read the menu. "You got a kraut dog?"

Duck laughed.

"What's that supposed to mean?" the guy with the sunglasses asked.

"I got regular hot dogs."

"Oh, you got regular hot dogs. Well, I don't want a regular hot dog. I want a kraut dog."

"Take it easy, Phil."

"Hey, Jimmy, you take it easy. I want to get something straight here, okay?"

The one named Phil walked over to a stool and put his foot on it. He adjusted his sunglasses.

"You think I'm weird because I want a kraut dog?"

"No sir."

"Why'd you laugh?"

"Thinking about something else."

"So you don't think I'm weird? I mean, I'm not a weirdo cause I want a kraut dog?"

"No."

"Good." He reached over and patted Duck's face.

"We're looking for a Mister Joe Pennies," Jimmy said.

"Don't be a wise ass," said Phil. "His name is Joe Panetti."

"Don't know him," Duck said.

"He's a big, fat, bald-headed guy," Phil said.

"Haven't seen him."

The one named Jimmy smiled, pointed at me. "Have you seen him?"

"No."

"He'd just be passing through. Drives a black Caddy."

"Haven't seen anybody like that," I said.

Phil swept back his hair. "Well, if you see him, tell him his cousins are looking for him, okay?"

"Sure thing," I said.

Phil smiled and turned around and they left.

"That don't sound real good," Duck said.

I waited, then opened the door and looked around.

I walked up to Thompson's boarding house. It was beginning to get dark. Azaleas were blooming in the front yard.

Joe was sitting out on the porch. The door to his room was open. He was sitting at a wicker table playing cards. There was a cassette recorder beside him.

"Hey, paesano," Joe said.

I sat down. "There're two guys looking for you."

Joe kept turning the cards.

"They said they're your cousins."

"Yeah, right."

"If you left now, I think you'd be okay."

"I'm tired of this shit, you know. I'm tired of it."

I watched him turn the cards.

"I could stay here with you," I said.

"No."

"It might help."

"Nope."

"Why not?"

"Cause you'd get killed, okay? You want to know? You'd get killed. Bam-bam. Now beat it."

It was dark now. Joe got up and went to his room and closed the door.

I sat for a few minutes and then walked back to the apartment.

I stood in front of my window and looked out at the town a long time. Then I went to the closet and opened it up. I kept his things here. Everybody told me to get rid of them when he died, but I didn't.

My father had been forty-three when he died. He had two suits and two pairs of shoes. The rest was overalls and work shirts.

He went to Atlanta twice. He said it was something. He said he was going to take me and he would have, but his brown lung got worse and he went down fast.

I stood there and thought about it, then I reached into the corner for his shotgun. I loaded it and got some extra shells.

On the way back, I saw the two guys in white suits walking into the Ramada.

I went up the steps to Thompson's and tapped on Joe's door.

"Yeah?"

"It's me."

He opened the door.

"I got something for you."

"What's that?"

I brought the shotgun into the light.

He looked at it, then nodded me in.

There was a bottle of red wine on the table. Joe got another glass and poured me some.

We sat down. I put the shotgun across my knees. We drank some wine.

"You ever listen to opera?" Joe asked.

"Not much."

"Oh, you gotta do that, kid. You really got to."

He pushed a button on the cassette recorder. "This is Verdi. He's the best. He'll take you away." He turned up the volume.

I sat and looked at my blue hands and listened to the music.

Alyson Hagy

THE FIELD OF LOST SHOES

I met her at New Market just like she asked. She thought it would
look good to her husband that way and good to me, the road scholar,
the able guy. She had promised she wouldn't pull any punches; this
would be an honest get-together. We really would meet halfway. She
would bring Timothy along too, she said. For her protection and mine.

It took me four hours to get as far as Lexington. I'd taken a five-mile
run at dawn, a crazy, beautiful thing to do in east Tennessee, and had
some coffee after my shower, while the sky was still lead-colored and
cold. But I wasn't hungry. All I could think about was Ellen having
lunch in the restaurant on Afton Mountain, explaining to her son how
they were going to eat ice cream, then drive into the valley for some
history.

I hadn't seen Ellen in three months, not since I'd packed my books
and files and left for East Tennessee State University, my first teaching
job. Ellen had been proud of me—was still proud of me, I thought, if
you could say pride slid in that direction. And though she had written
to me every Wednesday, while her husband Denny was teaching his
seminar on Jefferson Davis, what I felt behind her words was only the
very edge of things. *It's over, it's never over.* Her letters said both,
written as they were in the hard varnished smell of Denny's study. So
when she called me, a reckless thing to do, and said *Meet me at New
Market battlefield, it makes sense, you could be there,* I said yes, even

though I knew it could go wrong. She was bringing Denny's son; she was playing Denny's wife. Ellen and I could talk all we wanted, but her husband would still be there, casting shadows as dark and heavy as his moods.

And yet, Ellen had made me feel exhilarated, poorly aimed and powerful the whole time we were together. So she didn't have to sound desperate to convince me of anything. I'd be there. If she wanted to stake something—her time, her marriage, the wide eyes of her son— on seeing me again, that was her gamble. I didn't have anything to lose.

I'd never been to the battlefield, though I'd driven by it plenty of times. Ellen seemed to think it would be the perfect place for me—for us—because I was a historian just like her husband. But the Civil War was not one of my interests, a fact she would have taken into account if she'd been thinking clearly. Appalachia was more my line—the history of the mining companies, oral folklore, etc. Denny was the political buff, whether she realized it or not.

The New Market Visitors Center stood out among the modest farms near the highway, as proud as a mausoleum on a backlit hill. Its slanted stone walls were so stern and confident that I parked my car a respectful distance away. I knew that the South had celebrated one of its last victories here, a win fashioned from true and mythical Rebel strengths. The Confederates had been outnumbered and outgunned. Lee was across the mountains. Stonewall Jackson was dead. But the Yankees had been turned back, the farmers left free to cultivate their wheat and corn.

I stepped through the double doors, and a young woman with badly frosted hair offered me a crisp, metallic-smelling brochure in exchange for my donation. The woman barely glanced at me; I might have been one tourist in a million, except that the building looked empty. I knew Ellen would be late—she enjoyed the drama of delay—so I decided to go ahead and see the sights. There was no way we could miss each other in all this hush.

The exhibit hall was carefully organized. I heard marching music, then cavalry hooves, then cannon fire. Miniature men rushed frantically across miniature terrains. As I studied the maps that traced Confederate strategy in bold color, it was easy to see how victory had been preserved for more than a century. Forget the fact that Sheridan had burned his way down the valley before the summer was over. The Yankees had been whipped before that, right here.

I'd seen everything but the feature film by one o'clock, and since I thought Timothy might like to see the film with me, I went back to the lobby to wait. Ellen would appreciate the fact I'd thought of her son. Then again, Ellen tended to take such things for granted. What I probably wanted to do was reassure her, let her know that I remembered her and respected her and loved her. The fact that Timothy was with her only increased my care.

The lobby was quiet and wood-trimmed and topped with a cathedral ceiling; it reminded me of church. There was a stained-glass window— a blue, gray, and red tribute to the battle that stretched along the southern wall. The glass was thickly textured, and the colors were more vivid than any I'd ever seen in churches, where the windows tell a simpler story.

New Market was a matter of pride and romance, and romance was something Virginians understood, just like their Scotch-Irish fathers. It was an excess they enjoyed. An old claw hammer banjo player I once knew had put it like this: *My dead daddy played best and his daddy played better before him, I done lost the good songs behind me.*

I was looking at the window, watching the crossbar flags absorb the clear afternoon light, when the janitor interrupted me. It occurred to me later that maybe he wasn't a janitor, maybe he was the curator or an eccentric academic. I hadn't seen anyone except the frosty-haired woman; I wondered who ran the place. This old fellow was pushing a broom across the smooth slate floor as he talked.

"Brings tears to your eyes, doesn't it?" he said, swinging his broom close enough to brush my heels. "I've been here a long time and I still cry."

"It's impressive," I said.

"Have you been outside yet? Seen Bushong's farm and the old turnpike? The house still has holes in it."

"I'm waiting for someone," I said. "Maybe we'll take a look when they get here."

"I can't recommend it enough. Nothing like it in the whole war.

Those boys marching up from Lexington. Nothing like it at Bull Run or the Wilderness either. I've seen them all. I know."

I guessed he was in his sixties, a small man with leathery hands like you'd expect to find on a farmer. The skin on his face was slack in places, especially around his jaw, but his eyes were sharp, though a little bloodshot. Once he dropped a hand into his pocket and pulled out a big white-faced watch. I couldn't shake the feeling that he was more sophisticated, or maybe just crazier, than he seemed.

"I noticed you were from Tennessee." His head wobbled on his neck. "The Volunteer State. Bloody Murphreesboro."

It bothered me that he'd noticed my car. It shouldn't have mattered, but the old man made me nervous. He swept the floor with huge, shoving strokes, then shuffled away, his eyes on the ceiling beams that were speckled with refracted light. He clenched his jaw as if he were counting something in his head, and suddenly he was gone, shut off by a paneled door marked Private. His absence brought the hush back to the lobby, and I was alone again, hungry, jittery, wondering if I should laugh or break into a sweat. I was in an elegant shrine to a little piece of war famous for changing boys into men, and I was shivering.

Ellen drove up a few minutes later. She was in her car, a boxy Ford hatchback, and my heart went as flat as a crushed can when I saw it. I remembered the last time I'd seen her, the day before I left town. I'd gone into the A&P to buy some tape, and there she was, choosing grapefruit. We'd already said our good-byes. Yet I found myself close behind her, gazing down on her pale, bare neck, thinking that she was still young and beautiful. I wanted to watch her, secretly, for as long as I could. Holding my breath, I collected a memory.

This time, I waited for her. I wasn't going to try to fool Timothy, but I wasn't going to make it worse for him either, not by rushing up to his mother with my eyes bright and my hands whirling. Ellen was wearing a chocolate brown skirt and high heels and a creamy, tailored blouse that emphasized her breasts. Her dark hair was pulled back in a French twist, and she walked as if she were very self-assured, like the lawyer or broker she sometimes wished she could be. Timothy trailed behind her with her purse in his hands. She let him handle the donations while she headed straight for me, her shoes sounding hard and fast on the slate. I smelled the gardenia in her perfume before she stopped.

We looked at each other for several seconds, both of us wondering who was going to set the first stakes.

"You can hug me, you know," Ellen said, pressing on her lower lip.

I stepped forward and kissed her on the cheek, but the hug was all wrong. I hooked her too high across the back and pulled her to my side as if her body were shapeless. Sometimes, awkwardness can be sweet. Ellen had said that on the first afternoon we found ourselves in bed, though I'd always wondered if she really believed that she over-looked such things.

"Hello, Tim," I said, waving to him over Ellen's shoulder. "How've you been?" He didn't answer, just stood there clutching his mother's purse and two brochures as if he wanted to be somewhere else. He was a thin boy with freckles and reddish-blonde hair—a small, wiry version of his father, except his eyes, which were round and hazel, like Ellen's.

"He's a little shy," Ellen said. "But he's like Denny, he'll be completely absorbed in detail before long." She put her arm through mine and guided me toward her son, her head tilted at an angle that was supposed to be coy. I hadn't expected this, not a frontal assault. I thought I'd hauled myself north for understanding, the sweet resolution of loss.

I held out my hand and Timothy shook it with a quick, formal snap. I could see that he didn't remember me though he'd met me once when I'd dropped off some papers for Denny. He turned to stare at the high wall of stained glass, deferring to his mother. Ellen had always described him as an obedient child, a child she adored until she decided it was selfish of her to depend on him.

"Well, you were here first." Ellen raised her hands in an animated shrug. "Where do we start?"

"The movie," I said, remembering my plans. "It gives the overview. Then there are the exhibits and the battlefield. I think that's the way to go."

"Sound okay?" Ellen bent to remove Timothy's jacket.

"Yes ma'am," he said.

"Fine. Professor Marlowe, you're in charge." She spoke with a hint of a giggle, but I saw the skin around her eyes go tight, and realized what her lips would look like without the bronze gloss of lipstick—thin, drawn, vaguely worried. She could say what she pleased, but I wasn't in charge. And neither was she.

The theater contained about two dozen seats. A large white button on the wall allowed us to start the film when we were ready. Ellen glaced around, then excused herself. "Y'all go ahead," she said, smiling for Timothy and vamping for me. "I'll be back when I can."

I let Timothy choose our seats, a decision that loosened him up a little, and we settled in the front row before the house lights went down. He saved a seat for Ellen between us.

The movie warmed up with fife and drum, the same tune that heralds every Civil War battle as something distinctly American, innocent and brash from the beginning. At New Market the fife announced the coming of the VMI cadets, a thirty-seven-mile march by schoolboys who saved the day. I noticed how the music was setting me up for a tragic thrill, the gut-tight rush before sorrow.

While the narrator explained the Southern troop shortage and the need to defend the turnpike, I slipped down in my seat, my legs stretched out toward the screen. Before long I was the same height as Timothy, who was also slumped, face lifted, eyes open and rapt. "Hey," I said, as a few bearded actors and prancing horses staged Imboden's advance cavalry raid, "this is pretty good."

"Yeah," he said. "I can't wait to see it again."

I understood then why Ellen was missing. She knew her son; she'd raised him. She knew he'd stare at a screen filled with advance and retreat for at least an hour. Maybe she'd told him to stay put; maybe she'd planned this. I could feel myself getting tense, so I refocused my eyes to let it pass. Above me, the screen was covered with the sepia-toned portraits of Yankee commanders, square-faced, deep-eyed, and grim.

I reached across the empty seat and touched the boy's small elbow. "I'm going to check on your mom," I whispered. "You sit tight. I'll be back for the good part." He nodded without looking at me, but I knew I'd been acknowledged because he hadn't flinched when I touched him. I drew in my legs and left on tiptoe, preparing to sidle out of certain confrontation.

She was sitting on a blue padded bench in the hallway, smoking a cigarette, which would be her excuse—that she needed to relax. But the Ellen I'd known smoked only when she drank. Cigarettes were part of an old pose, she'd told me, something she'd picked up from her roommate at Hollins. She winked when she saw me and tapped her ashes into the silver basin of a water fountain. I felt as if I'd been waved off the dance floor by the homecoming queen.

"You're missing a pretty good show," I said.

"So are you," she said, swinging her knees to one side to give me her best profile. "Besides, I'm tired."

"Maybe I should go back to Timmy then. I just thought you were lost."

She laughed, and I noticed that her lipstick was fresh and perfect. She really could be lovely, a fact brought home by the neat curve of her throat. I remembered her startled blush when I lifted that A&P grapefruit from her hand. She hadn't had a single second to think. She'd reached up to touch my breastbone, her eyes a soft liquid brown. Then she'd recovered, her pupils going blank and hard.

"Don't go anywhere," she said. "Timmy's fine."

"So what's the rest of your plan?" I asked. "Should we talk? How are you?"

I'm not much for sarcasm, so my concern—and that's what it was—surprised her. Sincerity tended to confuse Ellen because Denny considered himself a polished wit, an ironic intelligence with an acid tongue; he always undercut her. I wasn't so predictable, or so sure of myself.

"I miss you," she said, dousing her cigarette in the fountain. "It's not easy to say that. I feel silly."

"I think about you, too. There aren't any beautiful wives in Johnson City." I smiled, trying to revive our best joke, the one about ourselves.

"You're sweet," she said, "but let's just stick to today."

"Here I am."

"I know. I pretend to leave Denny every day," she said. "Now I remember why."

It was familiar ground, an indulgent tangle of wishes and denials we had both wanted a few months earlier. Ellen's voice became softer, more tentative, and she turned to face me. I saw that she was prepared to worry the idea of leaving Denny as though it were a shiny stone in her hand that had the power to conjure my resolve and bring me back to her.

"You don't have to flatter me," I said. I sat down beside her and reached around her waist. "I'd rather not be full of regrets. The film will be over soon. Is there some real trouble somewhere?"

"Don't worry about Timmy. He loves places like this. He can take care of himself."

I raised my hand to trace the edge of her chiffon collar, my fingertips tingling. "I don't want to confuse him, that's all."

"He could use some confusion. So could you." She kissed me hard then, her hands touching my knees, her weight coming behind the push of her lips and tongue. I felt the blood heat up in my chest and thighs.

"You want to know the truth," she said, breaking away to let me know she was kissing me out of anger as much as anything else. "The truth is, my car is going to break down this afternoon, and Timmy and I are staying over, and I'm going to be with you tonight. That's my so-called plan."

She looked at me, her forehead set and smooth, her mouth pressed closed as if she had given me a choice and was waiting for my answer. In or out. Yes or no. But there wasn't a choice. Part of me wanted the night at Howard Johnson's, the long, muffled night down the hall from where Timmy would be sleeping in a room littered with candy wrappers and comics, whatever would appease. Ellen would be warm and slippery, at her best, most fragile peak. And I would feel it again, the thin, dark plumb line of taking a turn that cannot be retraced. There was depth to that; it could be a night I'd never forget. But it could also be a night without end, a deed without boundary. Because Ellen would want it again and again, maybe only in miniature, maybe only on the phone, but she would consider it a promise wrapped around a core of hope, and she wouldn't let it go. Not for a very long time.

"It'll just hurt you," I said.

"Hurt me? Who said I wanted anything more than a good screw?" She stood up then, her hips tucked forward as she threw back her head and glared. "You don't want to understand, do you?"

"Ellen, honey. I said that wrong." I put a hand on her hip, taking a chance. "Let me tell the truth. It'll hurt me. I love you, but it can't work."

"Who said anything about love?" She swallowed between her words. "I'm keeping this simple."

"You know it's not simple. And Timmy's here now, I'm not going to involve him." I ran my hand down her arm, trying to soothe, trying to regain the woven feeling in my skin.

"Timmy's not your decision, you bastard. How dare you make him an excuse. I suggest one thing, and you ruin it, you ruin it for us all."

She was crying then, and so was I, my eyes burning, my throat feeling round and hollow. I wanted to hold her. I wanted to make love to her for a hundred dark and separate nights. But the truth was there beneath the light, powdery makeup that had softened on her cheeks. My Ellen was old—not so much in body as in heart. She wasn't prepared to love me or leave Denny. She'd resorted to a wheedling revenge because that was what she knew; it was Denny's own medicine in triple dose. She had stepped out of bounds with me, but she would never stay there. Because that would leave her with nothing—not her son or her simmering, necessary anger.

"I can't stretch things out," I said. "It's wrong."

She screamed at me then, cursing what she called my horny morality. Before she left, she asked my why I'd come, what I thought I'd get besides her ass. And I told her what I suppose I had known since my run through the football stadium early that morning when I made my legs carry me high into the bleachers while my guts knotted and rocked. I'd come to get what I deserved, to take the kicks and blame I'd truly earned.

I watched her stumble up the carpeted stairs, her sobs buckling against the wall behind me. I thought first of the old man with the broom, wondering what he would think of such behavior. He would probably find us profane—whispering and shouting about love in a hall of valor and death. Then I thought of Timmy, alone with his cannons and heroes. I knew Ellen would be back before long. But for now, because of the vagaries of quarrel and trust, Timmy was mine.

He had started the movie a second time, so when I walked into the flickering theater, I heard the shrill fife and witnessed the wild ride of Imboden's cavalry once more. The horses swirled like leaves on a biting wind. It occurred to me that Timmy didn't like silence. He could handle being alone, but silence—a confirmation of his mother's bitter eyes—was too much for him. I imagined him pressing the white button with his oval palm, evading the strained voices in the hall, edging away.

"Hey," I said, settling next to him. "Your mom's not feeling well. How's the movie?"

"It's good," he said.

"All right. What do you say we go outside and see it live. Rude's Hill, the orchard, the places where the artillery was set up. Until your mom feels better."

"But you missed the movie," he said, reminding me of my promise.

"That's okay," I said. "I've heard the story before."

The famous bottleneck between Smith Creek and the rise of the Blue Ridge Mountains was planted in wheat, and except for the plateau of the interstate, the battlefield was so featureless that I became disoriented. Timmy found a plastic-framed map, and together we scouted the land for points of interest. Though I expected Ellen to return at any moment, straight-lipped and firm in her claim to what was hers, I was able to relax a little. Timmy was chest-high and talkative; he seemed to like me because of what we currently had in common.

It was his idea to walk to the farm. The Bushong house was maybe a half-mile from where we stood, surrounded by wheat and perfect four-board fences. There weren't any sidewalks or trails; the Historical Commission seemed to hope no one would take the trouble. But I decided that a couple of visitors wouldn't bother anyone. And Timmy was right. The Bushong farm was where the action was, or had been.

I swung him over a creosote-stained gate. He laughed out loud, his mouth wide open in the air. Denny wasn't a large man—Ellen said his presence never felt physical—and I wondered how Timmy saw his father, if he thought of him as old and brilliant, the kind of man people listened to, a man who got his way. I knew I must seem very different to him with my scuffed jacket and flyaway hair, a young man without certainty on his face. And it suddenly became clear to me that Ellen had brought Timmy along for his own protection, not hers or mine. She'd brought her son to save him from the lies, the webs she'd have to weave back home in Charlottesville. Watching him run into the field with wheat up to his elbows and the beat of an imaginary drummer on his lips, I knew what cruelty was. Cruelty was forgetting the delicate paper heart of a child. Cruelty was dropping the shield.

"This wouldn't have been so easy with the cannons and bullets going," I said. "Even the Yankees were pretty good shots."

Timmy hoisted a pretend rifle on his shoulder. "It would've been noisy," he said, "like the movie." He imitated the whistle of an artillery shell, his freckled cheeks exploding with the shrapnel of sound.

"And scary. There's nowhere to hide."

"Would you have been scared, Mr. Marlowe?" He glanced up at me, then ran forward a step, two steps, waiting for my answer. I saw that Denny had been the fatherly model for a few things. Glory, heroism, certain historical hurrahs. "Yes," I said, "I probably would have been. I wouldn't want to die."

"I wouldn't be scared." He slowed his choppy pace to fall in line with mine.

"That's the thing about this place," I said, laughing a little. "The Yankees attack. And the South wins because of the perfect courage of boys."

I looked past the clean white farmhouse toward the orchard where teen-agers had plugged a busted line and kept the bluecoats from spilling through. "We don't fight like this anymore. Nowadays, we fight almost blind. In jungles."

"I could go to VMI," Timmy said. "My father almost did."

"Would you like to?"

"When I'm older," he said. "I'm only ten."

"And I'm almost thirty." I leaned against the barnyard fence. "An old man."

"My mom got mad at you, didn't she?"

I looked into his round, gold-flecked eyes, discovering what every parent must know a thousand times over, that sons and daughters are aware of more than their tongues can say.

"Yep," I said.

"But you like my mom, don't you?" His words folded into a shy stutter. "You don't hate her now?"

"I don't hate her. To tell you the truth," and he seemed to deserve this much, his face so frail with expectation, "I probably like your mom too much. That makes it even harder."

He tried to seem serious for a moment, but he was soon pulling himself onto the orchard fence, aiming his fingers toward Yankee territory. "I love her," he said. "More than anything."

Watching him fire distracted blanks, I knew that Ellen and I had wrought something dangerous and alive. She was wholly prepared to draw her son into our maelstrom, to teach him the truth of the whirling, sucking love that could not hold. But what he already knew was sufficient for any boy.

"Timmy," I said, "let me tell you about the fight for this orchard."

"What?" he said, swinging a narrow leg across the fence. "I learned lots from the movie. Like how they were only a few years older than me. Like how they won the whole thing."

"It happened out there," I said, pointing vaguely beyond the bare apple trees. "When the boys, the cadets, were heading toward the ridge, they ran into a swamp of mud because it had been raining hard, like in the movie."

He tilted his head—curious and impatient, just like his mother.

"They hit the mud and stuck. Some of them died there. Some of them made it through barefoot, they lost their shoes and boots and everything. But they didn't stop. They kept running and firing and swimming through mud until they silenced the cannon." I looked across the fence into his well-combed reddish hair. He was fidgeting a little. I dropped my hands to my sides. "It's amazing when you think about it."

"I could do that," he said. "Even if I wasn't really a cadet."

"I know you could," I said. "You'd have to be very brave, but you could do it."

He smiled then, a big toothy smile, and took off through the twisted orchard without waiting for me, rushing forward with sounds and ghosts of his own. And I wished I could explain everything to him— his mother, my broken feelings, myself—before he ran. I wished hard for the impossible: that I could tell him about the inevitable douse of failure and the struggle to capture even one inch of our lives. But I didn't. Given the burdens of my age and the buoyancy of his, I could only follow his launch into the fife melody of a lie, watch him run with its simple purity across that field, gold and green and now untrodden, barely led by the twin barrels of our long, misshapen shadows.

Cathryn Hankla

DOMESTIC UNDERSTORY

Hunched on the flaking linoleum, Boything poised somewhere near the kitchen's dead center. The rustling of a mouse reached him; forced air from the heat ducts ruffed his whispy hair, and still he went on eating. Scattered around him like a collection of pinned butterflies were the colorful, empty tin cans of his night's forage. If he felt guilt, it was so tempered by stealth as he quietly punctured a can of condensed tomato soup and listened to its hush of air that he only felt hunger, was only aware of relief when the lid of the red can ticked fully open. The teaspoon felt wrong. He placed it on the floor and selected the soup spoon with the care of Arnold Palmer's lifelong caddy. As he slurped tomato globs, he remembered to tilt his large spoon toward his lips, remembered not to place the spoon entirely into his mouth.

After the Green Giant corn and the fancy asparagus, the Progresso split pea, the small tin of deviled meat, the tomato soup tasted faintly of dessert, though he'd lined up a can of Hershey's syrup and a jar of maraschino cherries.

As he lifted a last spoonful of tomato to his mouth, he started. He thought he heard his mother stir in her sleep. With the spoon just touching his lips, he froze in his furtive pleasure. Yet with the tip of his tongue he could not resist another taste of soup while he waited for another sound, or for silence followed by snores. If his mother were waking, he could only grin and greet her where he sat—too many empty cans to dispose of the evidence before she made the trek down the short hall. He heard the toilet flush, and at that instant the refrigerator kicked into its cycle, a loud purring. Without finishing the soup or thinking again of the chocolate syrup, he scrambled to gather up the tins for the trashcan and to replace the untouched dessert items on the shelf where he'd found them behind the spaghetti.

"Have you heard? Of course you haven't, you're still fanning around in your robe and houseshoes. She's doing it again, this very minute. I thought I'd never get out of there. Since nine this morning—and I was standing at the magic doors when they opened. When they opened! I walked inside and not a soul ahead of me. I got the first buggie and went to town. Straight into produce and up and down, and not a single other customer until I hit the meat counter. I didn't like the looks of the chops—too thin—so I rang. What a mistake. Mr. Hatcher—can you imagine, but that's his name, I remember his brother from grade school—came out of the back, finally, after I rang again, and opened the little door. 'What you want?' he asked cheerfully. His voice just doesn't go with the way he lumbers around. I tell him I want some chops and of course he motions to the bunch of chops in the case. I pretend he had nothing to do with them and ask for some nice thick chops like I know he knows how to cut. He beams at me and disappears. He comes back with the nicest looking chops. Here, look at them, believe me these are the pork chops, when we tear this paper off. Just look. Look at this!

"When he handed me the chops I realized there was a customer behind me waiting for service. I smiled at her, such a small old lady, like she'd shrunk. Well, I guess we all will someday. Here's your newspaper, and your mail, Dear. She was wearing a kerchief and a wool coat and looked chilled to the bone. As I wheeled my buggie toward the dairy case, I heard her say to Mr. Hatcher, in a voice not much above a whisper, 'Cut me a T-bone fast.' What do you think a little old lady is going to do with a T-bone steak? Everything else in her buggie was canned goods, believe me, that and some pink hair bobs on a card like prissy little girls wear. Those took me back for a minute. Who were they for? She probably keeps one of those French dogs with a rhinestone collar for all I know.

"To make it as brief as possible I found the rest of what I needed and by the time I got to the checkout it was backed up—no, thank you,

I've had all the coffee I can stand—only one register open of course because it was so early in the morning, only 9:30 at the latest. Backed up! I promise you I hadn't seen anyone in the store but that old lady, but I guess I'd been thinking of other things. I don't know what, but you better believe me the line was here to kingdom come, and she was doing it again, and for a while everyone was patient. Then they began to whisper up and down the line. Mrs. Pollit said she was going to leave and go to Winn Dixie. 'I'm going to *replace* the spinach and the winter squash,' she said; but of course she never did. She stood there like the rest of us, and eventually we were all shaking our heads and hushing each other if one of us raised a voice against Mrs. Westmorland. Mrs. Crocket started telling me all about Buddy's triplets like she always does. And not a word about his divorce. I swear I've heard that story about little Amanda's front teeth getting knocked out by a softball Stephen didn't mean to throw so many times I could scream, just scream. But it passed the time. Of course I didn't ask her about the divorce. Those triplets are the ugliest children I've ever seen. Mrs. Crocket had a studio portrait in her handbag—that bag's the size of a suitcase. She hunches over it's so heavy. Please tell me if I'm slumping, will you, it's so ugly looking to see ladies slump. Amanda, that's the only girl, looks better without her teeth, you'll have to take my word for it. I told Mrs. Crocket so.

"Just look in this bag! Here, help me unpack this stuff. You can't guess a single item until you rip off the Christmas wrap. Look at this one—so pretty we could put it under the tree and I believe it's only a three-bar special of Lifebuoy soap! Mrs. Westmorland even took pains to curl the ribbon. Imagine. Don't tear the paper like that! I don't care if the darn milk spoils! I think I feel like crying. That was the loveliest package I think I've ever seen in my whole life and you ripped the ribbon off and tore against the grain of the silver paper. The white underneath the silver looks like a fish belly. How could you wound the pretty paper in that thoughtless way? Let me put everything up. I'm sorry for yelling, I just don't know sometimes. It all seems so ridiculous and then I feel like crying and I can't go on pretending. Pretending what? Well, acting like it's more important that the milk doesn't spoil. I know you like milk in your coffee. Let me, Dear. The lives all around us are impossible to imagine and there are things about me you will never understand. Don't look at me like that, like you don't know what I'm thinking or who I am. It gives me the creeps. I think I'll just put everything into the refrigerator as it is. We'll unwrap it later, if that's all right with you? I have no idea why Mrs. Westmorland does it. Somebody in the checkout line whispered that she was out of her mind again, that she lost her son in Korea and she'd never been the same—I need to lie down, you really should take your shower and dress. For God's sake quit looking at me—is she a nut? What do you think?"

At an early age, Boything had rocked on the floor as if in a chair, singing to himself a steady song. And whenever he had been upset or hungry, he had rapped his head carefully against the wooden floor, knock, after knock, after knock. If his mother watched and he felt her eyes on him, he rapped his head with more force. Once, while his mother stood in the doorway and begged him to eat just one bite of cheese soufflé, he made his forehead bleed by pounding his head hard on the splintering floor. The blood trickled, then streamed. He tasted some of what lived inside of himself. His blood tasted different from food, different from anything, but he thought he might like more. Then his mother's arm jerked him to his feet and her voice said, "Lawd, lawd, Boything, what you done to yourself." And a little later her fingers smoothed a Band-Aid over what turned out to be only a scratch. From the corner of his mouth, his mother dabbed the rusty color clean. He cried, and his mother said, "Be still, just be still."

He turned to the mirror when she'd finished with him, and he no longer recognized himself. It looked to him as if an eye had sprouted in the middle of his forehead, too far down for his hair to conceal it. He took a lipstick from his mother's shelf and drew an eye while looking in the mirror and being careful to stay within the boundary of the Band-Aid. Some thick red eyelashes strayed above and below the bandage. Before replacing the blunted lipstick, he blinked at himself and tenderly smiled.

Dear Buddy,

It's such a beauty of a day I just had to write You and The Triplets! Do you remember how you used to go down to the creek and muck around when it was too cold to do much else, well it's that kind of a day. I just got back from doing my shopping for this weekend when you bring up the children and I sincerely hope I do not have to go back there because it took me all morning! Mrs. Westmorland is being strange again and no one has the heart to stop her. Well, it is her store afterall, and she has owned it all by herself for twenty years, bless her heart, and nobody should interfere if she wants to giftwrap a head of green cabbage, I suppose. Maybe the children will enjoy unwrapping the groceries, so I just put them away as best I could. If something felt chilly I put it in the refrigerator and if it was beginning to sweat I put it in the freezer. When you were a little boy Mrs. Westmorland said you were the handsomest young man she'd ever seen, I'll never forget that. Somebody said it was on account of her son being M.I.A. in Korea, but I swear this has been happening on and off as long as I can remember and it was happening before that boy, who was in my class at school by the way, went to War, but I just kept my mouth shut, you know me.

Mrs. Rimmer was standing in line back of me—do you remember her? She said Amanda had a sweet smile even without her teeth. I feel so sorry for her, without any children, and with her husband at home on disability. I think maybe she goes shopping just to ease her mind. I don't know what I'd do without my grandchildren. Just remember that everything will somehow work out. There's a plan for everybody's life and I know there's a plan for yours, Buddy. I can't wait to see you!

Love,
Your Mother

Mrs. Westmorland hovered over the array of items spilled by the conveyor onto the sloping metal lip of the checkout lane, thinking of nothing but the geometry of planes of colorful paper folded into three dimensions. A can of creamed corn, two cans of lentil soup, four cans of carrots, three tins of deviled ham, a tin of sardines, two cans of peas, three of candied yams, one of New Orleans-style red beans, a card studded with hair bows, and a thick-cut T-bone steak. Mrs. Westmorland, who had had years of practice surmising the stories behind groceries, selected the red and white candy-striped paper in which to wrap the steak. She measured, cut, fitted the paper, and taped it neatly in place. Taking up both red and white curling ribbon, she encircled the package and tied the twined ribbons taut, but not too tight to hurt the meat. When the two-color bow was attached like a medal of honor and the loose ends curled with the scissor blade, she lowered the package into a brown paper bag.

For the canned goods she selected dark green and silver striped paper and left off the ribbon, hoping the pretty red and white wrap might tempt the little old woman's odd son to try cooked food.

The next customer's groceries rolled toward her, a winter squash wobbling down to her hands. Mrs. Westmorland could only glance at Mrs. Pollit's expression for an instant, as the grim, tight smile went through her like a sad, dull knife. But she knew how much little kindnesses could mean, so she selected the brightest papers, the most exquisite ribbons. Mrs. Westmorland spared no expense of wrap or ribbon and gave herself over entirely to her task while her customers waited their turns, chatting merrily, in the ever-lengthening line.

William Harrison

THE MAGICIAN OF SOWETO

First I swiped this peach and ate it, then I took a package of almonds and ate those while I shopped for my main course.

This was a supermarket on Wanderers Street—great name—right in the middle of Johannesburg, and the clerks were busy, my movements were unhurried, I was taking my time.

Then this little guy starts following me around the aisles. He pretended to read the labels on things, but there he was, always behind me. What did I care? He was just another piece of dark background: a scrawny black guy who would get in trouble himself if he told anybody what I was doing.

There was this barbecued chicken on a rotisserie, just like in some big supermarket back home, so I took that, then picked up some cheese, a carrot, milk, and candy bars. Everything went into my backpack, and this little guy was watching talent, trying to see what the hands were doing, but I was too quick.

After I finished, though, he was waiting for me outside. He had lots to say, but I was moving on down the sidewalk.

It was a cool, breezy morning with a slight odor of cyanide in the air: the residue of those big mounds around town. In the old days they used cyanide to leach the gold away from other minerals out at the mines, so now the wind blew it in the air, everyone getting his nose and eyes burned, everybody here sort of waiting around in the poison for things to get worse.

This little guy fell into step with me, saying, "Work for me, see, and we make ourselves rich?" I paid him no attention, but he kept on. "You're American, aren't you? You look American and my name is Moses Kawanda? I operate this stall in Soweto? But I plan to open a shop here in the city?"

He talked in questions. As we made our way toward the railway station, the stores got cheaper. After Woolworth's came the used clothing outlets.

"The new law?" he went on. "It says a black man can open his own business in town? So the shop owners don't have to be white or Indian now? And why should the rest of us work out of open stalls in the townships?"

I ate a barbecued drumstick, pulling it out of nowhere just to impress him. We sat on this patch of grass near the station, the little guy kneeling beside me while I ate.

"I know you've been sleeping outdoors because of how your jeans look? But the nights are getting cold, I know that, too? So I have this room in back of my shop? I signed a lease? And there's a bed, nothing fancy, so you can stay there while we get items to sell?"

His voice rose with every sentence and he had this crushed-down face, as if somebody had stepped on him and mashed his brow, nose, eyes, and mouth all together. He also wore a mismatched suit: brown pinstripes, but not the same coat and pants.

"African artifacts, that's all I need? The easiest things in the city to shoplift, you see? Beads and bracelets? A little ivory? Or if you find something really valuable, we can sell it? But for your room rent and salary—a very small salary—you can just bring me cheap rings, ebony trinkets, all those things they put in open bins, see? It is such an easy matter for you, correct?"

"You're a crook," I told him.

"Who can do things honest here?" he asked, turning his palms toward the sky as he would do when he talked politics. "This land came from cheating and killing, didn't it? And is governed by lies? No, think about it, who can play fair?"

Traffic honked around us. As the midday clouds built up, the air became chilly with the scent of rain: the month of June and the coming of winter in South Africa.

"Well, okay, show me the room," I said.

I followed him back toward Wanderers Street. I didn't even need the room or money all that much, but it was something to do.

For two weeks I worked the suburban shops in Sandton, Hillbrow, and Melville, then I worked the western part of the city, then shaved my stubble, bought a change of clothes, and doubled back to some of the easiest places. Moses Kawanda's shop picked up quite a bit of merchandise and in the evenings he arranged for me to have girls from Charmaine's Escorts. I had the room, food and drink, ladies, and worked only a couple of hours a day doing what I enjoyed: strolling around, sitting in outdoor cafés, going into shops and letting my fingers trail across the goods. I was having a good time.

"These, look, what did you do?" he asked one day.

"When there are big crowds at the Carlton Centre, I can pick up anything," I told him. "These are gold. That, I think, may be a real ruby."

"Don't you know we will have to sell these tonight?"

"What I'm thinking, Moses, is that we should have one case of nice stuff."

"Dangerous and crazy? Is that what you want?"

"Half of the shops don't even know they have pieces missing."

"Tommy, we should stick to cheap items, please, like I told you?"

"No pain, no gain," I said. "See, we could put our class merchandise in this case right here."

I had my pride. A talent can only swipe so many elephant-hair bracelets and plastic Zulu masks.

We were arguing all this when Mr. Rashi, the Indian rug dealer in the shop next door, stepped into our place. He wore his silk Nehru suit and folded his hands across his belly as if he might soon break into prayer. We got a little nod hello, then he sniffed around through the goods. Moses wanted to stay cool, but failed. Mr. Rashi was big time: a blue sapphire on his finger and a blue Mercedes to match.

"I was going to expand," he said to the walls and ceiling. "I meant to lease this place myself."

He had a way of addressing blue space.

"This is Tommy, my partner?" Moses managed, and he bowed and smiled as if he expected a blow from Mr. Rashi in return.

Mr. Rashi just tilted his head back and talked. He was used to being listened to, so Moses paid attention while I sorted through the day's take, spreading everything out on a piece of old velvet. Mr. Rashi discussed his daughters, the falling value of the rand, and how the Transvaal winters seemed so long. When he spotted a ring he liked, his eyebrows went up.

"See, gold, you see?" Moses prompted him.

"Nice design," Mr. Rashi admitted.

"Take it, will you? A present? From your new neighbor?"

The ring was two serpents entwined, their mouths and fangs locked. Mr. Rashi liked it a lot, though it looked puny next to that big sapphire of his.

"I could give a rug in exchange," he said to the ceiling. "Something small. To wipe the feet on."

"Hell of a deal," I said with a smirk, but Mr. Rashi just held the ring up, admired it, and paid me no attention.

Worried that Moses might give away the ruby as well, I wrapped up the rest of the stuff and tucked it away.

Mr. Rashi, gazing over our heads, described the rug he had in mind. Moses countered by bragging that we would have ivory, fine jade, gold, semi-precious stones, and the usual Africana. They talked about security: alarm systems and guard dogs. As I watched Moses move up in class, I calculated that I'd eventually have to knock off the Kimberley mines to compete with this snob next door.

Before Mr. Rashi left, he and Moses talked about Soweto, where they both lived. I tried to figure Mr. Rashi and his Mercedes out in the ghetto, and after he was gone I asked Moses about it.

"You know Lenasis?" Moses asked. "Where all the Indian merchants live?"

"No, can't say that I do."

"Big houses with swimming pools and black servants? You don't know Lenasis?"

"That's part of Soweto?"

"You come to my house?" he said, turning his palms up. "We can eat soup?"

"Sure, okay," I agreed.

Both of us looked around the shop as we talked. Through the doorway with its thin curtain of beads we could see my unmade bed in the back. Everything needed fixing up.

Moses disapproved of all the girls from Charmaine's and hated paying the bill, but got local prices.

"Don't get emotional," I told him. "Those girls are like fast food. And what else am I going to do?"

"Do you think I'm proud? Having a partner with low habits?"

"Look, so what? You cheat in business and I buy my romance."

Only a couple of things got me high, never girls, I told him: one was good surf and the other, lucky for him, was shoplifting. It was a buzz swiping things, it was like the top of a good wave. He could understand sport, but he got upset when I told him about Cape Town, how I went there for the surf and hung around Sea Point making out with the high school girls.

He asked didn't I realize he was a Methodist?

I did get soup, as promised, that first time in Soweto. Mrs. Kawanda, who was twice his size with that same mashed-down face, spooned it out for me and maybe ten kids. I never got it straight how many of those kids were theirs.

They lived in this two-bedroom frame house, and if you stood on some of the junk in their backyard you could see these same houses all the way to the horizon in every direction. Soweto—which I thought was some shantytown ghetto—turns out to be fifteen miles long and six miles wide and filled with these little government bungalows. There are also neighborhoods of three-bedroom brick houses with wide lawns. And Lenasia: the biggest houses of all and a mosque with a gold dome. And, of course, White City: a pretty punked-out neighborhood. And floating over everything was this coal dust and soot pouring out of the Orlando Power Plant, lots of smoke in the air including more cyanide, and hundreds of busses hauling everybody to jobs in the city and back again.

At supper we talked about the rent boycott.

"Half the people here don't pay rent?" Moses carried on. "Good idea, right? Who wants to pay the government for this? But I say, let somebody else get evicted at first, let me see if the boycott works, then I'll stop paying, too?"

The big kid at the table, a sixteen-year-old with some hair on his chin, wanted to burn down the schools.

"There's no leader for them to arrest, is there?" Moses went on. "They've got all our leaders in detention, don't they? So nobody pays rent and nobody thought of the idea? It just happened, didn't it?"

Everybody ate bean soup while Moses, palms up, talked politics. Then, afterward, I did magic tricks for the kids, except for the sixteen-year-old, who went outside and stood in the cyanide. I pulled cards out of the girls' ears and made coins disappear until Moses got concerned about how his daughters sat too close to me on the couch. He suggested that we go to Klipstown to see his stall at the market.

Under some drooping eucalyptus trees at this big flea market, Moses had five wobbly tables piled with clothing, hardware, plastic kitchen utensils, and secondhand plumbing fixtures: corroded faucets and coils of dirty copper tubing. A rooster pecked around on top of all this.

"A dump," I told him.

"My daughters are damned young?" he said in defense. "You kept touching their ears with that trick, didn't you?"

"Up yours, you crook," I said, not giving him the edge.

As we bickered, the Klipstown market depressed us even more, so we went to a makeshift bar constructed out of old oil drums and corrugated tin where we drank glasses of warm lager that almost gagged me.

"Do you know I'll make more off those old plumbing fixtures than I'll ever make on Wanderers Street?" Moses asked, gripping his beer in both hands.

"So why open a shop in the city?"

"Years ago all those fixtures were stolen? Families moved into a new housing development here and their toilets weren't attached to any pipes? And eventually I'd had it and everybody in Soweto knew it, so they bought from me? But a shop in Wanderers Street, Tommy, ho me, think about it, why do I want that? When the law finally changed, who was the first kaffir to lease himself a shop? Moses Kawanda!"

Soon I ought to move on, I was thinking. Maybe I would go see a lion in Kruger Park before going home. I'm halfway around the world, I decided, working as a necessary evil for a little black crook's upward mobility.

In the big shopping mall out in Sandton suburb I waited until all the jewelry stores were filled with Saturday shoppers, then I asked to see the trays of rings. While the clerk bent over the trays with me, I picked up four, five, six rings at a time, looked at them, then said no, thanks anyway, these aren't for me. They never figured it out. Once I got this nice silver bracelet because the salesgirl worried about another bracelet with diamonds. Another time this guy just walked away, leaving me under the rotating eye of this camera on the wall. Just me against the camera, I liked that a lot.

Mr. Rashi now came into Moses's shop every day to see what we had. He folded his hands on his belly, cocked his head, and looked at the ceiling as if to say, great holy krishna, I know exactly where you're swiping this stuff.

I gave him my blank stare, showing him nothing.

The shop looked good by this time and Mr. Rashi told Moses he'd help with the opening, which made the little crook giddy with pride. Mr. Rashi also suggested that Moses might want to sit in on a weekly poker game out in Lenasis.

"Card playing? At your House? But, see, I don't play cards, do I?" Moses said, his voice getting squeaky with excitement.

"I play some," I offered, butting in.

"Then you should both come," Mr. Rashi told us. "You can be our American cardshark. Cash only. Table stakes. Do you know table stakes, Tommy, my friend?"

"You can explain it," I said.

Mr. Rashi looked at the silver bracelet, shaking his head slowly from side to side as if he recognized an old friend.

To pay back the Kawandas for the meal at their house, I took them to the Carlton Hotel—not the coffee shop, not the lousy café with the Spanish motif, but the main dining room with the heavy silver and all the candlelight. We were thirteen at the table and we were noisy. The big sixteen-year-old looked around like this had to be a trap. Moses and his wife got small and quiet. I did a fork trick for the girls.

We had soup, two starters each, the lobster, a cheese course, two desserts, and three kinds of Cape wines. By the time I ordered cognac for Moses and me, he was getting worried.

"How will you pay for all this?" he wanted to know.

"Oh, we don't pay," I said. "We walk out of here one by one. Women and children first."

"Tommy, how can we do that?"

"Then loan me some money."

"Tommy, don't fool me," he said, sinking lower in his chair.

"Look, Moses, what are we? We're gangsters, right? Gangsters don't pay."

Across the room these two businessmen and their dates got up to leave. One of the girls was from Charmaine's, a Maylasian named Kiwi, and she gave me a tiny wave of the hand as they went out.

Moses talked with his wife about how we might have to escape. I was about to tell him I was just joking when the waiter appeared and gave the kids a sneer of a look.

"To whom do I give the check?" he asked in his crappy British accent. Because of the way he said it, I went on with the joke.

"We can't pay, but we're willing to leave one of the kids," I told him.

He took a deep breath and tugged at the lapels of his dinner jacket. "We obviously have a liberal policy here," he said, viewing the Kawandas with a smirk. "But we must all pay, mustn't we?"

I popped my American Express card at his nose.

"Write yourself a one-percent tip," I said. "And hurry up with our cognacs."

Moses wanted to leave right away, but we sat there as the kids got squirmy. As he finished his cognac, he asked to see the American Express card and he studied it and rubbed its letters and numbers. Mrs. Kawanda said, no, she didn't want to touch it.

"My dad allows me three hundred a month on it," I admitted. "You guys just ate up my July allowance."

My confession was translated around the table, each kid looking at me as it became clear how rich I was.

It was so late when we went outside that the busses had stopped running. We found two black taxi drivers, but had to argue with them about fares to Soweto and about overloading their vehicles. Moses made a deal with one of them, something about used pipe from his stall, I didn't hear all of it. The taxis cost him plenty, but he shook my hand and told me that he never thought he'd eat lobster or have a friend with an American Express card. The big kid gave me a good-bye nod, raising his hairy chin maybe an inch.

Mr. Rashi's house had lots of marble and was padded with rugs, pillows, and fat women. His daughters, aunts, cousins, and a grand-mother carried trays of food from one room to another.

The victim that night was supposed to be this Afrikaaner salesman with a roll of hundred-rand notes. The game room had old movie posters on the walls—Bogart and everybody—and the poker table had a green hooded light over it. Mr. Rashi took off his Nehru coat and underneath was more silk, silk all the way to the bone, I supposed, and I knew I had to win early in order to stay around.

Moses gawked at everything, being too polite, and ate chocolates off some fat woman's tray.

When the Afrikaaner pumped my hand I told him that I loved his beautiful country and that I was here scouting business investments. There was Mr. Rashi, the Afrikaaner, me, and these four Indian geeks who smelled like talcum powder. One of the fat daughters ate this fruit and gave me a slow wink. Moses sat on a high stool so he could see the table, and he was getting wasted on chocolates and the fear that I would lose our operating capital, but I was happy when I saw the deck Mr. Rashi put into play: those standard blue Bicycle playing cards.

I won six of the first nine hands, staying alive in little pots. Mr. Rashi observed—not without sarcasm—that I paid very close attention.

"Because I'm a beginner," I told him, and actually I was counting aces when he interrupted me.

"You're a strong boy," the Afrikaaner said, slapping down his cards as I won again. One of the geeks took up whiskey drinking.

We played for an hour, nobody talking much, and I sat out three big hands that Mr. Rashi won. Playing with their money, I tried to look interested and hide. I dropped out of another hand when the geeks and Mr. Rashi started all their signals. They took the salesman pretty good, everything rehearsed, and my host wouldn't look at me as they did it.

After another hour, I decided to have a little run. I pulled stray cards into my hand at every opportunity. One of the geeks went head to head with the Afrikaaner, neither of them paying me much attention, and I turned four deuces for the biggest pot so far.

Then we took a break. The fat women pushed sandwiches while everybody tried to smile and act social. Moses was sweating too hard to make much conversation, but Mr. Rashi, speaking to me and yet to the whole room, asked, "Tommy, do you agree with the philosopher who said that in an immoral society, only the criminal is moral?"

"That's a good one, Mr. Rashi. I don't know."

"One could offer that this also defines the terrorist or the revolutionary in any evil regime," he went on, gazing at a slow ceiling fan above us. "Or it could perfectly describe a simple thief. Thieves have their own small way of correcting inequities in corrupt social systems, wouldn't you say?"

"You're over my head," I told him.

The Afrikaaner added his genius to the topic by declaring that thieves were no good in any situation.

Mr. Rashi chewed a chicken sandwich and peered into the darkness above that hooded light. "Evil against evil can become a good," he went on. "And I suppose the lines between the two are thinly drawn."

"These are certainly bad times," the Afrikaaner stated, turning his gaze on me. "But I say they'll pass away."

"Quite so," Mr. Rashi answered. "But where, Tommy, did you learn to play cards?"

"On the beach in California," I lied. "We used to play slapjack on top of our surfboards."

The fat daughter who had winked at me led me toward the toilet down this long hallway. There was a lighted statue of two naked lovers with snakes in this alcove, but I didn't want to stop there with her.

Now that I knew where everyone sat at the table, I fixed two decks— allowing that one geek might soon quit the party. This ought to be enough evil against evil, I decided. I flushed the john and tried to clear my head. I did have this one twinge of doubt, wondering if I'd spill cards everywhere since I hadn't practiced this, but by the time I got back to the table I felt like pure talent.

Moses asked if we shouldn't quit, but I explained, no, hold on, so he went back to his perch.

The Afrikaaner won a nice hand that put him in a good mood. He started giving me glances like, okay, we're the white guys here and we should stick together.

Then it was my deal. I took a sandwich off a passing tray, got a beer and some napkins, and stacked all this and my chips in front of me: lots of props. I shuffled and shuffled, then switched decks and dealt real slow, giving everybody a good hand with special service to Mr. Rashi, one of the geeks, and the salesman.

Somebody kicked my leg.

"I'll just play these," Mr. Rashi announced.

"So will I," said his geek friend who only had a flush.

As I planned it, everyone else dropped out and I took one card, the same as the Afrikaaner. When everybody raised, I got another little kick. Mr. Rashi wanted to bet his shop, sapphire, Mercedes, and marble house. I could hear Moses sweating over all our money.

"Get out, kid," the Afrikaaner salesman said, giving me another friendly kick. "You can't beat me." He thought we were in this conspiracy together, but I hurt his feelings by raising with all the money I had. When the cards were down, he was second best: four nines against my four queens.

It got pretty uneasy after this.

"Tommy, I believe you are a magician," Mr. Rashi told me.

"You haven't seen his tricks?" Moses put in, helpfully. "He entertains my children? You didn't know?"

Mr. Rashi paid this information little attention because the Afrikaaner was leaving. The other losers began putting on their jackets, and the host accompanied them to the door. I drank my beer, moved my chips and cash around, and managed to get rid of that extra deck of cards.

"You play too good," one of the geeks complained, looking over his shoulder in my direction.

"Up yours," I said. "You give out signals."

Mr. Rashi came back to the table during this exchange.

"Moses," he offered, "allow me to give you and your partner a ride home."

The Mercedes crossed Soweto Highway and turned toward White City. The driver was this Untouchable who wore a chauffeur's uniform that looked like it was padded with muscles and weapons.

Mr. Rashi spoke in a reasonable tone. He wanted ten thousand rand—his estimate of our night's take—and he wanted me to never show my face on Wanderers Street again. He also wanted Moses to sign over the lease to his shop and move out.

"No way," I said, braving it out.

"Please," he said with a long sigh. "I'm taking you into White City, don't you see that? Do I have to threaten you?"

Moses and I agreed to pay up. With a certain amount of protest, I fumbled in my pockets for the cash.

"You and your buddies signaled back and forth all night," I told him. "You took mine and I took yours. You should let us keep our stake."

"You thieves cheated me in my own house," he argued. "You gave me a stolen ring. You took money from my Afrikaaner."

Moses was pleading with the driver. "See, this is the wrong place? Don't you want to be back on the highway?"

The driver gave him a grunt in reply.

"Make a fuss about paying and we'll put you out here," Mr. Rashi said calmly. "Try explaining what you're doing in White City after midnight: a white boy and a little black man from the wrong tribe!"

"Here, that's everything," I said, dumping a handful of crumpled bank notes in his lap.

"He's paying you, isn't he?" Moses pointed out. "So don't we want to turn around?"

Mr. Rashi counted the cash as the Mercedes turned a corner and slowed for a roadblock. Two dozen black figures danced behind a barricade while a bonfire spewed ash and gobs of flaming paper into the dark sky.

The Untouchable grunted again, hit the brakes, and attempted to shove the car into reverse, but too late. A kid beat on the window beside Mr. Rashi's face with what looked like a piece of Moses's secondhand pipe. Then the door on the driver's side flew open and the

Untouchable was among the enemy. As he reached inside his uniform, he was dropped: struck from behind with a cricket bat.

Then Moses was outside the car, too, his palms upturned, talking politics with the rabble. A missile flew by his head, but he kept jabbering. Mr. Rashi attempted to lock his door, but two kids pulled him out. As his shiny silk suit caught the reflection of the bonfire, I thought, get ready, it's evil against evil for sure, think fast, it's the revolution.

"Who doesn't hate the landlords?" Moses said, addressing the crowd in his usual interrogative. "Do you think I'd pay rent? I haven't paid for weeks, have I?"

The kids around the bonfire looked maybe fourteen years old.

I came out of the car with my hands high. At the top of my reach, at the very tips of my fingers, I produced an ace of diamonds and sailed it off into the darkness. Eyes widened. But to make sure they caught my act, I did it again and again: my queens, my deuces, another ace. Mr. Rashi's tormentors stopped to watch.

Next, a cigarette lighter with flame aglow—swiped from Charmaine's. I pitched it toward the kid with the cricket bat and he caught it. The whole crowd had gathered around me now, so I tossed out the money—picked up in the car after Mr. Rashi had been dragged away. I heaved a handful in the air, putting it up there with the floating cinders and glowing ash. With the last handful, I yelled at Moses, "Let's get out of here!"

As we started running, a security force arrived. They came out of the darkness, jumping out of lorries without headlights: big, uniformed men with nightsticks and long quirts. But rand notes filled the air along with burning debris, so nobody knew exactly what to do. This fat soldier arrested me, then ordered me to help find the money. When I found some, he stuffed it in his pockets.

Mr. Rashi kept telling the security men that he lived in Lenasis. "What riot?" Moses asked his soldier. "You think this is a riot? Don't you know a riot?"

At the station, I was placed in this lounge with purple walls, a television set, and a coffee maker. The police sergeant explained that

I was the first American ever "involved in an incident of unrest." They phoned my embassy, so someone could take me away.

I wandered the hallway, drinking coffee and looking for something to swipe, some little souvenir, but there were only police manuals.

They had arrested nine kids, Mr. Rashi, and Moses, but nobody knew anything about the big driver. Breakfast was this hard biscuit and more coffee, then I saw the sixteen-year-old, Moses's kid, and when I asked him about his father he didn't seem to speak English.

Toward noon this embassy representative in coat and tie arrived. He asked me if I wanted to leave the country.

"What do you mean?"

"In these circumstances," he said, "it might be less delicate for you to leave. We can advance you plane fare."

"Sure, I'll take the ticket. But can I see Moses Kawanda first?"

He wrote the name in a small leather notebook.

Then there was a long conversation in the hallway with the security officials until, eventually, Moses appeared. Somebody had hit him in the stomach and he was feeling sick, but they had allowed him out of his cell to sit with me on this bench.

"Yeah, I'm flying home," I told him.

"But what about our shop?"

"You've got plenty of stuff. You don't need me anymore."

"And what about Mr. Rashi? Won't he report all the stolen jewelry?"

"Nah, he won't bother you."

"How do you know this?"

"Because he's crooked like everybody else."

"I don't feel too good?"

"You'll get better." I patted his knee, but he looked bad.

"And we lost our money? And I'm in jail? And my son is here, so I'm embarrassed because he'll never believe me?"

"I'm sorry, Moses, I really am, but you'll be out soon."

"And look at you: you're a thief and you go free?" he said. "You go free and here I am?"

"Moses," I said, "it's the way of the world." I gave his bony knee a last slap, then got to my feet. "And I'm doing my disappearing act," I said, and I did.

Madison Jones

RAGE

The rumor circulating among the white people of Okaloosa that the Strangler was known to be a Negro found its way to black ears too. When Herman Coker, Sim Denny's son-in-law, heard it, he said, among other things, "Yeah. *Knowed* to be. Got to be a nigger. It's me, maybe. I hate them white som'bitches bad enough to done it."

Herman's response was predictable—and understandable too, up to a point. He had grown up in a black slum in Birmingham, in a two-room tenement apartment that, as he said later, a farmer wouldn't keep his hogs in. There were six children and the mother but no father that Herman could remember. Until she died when Herman was seventeen, his mother worked as cook and maid for a white woman, a job that made her have to travel twenty miles by bus back and forth every day except Sunday. Herman saw the white woman two or three times and later, after he learned to hate, remembered her with hatred both for his mother's toil and for the ugliness of that wrinkled old white face.

The mother, who was both pious and ambitious for her children, managed to make them all go to school for a while, and Herman, the brightest one, longer than any of them. By the time he got to high school, the first whispers of racial troubles to come were already in the air. By the time he got out, quit in the middle of his next-to-last year, he had a seething bitterness toward all white people and a cynicism that made him mock his mother's piety and her stupid ambition for him. She died not long after that and Herman had to go to work.

There were several years of jobs like loading trucks and stacking lumber and putting down pavement. The jobs mostly ended in about the same way, with Herman quitting in a rage or getting fired because he made his hatred of whites too plain. He drank too much and got in fights, though always it was black people he fought with. By the time he was nineteen, he had a big pale ridge of scar tissue on his neck and also a reputation. Most people steered clear of him. When the real racial protests got started in the early sixties, Herman was right in the middle of them. He was put in jail twice. Even after the blacks won some victories and things generally had cooled off a good deal, he was not much less bitter than he used to be. But then he met Maybelle, up from Okaloosa.

Herman was ripe for the meeting. By that time he had practically lost touch with his brothers and sisters, and lonesomeness had taken him to, and brought him back from, two or three cities where he did not find anything. Then he met that glad timid grin of Maybelle's that fled away and suddenly came back and astonished him. It was as if she had come, bringing some of it with her, from a place that was brand-new and fresh like a garden on the old soiled map. That was how it was for a while. It was long enough for Herman to marry her. It was even long enough for him to go with her, a few months later, back to her home in Okaloosa.

It seemed to Herman that he had stepped back in time a few years. What had already happened in Birmingham appeared to be just getting under way in Okaloosa. But Herman was more prudent now, if not less bitter, and he managed to get and keep a job at the Rayburn Textile Mill. He was a doffer, supplying loaded spools to long rows of rumbling clicking machines that passed the yarn from spindle to spindle like running webs. It was easy work, forgetful work. Except for the white people he had to work for, and sometimes with, he liked it fine. And he would have liked living in Maybelle's house in Creektown if the house had not really belonged to his father-in-law, Sim Denny, who was nothing better than an Uncle Tom. After the first few months, even after Sim started trying to act as if he was part of the Movement too, Herman had got so he couldn't speak a word to the old man without there being a sneer in it.

"Leave him be," Maybell said. "He old."

"Yeah," Herman said. "Leave him be. If niggers like him hadn't been sucking up to honkies all their life, we wouldn't be where we at. He ain't earn *nothing* from me."

"This his house," Maybelle said, but mildly, not looking at Herman any longer. Her sullen expression, the out-thrust purple underlip, did not quite hide the fact that she was afraid of him.

"*His* house, yeah. Till a white man decide he want it for something. Ain't nothing *his.*"

More and more nowadays that tone of his voice was like a signal to Maybelle. She hushed, and if Sim was present, she always cast a warning glance his way. There was no need for it. Sim was afraid of him too, and at supper, almost the only time he had to be in Herman's presence, he sat in silence with his gray bullet head bent over his plate eating. Those meals were mostly silent. If there was other talk than a necessary word from Maybelle now and then, it would nearly always come from Herman. The chances were it would be some angry or mocking thing ending, as likely as not, with a cut at Sim or the question: "Ain't that right, Uncle?" A grunt from Sim, an agreement and a protest both, would be the only answer. And Herman would grin, maybe, a hard little flash of a grin, and go at his food again as if he had forgotten until now what he was at the table for. He wolfed the food, quick with his hands, forking up beans and cornbread or a piece of pork at random. His mind was busy, and under the hanging light bulb, weakened by the paper shade, the white in his eyes suggested eyeballs reversed and gazing backward into his head. For Sim it was a little like sitting at the dinner table with something that just might all of a sudden spring at him.

After Herman's first few months in town, the feeling that he was somebody to be avoided was pretty general among people who knew him even fairly well. And this was true in spite of his deliberate efforts to be friendly. He tried to enter into things and he kept his rage in check. A week after he came to town, he joined the Improvement Association. He made contributions and went to all the meetings, and when he talked, seeing how things were in Okaloosa, he always throttled the violent words that had used to come boiling up like acid in his gullet. Sometimes he had even gone to church and sat nodding agreement with Brother Dick's pale diatribes. Finally, though, it was all no good to him. There was not any curtain he could draw against their glimpses into his soul.

Herman had not quite stopped hoping, though, and several times in the course of that spring and summer, there were occasions when he thought his hour was at hand. A row between blacks and whites at the high school was one of these. There was anger in Creektown and words spoken with feeling that might have come straight up out of Herman's own heart. The aftermath of that second old white woman strangled made another occasion. A Negro, the white people said, and said it this time in the newspaper, as though it was a fact already proved. Hershel Rawls answered. He answered from the steps of the First African Baptist Church and made a speech out of it that blasted Whitey the way he ought to have been blasted and lifted Hershel's voice quite out of its old suave accents. For Herman it was like a friend's voice speaking to him. And the crowd around him, touching him, the black heads nodding and murmuring and shouting Amen where Hershel left a pause: suddenly they too, all of them, were his friends. At least for a while they were.

But the big moment, the one that seemed to be *it*, came at the end of summer when the white police killed poor old deaf and dumb Earl Banks. It was not just a moment, either; it was two or three whole days of moments running successively. Herman had friends everywhere. He met them on Creektown street corners talking in noisy threatening voices under the streetlights and saw them pass by in speeding cars and heard, against the wail of police sirens, their shouts in the distance. On into the night and all the next day and into that night too, Hattie's Cafe was crowded. Bottles of whiskey, pillaged from the white-owned store at the west end of Creektown, stood openly on tables or passed from hand to hand through the drifts of smoke. One of the hands was Herman's. His voice, running unbridled now, sounded no different from other ones made audible in the break when his own voice stopped. "Yeah," he said, lifting the empty paper cup almost to his lips. "*Had* to be a nigger. So they got them one. *Any* one, it don't matter, niggers is all the same. Little bad luck and it'd been me," he said, addressing the big black man with the missing tooth.

"That's right. Sho it would," the man said. He pushed the bottle of whiskey across the table to Herman.

Pouring, Herman said, "Yeah. And you know what they going say when that Strangler kill him another old white woman? This here was just a little *mistake*. A little *mistake*," he repeated slowly. "and what *we* going do?" He lifted the cup and tossed the raw whiskey into his mouth. It burned, seared its way down his gullet. Through watery eyes he saw the faces watching him now, waiting, making around him a pool of quiet among the strident voices in the room. "Yeah," he breathed, with a breath that felt like flame. "I hate them som'bitches. I hate them goddamn white faces." The bottle was empty. He held it by the neck, gripping until the knucklebones whitely defined themselves through the skin. When he suddenly threw his head back, they could all see the pale ridge of scar above his collar line and they were still looking at this when, too quick for thought, he raised and hurled the whiskey bottle with all his strength against the wall. The explosion made a hush in the room that he remembered afterward.

They put him out of the café, though not roughly, and somebody with a hand on his arm walked the three blocks home with him. Drunk, in the dim streetlight, Herman did not know who it was or what raging words he had said to the man. He seemed to recall this much only. The hand on his arm and the low voice had answered in spirit to the violence pouring out of his mouth. On the front porch alone, standing propped against the door, Herman could feel yet the pressure from that hand holding his arm, holding him upright.

But that interlude was illusion like the others—just bigger this time and longer-lived. About three days, little more, and again the streets were quiet at night. There were bursts of laughter once more and mellow voices and clusters of boys instead of men standing under the streetlights on the corners. As if it had not happened, Herman thought, seated at Hattie's counter with his glass. There was no crowd at nine o'clock, and eyes that stopped for a moment on his face seemed barely to remember. A few did. He got a greeting or two. Wait a day, a week, he thought, and knowing how anger would pitch his voice too high, he did not answer the greetings. A few days more and not one pair of eyes but would look at him in the old way, uneasy or afraid of him, lingering a moment on his scar. Slowly he lifted his chin and made the scar like a badge plain to see. And he remembered, when he had hurled that bottle against the wall, the stillness of all those faces looking at him.

Herman remembered something else that night. He remembered it at Hattie's and he remembered it again afterward as he passed along the deserted street, walking a little unsteady because of the whiskey. It was the man who a few nights ago had walked him home from Hattie's. Herman had no memory of anything except a dark figure, maybe tall, and a hand on his arm and answers that appeared to second his own raging words. What words, though? It seemed to matter and he tried to recall. No use, the words were gone: no memory but the sound of his own voice pouring out his soul. It did not matter.

This was what Herman told himself then and also later when the thought recurred. Somehow it did matter. It mattered enough to keep on calling that question back, as if in his drunkenness he had laid bare a dark and ugly secret about himself. What secret, though? He had no secret. Even so, this answer was never good enough to finally silence the question. It came back in his sleep that night and still the next day, through the forgetful clicking hum of the doffing machines he tended, went on repeatedly asking itself like a voice from over his shoulder.

He was at Hattie's again by eight o'clock. In fact now he was at Hattie's every night, seated where the counter met the wall, an elbow propped beside a glass of beer or moonshine whiskey. Somehow he thought he would know the man who had walked him home that night. The one still figure in that room full of voices and movement and dinning jukebox music, Herman sat and watched. His eyes were secretly busy, passing from face to face, lingering when a new one entered the room. After the first few nights, of course, not many new ones entered. It made no difference. By eight o'clock he was there on his stool and busy with his eyes.

That was the week Sim Denny died. Of course it was expected, it was only decent that Herman go to the funeral of his wife's father. He did not go. From the first, feeling the way he did about Sim, even Sim dead, he did not want to. And he wanted to less and less when he thought about how it would be watching Brother Dick, the preacher, by the coffin with his black face turned up to where he could see, he would say, old Sim's soul already washed clean as a lamb and on its last bright journey. And Jesus waiting, holding his hand out. A white man's hand. Like all those notions were white man's notions cooked up to keep the niggers quiet. Precious Jesus. Those black voices wailing it out in that old nigger graveyard where you had to pick the cockleburrs off your ass before you could sit down on your chair. While Jesus looked down. Just like He had looked down when Herman was one of six little pickaninnies in two hog-wallow rooms in a stinking tenement house.

The clincher came when, the evening before the funeral, an old white woman showed up at the front door. It was Mrs. Mister Will, old Sim's white man's lady. With some flowers she had pulled somewhere in that big green yard of hers and looking tearful, sad about the good old days when niggers were niggers and Sim was Mister Will's own personal nigger. Except the ones in that living room were still acting like such niggers, jumping up all around like giving that old white woman a chair was the biggest thing that could have happened to them. Herman left the house.

He left the house but he did not leave that white face behind him. Even his vigil at Hattie's and all the whiskey he drank that night did not dislodge it from his memory. As usual his eyes were busy, though half the time they were looking inward instead of out, seeing the folds and creases in those pink-white cheeks and the melted look in the eyes and the tight mouth that had no flesh or color either one. He remembered that woman his mother had worked for. He remembered a hundred, thousand old white women's ugly faces that looked at him like they were blind when they passed him by. Finally, late that night, he kept seeing the face like an image printed on his eyeballs, as if his eyes had been mirrors holding it. The whiskey was the reason. He left Hattie's and made his way home in the swimming half-light from the street lamps.

The walk did not clear Herman's head. When he saw the lights on and then, as he stumbled up onto the porch, people in the living room, he stopped and stood there confused for a moment. Through the door the people were all looking at him, all silent, and the shiny head of the coffin reflected the floor lamp by the wall. Swaying a little, he pulled the screen door open. A voice and then another one spoke. Herman only stood there against the doorjamb making the round of faces with his gaze. The white one was gone. They were all black faces, all turned on him like masks with living eyes, evasive eyes. "Yeah," Herman said in their stillness. "Yeah," and settled his gaze on the motionless head in the coffin in the lamplight. A mummy's head. "Old Sim, there," Herman said. "Gone to white folks' heab'm." Around the room the eyes fled from him. "Yeah," he said and after one uncertain step, watched by the eyes, passed among them through to the kitchen and entered the bedroom door. He slammed it shut behind him.

Maybelle's startled face from the pillow met him in the first stroke of light. Herman looked back at her, waiting, waiting for her parted lips to move. Then he said, "Act like you ain't never seen me before. This here your husband done come home." Swaying above her on the balls of his feet, he felt like something fiercely perched and waiting. The parted lips went shut, said nothing, and the eyes escaped behind her fallen lids. "Better look see is it Herman," Herman said. "Might be some bad guy come in on you."

"I know it's you," Maybelle murmured and did not open her eyes.

"Like that Strangler dude. White folks say he black just like me. You better look see."

A long breath lifted Maybelle's bare shoulders but her eyes stayed shut. "Wish you'd get to bed, Herman. I tired."

"Yeah," Herman said. To steady himself he put a hand on the iron frame at the foot of the bed. A low voice from the living room was audible but he was still looking hard at Maybelle's face. "He don't go for black, though. It's white he after. Like that ugly old white woman come in this evening. Crying for good old Nigger Sim." Herman drew a breath. "I knows just how that Stranger guy feel."

He saw how Maybelle's body had got stiller on the bed—except her underlip, poked out a little. He said, "I reckon she be at the funer'l. With some more tears in her eyes. . . . I ain't going to no funer'l." Herman's hand had tightened on the bed frame.

"She ain't hurting nothing." Maybelle's voice was so low he could barely hear it. "Her old man, he dead too."

"*Mister Will*," Herman said in a voice much louder than hers. The knuckles of his hand were almost white. "You think you going get me at that funer'l? I might do like that Strangler, I might wring that old white woman's neck."

"Hush up, Herman, they hear you in there." Maybelle's eyes were open, her head lifted.

"Like a chicken," Herman said louder than ever. "I hope he do it to her. I be glad if he do."

"Hush up, Herman."

"Yeah," he said, very loud. "I might just do it for him." He suddenly gave the frame a yank that pulled the bed out from the wall. Then he found that he had to hold on with both hands, because now the walls were slowly wheeling around him. Maybelle's face was in it, with eyes showing white, passing and not passing across the track of his vision. The walls were spinning, getting closer. He opened his mouth but nothing came out. He handed himself along the bed frame and plunged facedown into the mattress, feeling the walls come down dark upon him.

Herman waked up almost blind, with something like a wedge embedded in the middle of his brain. Once he could remember things, the pain made fragments of them. Maybelle was gone, there was stirring in the house. He lifted himself slowly and felt between the flashes inside his skull last night's rage coming back. No need to dress. Walking with caution, balancing his head, he went into the kitchen and, watched by eyes from the living room, out into the backyard. Mid-morning sun glazed his vision. After a minute he saw the big black hearse and people dressed like Sunday standing out front. The flicker across his brain was pain and rage at once, and watched by the eyes, he went through the hedge into the yard next door and away down the street.

As late as it was, Herman went to the mill, walking the whole two miles in the sun, with lights that would not stop flashing inside his head. A brief hassle with pop-eyed Pinky Danford in the office and Herman was back among his machines again and it was better. Down the long deserted aisles, neon light from the ceiling bulbs fell bland and dreamy clear. An empty spool. He replaced it and farther on replaced another one and turned at the end from this aisle to the next. The hum and click and web after web of yarn running from spool to spool became after a while like something that went on inside his own skull, crowding thought, purging his mind. At least it was this way for a time, an hour. Then something happened. He did not know what had happened but suddenly he was nervous and his hands, when he changed a spool, trembled a little bit. He could not think of any reason except the white woman who tended the section next to his and whose boiled wary face, frightened of him, had peeped at him through the webs a while ago. No matter. All afternoon he could not shake the nervousness that followed him like a presence from aisle to aisle.

Herman did not go home that evening. He ate a sandwich at a place on Bean Street and sat until nearly eight o'clock. At Hattie's the whiskey burned his throat but it cleared his head. It seemed that his ears never had been sharper or his eyes more able to read the meaning in faces that answered his gaze. All hostile. Even Hattie's when she served him, always in silence, her stove-black face drawn up in wrinkles around her bulb of a nose. Herman was used to this. The new thing, getting slowly worse, was his nervousness. He began to feel trapped in his corner where the counter met the wall, and his hand on the glass began to tremble slightly. He was sure that something was about to happen.

It was a while later when it happened. It came in a lull when the jukebox had stopped, when even the voices had seemed to fade and then to hush for a moment. The clap of the screen door was unmistakable. Blurred in the corner of Herman's eye a figure stood hesitating, then moved out of his sight. The jukebox came back, thumping, screaming in the room. When finally Herman turned his head, it was only a little, a fractional movement, but it was enough. The man, seated not far away at a table with two other men, was facing Herman, and the smallest elevation of his gaze would bring it squarely up to Herman's face.

A whole half-hour must have gone by. There had been lulls when Herman could hear the man's voice though he could never hear the words. It was a low voice, and once, for several minutes running, it hovered just at the margin where hearing stopped. Those two heads at the table with it heard, were bent to hear. And that was when, the voice pausing, those two heads turned to look at Herman. He thought they had: his glance came an instant too late to catch the certainty of it. He had caught one certainty, though. *That* man was looking at him, looking straight, from under a knitted bone-ridged brow.

This had been a while ago and now a wild voice out of the jukebox made a featureless babble of voices talking in the room. Herman was waiting for it to stop. Then it did. A glance showed him an empty chair where the man had been sitting. Suddenly Herman was on his feet. Hattie's cry pursued him but it did not make him pause.

The street was empty. At the intersection below Hattie's he looked down each dim street, then turned and hurried back up the block to the intersection there. He was too late, there was nobody. He set out at a venture down Jacob Street, at a walk that kept breaking into a jog, slowing only for a look when other streets crossed Jacob. At last for no good reason he turned onto one of these. Two blocks on and he turned again and did not even know where he was anymore. There was a police car. He saw it under a streetlight prowling toward him and he stopped. There was a tree in the yard beside him. He lunged for it and stood behind the tree trunk while the car went past. He stayed there catching his breath, beginning to think again.

He was outside Hattie's when it closed for the night. He had been waiting where he could see through the door the two men still at the table, and when he saw them stand up, he took a few steps backward into the dark. He was lucky. They were the last two customers, and when they came out, the door shut behind them. Finding Herman in their path they stopped, peering at him in the gloom. He had a speech but it failed him. What came out was, "Who that guy was setting with you all? While ago. Hour ago."

It was wrong. The men just looked at him and finally one of them, the big one, said, "What you want know for?"

Herman's mouth opened and shut and opened again. "Wants to talk to him." It came out too sharp, staccato. "Wants to tell him something."

The men peered at him. "What?" the big one said.

Herman's throat had shut down on him.

"I tell him you looking for him," the big man said. He meant for Herman to get out of his way but Herman did not move.

Instead, in a voice still pitched all wrong, he blurted, "What he tell you? I seen him telling you something. 'Bout me."

The men just looked at him. He tried to see their faces. "I never meant nothing, telling him that. Just drunk talk, I was drunk. He telling it on me, ain't he?"

"Telling what?" the big man said.

Herman tried to read his face and then the other face beside him. It was too dark. They were waiting. It was a trick.

"Get out the way," the man said, advancing, brushing Herman's shoulder as he passed. The striding figures drew away, receding in the dark, with muttered inaudible words passing between them.

There was no light burning in the house. Tonight Herman was glad for this, and even when he entered the deeper dark of the bedroom, he did not reach for the light switch. He did not mean, at first, to speak to Maybelle at all and he moved quietly, hoping she was asleep. But her breath that came heavy always when she slept made no sound in the room and this told him she was awake—awake and lying with her eyes open. Unfriendly eyes. He unbuttoned his shirt with nervous fingers and laid it over the shadowy chair. Some words, almost spoken, died on his tongue. Seated on the chair he bent over, lest even in the dark a glance might show him what her expression was like. It was a long while and the second or third try at it before he said, "It go all right today?" It was just a murmur, so quiet it might have escaped her. He said it again, and he was almost ready to add something else when her silence struck him. His anger flickered palely and went away.

Later, still sitting bent over in the chair, Herman said, "You got to listen to me, Maybelle. They b'lieve any kind of lies on me. They lay it on me if they can. Police will too. You the one got to tell them. It's some man, I don't even know him. I never meant nothing, just talking. . . . You listening to me, ain't you, Maybelle?"

There was no reply, nothing.

"Ain't you even going answer me?"

Again no answer and after a moment Herman lifted his head. There was such a stillness where she lay, no breath, not even the faintest stirring, that he stood up and leaned over the bed. Where Maybelle ought to have been, there was a wadded garment lying. He switched the light on. He called her name, but not loud. He did not find her in the little back bedroom or anywhere else in the house. Nothing, gone, no message. Where? He looked again for a sign, looked harder. He turned the lights off and stood in the dark with his heart beating.

In the night Herman kept thinking that soon he would leave here and he thought about how he would go and what he would take with him. He did not think about where he would go. On this his mind shut down, too tired, as though whichever direction he looked would show him still another Birmingham. A little rest and then he would leave, and in the dark, stretched out, shoes and all on the bed, he kept thinking that each next minute would be the one. A police siren he heard, or thought he heard, kept making him lift his head. He always settled back again, too tired, still waiting for the minute to come.

What Herman was really waiting for came to him late in one of his fits of sleep. Maybelle entered the room. Even in the dark he could see her plainly and see the glad timid grin that pouched her cheeks. Her eyes, as used to be, kept fleeing and coming back to him—the look that once in Birmingham had astonished the evil mood clear out of his heart. He reached out his hands to take her. This ruined everything. First her underlip pouting, swelling, and then unmistakable fear blooming in her face. Her cry was real terror, a bolt of sound that left the room empty in its wake. Herman woke up with his hands extended.

Even just to run away again Maybelle did not come. The dream was what made Herman think she would and kept him suspended there in the house all morning pacing the rooms and thinking of words that never in his life had passed his lips. It was noon when he gave up and went next door. But Lena Brooks said no, she couldn't help him, and so did Mary Gaines across the street. Or wouldn't help him. His last try, at Mildred Echols's front door, was a little different. She didn't know, she told him through the screen she kept latched shut, then added something else. "I wouldn't tell you if I did. She want you to know, *she'd* told you."

It was the same tone, the same face as the others, clamped shut. Herman said, "I ain't never lain a hand on Maybelle."

"Well, now you aint' got no chance to."

At dark he would leave. Back in the house he stuffed some clothes into a laundry bag and money from deep in a dresser drawer into his pocket. His switchblade knife was there. He put that too in his pocket and stood with his hands empty, looking around the room. Maybelle's things, everywhere. She would have to come back. Later when he heard a woman's voice from someplace, he lifted his head and focused his ears to listen.

They were nervous hours. Voices from the neighborhood sounded much closer than they were, like muffled voices just outside in the yard. There were passing cars that seemed to slow down in front of the house, and once he thought he recognized a car that had passed by two or three times already. About four o'clock, for a space of fifteen or twenty minutes, a man Herman did not know stood on the other side of the street talking to Leon Echols. Except for a snatch now and then, he could not even hear their voices and he saw that they kept looking toward the house.

But Herman did not leave that night, or any night, as he had planned. Suddenly, late in the afternoon, he had heard Maybelle's voice. That was what he thought when, thinking it had come from out on the porch, he got up off the bed. There was nobody on the porch, though, or anywhere else in the house or the yard, but these moments nevertheless had made a difference. It was as if something, a passion, had got hold of him. Minutes later in the full light of sunset, he went out the door and up the street toward Hattie's.

It was around ten o'clock when Hattie finally telephoned the police. Ordinarily, being afraid of the police herself, she never did this even when things got right up nearly to the cutting stage. She had never had to because, just as was the case tonight, there had always been enough other people around who were willing and able to put a stop to it before the blood got flowing. Tonight she did, though, and did it even before Herman came out with the knife she had already known he would have. She had thought for a week and more that, besides his being just plain a mean nigger, there was something wrong about Herman. In fact she had heard some funny talk about him only this afternoon. And then he had come in, two hours before he usually did, and said some things to her that fitted right into what she had heard.

Herman had not said anything at first, not for most of an hour, but Hattie noticed the difference in him. Before, he had always sat there at the counter very still, just drinking and watching, sneaking long hard looks at first one person and then another. This evening it was Hattie he kept sneaking looks at. But at that early hour, there was nobody else in the place and his looks were not what she noticed especially. What she noticed was how nervous he was, with his hands and his mouth and the way his Adam's apple kept jumping. He had Hattie nervous too, before he ever even said anything to her. She had her back turned and she kept it that way, only moving her head sometimes so she could watch him out of the corner of her eye.

"They telling lies on me," Herman said.

"Who is?" Hattie mumbled. She was drying glasses. She wished somebody else would come in.

"Ev'ybody, now. It's a man. I just seen him in the dark, and me drunk. He mistook me . . . what I told him." Herman pressed his lips together and then, still watching her, took a drink from his glass.

Finally Hattie said, "What you tell him?"

"It's what he say I told him. I never meant that. He telling it on me. . . . All of them is, now. Ain't they?"

Hattie did not like the quiet in the room. "How I know?" she said, carefully wiping the glass in her hand.

"Don't tell me you ain't heard them talking." It was practically a threat.

"I ain't heard nothing," Hattie said quickly. She heard him move and this made her hands stop. When he spoke again, his voice was pitched higher, excited, as if it might break into a yell.

"They wants to lay it on me. All them old white women. 'Cause I won't be no nigger uncle like they is. Ask Maybelle, she know it ain't me. She be back, she. . . ."

What stopped him there and what stopped Hattie from making the retreat out the back way she had already planned was a man, two men, coming in the door. She thought at first, right after the interruption, that he was about to start up again, but he did not. He only stared, with eyes that in just the last minute or two had got almost crimson, at the two men who came up to the counter and ordered beers. He had forgot about Hattie. For a long time after that, while the place filled up with customers, except to order a drink once in a while he did not speak again.

By nine, there was a good crowd for a weeknight. Hattie, serving up beers, was too busy now to think much about Herman. Or was except when he signaled for a drink and she saw again how red those eyes were, as if they had a glaze of blood across them. In fact she was back in the little pantry reluctantly getting Herman still another drink when she first noticed that something had happened. It was a matter of sound: not the music but the voices had suddenly gone quiet.

When Hattie got back in there, the first thing she noticed was heads turned and the next thing was Herman seated at a table with three men. Their faces were anything except friendly, watching and not watching him, while Herman, leaning over the table, turned from one face to another with his red eyes. The jukebox was blaring but Hattie could hear his voice and sometimes snatches of the words, words she recognized. She heard Maybelle's name. The men kept swapping glances, while Herman's voice rising broke in a sort of plea and sank again. One of the men got up and left the table. This left two: the voice went on. Until, in the quiet when the jukebox hushed, these men also got up from the table.

This had seemed to be the end of it. After a little while, seated at the table he had emptied, glaring around at faces in the room, Herman got up and left the café. He was gone for maybe half an hour. Hattie was taking beers out of the cooler and when she turned around he was standing over a table where there were four men. Just the look of him, the way his head jumped and his voice rose and broke in the hush, set off something like an alarm in Hattie's brain. It was not just that she knew he was dangerous drunk and would have a knife somewhere in reach of his quick hands. It was something worse. She went to the telephone by the pantry and called the police. Even from back there, she heard Herman's voice before she put the phone down.

Everybody was standing up and it took Hattie a moment to move where she could get glimpses of Herman backed up there in the corner of the room with his knife out. She could hear him plain enough, though, his voice broken, as if he had something in his throat, crazy. "Yeah, me, lay it on me. Couldn't been no *Tom* nigger. . . ." He seemed to swallow something. His red eyes burned and that shining knife blade, held at ready, quivered under the light. "Not none of you . . . white folks' niggers. Yeah, I the one. That's right, that's right. Call the *police*. . . ."

"You crazy, man," somebody said. "Put that thing down."

But he lifted it higher. A swipe of his hand made the blade flash. "I the one. Choked them. All them wrinkled old white necks. Go 'head. Call the *police*."

"Man. . . ."

There was the wail of a siren, startling, pitched like a scream that gathered force as it approached the café. Then heads that had turned away turned back and saw, just for a second, Herman with his red eyes and knife-hand frozen standing like a man impaled in the corner. Blue light flashed in the room. Herman's eyes moved suddenly, sweeping the rank of bodies in his path. Just to his right, there was a half-shut window. He made a leap and then another and took both glass and window frame out with him. He hit the ground on his face but there was not even a pause before he was on his feet running, straight through a hedge, disappearing into the yard next door.

What Hattie told the police right after that was enough to get them heated up and within a few minutes there were three or four cars prowling the area. But if it had been only escape Herman was thinking about, probably he could have got away in those few minutes. At least he could have got out of the neighborhood. Instead, after that initial burst of panic fear that carried him through Hattie's window and the next-door hedge and straight on through many other hedges and yards, he changed his mind. Or, better, his mind changed itself, because he was still not very clear about what he meant to do instead of keep running. He was clear enough to move with caution, though, and nobody saw him again until about half an hour later when he turned up at Mildred Echols's house, where he had gone that day at noon. He came to the back door and he had knocked softly at first. The yelling and banging started only when Mildred, from inside the locked door, told him for the third or fourth time that she did not know where Maybelle was. Then he was yelling that Maybelle, she knew, and would tell them it wasn't him. Herman tried next to break the door open with his shoulder and Mildred's husband Leon had to stand there holding it while she called the police. Herman was gone when the police got there a couple of minutes later.

They found him at home. The house was all dark but they thought he might possibly be in there and they went in to look. He was in the bedroom standing on the other side of the bed when they switched on the light, and he had his knife out. There was a window he could have gone through, as he had done at Hattie's. He never even glanced at it. He stood there warning them. He had cut white throats before, he said. And then, like an afterthought, he said, "Choked some, too. Ugly old white-woman th'oats." With the blood and gashes all over his face and the wild red eyes and that knife in his hand he looked, the policemen said, like the devil himself.

They brought Herman in alive. After the Earl Banks uproar they were afraid to use their guns and so they went for him, three of them, with billy clubs. It was costly, though. One of the policemen got the knife in him, or rather across the side of his neck, and was taken out of there squirting blood. That was what Herman got sent to prison for, because they finally came to the conclusion that his claim to be the Strangler was probably all lies. For one thing, the details he brought in support of his claim were garbled and never were the same the next time he was questioned. He could not identify a single one of the houses where the women had been murdered or cite one piece of solid evidence. These things along with others mounted up. So, after a week, they dropped the charge, even while Herman went on claiming that he was the Strangler. It seemed he really did want what such a conviction would have got for him. As it was, however, he had to settle for five years, and the permanent loss of Maybelle, who never came to see him even while he was still in jail in Okaloosa.

Beverly Lowry

OUT OF THE BLUE

Secrets made Jocko happy. Alone in Bonnie's car, parked at the mall
celebrating the continuation of that part of himself he shared with no
one, he felt like a man throwing himself his own private party. Bonnie
had sent him to the store for a few last-minute things, milk, confectioner's sugar, lemons, cardamom. Whatever cardamom was. Some
new recipe she was trying.

He pulled up the ringtop of a beer. He could have gone to Pay'n Tak.
Pay'n Tak was closer, quicker. But they wouldn't have had cardamom.
Or all these people. Jocko had circled the parking lot until he found
the great parking spot, in front of Target where crowds were thickest.
Carefully, he scanned eyes. Brown ones, those with glasses. She was
out there somewhere.

The AC blew cool in his face. Bonnie had told him not to leave the
AC on when the car was parked, it ran the battery down. The Buick
belonged to Bonnie, she had the right to say. But the day was too hot
for rolling down the windows, and besides, Bonnie would never know.

He swallowed a long deep gulp of beer. For a treat, he had bought
Heineken, the best. Mexican beer was all the rage these days. Jocko
thought it was the lime juice people went for. He didn't like much of
anything Mexican except food.

She'd been gone three years. Friends said he was lucky to be rid of
her and in a way they were right. Those last months, friends told him,
Tee showed her true colors, not doing a thing in the world to hide the
fact that she was sleeping with every other man she passed on the

street. Some of them Jocko should have known about, the TV repair-man especially when he replaced their picture tube for next to nothing. Others were a surprise. Jocko had a way of shutting out what he didn't want to think about.

Once Tee left, his friends seemed to feel obliged to tell him everything they knew about exactly what she had done with exactly which person—whether Jocko wanted to hear it or not. Finally, he stopped asking. People thought he'd gotten over Tee and in a way he guessed maybe he had. Over but not past.

He took another slug of beer. Target was amazing. All these people. Everybody with a sack. Houston was supposed to be in a slump. Out here, all anybody did was buy, buy, buy.

The neighbor keeping Jennifer saw the whole thing. She said the motorcycle roared up and Tee ran out, carrying a suitcase. "She never looked back," the neighbor said. In his mind Jocko watched the scene over and over again, like a videotape you keep rerunning. Tee runs out, silver-blond hair flying, slips her warm soft butt onto the seat of the Harley, puts her plump white arms around the leather-jacketed chest in front, lays her angel-round face on his back, and the Harley takes off. "There goes your mother," the baby-sitter told Jennifer. Not that Jennifer understood, her being fifteen months old at the time, barely three months weaned.

That was another line he'd heard too many times.

Got her teeth fixed, weaned the baby, hit the streets.

People didn't just vanish into thin air. Whatever his friends said, Tee had been special to Jocko, his dream first girlfriend. He had loved her like ice cream. He couldn't just give her up.

Shoppers walked by at a careful crawl, setting their shoulders against the heat as if it were a solid wall. In Houston, August was the worst, the air wet as water and there was no breeze at all. Bonnie had those terrible allergy headaches. She was always listening to the weather, to catch the spore count.

Not that Bonnie wasn't great. When Bonnie found out she was pregnant, she went to Seventh-Day Adventist that day to stop smoking. When she was six months gone, she quit her job. She had amniocen-tesis even though she wasn't old enough to need it. She was careful and she cared. He didn't know what he'd have done without Bonnie.

But Jocko thought there was room in a person's life for only one sparkling love, and his was Tee. Shiny, light-fingered—Tee. He loved Bonnie too but it wasn't the same.

An old woman in a fishing cap came out of Target. The woman wore running shoes and half-socks with fuzzy balls hanging over the backs of her shoes. She walked in a stoop, as if her joints had rusted. Jocko hated seeing old women in sleeveless shirts. When she got to the Buick, the woman looked at Jocko for a full beat, frowned hard, then went on down the sidewalk toward Sav-On Shoes and Kroger.

Jocko chuckled to himself. People were great. Dressed every kind of way, every one of them thinking I am the one with the great look.

When he first got out of the car to go to Kroger with his list, Jocko had thought he heard somebody call his name. He'd looked around. There was nobody. Except all these strangers. But he'd had a funny feeling across the back of his neck. Like something was about to happen.

One day it would. He'd be in the supermarket with his basket, waltzing down some aisle, and there she'd be, rounding the end of the aisle, buying Cheetos or bite-size Snickers. Tee liked a candy bar and a Coke for breakfast. Or she might be shoplifting. Something small and expensive, say capers, or marinated artichoke hearts. Her round hips would be swaying, her blond hair would fall in her eyes. She'd be taking those short quick steps. Whisking cans into deep skirt pockets.

Out of the blue, that was how things happened. When you least expected it. The dentist told Jocko that Tee's mouth was a potential death trap, those two root canals half done and only a temporary filling for protection. The slightest infection could go straight to her brain. That was another reason to find Tee, to let her know. Jocko turned up his beer.

He checked his watch. Five of five. He would stay until five-fifteen, say he got stopped by a train and had to go to Kroger for the cardamom. He used the train all the time, at all hours. Bonnie never noticed. People, Jocko had come to believe, either wanted to know what you were up to, or they just didn't.

She had to have gone off the beam. One day she's the perfect mother, watching "Sesame Street" with Jennifer, the next she's hit the streets on a Harley? And with her teeth half-fixed? It didn't make sense.

A red-faced man in lime green pants and purple T-shirt came out the automatic exit doors of Target empty-handed. He walked unsteadily, bumping into other passers-by. Jocko made a silent bet with himself. Dime to doughnuts the staggery man was headed for Thrifty Liquors. This was why Jocko had turned out to be a good salesman, because he liked to figure people's stories. He could go to the beach and never get wet for watching the parade. The man in green pants strolled into Thrifty as if he'd just had the thought.

Bingo. Jocko congratulated himself.

Bonnie wouldn't be caught dead in a discount store. Jocko didn't like them either. Tee was an expert. She could spend three hours in K-Mart and come out with the one great buy in the store, maybe socks with silver flecks in the weave or a gold-spangled strapless blouse. Tee had a fantastic dime-store way of dressing. Ruffled skirt, drop-shoulder blouse, shoes with ankle straps. Tee never wore jeans, only skirts. And nothing underneath. When Jocko found out, he was shocked at first. Tee just laughed.

Two odd-looking boys in hats approached the Target door. One of them, darker than the other, carried a wrinkled Target sack with something long inside, like curtain rods. The boys looked behind them. The dark one carrying the sack had skin as pale as a cave rat and moles up and down his arms. The other one was blond, with a scraggly goatee. Both of them had the lean stringy look of a hillbilly. The dark one stepped on the black rubber mat which activated the automatic doors. The blond one started in. He had a funny walk, not crippled exactly but something. The walk was familiar to Jocko in a way he could not pinpoint. The dark one took another look around, then followed the blond boy in.

The boys were up to something. Hats on a day like today made no sense. Hillbillies were all over this part of Houston. Jocko steered clear of them. They would rip the skin off their grandmother for fun. Like she was catfish.

When Tee first left, Jennifer used to wake up in the night, screaming bloody murder. Jocko was trying to keep it together by himself then, taking the baby to a day-care center every morning, picking her up after work, thinking Tee was bound to come back any minute. Every afternoon he'd find Jennifer standing in a playpen sucking the rail. He couldn't take it. Jennifer had Tee's eyes, like down-turned almonds about to slide into her ears. Tee and Jenny both had this sad look, even when they smiled.

Day care was bad; evenings were worse. Jocko would fix dinner, he and Jennifer would eat, maybe play a game or watch a show. Taking her bath, Jennifer would look up at Jocko with that down-turned look and his heart would melt. The heavy loss of Tee was between them all the time.

When he went to her in the middle of those nights, Jennifer would be lying in a pool of sweat and urine, eyes wide, wide open. If he called her name, she wouldn't answer. She was asleep and awake at the same time. Something in her was awake; something else was determined to stay asleep. He didn't blame her.

When she left, Tee took all the pictures, including the ones of her and Jennifer. The only one she left behind was a black-and-white school-day picture Jocko still kept in his wallet, behind one of Bonnie. She was about twelve. Her hair was curled in fat sausages and she was smiling like there was no tomorrow. She had her sparkle even then. To Jocko, Tee sparkled like 7-Up.

Jocko stood over Jennifer's bed those terrible nights and wondered what memories were left in her baby head. He imagined her thinking, "There was a lap I sat on. What happened to the warm safe lap?"

Bonnie hadn't looked like what Jocko thought of as the motherly type. With a responsible job at a bank, she dressed like a woman on the so-called corporate ladder to success. But Bonnie went for Jennifer in a big way. The spanking almost killed Jocko, but Bonnie said Jennifer would thank them later on and Jocko went along. The thing about Bonnie was, Jennifer knew where she stood. Bonnie would never up and disappear. Never. Jennifer didn't wake up screaming bloody murder anymore. She called Bonnie Mom.

The boys in the hats came back out. The blond boy slung his right leg out in front of him as he walked, as if he had gum on the bottom of his shoe he was trying to sling free. Their hats were identical except for color. The dark-headed boy wore a red one, the other's was army green. The hats had high crowns and floppy brims with black splotches in the fabric, like those tie-dyed clothes hippies used to make. The dark-headed boy with the moles was still carrying the Target sack. On the sidewalk, the boys stood close, conferring behind the hats. They were about the same size, medium height and skinny with long narrow waists that caved in at the stomach. The blond boy wore a tight cowboy shirt. Both had on jeans and brown lace-up work shoes with thick rubber soles. A dangerous pair. Probably kin. Maybe double first cousins. Families like that intermarried, producing idiots and no telling.

Jocko checked his watch. Five-fourteen, time to go. He polished off his beer and threw the empty into the Kroger sack.

The sun hovered above the roof of Kroger, a fuzzy red-orange ball in the haze. In Houston, late afternoon was the hottest time of day. Bonnie's doctor said she'd be better off living somewhere drier but they couldn't leave now. They had both come to Houston for the money, Jocko from Georgia, Bonnie from Illinois. They had bought the new house, thinking what a profit they could make if they decided to move. Now the bottom had fallen out, not only of the real-estate market but Jocko's business as well, selling computers related to the oil business. Bonnie had quit her job to have the baby.

Jocko had worked out a system which kept them two steps ahead of the collection agency. To make sure Bonnie stayed in the dark—if she knew the truth about their situation, they'd be living on baloney sandwiches instead of trying fancy new recipes from the paper—he gave her lavish presents. The cashmere blazer, the Samoyed puppy, the ruby ring, this car.

When Jocko turned back to take one last look at the boys, they were looking at him. The dark one had a scooped-out dishpan face with a hatchet jaw. To avoid Jocko's eyes, he turned quickly away. The blond one was slyer. He slowly, casually lowered his eyes to the hood of the car. Bonnie's Buick was not new but it was racy, a '72 Riviera, sleek and heavily chromed, with the swooped-down tail Rivieras had that year. Bonnie loved the car. She kept it washed and waxed, the interior meticulously Dust-busted and groomed. The boys in the hats looked away, each turning his ignorant hillbilly head in the opposite direction.

Jocko had news for them. They weren't about to get their idiot hands on Bonnie's car. He twisted back to look through the rear window. He was waiting for a brown pickup with California plates to move out from behind him when it hit him why he recognized the blond boy's walk. He looked back toward the sidewalk but the boys were gone. Someone was walking beside the Buick, too close. The hatchet-faced boy with the moles. Down the passenger side, the blond boy moved more slowly, resting his hand on the hood of the car with each step for balance, making palm prints in Bonnie's wax job. Jocko put the car in reverse, turned to see if the brown truck was gone . . . then his door was open and the cave-rat boy was there.

Something in him knew it was going to happen, something else said no it couldn't. Both possibilities seemed true at once. And then pow, there it was.

"This ain't a game," the boy with the moles said, and he shoved the wrinkled sack in Jocko's ribs. When Jocko felt the hard round muzzle of what was unmistakably a gun jab at him, he was as good as gone. It was as if that sharp prick had suddenly relieved him of all his weight and suspended him there, light as a balloon. He might have floored the accelerator and backed into the brown pickup. Might have . . . what? You never know what you'll do until a thing actually happens. Jocko sat there.

At the passenger door, the blond boy punched the button on the door knob, tapped the glass and looked around.

The other one shoved the gun in deeper, punching into the soft place between Jocko's ribs.

"I said this ain't a game," the boy repeated in his high nasal East Texas twang. "This here's a sawed-off twenty gauge. Now put that car in park and move over."

In some situations Jocko took a stand, made a move. Like taking care of Jennifer himself instead of moving in with his mother the way everybody said to. When his father died, his mother had moved to Houston to be close to Jocko, her only child. It seemed only natural that Jocko move in with her and let her take care of the baby. But his mother had never approved of Tee. Tee came from a family Jocko's mother considered trashy. Jocko didn't want to hear the I-told-you-so's. When he said no, he meant it.

Other times he did as he was told. When things got out of hand at the office and his boss—a former Marine officer who dedicated an entire room in his house to glass cases filled with Vietnam memorabilia—first smashed his fist into Jocko's desk, breaking pictures, and then into the wall, sending a spray of plaster across the room, Jocko's future in the company was set. In the face of too much trouble he sulked. Bonnie said she'd have quit that job a long time ago, and Jocko knew that that was so, but he could not.

He took the car out of reverse and slid across the car seat. The plush velour seat cover moved against him like velvet. In the middle of the seat, Jocko sat very still, looking out the windshield, not afraid exactly, just blank.

Again, the blond boy punched at the button of the door knob to let his partner know he could not get in.

"Lift that latch," the dark one said as he slid beneath the steering wheel. Although he was no taller than Jocko, the boy pushed the seat back as far as it would go. Jocko let the other one in. The boy opened the passenger door and sat with his legs out the door, feet on the pavement. He swung his left leg in, then pulled the right one in with his hands.

It was a false leg. The knee didn't bend right. The boy had had an a.k. amputation. Jocko's father had been diabetic and, late in life, had had to have first one leg and then the other one cut off. When Jocko visited his father in the hospital and later the nursing home, he watched the amputees learning to walk. They threw their prostheses out the same way as the blond boy. A.k. or b.k. was the crucial difference, whether the cut had been above or below the knee. His father's had both been b.k.'s, two inches below. The blond boy was not so lucky. Jocko could tell from the cranky knee and the location of the crease in his jeans, just above his knee.

Blood sugar did its work. Jocko's father died a long slow death. His hands grew numb, his eyesight went, finally his kidneys failed. Poor health and dying did not alter a person's nature. Jocko's father remained sour to the end, when he panicked and changed his mind about going on dialysis—too late—blamed Jocko and his mother, then died.

"Ooo-ee," the blond boy said when he was in. He ran his hand along the padded vinyl of Bonnie's dash. "Fancy," he said, nudging Jocko, "ain't we, Riviera."

Jocko smiled, shrugged. The blond boy's voice was softer than the driver's. Jocko didn't exactly look at the boy, but he could see from the corner of his eyes, the blond boy was what he would have to call pretty. His lips, set off by the scraggly goatee, were full and pink as a girl's, his skin soft and rosy.

The boy closed the passenger door, and for a minute the three of them sat side by side looking at Target. A girl wearing a Madonna T-shirt came out carrying a Target sack with the big red bull's-eye on it. She held the sack loosely, twirling it in front of her like a sharpy twirling a watch chain. She wore running shorts, low white socks and aerobics shoes, nothing else. One breast poked at the M of Madonna. The other one distorted the *a*.

"Ooo-ee," the blond boy said. "Ain't she a fox."

Jocko thought of Bonnie at home, waiting for the milk and carda-mom, her cheeks flushed from the pregnancy, her eyes red and puffy with allergies. Jennifer was watching reruns of "Scoobey Doo" when Jocko left. When she saw Jocko going out, she asked to go, but her heart wasn't in it. "Scoobey Doo" was still Jennifer's favorite.

The truth slid down Jocko's spine. He would never see Jennifer again, or Bonnie. He would not see the new baby at all. He would not know how Jennifer turned out or if the psychiatrist Bonnie took her to was right when he said Jennifer was in for trouble in her teens from having been abandoned early on by her mother. Now Jocko would abandon her too. Tee would die from her teeth.

The boy with the moles cradled the gun in his lap. He had pushed the barrel out of the sack so that Jocko could see it. He put the car in reverse.

The bottom edge of the sun grazed Kroger's roof. Like it was resting there. The man in the purple shirt staggered out of Thrifty Liquors clutching his half-pint.

When the boy driving turned to look behind him before backing up, Jocko glanced in his direction.

"Don't look at me," the boy screamed, and he turned his hatchet face in the other direction. Reflexively, Jocko bunched up his shoulders and ducked his head.

"I'll hold Bessie, Rick," the blond one said in a voice meant to calm the other one down. The dark boy—Rick—handed the gun across, then took his foot off the brake. The Riviera eased into the parking lot. The dark boy drove with the tips of his toes.

A dead man, Jocko thought. *I am a dead man.*

He stared out the windshield, trying to catch somebody's attention. It wasn't every day you saw three grown men in the front seat of a car, especially two rank hillbillies in hats with an ordinary honest citizen in the middle.

A boy with his arms out whizzed by on a skateboard. A man came out of Target fast, as if on urgent business. When the man got to the sidewalk, he stopped abruptly. Jocko held his breath. The man wore a white short-sleeved shirt and a plain dark tie. On his shirt pocket, he wore a plastic name-tag with a Target bull's-eye on it. Maybe the man was looking for the hillbillies. Maybe they'd stolen something. The man looked up and down the sidewalk, then threw up his arms without ever glancing in the direction of the Buick. The automatic doors swallowed him up.

"Wait," Jocko said. His voice came out shrill and tinny.

"What you want, Riviera?" the blond boy asked. He patted the gun.

"Take the car," Jocko said. He cleared his throat to lower his voice. "Take my wallet, my credit cards, whatever you want. I won't tell. I have a baby daughter to live for. Another on the way. Please."

The boys didn't say anything. Jocko's breath made a whining noise somewhere in the back of his throat. His nose and eyeballs felt as dry as if all the moisture had been sucked from his face.

The dark one put his foot on the brake.

"Fuck your daughter," he said.

Jocko thought of Jennifer and shivered.

The blond boy chuckled. "Aw, Rick," he said. "Don't be strict." He shoved the gun barrel farther out the sack. The dark boy had not lied. The gun was a sawed-off single-barrel twenty gauge. "Don't worry none, Riviera," the blond boy said. "You be quiet, everything'll turn out."

The one called Rick let his foot off the brake and backed up. Target and what felt to Jocko like his last hope begain to recede. The boy driving turned in the direction of a blacktop road running down the side of the shopping mall.

Jocko looked down. His hands were between his thighs, palms

against one another like a child trying to keep from wetting his pants. He lifted them, then placed one on each thigh.

He had to do something. He had not gone from being a mediocre computer programmer to a cracker-jack commission salesman for nothing. On the road, making cold calls, Jocko had learned. You couldn't just *sell*, you had to know who to sell *to*. In a group there was always one person amenable to the touch. Learning to identify the prospect was one of the keys to good salesmanship . . . rule #2 after confidence in your product.

Rick had to slow down to let a frail old couple on foot cross in front of him. The woman held her husband by the elbow. The man shuffled his feet.

"Frigging old people," Rick said. He shook his fist at the couple. "If you're too old to cut it," he yelled though the windshield, "then get on back home."

"Shoo, Rick," the blond boy cautioned. "Let them alone."

If he had a prayer of helping himself, Jocko had to sell the blond boy with the gun and not Rick. Rick was stark raving idiot crazy.

When the old couple had barely passed the right bumper of the Buick, Rick floored the accelerator. The tires squealed. The old couple looked around. The man stumbled. His wife caught his other arm and pushed him against a parked van for support. As they passed her, Jocko saw the woman's eyelashes blink.

The boy drove the Buick to the edge of the parking lot and turned down the blacktop road. Jocko had driven the road himself once, to see what was down there. The road led nowhere. After a mile or two, blacktop turned to shell. After another two miles, it ended in a turnaround in the middle of a field.

That was Houston. Go to a shopping center, there were all those people buying TV's and microwaves. Turn down a blacktop road and nothing. Junk trees, rocks, dead grass, bags of trash. Jocko's house was maybe three miles away, a two-story American Colonial brick with pine trees, a playroom with a wet bar. Turn down the wrong road and nothing. Buzzards. Fire ants. Houston was on the edge in more ways than one.

They came to the end of the blacktop. The mag wheels of the Riviera took the switch to shell with ease.

"Ooo-ee," the blond boy said. He sounded like a child riding the down swoop of a roller coaster. "This is some car you got here, Riviera."

"It's not mine," Jocko said.

He was trying to sound casual. He had no reason to be, except for a distant memory of horses. When you were afraid, the horse was supposed to know. Jocko hadn't understood the lesson about horses either.

He deepened his breath to settle his nerves. "It was a gift," he explained. "For my wife. I gave it to her."

"Whoever's," the blond boy said. He reached into the back seat and felt around for the grocery sack. He pulled out the box of confectioner's sugar, read the label, rolled down the window and threw the sugar out. Jennifer loved strawberries dipped in confectioner's sugar. Bonnie had bought a quart of strawberries. She'd forgotten they were out of sugar. The boy did the same thing with the milk and the cardamom. The cardamom was stunningly expensive, $4.69 for a two-ounce bottle. Jocko heard the milk carton burst in a splat. The boy rolled the window back up.

"Hot out there," he said, fanning his face. The brim of his floppy hat lifted and then dropped. He took the six-pack from the grocery sack and set it on his lap.

"Ooo-ee," he said. "Buried treasure. Hey Rick, want one? It ain't Lone Star."

Rick shook his head. The blond boy opened a beer and pulled off the price tag. "Wooo!" he said. "$4.95 for a six-pack." He pulled up the ringtop, drank the beer in three long swallows, belched, said, "I needed that," then threw the empty into the back seat.

Jocko did a quick inventory. In his wallet he had probably thirteen dollars and his few remaining credit cards. He wore a good Seiko watch. Clipped to his shirt pocket was a gold-filled Cross felt-tip pen. The plastic didn't mean much. Until he paid them something, the charge companies had put the lid on. The boys wouldn't be able to charge a tank of gas. Bonnie's ruby ring was the last straw. American Express was stringing along until he bought that.

The road didn't last much longer. It was now or never.

"Tell you what . . . ," Jocko started to say.

Rick cut him short. "Can it," he said. "We don't want to know."
The blond boy giggled.

Jocko clasped his hands in his lap. And suppose their game was not just robbery, or even murder? Suppose the two boys were lovers out for a thrill, then what? Jocko closed his eyes. Anything could happen. He was a dead man.

Suddenly Rick shrieked, "Snake!" and jerked at the wheel. To keep from jostling the shotgun, Jocko caught himself by holding on to the edge of the dash. Dust from the shell road spun out from behind the car.

The blond boy looked back. "Missed," he said. "There he goes. Rattler, I bet. Ooo-ee, but I hate a snake."

"If you don't quit saying ooo-ee," Rick said, imitating the blond boy's falsetto, "I'm going to snake you." The blond one giggled.

After Tee had left, her friends all reported thefts—money slipped from purses, blouses from closets, cosmetics from bathroom cabinets, also pills. Tee loved cosmetics. Before they married, she had worked in a drugstore back in Georgia. She was fired for stealing. Knowing that Tee and Jocko were going together and that Jocko was thinking of getting married, the drugstore owner had called Jocko in to explain. "She can't help it," he said. "All her kin is thieves and no-goods. There ain't a stud in the lot. Their blood's thin, that's all." Tee's real name was Bettina, but Jocko never knew anybody who called her anything but Tee. Jocko broke up with Tee and moved to Houston. But when Tee called and said her stepfather was making passes, Jocko gave in. She never did finish high school.

He said nothing about the stealing. Every time he imagined himself doing it, he saw those sad, almond eyes looking back at him, and clamped his mouth shut.

Rick slowed down and pulled over. White dust rose up to the car windows and then settled. The minute Rick switched off the ignition, the car began to heat up.

After Tee left, Jocko found a scratch pad by the telephone where she'd been doodling. "Casa Bettina" was written up and down the page. The tails of the t's were long and swirled, the i dotted with a daisy she knew how to draw. Jocko looked up Casa Bettina in the phone book. It was an apartment complex, west of Chimney Rock. Tee wasn't there.

The summer had been dry, no rain in weeks, only this solid, smothering humidity. Jocko looked around. Far off in the distance he could see another shopping center, a radio tower and, to the north, the light on top of the Astrodome. Rick opened the door and got out. His head hit the door frame, knocking his hat to one side. Jocko got a glimpse of the boy's eyes, deep-set under an ape-like, overhanging brow. The boy jammed his hat back down and pulled at Jocko's elbow. Jocko got out.

"Let's see what we got," Rick said. The blond boy came over. They told Jocko to lie flat across the hood of the car, face down. Jocko spread his legs the way he had seen criminals do on television. There was a ditch beside the road. Beyond it, a stand of scrub oaks. No one would ever come down this road; there was no reason to. A person had to be lost to come down here.

The dark-headed boy went through Jocko's pockets, taking his wallet and his change, his pocketknife and the gold-filled money clip he'd bought in Hong Kong when he won the trip. The clip was a miniature abacus which actually worked. When the boy's finger grazed Jocko's groin through the cloth, Jocko flinched. The blond boy slid the Cross pen from Jocko's shirt pocket. Jocko put his cheek against the car hood. The heat of the burning metal consoled him somewhat.

"Let me just get this, Riviera," the blond boy said. He slid Jocko's watch from his wrist. Bonnie had given him the watch, a digital which did everything short of cooking your breakfast.

Jocko turned his face in the boys' direction. Rick went through his wallet, taking out credit cards, throwing away receipts he'd saved for expense-account reimbursement and income-tax files. The blond one watched. When they found out how little there was, they'd be even more in a rage than they already were. Jocko straightened. He'd left the wet shape of himself in Bonnie's wax job. Engrossed, Rick had let the gun go slack. It now pointed down at the shell road, instead of at Jocko.

Jocko knew a little something about guns. All Southern boys did. In Georgia, his friends loved hunting: the drinking, the jokes, the bloody birds and deer. As a boy, he'd gone along. Since leaving Georgia, he had not picked up a gun. But he did know a little something about how they worked.

He looked around. He could make a run for it, but where? There was nowhere to go. They would have only one shot before they had to reload, but out here, one was enough. He might as well have a Target bull's-eye painted on his back. He didn't want to die and leave Jennifer alone again. He didn't want to die period. He didn't know what to do but wait. He'd seen some women on a talk-show once; the women had been raped. This was how they said it was. Scared to stay, scared to run.

Rick put the credit cards in his bluejeans pocket. He held up Jocko's plastic bank card and asked for the number. Jocko gave it to him. With Jocko's pen, the blond boy wrote down the number. It didn't matter. The account had less than a hundred dollars in it.

Jocko felt terrible for the women on the talk-show. Like he was personally responsible for what had happened to them. Sometime he thought that was why he liked women so much. Because he understood how they felt.

Having examined the take, the two boys nudged one another, trying to boost their spirits. The hatchet-faced boy kicked at the shell, sending up a puff of white dust.

"How come there ain't more?" he asked Jocko.

Jocko shrugged, trying to appear charming. "You boys caught me at a bad time," he said. "I'm busted."

"With a car like that?" the blond one said. He held up the watch. "This watch?" He held up the abacus. "This pure-gold money clip? Come on, Riviera. What do you take us for?"

Jocko shrugged again. "Well," he said, "It's true."

"What about your house? Maybe you got a safe."

"No. Nothing. There's nothing there. You don't want to go there. Believe me. I'm broke."

The boys looked away.

They took out Jocko's driver's license, then flipped through his pictures. The blond boy took his picture of Bonnie and the one of Jennifer and slid them both into his shirt pocket. He closed the pocket's pearl snap. Coming to another picture, they stopped. Rick leaned over; the blond boy pointed. It was Tee. She was behind Bonnie. Jocko had that funny feeling again, across the back of his neck. And then it hit him.

Tee sent them. He didn't know how it could have worked out that they had come to Target during the very twenty minutes he was parked there; it just had. Blind luck probably. Pure dumb blind luck. Or else maybe Tee had been spying. Maybe she knew what he was up to and where he went all the time. Maybe she watched out for him, same as he did her.

Another funny look passed between the boys. The blond one took the picture of Tee and slid it into his other shirt pocket. That one actually even looked like Tee and her family, the idiot Crossetts. He snapped the pocket shut. Maybe he was one of her ignorant nut-church cousins.

The dark boy whispered something. The blond one motioned Jocko over and told him to go down into the ditch next to the trees. Jocko did as he was told. The blond boy followed, catching hold of limbs and rocks to keep his balance.

Why would Tee do this? And had she? Just as when the two boys first approached the Buick, Jocko felt certain that both ends of opposite possibilities might be true. Something in him knew how outrageous the connection was; still, the suspicion rolled on, gathering the heft of truth in his mind. At least it made sense.

Leaning on the Buick, Rick held the shotgun. "Don't try nothing funny," he warned.

"Right here is fine," the blond boy said.

He pulled a roll of silver air-conditioning tape from his pocket, then went around behind Jocko, grabbed his wrists, and pushed the insides of his arms together. He began to wrap tape around Jocko's wrist . . . tight, leaving no slack. Jocko felt his fingers begin to swell. He wondered if they looked like his father's, pale blue and useless. The boy cut the tape with Jocko's pocketknife.

"Okay, Riviera," he said. He came around and stood in front of Jocko.

Man to man, Jocko knew what to do, kick the bad leg out from under the boy, then take off running. He looked up. The one with the moles had taken aim. Then what? Target practice?

Suddenly the blond boy threw his right leg out and with surprising, practiced grace swooped down in a squat on his left. The move was beautiful. Like the descent of a large bird. He began to pull more tape from the roll.

When he used to go goose hunting with his father, all Jocko wanted to do was watch the geese land in the rice field. He didn't want to kill the noisy birds, he just wanted to watch them sail down and, gabbling among themselves, peck for food. He had to shoot. His father checked. He used to close his eyes and squeeze, hoping to miss.

Jocko looked down at the boy's red hat.

"How'd you lose your leg?" he said.

The boy slapped at the outside of Jocko's ankle until Jocko got the idea and slid his feet in together.

"How'd you know?" The boy began to tape Jocko's ankles.

"My father," Jocko said, "had to have both his off. I recognized the walk."

"Tractor ran over me," the boy said, making another round with the tape. "I fell off, rot set in. I was six. Don't remember having a real one, it's been so long."

"That's terrible," Jocko said—heartfelt now, in the groove; he was cooking now. The boy circled his ankles once again. "Especially," Jocko said, "an a.k."

The boy cut the tape and, with the same agility as when he squatted, stood.

"Could be worse," he said. He stretched another length of tape from the roll.

From the road, Rick socked the hood of the Riviera and yelled for the boy with the cut-off leg to speed it up.

The blond one looked up in Rick's direction and folded back the brim of his hat.

"You talk too much, Riviera," he said. His cold blue eyes did not blink. Not so much like Tee after all.

"One thing," Jocko said. "Please. Did Tee send you?"

"Who?" The boy narrowed his eyes. It was a long shot but Jocko had to take it.

"Tee. Bettina Barnes. Bettina Crossett. The blond girl in my wallet. She was my wife. Are you maybe kin, or do you know her?"

"I know lots of girls," the boy said. He brought the tape closer to Jocko's mouth. "And," he added, "I do them all."

"But I need to tell her something." Jocko didn't mean to shout but he had lost control of his voice. The boy held the strip of tape between his hands. Jocko feinted left, shifted. "I need to. . . ."

The boy moved too quickly. A dead branch caught at his leg. The boy grabbed at Jocko's shoulder to keep from falling and then drew back his fist. The punch landed quickly, in the soft part of Jocko's middle, just above his waist. Jocko fell to his knees and then on down.

Inside his chest, it felt like something had burst.

From the road, Rick laughed his ignorant head off.

The blond one bent down and put his lips beside Jocko's ear. Jocko could feel the wetness of his breath. "We got your address, Riviera," he said. Jocko heard a clucking sound in his own throat. He could not breathe. "It's on your driver's license. We know where you live. You and your precious fucking baby girl. And the one on the way."

The blond boy pulled Jocko to his knees and spread the tape over his mouth, then reached into Jocko's shirt and grabbed Jocko's breast in his fist. The hat brim fell back down. With his thumb and forefinger, the boy pinched Jocko's nipple.

"Like that, don't you, Riviera," he said.

Jocko felt the pain clear back to his spine.

"I know you like it," the boy said. He let go of the nipple "You want to know about your fucking a.k. Tee?" he said. "If I knew I wouldn't tell you." He shoved. Jocko fell backwards, then rolled on his side.

The boy went away, double hopping on his good leg. "Think about it," he said as he went. "We got your address, dumb bunny."

The ground was covered with stickers and burrs. Small points pricked Jocko's cheek.

The car doors slammed. The Buick took off. From the road, Jocko—lying on his side, curled up into himself—was a sitting duck. They could do what they wanted, shoot, not shoot. The turnaround was less than a mile away. One way or the other, they would have to come back.

The sun hung in the smog above the radio tower. Light enough to aim by. Jocko had made a mistake asking the boy about his leg. The boy didn't know what a.k. meant. Jocko shouldn't have gone along. In

Bonnie's self-assertion class they taught her to scream, run, do anything except go along. He should have made a run for it. He should have done something—anything—instead of trying to make the whole thing make sense. He had never known how to be a man, not in his whole stupid life. He should not have been at the mall in the first place.

His breath settled a little. Reason was on his side. They had no cause to shoot him now. But then, so what reason; reason meant nothing out here. He heard the Buick coming back. The sun looked stuck on the radio tower, like a bug pinned to a corkboard.

Jocko turned his head toward the trees and closed his eyes. He felt like a prisoner facing the firing squad. Given the choice, unlike that murderer out in Utah, he thought he would ask for a hood to cover his eyes.

He drew his knees to his chest and rolled himself into as tight a ball as he could make. His life did not flash before him as he waited; he spent the time instead reciting something like prayers in his mind. He asked God, to whom he had not spoken in years, to spare his family. He begged Bonnie not to be home, to have taken Jennifer somewhere, anywhere in the car. He asked for her forgiveness for looking for Tee. Her kind of love, he assured Bonnie, the stable, caring kind, was the only love worth having.

Jennifer. . . . Oh Lord, well, Jennifer. It was too horrible. He put the picture of her straight out of his mind.

He tucked his chin and rested his forehead on his knuckles.

He did not want to think about Tee, not now; Tee was gone; he was over her. But want-to was a so-what issue now. In a flash in this, the worst moment of his life, there she was, not distant and moony like at the end, but *right there* in the flesh . . . laughing; sparkling like 7-Up, clear as the light on top of the Astrodome.

Life was a mystery. Jocko did not get it and he never would, who did what and for which reasons and what it all came to. Just there it all was. Blank and making no sense at all and just . . . out there.

Tee, he said to his first dream-girl love, *I know you were happy. I remember you with the baby, holding her on your lap. I remember you laughing. For a time there, I know you were happy.*

Jocko thought if he made himself small enough, he might actually roll away into the distance, turn into a tiny speck of nothing and eventually disappear.

Fat chance, he said to himself as the Buick arrived. But he had to try.

David Madden

THE LAST BIZARRE TALE

On July 23, 1921, a young Italian troubador came rolling into the East Tennessee mountain town with a one-ring circus and by nightfall lay with a tent stake in his chest. On August 14, 1989, he was to be buried in a hillside cemetery by the railroad tracks.

The young man mowing grass had never heard of the murder, nor did he know why the man on the hillside below was breaking the rocky ground with a spade. The sun rising, he was wondering why he had accepted this job instead of going back home to Bristol. He didn't want to be reminded of Ricky. Things like the mausoleum were what had driven him over the mountains into this remote and very different region. He did not mind remembering Ricky's funeral. But without ever seeing it, the mausoleum Ricky's mother had erected had disturbed him.

What kind of mind and heart, he had often wondered, did it take even to imagine a replica of Ricky's room inside a mausoleum? Doing it took a year and almost wrecked the family business and Ricky's parents' marriage. On the day he would have graduated from high school, it was ready for Ricky's mother to enter. Over the past year, she had visited it, sat in the room, according to talk around Bristol, and kept it clean herself. Jeff would go out of his way to avoid even passing the gates of the cemetery. Of the five in the car, Jeff alone had survived the crash. He sometimes wondered how he would survive in a world where people like Ricky's mother did such bizarre things.

Precariously riding the mower across the hillside past photographs of the deceased set in the gravestones, past urns of plastic flowers, Jeff could not help but imagine Ricky's mausoleum and wish all the harder that there had been a job opening for him when he arrived in South Mountain yesterday afternoon.

Word had reached the streets of Bristol that the South Mountain city fathers, with help from the federal government, had funded the restoration of the town as a way of drawing tourists off the major artery that came from Washington, D.C., down the Shenandoah Valley through Bristol to venture over two-lane mountain roads to South Mountain. After a year of indecisiveness, he needed to make some money so he could make a move—into the university to study engineering or into Europe for a bike tour so he could think over possibilities. No money at all left him open to the temptation to join the Air Force to learn how to fly a helicopter.

He had delayed too long; the jobs were all taken. But as he watched men tearing up the streets and laying brick sidewalks, he heard two other unemployed men saying they'd rather starve than cut grass in the cemetery on an open hillside in the hellfire of August. Jeff asked where to go, and got the job. So far, the morning heat was bad, but not horrendous. Being forced to imagine Ricky's mother's private freak show was.

Jeff wondered why the man digging the new grave below by the railroad track kept looking up at him. Maybe he's just suspicious of strangers. Or maybe I'm cutting into his work.

After three passes above where he was digging, the man yelled up at Jeff, "You be careful now!"

"I am, don't worry!"

"You the one better worry! The regular mower tipped it over on himself and he's in intensive care right now!"

Jeff felt a chill in his scalp.

"Where's your cap?"

"Don't have one!"

"None of my business, but that sun'll turn your brainpan into a hot skillet 'fore you even know what hit you!"

"Hope not!"

"Come take mine! I'm used to it!"

Jeff said no thanks, but the gravedigger insisted so bossily, he caved

in, parked his mower, left it idling, and trounced down the steep
hillside to the level ground by the railroad track.

"Three years in 'Nam will 'climatize you for the rest of your life,"
the gravedigger said. Long exposure had burned him dark, but his
hollow eyes and sharp jawbones made him look like death warmed
over, as Jeff's grandmother used to say.

Jeff took the cap the Vietnam veteran handed him and, putting it
on, asked, "How long does it take to dig a grave?"

"Forever, seems like, but by noon it'll be ready for him."

"Who's that?"

"Old Spaghetti."

"Did you say Old Spaghetti?" Jeff always played along with older
people who like to talk that way.

"Called him Spaghetti 'cause he was a wop."

"Not many Italians live around here, I bet."

"Right. But this one didn't live here either. More like here was just
where he was being dead all these years."

"Well, how old was he?"

"They say he was twenty-one when he was killed, but if he had
lived, he would be about ninety by now."

This man is not worried about whether I have a heat stroke or not,
Jeff thought; he just wants somebody to tease. If I were twenty-one he
probably wouldn't do it. "I don't get it."

"Where you from anyway?"

"From over at Bristol."

"Tennessee or Virginia?"

"Virginia side. What difference does it make?"

"Makes all the difference in the world, but either side, you bound to
have heard of Spaghetti."

"Never did. Or if I did, I forgot."

The vet went back to digging, and Jeff sensed that telling it would
take him a while. He wished he had turned off the mower. The sound
of the motor forced him to strain to hear, and the exhaust drifting
down the slope stung his eyes.

"Well, he was a wandering singer and violin player who took up with
a little one-tiger circus and come rolling into South Mountain July 23
in 19-and-21, and they found him that night dead out back of a

tobacco warehouse that used to be on the west side of town. Somebody had stobbed him in the chest with a spare tent spike, they never knew who. Didn't nobody know his name, but they knew he was Eye-talian, so they just called him Spaghetti—well, that was later because at first there wasn't any reason to call him anything. He was just your everyday corpse lying at Smythe's Funeral Home on the third floor of the Smythe building, over Smythe's hardware store, by the railroad track where nobody paid any attention at first. No reason to.

"The circus broke camp and moved on and sent word to the young man's father in Chicago, who promised to send money to ship him home."

Suffering the heat of the rising sun, Jeff watched the Vietnam vet, the digging and the telling synchronized.

"Didn't come, and it didn't come, so there being a law you had to bury or embalm within three days, Smythe embalmed and left him in the coffin, hoping the money would come after all. Them Smythes. They're the ones behind this restoration scam. Who's gonna come to see it? They used to come to see Spaghetti all the time, though.

"After about a year of laying in that coffin and turning black as a Nigerian, they couldn't spare the coffin if they was to stay the richest family in the county, so they trussed him up on wires against the wall." His digging-talking rhythm seemed hypnotic. "That's how the choo-choo train curving over the trestle threw its beam through one bare window and out the other, swooping across the room, exposing, only to the engineer of course, what they called the Mummy of South Mountain. That light like threading needles. The engineers carried it from town to town, and this is a major line, you know, from Richmond, and so it got to be a scary story that got all over in those days, until the engineers would let you come up there with them in the cab so you could see what they saw, for a price. But the railroad made them cut it out after a few years.

"By then, you know, the word was out and some folks passing through would get out of their cars or off the bus or even off the trains and show up at Smythe's hardware store and ask could they see it. Why, sure, they could see it. And they would climb up to the third floor and look at it, and look out at the tracks to see how the light they had heard about must have shot through the windows. And those

Smythes would ask for a donation to help send Spaghetti back where he came from. They say it was some sight."

Jeff was appalled by what he was hearing. "Did you ever see it?"

"No, I never got to see it because by the time I come along, they had quit showing it except a for a select few, and my folks were not among the select few. And after I had been to 'Nam and back, I didn't have any desire to look at it. I've lost my interest in human interest sights like that."

"So you're digging his grave now?"

"I'm digging Old Spaghetti's grave because the town wants to turn into something cute and mummies ain't cute no more, and tomorrow the new mayor and some state representative from Memphis who's a relative of the dearly departed and a few others will come here for a little ceremony, and after the grave settles, in about a month, they'll erect a monument to him."

"Do they finally know his name?"

"Yes, I heard it said, but I can't recall it. You'll have to stick around or come back and read it for yourself right where you're standing. No, don't move. You're casting a nice shady shadow on me."

"Well, what I don't understand—"

"What don't you understand? What? What? What?"

"Mind if I ask?"

"No, just run up there and turn off that damn mower. My nerves is frayed enough just on general principles. And that exhaust is too much."

Jeff gladly did it.

"What don't you understand?"

"Well, how the law would let them do it, for one thing."

"Do what?"

"Let him just hang there, wired up to a nail in the wall that way for the whole world to see."

"Smytheses was, is, the law. They're in everything around here. Some say they're even in the Klan. Guardian of morals right up to now. They want to censor the videos, they—"

"But didn't the singer's father ever send for him?"

"Never did. Maybe he died of a heart attack. Who knows. In the twenties, some said it was the Mafia that sent a hit man down here to

do it. See, it all depended on when you were born. Different generations had different attitudes about it. Like when I was growing up, it
was a dirty little secret. People were ashamed of Spaghetti. Now days
it's just P.R. pure and simple."

"And how about the church people? Isn't it blasphemous or sacrile-
gious or something not to bury somebody?"

"Probably, but that's just for homefolks, not for a double alien like
he was. Eye-talian plus being circus scum, way they looked at it."

"But would they have let that happen to a criminal?"

"Never did."

"Or even a lynched black man?"

"Of course not. Inhumane."

"Then I don't understand."

"What's there to not understand? People are crazy, don't you know
that yet, boy?"

Jeff watched him digging, thinking of Ricky's mother, sitting this
very minute, it being Saturday, in the replica of Ricky's room, inside a
mausoleum in the Bristol city cemetery. He wondered what the
Vietnam veteran would think of that bizarre tale. Bizarre tales. Jeff felt
stuffed full of them, from infancy on to this new one. The bizarre,
violent past. The Civil War tales. The World War I tales. The World
War II tales. The Korean conflict tales. The Vietnam stories on TV
that he could now barely remember. The folksy tales of the Southern
Appalachians, full of cruel jokes. Backdrop to the blandness of the past
ten years of his own life. The blank of his future. A profession in
engineering? Helicopter school inspired by this grave digger's era? A
bike trip through Europe, on an off-the-deep-end impulse? A crazy
world to have such people as these South Mountain people in it. All
those generations of mummy show-offs.

"Yeah, boy, the sooner you realize that people are crazy, the better
off you'll be."

"Hearing this story doesn't really make me feel any better off, I'll
tell you."

"It's just a story."

"No, it's not just a story. That man once breathed this same air like
you and me. First, somebody murdered him, and then the whole town
took away his dignity as a human being."

"A corpse ain't got no dignity. Now listen to what I'm telling you. See this hole? All corpses go in a hole just like this hole. Or they burn and blow away. Get used to it, boy."

"Don't it make you feel bad? Thinking of him all those years, naked, on exhibition like a freak in the sideshow?"

"Why would it make me feel bad? And he wasn't naked." The vet handed Jeff the shovel. "Here. Hold this a second." He pulled out his wallet and dug in it and came out with a photograph. "See?"

Jeff saw an almost naked, very skinny, coal-black man, with a huge white smile like the janitor of his grammar school had, and he wore a kind of diaper. "What's this?"

"See, he's wearing a thing like an Indian to hide his dingdong of doom."

"That's Old Spaghetti?" Jeff regretted saying his nickname out loud. "He looks real."

"Used to be lot of barroom jokes about what sex was he. And writing on the latrine walls, even in my grammar school, I remember. Smythe had to keep his eye on the kids, of course. But, hell, the Smythes tell it that they caught some of these high society ladies peeking up under his flap to see what it looked like after all that time."

"Who's that standing beside him?"

"That's my only surviving picture of my daddy."

"Your daddy? Why would he want his picture taken beside—the—?"

"To show off to his buddies in his outfit. He was home on leave. That's my only picture of him. He was killed in the invasion at Salerno."

Jeff wondered whether the vet showed the photograph to his own buddies in the Vietnam war as a joke. He wanted to ask, hoping not.

Jeff handed the gravedigger his shovel. "Well, hold it till I get it put away."

The vet put the photograph back, took the shovel, and continued to dig.

Nauseated by the heat and the lack of food and the last bizarre story he ever wanted to hear, Jeff started to walk away.

"So now do you understand?"

"No."

"What more do you want to know?"

"Nothing."

"Don't go away mad."

"I guess you need to finish digging and I need to finish mowing. . . . Here's your hat."

"You need that hat."

"No, I appreciate it, but I got a handkerchief I can rig up—tie it at four ends and fit it over my head. It'll do. Thanks."

On the mower, Jeff tried to go over his options for the future again, to imagine how each might work out, but the young Italian singer stayed on his mind. He tried to fend off images and thoughts of the murder and the desecration that followed, year by year. The young man could have lived on to this very day, a ninety-year-old man who had experienced the world as all those who had lived had experienced it. The Roaring Twenties. The Depression. The World War II Era. The Atomic Age. The Space Age. And some faint taste of the present vanilla age. Was the man who embalmed him still alive? Probably not. No, he didn't want to dwell anymore on those people, the curious who came by foot, and wagon, and car, and bus, and train, and airplane, who passed through here to take a look and go away to tell the bizarre tale, to call attention to themselves as the source.

Mowing, mindful of the danger of tipping over, mindful of the steady rhythm of the vet's digging down by the railroad track, the same track that crossed the trestle passed the third-story window of the building where the singer once hung by wire from a nail in the wall, he tried not to let the questions sink their hooks into him. Did a fellow Italian put a curse on him? The evil eye? How many thousands of photographs like the one of the World War II soldier, father of the Vietnam vet, had been taken with the mummy singer and put away in drawers or albums all over the world? Japanese, Germans, Russians, one or two at least, may have passed through here and heard about it and asked to see it and asked to be photographed so they could show it back home. Like those lawmen photographed with the corpses of the Younger brothers and later Dillinger's.

Did "Ripley's Believe It or Not" mummify him in a book? Wasn't it a violation of all known burial rights or rites in the recorded history of mankind? And yet he vaguely remembered that one of the bizarre tales his kin thrived on had been about the custom in remote mountain villages of hanging the family dead in the barn in cold weather until the ground was soft enough for grave digging. And didn't one man keep his wife hanging in the barn because he hadn't the heart to part with her? Or had he dreamed that? And yes, they had, in one town many long years ago hung a lynched black man in the show-window of a millinery shop on the town square for public display, but only for three days, not for over half a century. Why were other unclaimed bodies not treated that way? Thousands of funerals and decent burials over the many decades had taken place here, while the singer hung naked. Grave robbers and cemetery vandals had been sent to jail over the years. The banality of evil—he had heard that somewhere about the Holocaust and why and how it could have happened.

Maybe he shouldn't judge them by present-day standards. But he didn't want to condone that prolonged act of desecration. If he was to live in this world, he needed to understand how such things happened. Something in human nature made it possible? What? Too blazing hot to think! He would be delirious even before he realized it.

But he could not stop trying to see. The vet had talked about generations. Something happens to each generation. The generation in place when the singer was murdered allowed a process to get started, so that in the Depression years, the original generation had been displaced, time-the-neutralizer had dehumanized them, made them into clichés, stereotypes—all the people, and the singer with them, turning him into Old Spaghetti, a joke. But underneath it all must have been a steady sense, like the one he felt now, of nausea. Time displaced the mummy, too, and people living here and coming through could think of him in the same way you think of the Egyptian mummies on display in the Museum of Natural History in Washington, D.C. Even Boris Karloff as the mummy in the late movie.

The present generation feels shame, tries to bury the past, but it comes too late to rectify. Rest in peace, among the unloving living who are all in love with death.

Jeff stopped the mower. He had moved aslant, not straight across. He shut off the motor. He staggered down the hillside to the gravesite where only the Vietnam vet's cap showed above the rim of the grave.

"Hey!"

"You scared me half to death," he said, putting on.

"Do me a favor. Tell the keeper I quit. He doesn't owe me anything. See you."

Jeff walked down the railroad track toward the next road that would cross it, wherever that might be.

A road was not far ahead. And he caught a ride as soon as he stuck out his thumb. Coincidentally, the man was headed for Bristol. Jeff felt it would probably turn out to be a damned bizarre coincidence. The man asked if Jeff were from around South Mountain, and he said no, Bristol, the Virginia side.

They lapsed into silence, and he was thankful. Weak from the heat and the lack of food, he tried to sleep to keep from thinking about the singer who would be buried tomorrow. He felt guilty for not being there to pay his respects. But he was so glad to get out of that town, so glad. And when, six hours later, he knew he was only five miles from Bristol, from home, he was so glad, to have put that town and those people behind him, and even Ricky's mother seemed likely.

But he kept thinking of all the people who has passed through that town and collaborated with the townspeople in the desecration of the young circus singer. But wait, he thought, what about me? Don't I count? If I feel bad, that means one person on this earth feels something, whatever it is, for the wandering singer. But that prideful revelation made him feel ashamed of himself.

Wait now, if I feel that way, there must have been other people who did, too. Who went to see him eagerly or even reluctantly but did go, and then felt, when they actually saw him on exhibit, some compassion, and went away imagining him as a real human being who had lived and been murdered and then desecrated by his fellowman. Enough people like that after all, men and women, young and old, who did not laugh or feel a cheap thrill. Who resurrected him in their feeling of compassion and in their imaginations as they walked away, rode away—and some who lived on in that town—to all points, north, south, west, east of the world, with images in their heads, stories in their mouths. And so the singer has had a life in those responses, a life he wouldn't have had even if he had lived to this day, or tomorrow. The same rush of energy he felt in seeing that had been loosed into the world many times before by other people, hadn't it? Mind and body, he was totally awake. He felt too confined in the car. He had to get out and walk.

The man stopped and Jeff got out and the car sped on ahead and he continued on foot, walking, walking fast, feeling an intuitive sense of there being images of the singer in the heads of people in every corner of the world, as far as India, even as far as the South and North Poles, passed on from generation to generation. A sudden feeling that the singer lives everywhere, more intensely than Ricky had lived, than Ricky's mother, than the Vietnam gravedigger, than all those townspeople, than Jeff himself, lifted him into a leap of exhilaration.

Jill McCorkle

FINAL VINYL DAYS

I'll never forget the day Betts moved in. How could I? Open the apartment door and there she was with two suitcases, a purple futon, and two milk crates full of albums. It was 1984, the day after Marvin Gaye died. That's how I remember so well. I had just gotten home from my job at Any Old Way You Choose It Music, where the Marvin Gaye bin had emptied within a couple of hours. I'd spent the afternoon marveling at what happens when somebody kicks. For years, other than the Motown faithfuls and a brief flurry after *The Big Chill*, that bin was neglected; I had even *dusted* it back when everybody was BeeGee Disco Crap Berserk. Now Marvin is dead and there's a run on his music. Same thing happened with Elvis and John Lennon, always good sellers, but incredibly so when they died.

"You want me here, don't you?" Betts asked, her thick dark hair hitting her shoulders. Her eyes were always wide open as if she were seeing the world for the first time, every object catching her attention. She was staring at me; I was the object of her attention for the moment. "I mean I've been staying every night so I might as well have my things, right? And by the way," she was saying, "I could use some help." The purple futon was unrolled and halfway in the apartment. "We don't need this, but Helen said she didn't want it." Helen was the roommate, a physics major who liked to test all the physical properties during sex. Betts had said (before she started coming to my place) that it was driving her crazy (the shaking plaster and peculiar sounds). I didn't tell her but it was driving me *crazy*, for different reasons, the main one being that I was a wee bit curious about what took place on the other side of that wall. Betts's side was pretty tame: a bulletin board covered in little notes and photos and ticket stubs, a huge poster of a skeleton. She was majoring in physical therapy and was taking it all real seriously (too seriously if you ask me) or depending, *not* seriously enough. "I am not a masseuse," she said often enough with no smile whatsoever. Short on sense of humor but long on legs. Sometimes you have to pick and choose. Sometimes you buy an album for just one song, thinking that the others will start to grow on you. When she finally got that futon in, she pulled out her Duran Duran album and that's when I put my foot down. We were from different time zones. She had a whole list of favorite *good old songs*: "Afternoon Delight" and "Muskrat Love" to name two.

I played Marvin: "Stubborn Kind of Fella," "It Takes Two," "Mercy Mercy Me." She just shrugged and went back in my room to arrange her little junk all over the top of my dresser and all over the back of the commode. I just sat there with Marvin, tried to image what it must feel like to know that your old man is about to kill you like Marvin did.

"Why did he wear that hat all the time?" Betts asked, looking the same way she did when she asked me why I still wore my hair long enough to pull back in a ponytail. "IS he the guy who sings that 'Sexual Healing' song?" She was standing in the kitchen with a two-liter Diet Coke in one hand and a handful of Cheetos in the other. She's the healthy one. She's the one bitching about an occasional joint. It's okay for her to go downtown and pound down beer with her girlfriends but for godssakes don't do anything illegal. "We've got to fix this place," she was saying. "And did you say you were going back to graduate school in the fall?"

"No." I shook my head and watched her peek under a dishcloth like she expected a six-foot snake to pop out. She sounded just like my mother, asking me if I just said what she knows I never in the hell did. Those were her words, *graduate school*. When my mom does it, the secret words are electrical appliance store. My old man owns one in a town so big it actually has two gas stations, and he'd rather pull his nose off of his face with a wrench or beat up a new Maytag washer than to have me in his employment. Mom says things like, "Didn't you say you were looking for a job where you can advance in the business?" That's when I always click the phone up and down or flip on the blender and plead bad connection. It's a real bad connection, Mom. And there stood Betts, swigging her NutraSweet, eating her flourescent cheese, waiting for an answer.

"You know that night we first met, you said you had been in law school and were thinking about going back."

"I said that?" I asked and she nodded. "Did I tell you I quit law school and joined VISTA? Spent a year in the Appalachian Mountains with diarrhea?" She nodded a bored affirmative. "Did I tell you I loved it?"

"No."

"Well, that's because I didn't. But what I learned in that year is that I could do anything I wanted to do, you know?"

"So?" She took a big swallow of NutraSyrup, then wiped her mouth and hands with enough paper towels to equal a small redwood. "What are you going to do?"

"I'm doing it." I lifted the stylus off of Marvin and cleaned the album, my hand steady as I watched that Motown label spin. She was still staring in disbelief. It was a real bad connection. As good-looking as she was, it was a real bad connection. I left for five seconds, long enough to go pee and see her little ceramic eggs filled with perfumed cedar shavings on the back of the john, and in that brief five minutes, she put on Boy George. What we prided ourselves on most at Any Old Way You Choose It Music then was that we did just that, *chose it* without regard to sales and top tens and who's who. Like if I was in one mood, I might play the Beatles all day long, might play "Rubber Soul" two times in a row: I had whole weekends where all I played were the Stones, Dylan, or the Doors, and then followed it with a Motown Monday, a Woodstock Wednesday. Some days I just went for somebody like Buffy St. Marie or Joan Baez, which always surprised the younger clientele, people like Betts, people who might say who's that? Screw them.

"You mean you're going to work there forever?" Betts asked. Boy George staring up at me from the floor. Her fingers were tapping along to "Do You Really Want to Hurt Me?"

"I'm buying in," I told her, which was not entirely a lie. The owner, a guy my age who had already made it big in the local business scene, was considering it. He graduated with a D average from a small second-rate junior college, and found a small empire already carved out by his old man. I graduated from the University with a 3.7 in English and philosophy, highest honors for some old paper I wrote about Samuel Coleridge, and what I got was one of those little leather kits for your toiletries. *What toiletries?* I had wanted to ask my mom, who said she remembered me saying I needed one of those. Yeah right. I *need* a toiletries kit.

"I'm doing okay," I said and lifted the stylus from Boy George, searched in earnest for The Kinks so Betts could ask some more dumb questions. She came over and knelt beside me, put her head close to mine, little orange Cheeto sparkles above her lip.

"I know you're doing okay," she whispered and pressed her mouth against my neck. "You're better than okay," she said. "My friends all think you're interesting in a kind of weird way, you know, mysterious." Though her knowledge of gross anatomy was limited at that stage of the game, her own anatomy was doing quite nicely. Too nicely really because it made me a dishonest person. I was thinking *bad connection, bad connection,* and yet I let her play her albums and pull me to the floor. "Isn't it great I've moved in?" she asked ten minutes later, the needle hugging the wide smooth grooves of the last song, a long silent begging for the needle to be lifted. "Isn't it going to be wonderful?" she asked, but all I could think about when I closed my eyes was Marvin standing there in his hat, his old man with pistol aimed. Betts moved in the day after he died and he hadn't been dead three months when she moved out; she pled guilty to not *truly* loving me, and I turned on the somber brokenhearted look long enough to pack up her books and hand them out to the squat-bodied pathology resident who she had taken up with and who was waiting for her. "Here's a live one for you," I told him and patted her on the back.

I didn't really *miss her* so much as I just missed. The young jerky store owner was still dangling his carrots about *maybe* letting me buy in. I told him he was getting too far away from the old stuff, the good stuff, but he insisted that we *go with the flow*. He didn't want me monopolizing the sound system with too much of the old stuff; he said Neil Young made his skin crawl. He was just sick all over that he hadn't kept his Rick Nelson stock up to date. I figured what the hell, did I *really* want to be in business with such a sleaze? I took a little vacation to get myself feeling up, to get Betts out of my bones, and then I was back full force, nothing on the back of my john, no album that never should have been on my shelves. But before too long, there I was hanging up T-shirts of the Butthole Surfers. Things were getting bad.

I thought things couldn't get any worse, but let a couple of years spin by and they did. There were prepubescent girls with jewelry-store names running around shopping malls singing songs they didn't deserve to sing. It was plagiarism; it was distasteful. Where were the *real* women? Where was Grace Slick? Then there was a run on Roy Orbison's music, and once again my jerk of a boss was in a state of panic that he'd missed yet another good-time oldie post-mortem sale. He was eating cocaine for breakfast by then and had a bad case of the DBCs (Dead Brain Cells). I might sleep around now and then; I might even end up with somebody who was born after 1968, but at least I'm moral about it. He gets them tanked and snorted and then goes for the prize. One step above being a necro if you ask me. And what really pisses me off is that society sees me as the loser, the social misfit who's living in the past. The guy drives a BMW and owns a condo and a business, stuffs all his money up his nose, pokes teen-age coeds who don't remember that he did it, and he's successful.

I was just about to the point where I couldn't tune it all out when I landed up with a bad hangover that turned into the flu and landed me in one of those fast-food medicine places. You know; a Doc in the Box, planted right beside Revco so you can rush right over and fill your prescription. I felt like hell and I was about to stretch out on their green vinyl couch and snooze when I saw someone familiar. It was Marlene Adams, a girl from home, a woman of my time, no ring on her hand, good-looking as ever. I sat straight up and was about to say something when she turned calmly and called my name. "I was wondering when you'd recognize me," she said and laughed, her eyes as blue as the crisp autumn sky. "I had heard you were still living around here. Who told me that? Somebody I saw at a wedding not too long ago." For a split second I was feeling better, felt like grabbing a bucket of chicken and sitting in the park, throwing a Frisbee, going to some open-air concert. "You haven't changed a bit," she said, and I felt her gaze from head to toe. It was the first time in years that I was *worried* about how I looked.

"Neither have you." I sat up straight, smoothed back my hair. God, why hadn't I taken a shower? "Why're you here?" I asked and glanced to the side where there was a cloudy aquarium with one goldfish swimming around. "I thought you were some place like California or Colorado or North Dakota. I thought you were married." I thought that fish must feel like the only son of a bitch on the planet, thirty gallons of water and nobody to swim over and talk to.

"Divorced. I'm back in graduate school, psychology," she said and laughed. "And I'm in this office because I tripped down some steps." I turned back from the dismal fish to see her holding out her right foot, her ankle blue and swollen. She had on a little white sock, the kind my mother always wore with her tennis shoes, little colored pompom balls hanging off the back.

"Can you believe it?" She shook her head back and forth. "It was really embarrassing. There were loads of people in the library when it happened." She leaned back, her thick hair fanning behind her as she stared up at the ceiling. I kept expecting her to say something really stupid and mundane and patronizing like *so, you say that you're living here but not in graduate school, you sell albums and tapes to coeds who you occasionally sleep with, you say that you have a hangover, what I'm hearing from you is that you are in search of a sex partner who has possibly heard of some of the songs of your youth.*

"I'm just as clumsy as I was the time we went camping," she said, her voice light and far removed from that psychological monotone I'd just imagined. "Remember? You swore you'd never take me again?"

"And I didn't," I said. "I never got the chance." I turned back to the fish. It was an awkward moment. You don't often get to discuss breaking up years after the fact, but we were doing it. She dumped me, and now that I had reminded her of that fact, she was talking in high gear to cover the tracks. *Why does it take so long to get seen in this place?*

and *When have you ever been home? Does your dad still have the refrigerator store* and *Is your mom well?*

I was relieved when the door opened and the nurse called me in. "See you around," I said politely, half hoping that she'd disappear while I was gone. Marlene and I were the same age from the same small town, the same neighborhood even. I had known her since my family moved to that town when I was in the fifth grade and we had all run around screaming the words to "I Want to Hold Your Hand" and crossing our eyes like Ringo. That was the common ground that had brought us together that month in college to begin with.

I thought about it all while they stuck a thermometer in my mouth and instructed me to undress. Marlene had been pretty goofy as a kid, and though I considered her a friend, I never would have ridden my bike over to her house to *visit.* She had this dog named Alfie, who smelled like crap, thus leaving Marlene and her wet-dog-smelling jeans rather undesirable. In junior high, Matt Walker and I had suggested we put Alfie in front of a firing squad, and Marlene didn't speak to me for weeks after. No big deal, but then in high school we got to be pals just sort of hanging outside in the breezeway where you were allowed to smoke in between classes. Can you believe they *let* us smoke at school? That *they*, the administrators, those lopsided adults had *designated* an area? I spent a lot of time there and so did Marlene. She was on the Student Council, which most of us thought was a bunch of crap, but still, she was forever circulating some kind of petition. She was really into womanhood, which I found kind of titillating in a strange way, don't ask me why, though I never did anything about it at the time. She was a hard worker, a smart girl. That's the kind of shit people wrote in her yearbook if they wrote anything at all. Nineteen-seventy was not a big year for yearbook signing. But then, get the girl off to college and there was major metamorphosis; it was like I could watch it happen there in poli sci lecture, blonde streaks in her hair that hung to her waist, little cropped T-shirts and cutoff jeans, her tinted wire-rim glasses (aviator style like Gloria Steinem's) always pushed up on her head. Guys waited to see where she was going to sit and then clustered around her. God, she was beautiful, and then I had to take a turn just sitting and *listening* to all that was going on in her life just as she had *listened* to me there in the smoking area. I had a girlfriend here and there along the way, but I guess I was really waiting for Marlene to come around. Her boyfriend had been drafted, and though she told me how lucky I was not to have been taken (lucky break, legal blindness; my brother winged me in the left eye with a sharp rock when I was seven), I could tell that I was somehow weakened in her eyes. There would have been much more admiration had I had 20-20 vision and fled to Canada. It was a brief affair, the consummation of any likes we'd had for each other since adolescence, and then it was over, one fiasco of a camping trip, pouring down rain, Marlene spraining her thumb when she tripped over a tree limb and landed face down in the mud. It amazed me the things that that damn thumb *hindered* her from doing. It was a loss of a weekend.

"You have the flu," the nurse told me after I'd waited forever in my underwear, and I made my way back out to the lone-fish lobby to find her still there, though now her ankle was all neatly bound in an ace bandage.

"You don't look so great," she said. "Why don't I go home with you and fix something for lunch?" I just shrugged, thinking about what was in my kitchen cabinet, a molded loaf of bread, a couple of cans of tomato soup, one can of tuna. If she could turn it into something, I'd beg her to never leave me.

"What about your car?" I asked, and again she pointed to her ankle.

"I can't drive. My ankle." For a minute she sounded just like she had years before, *I can't do that, my thumb,* and I should have listened to the warning but I was too taken by her features, a face that needed no makeup of any kind, a girl who *looked* like she *ought* to be a perfect camper. "I rode the bus here," she said and extended her hand for me to help her out. "It'll be fun to catch up on things."

Marlene and I picked up with each other like we'd never been apart. It was like we could read each other's mind, and so we carefully avoided talking about the time we broke up. Instead we focused on all the good times, things we had in common just by being the same age and from the same town. Like I might say, "Remember when Tim Oates cut off the top of his finger in shop?" and she'd say, "Yeah, he was making a TV table for his mama." Things like that. We had things in common that might *seem* absolutely stupid to an outsider. After three glorious months, tripling our first time together, Marlene and I finally came around to talking out all the things that ruined us before. She was starting to kind of hint about how she was going to be a professional and how maybe I would want to be a *professional* too. I started singing that song, "I see by your outfit that you are a cowboy, you see by my outfit that I'm a cowboy, too."

"C'mon," she said and wrapped her arms around my neck. "I don't mean to give you a hard time, it's just I've heard you say how you really want. . . ." Bad connection, bad connection.

"So get you an outfit and let's all be cowboys." I finished the song, and she went to take her exam in a real pissed-off state. I did what I always do when I'm feeling lousy, which is to sort through my albums and play all of my favorite cuts. I should have been a deejay, the lone jockey on the late-night waves, rather than employee to a squat coked-to-the-gills little rich shit. I thought of Marlene writing some little spiel about *composure; heal thyself.* I was playing Ten Years After full blast. Sly and the Family Stone on deck. And then all in one second I felt mad as hell, as mad as I'd been on that pouring-rain camping trip when Marlene told me that it was hard for her to think of me as anything except a *friend.* She actually said that. It all came back to me when I saw that old Black Sabbath album, which is what she had left behind that other time she moved out. Thanks a whole helluva lot. Warms my heart to see a green-faced chick draped in scarves wandering around what looks like a mausoleum. She had said *all* the routine things you can think of to say. "I know you don't really care about *me,*" she had said. "I could be *anybody.*"

"Yeah, right," I told her. "I could cuddle up with Pat Paulson and not care. I'm just that kind of insensitive jerk."

"But you don't care about *me,*" she had said and pounded her chest with her hand, which was wrapped in a bath towel to protect the sprained thumb which had left her an asolute invalid. "I need to be my own person, have my own life." I found out a day later that she already had all the info on all these schools in the West; she had been looking for a good time to bale out and it seemed camping out in a monsoon was as good as any. It was hard to remember but it seemed I said something like, "And I don't need to have my own life?" and then the insults got thicker until before long I was told that I was apathetic and chauvinistic and my brain was stuck between my legs.

"So, that's why you're always asking what I'm thinking," I said in response. By that time we were soaking wet and driving back *down* the rest of this mountain in a piece-of-crap car I had at the time, an orange Pinto, with a Jimi Hendrix tape playing full blast (eight track, of course). "And what kind of stupid question is that anyway, and yet you always ask it. *What are you thinking?*" Yeah, that was how the whole ride home went, and of course any time I had a good line, any time I scored, then she got to cry and say what an ass I was.

By the time she got home from her lousy test, I was as mad as if I was there in the pouring rain, jacking that screwed-up Pinto to change a flat while she sat on the passenger side and started straight ahead at that long stretch of road we had to travel before I could put her out. Apparently she had been thinking through it all as well because she walked into my apartment looking just as she had when I dumped her out in front of her dorm years before. We had both played over the old stuff enough that we had independently been furious and now were simply exhausted and ready to have it all end, admit the truth. Nothing in common other than walking the planet at the same time. She was barely over her divorce, she rationalized (he had dumped her, I was delighted to find). I handed her that Black Sabbath album on her way out, and we made polite promises about keeping in touch.

And now I've come to this: Final Vinyl Days, the end of an era. Perfectly round black vinyl discs, their jackets faded, sit on the small table before my checkout and await extinction. I stare across the street, the black asphalt made shiny by the drizzling rain, the traffic light blinking red and green puddles in the gray light where a mammoth parking deck is under construction. There I see the lights in the store we compete with, Record City, and I can't help but wonder when they'll change their name: CD Metropolis. But what can I say about names? Any Old Way You Choose It ain't exactly true either.

"Record City doesn't have *these*," my boss had said just last week and began putting this crap all over the place, you know, life-size cutouts of Marilyn Monroe and Elvis, little replicas of the old tabletop jukeboxes that are *really* CD houses, piñatas and big plastic blowup dinosaurs. I work nights now, not as much business and I don't have to argue with the owner about what I play overhead. As far as I'm concerned, the new kids on the block are still Bruce Springsteen and Jackson Browne. My boss said it was a promotion, but I know better. Janis Joplin's singing now, "Me and Bobby McGee," and the Stones are on deck with "Jumping Jack Flash." The Stones are the cockroaches of rock. They'll be around when civilization starts over, and I cling to this bit of optimism.

I had no choice but to give in to CDs. And yeah, they sound great, that's true. It's just the principle of the thing, your hand forced to change. Not to even mention the dreaded task of *replacing*. It's impossible. Think of what's *not* available. I'm just taking my time is all. I figure if I just go from the year of my birth to the year I graduated from college, it'll take the rest of my life. I'm going alphabetically so that I don't miss anything, and it's a real boring calculated way to approach life. I mean, what if that's how I dealt with women? Imagine it: Betts, Erica, Gail, Marlene, Nancy, that one who always wore black, either Pat or Pam, Susie, Xanadu. Yeah right, Xanadu. I thought it was kinda cute that she had gone and renamed herself. Then I learned that she had never even heard of Coleridge, but rather had some vivid childhood memory of Olivia Newton John. Scary. We were in a bar and it was very very late so what could I expect? "Let's get physical," I suggested, and she raised her pencil-thin eyebrows as if trying to remember where she'd heard *that* line before. "Can I call you Xan?"

"Oh sure," she said, "everybody does." And when she walked ahead of me to the door, I noticed her spiderweb stockings complete with rhinestone spider. She wore a black spandex miniskirt, and I realized that my knowledge of women's fashions had come full circle. I looked at myself in the beer-can-lined mirror to affirm that, yes, I had hit bottom. Xan and I had *nothing* in common except cotton mouth and body hair.

Now Del Shannon has gone and shot himself, and no one has even asked about his music. I hear the song "Runaway," and I see myself, a typical nine-year-old slouch, stretched out on my bed with a stack of comic books and the plug of my transistor radio wedged in my ear. My mom made me a bedspread that looked like a race car, the headlights down at the end facing into the hallway where my dad was standing in his undershirt, his face coated in lather. "C'mon, honey," my mom said. "We've got to get down to the store," and then there we all were in front of this little cinder-block store at the edge of town, our last name painted in big red letters on the window. There must have been at least ten people gathered for the event, which my dad later said (while we waited for our foot-long hot dogs to be delivered to the window of the car) was just about the proudest moment of his life. He said it was second only to marrying my mother (she had a ring of vanilla shake around her mouth as she smiled back at him) and having my younger brother and me. My brother was in a french-fry frenzy, bathing in the pool of catsup he'd poured in the little checkered cardboard container, but he stopped to take in the seriousness of my dad's announcement. I was wondering even then how you *know* when it's the happiest moment. I was dumbfounded that anyone could build a life on refrigerators and stoves and be happy about it. It amazes me now to think that I had ever sat in the backseat of that old Chevrolet and looked at my parents (younger then than I am now) and thought how ridiculously *outdated* they were.

Now this coed comes in. Tie-dye is *back*, torn jeans, leather sandals. If her hair wasn't purple and aimed at the ceiling, I could just about console my grief. "Can I help?" I ask, totally unprepared for the high squeak of a voice that comes out. She sounds like she just inhaled a balloon full of helium.

"I want *The Little Mermaid*," she said, a high-school ring still on her finger. "You know, the video? It's for my little brother."

"Yeah right. Over there." I point to the far wall, the latest addition to my record/CD/video store, a menagerie of colorful piñatas swinging overhead. "We got 'em all."

Oh yeah. We've got a two-foot table boasting the end of my youth, leftover albums, the bottom of the barrel. It's all that's left, and nobody even stops to look, to mourn, to pay respect. I arranged them such that Joni Mitchell is the one looking out on the dreary day. I imagine someone coming in from the street and saying, "Oh I get it, *paved paradise and put up a parking lot,"* but no such luck; there is no joy in Mudville.

I try to make myself feel better. I think of the positive factors in my life. I recycle my cans and glass and paper. I ride a bike instead of driving a car. Though my old man and I don't always see eye to eye, I know that I'll never turn to find him with a gun pointed my way like Mr. Gaye did to Marvin. I sleep peacefully, all bills paid, no TV blasting MTV like the one across the street in the cinder-block house where a couple of girls come and go. One of them is real nice looking in a kind of Marlene way, wears gym clothes all the time, no makeup, hair long and loose. Though I know sure as hell if I slept with her she'd get up and put on lipstick and control-top panty hose and ask me why I don't cut my hair and get a real job. It's the luck of the draw, and my luck is lousy. "Give up the Diet Coke," I had told Betts. "Give up the fluorescent foods." I had told Marlene to give up the self-pity; if she wanted to be somebody, then to stop talking about it and be it. I had suggested to Xan that she give up the body hair. I told the boss to be *different*, not to cave in to all this new crap. The bottom line? Nobody likes suggestions. So why am I supposed to be different?

"What can you tell me about the Byrds?" My heart leaps up and I turn to face the purple-haired, squeaky-voiced girl, who has placed *The Little Mermaid* on the counter and has a twenty clutched in her fist.

"Yeah? The Byrds? Like turn, turn, turn?"

She looks around, first one way then the other. The she looks back at me, face young and smooth and absolutely blank. "The pink ones," she squeaks and points upward where flamingo piñatas swing on an invisible cord. "How much?"

I watch her walk off now, her pilgrim-looking shoes mud-spattered as she heads through the construction area, her pink bird clutched to her chest along with *The Little Mermaid*. It's times like this when I start thinking that I might give my dad a call and say, "I know you've been saying how you want me to take over your business some day. . . ." It's times like this when I start thinking about Marlene, when I start forgetting how bad it all got. I do crazy things like start to imagine us meeting again, one more try at this perfect 1970 romance. Like maybe

I *will* go to work for my dad, and in my off-hours maybe I'll get out the old power saw and make my mom a TV table (just like you've been saying you wanted, Mom), and maybe I'll circumcise the old index finger and end up in an emergency room and I'll look down that row of vinyl chairs and there she'll be. It's not the *perfect* fantasy but it's one I have. It's one that more and more starts looking good after I watch Marvin's music revived by a bunch of fat raisins dancing around on the tube, or after I see a series of women getting younger and younger, arriving at my door in their spider hose and stiff neon hair, their arms filled with little plastic squares, a mountain of CD covers dumped on my floor.

Bobbie Ann Mason

WEEDS

When he got home from work, Sam found his wife, Alma, in the garden. The sour smell of the composter—a green barrel in a metal frame—wafted across the rhubarb bed at him. A katydid buzzed off a squash leaf, making a bird-like noise. Delighted, Alma held up a cantaloupe for him to see. It was misshapen, something like their old living-room hassock. Her fingers were stained brown from pinching lice off stock peas. Alma's hair was frizzy and she wore no makeup and she was nearly fifty, but she never seemed to mind any of these things.

"Let's go back to the back field," Sam said. "I want to show you those weeds. I've never seen anything like them on this place in my life."

"I ain't got time." She flipped a string bean into a bucket.

"The weeds are higher than I am," he said, lifting his hand above his head. "You won't believe it."

"Snakes," she said.

"Not too many," Sam joked.

"I've got to work up peaches this evening," said Alma. "I've got a whole basket full of drops."

"Excuses," he said, exasperated. "One of these days you're going to run out of excuses."

The back field belonged in the government set-aside program. This year they were paid for not growing wheat, so the field had gone berserk with weeds. Bob Benson, who was growing some corn in one of Sam's fields, had promised to mow the weeds, but he couldn't get his tractor there now without blazing a trail through the corn. Laboriously, Sam had used his small lawn tractor to carve out a path along the edge of the field. Sam's family had been farming for generations, and he had never seen a field grown up wild like that. But now, small family farms were called hobby farms—meaning that the farmers had to earn their living outside the farm and didn't have time to tend all their land. Sam worked at an air-compressor plant. There was a lot of pressurized gas in the world, he thought. Sometimes he felt he would explode.

Sam fastened the garden gate with its whittled wooden pin. From the gate, he could see his parents' old house sitting forlornly in the trees, with a cluster of junky cars pulled up around it. He had rented the house to an older man and woman who seemed settled and dependable, but Sam hadn't expected the couple's kinfolks to descend on the place. Every day there were at least five cars coming and going. It was a strain on the septic system. More than once Sam had had to go out in the woods and dig out the drainpipe. He feared the overflow would kill the trees. Renters were like weeds, he thought, troublesome and impossible to get rid of.

It was a drought year, but weeds were flourishing. Pondweed was devouring the pond, spreading several feet out from shore already. Alma's fishing line kept getting hung up in it, and the fish weren't biting well because of it. They fed on the snails that fed on the weed. He had raked out the pondweed, spending hours grabbing at the tendrils with a garden rake and tugging them toward shore. He refused to use a weed-killer, but someone had suggested geese. On TV once, he had seen geese in France, weeding strawberry beds. It seemed funny at the time, but now the notion had seized him, and he planned to get a pair of geese.

Heavy-metal music roared up the driveway. It was their daughter, Lisa. Her horn blurted out a staccato greeting. She had swapped her Mustang for a red compact with broken air conditioning. Sam suspected she stopped by to visit them as often as she did only because their house was on the route between the plant where she worked and her apartment in town. Her dutifulness had a distracted quality about it, he thought. She shut off her engine, but the music continued to blare.

"Go with me to get some geese," he said when he and Alma met her at her car door.

The music stopped when she removed the key and got out. She had on a loud pink outfit with large pink earrings.

"Aren't geese mean?" she asked, pushing up her sunglasses.

"Yeah, but they're supposed to eat pondweed."

"That pondweed will take the place," said Alma, scrutinizing Lisa's appearance.

"You say that about everything, Mom," Lisa said, pushing Chester, the dog, away from her legs.

"What do I say that about?"

"You say that about cattails. And willow trees. And Wandering Jew."

"We had to get that willow tree out," said Alma. "It was causing the pond to leak."

Lisa rolled her eyes toward the sky, and Sam glanced down at the old house through the trees. A long gold Chrysler was pulling in down there. Two hulky teen-age boys and a woman in a green get-up slammed doors. "They're gathering in," Sam said.

"Why don't you kick them out?" Lisa asked.

"You can't fool with people like that."

"But it's your house."

He shrugged. "They know there's nothing you can do to them. They ain't got nothing, so they take advantage. Even if you brought charges against them, they'd get away with it."

Indoors, the blast of air conditioning and the peach-strewn table faced them. The kitchen was a mess. The house was jammed with what Sam called Alma's "savings." She saved cereal boxes, smashed flat and tied in bundles with strips of selvage; she had accumulated a gallon jug of twist-ties. The basement was crowded with jars of fruits and vegetables she had canned; the freezer was full of fish she had caught from the pond. In the winter she quilted frantically, like a farmer baling hay before a storm. She wouldn't sell the quilts, nor would she use them.

Alma said, as she ran her hands under the kitchen faucet, "The peaches are falling off with this drought, and the grasshoppers are all gone. But there's plenty of frogs, little pale ones in the garden. I think it's the shade. In the shade they can't get much color."

Sam said to Lisa, "I wouldn't have to rent out to strangers if you'd moved into your Grandpa's house like I wanted you to."

"I hate that old house! I think you should set fire to it," Lisa poked at a pale, dotted peach. She said, "Besides, I have some news."

"What?" Sam and Alma said simultaneously.

"I'm moving to Florida with Grayson. He's being transferred."

Alma gasped and accidentally sat down on a stack of egg cartons. They popped and cracked.

"Oh, excuse me," she said, rising; her hands, still wet, stuck out in front of her, dripping like sponges.

They never knew what to expect from their daughter. She had dropped out of college, quit her best jobs, enrolled in odd workshops. She even became a Catholic for a year. She was self-conscious about her overbite. In grade school, kids teased her and called her Squirrel-face. She had had a hard time, Sam had to admit. She was married once, but her husband drank, and her divorce hurt Alma deeply. For several years Lisa worked at the telephone company, but when the Bell system fell apart, she changed jobs. Families, like the telephone company, were more diversified now, she explained to Sam one spring when she moved in with a man and his three young children. That arrangement lasted the summer.

"I've always wanted to go to Florida," Lisa was saying now. "And this is my big chance."

Alma wasn't even listening, Sam noticed. She was peeling a peach, gouging out the bruises.

The woman on the telephone had said she could catch a pair of geese for Sam by the time he got there. Her place was several miles farther out into the country. Lisa agreed to go with him. They had finished supper, through Alma's silence and Lisa's nervous chatter about sea and sand.

"Don't you want to go too?" Sam asked Alma. He always made a point of asking her to go somewhere, knowing she would say no, but he kept hoping she would surprise him.

"No, I've got to work on these peaches." The peaches were pock-marked by worms, but Alma insisted they were salvageable.

In the car, Lisa said, "Grayson's going to finish training down there, and then they'll send him to one of their plants. They'll pay for his training and then his moving expenses to the new place where he's assigned. It could be Oklahoma, Atlanta, or Missouri. So I don't know where we'll end up."

Sam didn't dare ask if they planned to marry. That didn't seem to be the point nowadays, but he knew that for Alma it was a major point. Alma had actually believed that Lisa should have helped her former husband with his drinking problem, in order to save the marriage. Lisa had said she felt lucky she got out of it alive.

Sam said, "What do you think it will do to your mother if you leave?"

"I can't go on humoring her," Lisa said impatiently. "I think you ought to get her up in a jet airplane and take her to some big city. Chicago, say. Get her into the modern age. She acts so old, it's embarrassing."

"That's not what she needs."

"Then you should take her to a shrink. All that old-timey stuff is an act. She didn't grow up with all those doilies and pickle jars! They had television, for crying out loud."

"Don't talk about your mother like that," Sam said, coming down hard. "Let me tell you one thing."

He studied a road sign and made a deft turn onto a road partially hidden by an overgrown stand of sumac. The woman on the phone had said it was the old Caldwell place. A subdivision had sprung up on the road out to that farm—new houses, large and close together, without trees, more houses under construction. It was unusual to see a subdivision so far from town.

Sam hated seeing farmland eaten up this way by an impulse to live in the country that was not much more than a fashionable idea. But Alma had been serious about it. She told him long ago that she married a country boy on purpose. He recalled the time he was away in Louisville at a soil seminar and she had gone out looking for wild gooseberries, locating a quart of them in several hours of searching through some scrub acreage for a stray little bush here and there. Wild gooseberries had sharp thorns growing out of the fruit, and she had painstakingly snipped each thorn off with nail scissors. Instead of simply straining the fruit for jelly, she sought the sharp flavor and texture of the berry's skin. He praised her excessively, glorifying her extraordinary effort—like that of a craftsman who could still do delicate, almost-forgotten work. Her strength held him fast, made him never doubt her.

"What were you saying, Dad?" asked Lisa.

"I wanted to say something to you." Sam was fifty-one. He felt a choking in his throat, the sadness of being so old with living, wishing he could be headed for Florida with nothing but expectations instead of experience. "I just wanted to say—if you get down there, and if you need help—I don't want you to forget where your home is. If you get down there and get stranded, and if this guy does you bad, you've always got a ticket home, understand?"

"You don't have to treat me like I'm a kid! I know how to take care of myself!" She jostled his arm affectionately. The steering wheel bobbled.

Sam let the matter drop. Whenever he tried to express something heartfelt like that, it came off being corny. He thought she understood. But he didn't trust Grayson—a man with empty eyes, a bluffing manner, and a bushy little mustache that made Sam's flesh crawl. It made him think of the dirty brushes that he once used for horse grooming. Sam was always awkward with his daughter. He and Alma always knew they should have had more than one child, but she had refused after going through the Caesarean with Lisa. Ever since, their sex life had been sporadic and strained, punctuated with bouts of heavy passion that trailed off into forgetfulness.

"Here it is," he said, coming upon the farm suddenly. The farm had a large, rambling barnyard enclosed with white wood fences. It was a picturesque place, with a tree-shaded pond and well-maintained barn, the kind of place Sam would keep if he had time.

They were admiring the farm from the driveway when a woman came from the house.

"I done caught them geese for you," she said.

"Out on the pond the geese look like swan boats," said Lisa.

"Where'd you see swan boats?" Sam asked.

They followed the woman, Lillian Campbell, along the pond bank to the barn. On the pond a regatta of ducks and geese sailed. In the barnyard, a group of guinea hens—white as rabbits—trundled toward a trough, where some breakthrough discovery had been made, Sam judged by their chatter.

The two geese huddled together, quivering, in a corner stall of the barn. The male was white, and the female was a buff color with a multitude of related shades in layers of feathers as carefully arranged as playing cards in a game of solitaire. She was small, compact, nervous.

"How did you catch them?" Sam asked Lillian.

"You drive geese, just like you was driving cows. Nothing to it." She shoved the female into a mesh potato sack. Sam held the bag, feeling the woman's force as she pulled the drawstring tight and knotted it. Then, using a piece of baling twine, she bound the end of the bag the way Alma used to wrap the ends of Lisa's pigtails. The goose was upside down, her neck twisted and her head flat against the straw-covered dirt flooring. The woman swished the bag as if to settle its contents and handed it to Sam to hold while she started sacking up the second goose. The male, heavy and proud, sputtered and honked as the woman bunched him into the sack. Sam was afraid Lisa was bored. He saw her stoop to catch a scampering kitten, which rolled over, batting her hand playfully.

As they emerged from the barn, a car drove up and a man disappeared into the house.

"Hardy's come in late from the mill, ready for his supper, and when he don't get it right then and there, he growls," the woman said, apologizing for her hurry. She tucked Sam's $20-bill into a pocket of her stretchknit pants—pale blue, dotted with nap balls and snags, fibers probably plucked out by cat claws and splinters, the same as Alma's pants were. Lillian was once pretty, Sam thought. Her body was still hard, and her cheekbones glistened with color. A fantasy charged through his head—an affair with this woman, a stranger, while her husband was at the mill (the feed mill? the lumber mill?), and the complicated adventure of concealing it.

"You're a cutie-pie," Lisa said to the kitten.

"You can have it," said Lillian.

"No, I can't take it. I'm moving to Florida."

"I went to Florida last winter and I wouldn't give you anything for it. It rained the whole week and everything cost an arm and a leg."

Sam opened the hatchback and set the geese behind the back seat.

They honked—fierce, threatening squawks—as they tumbled onto the floor, their toes poking through the mesh of the sacks. The male, trying to upright himself, somersaulted. As Sam drove away, the birds fluttered around, the bags turning and jerking. The geese settled soon into a quiet fear. It was getting dark. A shadow ran across the road. Sam's eyes weren't great at night. He hadn't driven at night in at least five years.

"What do geese eat?" Lisa asked him.

"They're going to eat pondweed and like it," said Sam.

The geese were thrashing again, and Lisa seemed alarmed.

"What if they get out?"

"They won't get out."

"Will they attack us?" She gripped the handle on the dashboard.

"No, don't be silly. Hold on. We're having some fun now!" An ironic line he recalled from some movie.

At a stop sign Sam said, "Isn't this exciting?" He meant the night, the adventure, the geese, the drive in the dark with his daughter. It seemed that they hadn't done anything like this together since she was a child. As soon as she became a teen-ager, she had lost interest in anything that grew, animal or plant. And Alma had done the opposite, as if to spite Lisa's lone foray into the social world of school and church.

Sam thought he knew a shortcut through some back roads. He turned down a road he remembered from his childhood. In the dark it was lonely and twisted. They passed ramshackle houses and house trailers. In the twilight the chaos of their forms blended into the darkness, as if they were grown into the landscape—the old machinery and cars and other eyesores welded together into one large, shadowy organism.

He recalled this intersection, the next curve, then the little bridge that followed. He remembered playing in that creek once, long ago, after a storm when an uprooted tree had made a bridge above a churn of angry water. He drove on, the geese murmuring and flapping, Lisa holding on to her seat and glancing furtively back at them.

Sam slowed down before a house. "That's the house where I was born."

"I never knew that!" Lisa said, surprised.

"It's been bricked over and added on to. I remember one year we had guineas. And I remember a tricycle."

The geese honked and fluttered. A bad smell drifted through the car.

Sam said, "It was so far out they didn't make it to the hospital. I was dropped just like a calf in a stall."

"That's incredible," said Lisa. "I can't imagine you here. There are so many things I don't know about you and Mom. Now that I'm going away, suddenly it seems like I haven't paid attention."

"We'll miss you," he said, choking on the words.

He eased down on the gas pedal. The tank, he noticed suddenly, said empty. They made it home, on fumes. "Goose fumes," he joked as they raced through the night, feeling free.

Alma had turned the outside light on for them, and Lisa volunteered to help Sam stow the geese in the pen where he planned to keep them until morning. She grabbed the flashlight from the glove compartment and lighted his way as he carried the geese down to the pen behind the house. Then, grunting slightly, she supported their weight against the top of the fence while he cut the strings of the sacks and let the geese down into the pen. Then she played the flashlight on the birds' confusion as they explored the dark pen. Cautiously, they murmured like children whispering behind the teacher's back. They snaked their heads in and out of the light. Lisa laughed with pleasure, a laugh that reminded Sam of Alma in her youth.

Inside the house, Alma gave them steaming peach cobbler and watched them eat it while she tended the pressure canner. Alma said, "Why do you want to leave home, Lisa?"

"You've got to take risks sometime. Hint, hint."

"Is there something the matter with you, Lisa?" said Alma. "Something you're not telling? Cancer? Are you pregnant?"

Lisa signed. "No. No. And no. I'm just tired of this town—the way people treat people; those old biddies I have to work with; and the way people in the social set turn up their noses and look down at the people who do all the real work in this town. I never had a chance to get out till Grayson came along. Grayson's my ticket out."

"Prince Charming," said Sam dryly.

Lisa said, "I want to get away because all the women I know here are alcoholics and the men are high on themselves."

Sam let a warm peach loll on his tongue. He felt oddly relaxed at this moment. Lisa had been a cranky baby—bottle-fed because Alma's milk wasn't good and she didn't have the strength to nurse. Alma always said bottle babies were spoiled, expecting to be given presents all the time. He was still luxuriating in the warm feeling he had about the evening with his daughter. In that moment when they had released the geese, he had felt they were sharing something special for the first time since she was a small child. It was that moment when parent and child come together as people—adults—for the first time, he thought, hoping he wasn't reading too much into it.

In the morning, Sam sacked up the geese, and Alma helped him carry them down to the pond. He loved the reflections on the pond— the sky, the fluffy marshmallow clouds, the sycamore trees, the still darkness of the mowed field, the spindly patch of cattails like roasting wieners shining in the water. In the distance was a glint of metal—one of the renters' cars arriving. Sam caught Alma staring into the pond reflections as if she expected to see her future.

Sam released the female first, then the male. He had decided to name them Lillian and Hardy. Startled, the geese honked and splashed into the water. They swam in unison, swooping together. The dog, Chester, barked at them, and they lowered and extended their long necks, huffing menacingly at him.

"Eat that pondweed," Sam urged them.

Sam and his wife headed for the field of weeds. She carried a tobacco stick with her to beat back snakes.

"Where in the world did you come up with a tobacco stick?" Sam asked on their way down the fencerow. "I haven't seen one of those in years."

"The renters had it in their things. They said they didn't have any use for it." She laughed and clawed at her blouse. "Look. I found a grasshopper so I can fish on the way home." She had pinched the grasshopper and wrapped it in a little piece of brown paper and stuck it inside her brassiere. The grasshopper was still alive. "Crappie like 'em alive," she said.

They followed the path Sam had cut with his small tractor along the edge of the cornfield. By hand he had cut back blackberry briars. Chester ran ahead, rooting into the blackberry bushes, which were growing out from the fencerow into the field.

Sam had spent most of his spare time cultivating—controlling weeds and pests, coaxing food plants to grow. They called that husbandry, he had learned in an agriculture course he took once at night school. Following the necessities of the seasons seemed natural and clear and easy, but when it came to being a husband to a woman, he had his worst doubts. Sometimes it seemed a passive role, like the way you had to accept a drought year. Other times, marriage seemed like the most artful of crops, requiring exquisite care. The notion that marriage produced something hadn't escaped him. But on the occasions when Alma shut him out, he didn't know what farming analogies applied. He once accused her in jest of using the no-till method of birth control. The joke had hurt her, and he had never challenged her again on the point. Sometimes they made love, and sometimes they *seemed* to be making love, when they shared some wonder she had found—those gooseberries, a bird's nest with four glistening speckled jewels inside, a new ear of corn. Sometimes that was enough. Today he thought showing her the field of weeds would be like that. He felt stirred, hoping.

The creek had dried down to a few puddles.

"Well, Lisa likes to get out and go," Alma said thoughtfully, poking her tobacco stick in the gravel. "And maybe she can learn to love that Grayson enough to marry him."

"That's pathetic reasoning," said Sam.

Something in him felt broken, cracked by Alma's irrationality. She stood before him—square-jawed, large-boned, with delicate skin like honey. They were well beyond the mid-life crisis, an idea she had thought was silly, but Sam knew he had to change something before it was too late. He loved her as much as ever, but he was afraid their love had gone into something so deep and unexplained—like the creek deepening from soil erosion—that it wasn't free.

"I used to think Lisa wanted a nice house and a family and a dependable man who'd take care of her," Alma said. "But they don't want that anymore, girls don't. I don't know what they want, and I don't think they do either."

Along the creek bank, dried blackberry briars crunched underfoot, and occasionally some of the briars grabbed at Sam's jeans. A squirrel darted out in front of them and disappeared. The ground was covered with hickory nuts the squirrels had cut down.

Alma said, "For a drought year, I never saw so many hickory nuts."

She flew toward them, stooping to gather them, flinging aside the split green hulls and stuffing the nuts in her pockets.

"Leave them for the squirrels," he said sharply. "Can't you leave well enough alone? Do you have to save everything you find?"

He kicked at a few nuts. There were so many thing he didn't know and didn't have time to know and would never understand. The drought caused some things to dry up and some to overproduce—much like Alma, whose attentions to people had dried up, while her garden was bursting. He felt heavy, heavy as the ground cover of hickory nuts. He hoped what he was feeling was only another phase, but he knew that this was the first moment in his life that he knew truly how limited time was. It was that age when you figure it's too late to learn French or how to play the piano.

"There they are," he said as they faced the forest of weeds. They were stately and wild, their thickness giving off a dusty, harsh heat. Sam guided Alma down the path he had mowed.

"Ain't these the tallest weeds you ever saw?" he said. "Look at that—there's jimson weed and sawbriar and horseweed."

"Ragweed," she said, touching the yellow floss.

"Look at that," he said. "Old foxtail and white-top weed and that old vine there. I never saw anything like it."

The weeds disgusted him. On television recently, he had seen an ancient ruin—some toppled statues and crumbling walls of an old temple in the Far East somewhere—and the weeds were growing through the stones, right through the eyes of the statues.

"There's that purple-flowered weed that used to be so bad in the garden." She touched a dark green plant with pointed leaves. "Nightshade."

"Poison," he said, feeling slightly sick.

She plucked a seed pod, a green paper lantern, from the nightshade.

She opened it at its seams and turned the petals down, exposing the hard green ball in the center. She opened a second one, then held the two a certain way for him to see.

"My grandmother used to do this," said Alma, smiling. "This is the boy and this is the girl." She had fashioned one of the seed pods into a girl with a skirt and the other into a boy in pants. "In the old days, these were toys," she said.

Alma had plunged ahead of him. Now she was studying another tall weed, with a thick-headed purple flower, a flower he didn't know. Miraculously, a dozen tiny hummingbirds were feeding on the purple flowers. They had unusual markings—green heads, sienna stripes circling their black bodies.

"They're not birds," Alma said, reading his thoughts, without even looking at him. "They're hawk moths."

Sam moved closer, and the little birds turned out to have six legs and long, rolled tongues. "How did you know what they were?" he asked.

She shrugged. "I lost my grasshopper," she said, touching between her breasts. "Reckon one of these hawk moths would do to fish with?"

"How did you know their name?" he demanded.

She walked on. "Maybe we can gather some of Bob's corn on the way back. He said for us to get some since our corn didn't make."

He followed her, his heart high, and the pond came into view. He could see a large heron on the pond bank—a tall, dusky bird, maybe a great blue. As he watched, the heron stalked curiously toward the geese. The geese fled to the opposite shore, honking like visitors arriving.

Heather Ross Miller

UNCLE PRESTON

Paint dabs across the rough canvas, fleshing out Kate Poole's arms, her dark eyes that flash and dart, her short hair cut in dark bangs thick to the brow, and her grasping, claiming little hands. Seven years old, she does not want to pose like this, like some kind of baby.

"Preston!" prompts her mother Zandra, the painter. "Make her be still."

And Uncle Preston, her daddy's younger brother with whom they share the house, takes charge of Kate, holds her on his lap and tells ugly little stories to calm her down while her mother paints the portrait.

Outside their pale yellow-boarded house, North Carolina sweeps off into thin blue distances. Old women who have lived into the 1990s, tough old women nobody wants to take care of, root up potatoes in flat gardens edged by plum thickets while the aluminum smelter in the middle of town pours out long, malleable, silver-white ingots breathing flame. They become part of the ugly little stories.

"Once a big old billy goat belonged to a farmer and his wife and little girl," begins Uncle Preston over Kate's busy head. She bumps her head against his gray sweats, rolls her eyes back to look.

"Kate!"

She returns her gaze to the front, still listening to the story.

"This billy goat was bad news. He played tricks and cut up all over the place and took advantage, and the farmer said he would punish him if he didn't quit it."

Light blooms in the open windows of the studio, which is just a big upstairs bedroom from which they can see the towers of the aluminum smelter. The sour smell of paint loads the air and Kate's mother smiles, dabbing at the rosy skin beneath the brush.

Uncle Preston shifts, kisses the back of Kate's dark head. Already she is mellowing under his syllables, eyes wide-fixed, listening and waiting.

"It didn't make any difference to the old billy goat what anybody said. He kept on doing things, kicking over the milk cans, butting stuff off the table, scattering the chickens in the yard. 'I have warned you and warned you, goat,' said the farmer. 'Now you have to pay for this.' And while his wife and his little girl held the billy goat down, the farmer started to skin him alive with a big sharp knife."

Her arms and the back of her neck prickle at this, and Kate shivers. "That's a lie," she says. "I don't believe it."

Uncle Preston kisses her head again. "You don't have to," he affirms and picks up the story.

"But the billy goat was too smart. He got away from the farmer's wife and his little girl and started running, half-skinned, down the road from the farmer. And he ran away to the woods and stayed there. The woods right outside." He nods toward the window. Kate stretches her eyes toward the windows, too.

"Preston," says her mother, "turn her a little to the left."

"Did it bleed?" demands Kate Poole as she is being turned a little to the left.

"You bet," replies Uncle Preston.

"Did it hurt?"

"Like the *devil*."

"How did he get well?"

"Listen," says Uncle Preston, "the farmer and his wife and his little girl got along okay and nothing bad happened. Then after a whole year, one night the billy goat came up and knocked on the front door. When the farmer opened up, he was shocked to see that old goat, still half-skinned, still alive. No hair growing on the skinned part, though. It was just kind of bald and like a scar."

Kate blinks, smells the comforting stink of Uncle Preston's gray sweats, warm and rich. "Oh," she says, again, "oh," feeling her arms and neck prickle more.

"Listen, 'I am your old half-skinned billy goat,' the goat said to the farmer." Then Uncle Preston jogs out a little rhyme:

> *My horns are sharp, my hooves are bright.*
> *Give me what I want tonight,*
> *Or I'll cut your throat,*
> *For I am the old half-skinned billy goat!*

Kate sits like a stone, imagining the horror of opening the front door and finding a half-skinned billy goat. The shock of having this old goat say a little rhyme to her, jog it out at her that way. Like Uncle Preston.

"What happened then?"

"You should ask, 'What did he want?' " chides Uncle Preston.

"What did he want?"

"He said 'Give me butter and milk. Give me satin and silk.' 'I don't have satin and silk,' said the farmer, scared to death. 'Well, then—' " Uncle Preston jogs again:

> *Give me what you have tonight,*
> *Or I'll carry you away out of Christian sight!*

"What did he give him?" asks Kate. Her fingers twist a fold of the gray sweats. She wants to make sure Uncle Preston stays there. She is half mad at him for starting this.

Kate's mother's brush spreads curiosity, wonder, excitement, a tinge of horror across the canvas. She listens to her brother-in-law's story with the same attention as the little girl. It enhances her stroke, sharpens her eye.

"Well," says Uncle Preston, shifting a leg, "he gave him all the butter and milk out of the refrigerator and then the billy goat went off. But the very next night, he came back and knocked on the front door. And the billy goat said all over again:

> *I am your old half-skinned billy goat.*
> *My horns are sharp, my hooves are bright.*

Give me what I want tonight,
Or I'll cut your throat,
For I am the old half-skinned billy goat!

"What did he give him then? More butter and milk?" Kate pinches up folds of her skirt along with the gray sweats. Her legs itch and she wants to get down, run outside and look at the real goats in the yard behind the house. She wants to look very hard at all of them.

"No." Uncle Preston smiles. "This time the goat said:

Give me strawberry jam and a roll,
Give me silver and a bag of gold.

'I don't have silver and a bag of gold,' said the farmer.

Well, then give me what you have tonight,
Or I'll carry you away out of Christian sight!

"Preston," asks his sister-in-law, "where did you hear this ugly little story?" She puts down her brush and waits. Light coming from the windows behind throws a bright crown around her head, and she looks like a holy picture to Kate. One of those things on the front of the Sunday School books. "Where did you hear it?"

Uncle Preston shifts Kate on his knees. "From Michael. He made it up. I think to make me shut up when Mama made us take a nap. He always wanted me to shut up and go to sleep so he could sneak out. It's Michael's ugly little story."

"I can't believe Michael Poole made up anything."

"What happened next?" insists Kate.

"I don't know," Uncle Preston shrugs. "I always went to sleep before the end. Michael knows what happened next. Didn't he ever tell it to you, Zandra?"

"I told you, I never heard it before, Preston." She turns away and snaps shut her paints.

So, thinks Kate Poole, it is a lie. Nothing happens in that old story. No old half-skinned billy goat is coming back again to get nobody, no farmer, no farmer's wife, no little girls. It's a lie. She cannot help it, though, that she shivers again on Uncle Preston's lap and demands, "Tell me the end anyhow. I want to hear the end."

"That's enough for today." Her mother moves around taking charge of things. "The light's moved already. Preston, you've sat there with her long enough. We'll work some more tomorrow."

Set free, Kate runs to the backyard to look at the little goats fenced there. She looks hard at their hooves, their curved horns, and their slanted yellow eyes. Small and playful, they follow one another jumping and butting. One of them stands on an old walnut stump, and the others try to crowd him off, baaing all the time.

Kate plucks the wire fence and threatens, "Give me what I want tonight, or I'll carry you away out of Christian sight!" The little goats blink at her, baa, chew their cuds. Stupid goats, she thinks.

Two white-brown does stare. One curious little dark buck trots over to butt at Kate's hand. She studies his head, thinking he ought to be painted in her mother's portrait, not her.

Give me what I want tonight!

She picks up a rock and throws. The little goats scatter.

The pale yellow-boarded house stands in the countryside about two miles from a small North Carolina aluminum-smelting town. They inherited it together, Michael and Preston, from their mother Sheila Poole, and neither will leave. The house, with goats and chickens fenced in the backyard, has green shutters pulled against the noon heat, and upstairs Zandra and Kate are lying down on cool bare sheets. Uncle Preston has gone out to interview for a job, he said, at the aluminum smelter. Kate slips closer across the sheets toward her mother, who sprawls, open-legged, a wet towel on her head, eyes closed. Kate's daddy Michael Poole, an exterminator, drives around with a big black spider stuck to the side of his truck. He mades good money and stays gone so much she can barely recall the look of him, the tone of his voice echoing in the house. He is gone now and will be gone for days.

"Mother?" she puts out a hand to trace the lace insertion of Zandra's camisole. "Mother, why do we have all those goats out in the back yard?"

"For milk, you know that. Because Daddy's allergic and he has to drink it." Her mother moves away from the child's hand. "You know that."

"Daddy's not ever here to drink it." Kate puts her hand back on the lace. She brightens, "Do we have them for butter?" Kate sits up, delighted with this new possibility. "Do we have them for goat butter?"

"Don't be so silly. People don't eat goat butter. What a stupid thing. Daddy's just allergic, that's all." Zandra turns completely over, away from Kate's hands and her new delight, leaving her utterly alone and unrequited.

Kate drops back down, turns the strange word *allergic* over and over her tongue, *allergic*. It sticks to the roof of her mouth, kicks toward her front teeth, *allergic*.

In the night, after Uncle Preston has returned and everyone gone to bed for good, the heat slacked off a little, Kate Poole wakes, hears whispering, her mother's laugh low and throaty, then her uncle's responding laugh.

"Mother? Uncle Preston?" She waits in the dark.

Nothing.

No movement outside her door. Only the faintest ba-baaing from the goats in the yard. She imagines their little yellow eyes, the little beards under their chins.

Or I'll carry you away out of Christian sight!

Stupid! Kate slips from her bed and pads down the hall to her mother's room. She barely opens it and sees in the soft darkness Uncle Preston lifting himself over Zandra, then thrusting down, Zandra sighing.

"What're you doing?" Kate pushes wide the door. "You stop!"

Uncle Preston does stop. Both he and Zandra crane toward Kate in the door.

"It's just Kate," whispers Zandra.

"What're you doing?" Kate demands again. "I see you!"

Uncle Preston laughs, pushes away from Zandra, pulls the sheet over him. "Come here," he invites, holding out an arm. "Get in."

Kate hesitates a moment, sliding her bare feet on the slick-polished floor. She does not entirely trust Uncle Preston. Then she brightens, "Tell me the billy goat."

"Why not?" he agrees, and she settles between her mother and Uncle Preston. "But I don't know the end," he reminds her.

"Michael does," she reminds him back. "You said."

At the mention of Kate's daddy's name, both Uncle Preston and her mother squirm. Uncle Preston hugs Kate closer. "Listen," he says, "this is a game we're playing, me and you and Zandra. And we're playing it against Michael. It's a secret game, you understand?"

He hugs Kate again. "You want to keep playing the secret game?"

She nods, flexes her toes under the sheet, drinking in the smell of Uncle Preston and her mother and herself. Nothing, she thinks, can be a good as this. Uncle Preston keeps talking about the secret game against Michael Poole and what the rules are, but Kate is not paying attention. She drifts, snores.

For breakfast Kate Poole likes eggs beaten with sugar until her glass is full of foamy yellow sweetness. She does not care that the egg is still raw when she eats it, her lip a yellow smudge. She loves it and smacks and declares, "I love this to *death!* Make another one."

"That's raw, you know," Uncle Preston teases. "You're eating a *raw* egg."

Her mother observes. "Sugar helps to cook egg. It's not really raw. Something happens when you mix up the egg with the sugar. It cooks it, sort of."

"Listen to the chemistry major," scoffs Uncle Preston. "Dr. Zandra and her Nobel Prize." He breaks more eggs into the glass, spoons great mounds of sugar in with them, and beats everything with a fork until it is all goldish air and sweet delight.

"We spoil her," he says, watching Kate eat.

"*You* spoil her," corrects Zandra.

"Somebody has to," he says, wiping off his hands. "And," he adds with a wise air, "it's good for her."

"Ha," scoffs Zandra. "It's not good for her. It's good for the chickens. Gives them something to do. Lay more eggs." She puts down her coffee cup. "Gives *you* something to do."

"And what, darling Zandra," Preston asks, smiling across the table, "does it give you to do?"

"I have plenty to do." She smiles back at him, her lips very full and firm.

"Does Michael believe that?"

"It doesn't matter what Michael believes." Kate's mother shakes a cigarette from the pack on the table between them, lights it, continues smiling.

Michael Poole, the exterminator with the truck, knows the end of the billy-goat story, Kate remembers. Her own big bald-headed daddy. And, she sits wondering, maybe when he comes back, he will bring the end of the story with him. After all, Uncle Preston already said he made it up in the first place just to make him, Uncle Preston, shut up and go to sleep. Right here in this house which they both own.

Kate snuffles the last of the sugary egg, well pleased. She will ask Michael the first thing, What happened to the old half-skinned billy goat?

But when Michael Poole finally gets there, he is not in a mood to tell stories. He roars into the drive, his truck throwing gravel, the big black spider hanging like some ugly abnormality from its door. Upstairs in the studio, Kate twists around from her pose and watches him walk toward the house. He pauses, lights a cigarette, then shoves the door.

"Zandra?"

Kate's mother ignores this. "Turn back around," she commands Kate. "Do I have to go get Uncle Preston to hold you still again?"

Kate does not turn. "Yes," she says, "go get Uncle Preston." She blinks against the light, listens to Michael's truck popping in the heat, follows his tread up the stairs. "Go get Uncle Preston to hold me still."

"Turn around!" Her mother raps a brush against the easel like a schoolteacher calling for attention.

"Zandra, didn't you hear me?" Michael is in the studio, and the stink of his cigarette floats with the smell of the paint. "I called you soon as I came in the front door."

Zandra dips her brush in dark paint, loads it, applies the dark to Kate's bangs. "I heard you. Everybody heard you, Michael. So?"

"So, I might like an answer. Something easy, like 'Oh, hello, Michael. I'm glad to see you, Michael. I love you, Michael.' "

With each example, Kate's daddy gets closer to Zandra, standing finally behind her. He flicks ash in the dark paint, then stubs his cigarette there.

Zandra looks at the cigarette. Smoke still wisping up from it stings her eyes. "Hello, Michael," she says. "I'm glad to see you, Michael. I love you, Michael."

Kate has turned now to sit and stare at both her parents. She is as good a model as Zandra could wish right then. Nothing moves. Her hands are clasped in the way Zandra wants, her face set, her dress spread, her ankles crossed, her bare feet. Kate is the best portrait anybody could ever paint right then. Still life. She is figuring out what kind of people she came from.

Michael Poole gazes a while at Zandra. Then he shrugs and leaves. Kate and Zandra listen to his steps down the stairs. Zandra says, "Fuck you, Michael," and crossing to the big mirror she keeps on the wall of the studio, studies her face. She picks the cigarette from the dark paint and uses it to paint one streak across each cheek, another down her nose and chin.

"Mother!" exclaims Kate, wriggling off her pose. "What're you doing that for? You look like an Indian!"

Zandra thinks awhile. "I am an Indian," she says. "I'm going to scalp him."

Kate thinks of her daddy scalped. She knows what that means. She has seen enough movies on television. Her mother with a scalp hanging off her belt. Except Zandra does not wear belts. Except Michael does not have enough hair to make a good scalp to hang off anything. Michael's hair, the same dark brown as Kate's, has slipped down behind his ears. What there is left clings thick and curled against his collar, the top of his head mottled gold and brown. He wears a dark blue Greek fisherman's cap to cover his head.

But Kate thinks about Michael Poole getting scalped anyway. Her mother would grab the dark blue cap, hack it under the brim, then with one sickening yank, scalp it off her daddy's poor old bald head. Kate grins.

"Wouldn't hurt him none," she says.

"What?" Zandra was staring out the window, the paint still gleaming on her face.

"Daddy," says Kate Poole. "It wouldn't hurt him none if you scalped him."

Uncle Preston is there for dinner, laughing, passing plates, like some kind of sunny generous clown between Michael and Zandra. Kate could almost scorn him for this, except she is fascinated to see it all happening. These are my people, she calculates. Zandra and Michael and my Uncle Preston, they all hate each other to death. Then quickly amends, They all *love* each other to death, too. Loving looks, to her, to be the same as hating right then. The secret game, maybe. The game against Michael Poole which has rules. But Kate does not bother herself about such distinctions.

"What's the end of the billy goat?" she blurts. Michael has just lit a fresh cigarette and sits propped over his plate, chin in both hands, eyes shut against the smoke.

"What?" He blinks at her, smiles slightly. She knows Michael likes her. In spite of everything, Kate can count on Michael liking her a lot. Uncle Preston and Mother can have all the secret games against Michael they want, she thinks. In the end, he will still like me.

"That old half-skinned billy goat you told to Uncle Preston." Kate holds her fork like a conductor's baton. "What happened in the end of the story?"

Michael clears his throat, laughs, takes a deep draw. "God," he says. "I hadn't thought about that in a hundred years." Then he looks at Kate, smiles again. "Why, baby? Doesn't *he* know the end?"

"Uncle Preston said you would!" Kate cannot hold back the disappointment, even though she sees how much it also disappoints Michael. "Uncle Preston *said!*" Her voice sharpens.

Michael shrugs, looks at Preston. "What else did Uncle Preston say?"

"He said you made it up."

Uncle Preston passes the rolls. "Look," he offers. "Maybe that old goat ran off and never came back. Maybe he got tired of coming to the farmer's house all the time and asking for stuff. Maybe he just kept coming back and asking for stuff until finally there was nothing left in the house to give him. You think?"

"Maybe." Zandra butters a roll. "Maybe he got married and aggravated his family for the rest of his life. Maybe." She breaks off a piece and lifts it to her mouth. "Maybe he drove around in a truck and killed bugs for a living."

"That's what Daddy does." Kate Poole is at first delighted with this observation, then she knows it is not good and shuts up fast, her lips clamped with the effort.

Michael and Kate and Uncle Preston all watch Zandra chew the roll, swallow, then sip some iced tea.

"Why don't you just say it, Zandra?" sneers Michael Poole. "Quit playing games and just say it."

At this, Kate perks. "It's a secret game against *you!* We've played it."

"Shut up," hisses her mother.

"What secret game?" Michael blinks, knocks the ash from his cigarette.

"Shut up!" commands Zandra. "I mean it, shut up."

"I mean it, too," says Michael. "Who played the secret game, baby?" He coaxes, and Kate is eager to give him what he wants.

"I got in the bed with them and we played it together against you."

"Michael." Uncle Preston puts a hand out, "Michael, it is not what you think. Zandra." He turns, a hand out to her. "Zandra, tell him."

"Oh, shut up, Preston." Michael's face is as venomous as the black spider on his truck. "Nobody needs to tell me anything. I can see. I can hear. I can, goddamnit, *smell*, Preston."

Michael rises, ashes the last of his cigarette. "I can smell you all over her."

"You beast. You disgusting animal." Zandra does not rise, does not even deepen her voice. She continues to butter her roll and sip her iced tea. "You can see and hear and smell whatever you want to."

Then she does rise and stares straight down the table at Micheal Poole. "But so can I, goddamnit, Michael. So can *I*."

"And what does that mean?"

"That means, Michael, that you don't come in here hollering and screaming at us and making insinuations when you yourself have been out catting around." Zandra balls a fist. "Smell? You want to talk about *smell*, Michael?"

Kate, fork still in hand, opens her mouth and bawls. It is all she knows to do when they are like this. Her face reddens and turns shiny with tears as her incontestable bawling increases.

"Now, look." Michael glares at Zandra and Uncle Preston. "It's not enough for you to carry on in my house behind my back, but you have to get my baby upset, too?"

"Your house?" Now Uncle Preston rises, sharpens his own voice. "This is not your house, Michael. This is my house, too."

"Well, then, Preston," Michael threatens, "see what you can do about getting your house in order. Because if you can't, Preston, I can."

"What does that mean?"

Michael Poole pulls on his blue cap. "That means someday I'm going to come back and you won't be here."

Uncle Preston follows him out to the truck, "Michael! Michael, *listen!*"

At the table, Kate's bawling subsides. She hiccups, snuffles in her napkin.

"Satisfied?" Zandra pours more iced tea, sits down again.

Kate nods. Michael's truck grinds off into the fading daylight. Uncle Preston comes back, the screen door slamming behind. "I can't stand this," he declares to Zandra.

"You don't have to," she says. "Just look at it the way Michael does."

"And how is that?" Uncle Preston takes his seat, watching her. Kate rolls her clammy napkin in a long bunny ear.

Zandra wipes her mouth. "Michael can't throw you out. He can't prove anything. That's the thing about Michael. He can't throw anybody out. He can't prove anything. All he can do is come back."

Kate watches Uncles Preston watching her mother and her mother watching Uncle Preston back, hard. All of them hard and intent. The long bunny ear flops open in her lap.

"He didn't know the end of the story," she accuses. "You said he knew the end of the billy goat."

Neither Zandra nor Uncle Preston look at her. They do not take their eyes off each other. And she knows, finally, there is no end to the billy goat story. It keeps going and going. Asking for things. Until you go to sleep. Stupid, stupid!

In the middle of the night Kate Poole sneaks down the hall to her mother's studio. The portrait stares at her from the easel. For a minute she hesitates, is not sure, then shakes off the feeling. Kate squeezes paint deliberately. In the pale light of the stars, the faint shrinking moon, she can tell it is alizarin crimson, her favorite, and she is encouraged to squeeze a long, long strand of it down Zandra's palette. She takes the heaviest brush and carefully, methodically, loads alizarin crimson all over the portrait, giving herself big clown lips, a cherry nose, bloody cheeks. And raises off the top of her head, out of those glossy dark and perfect bangs, two stubby but distinctive horns growing larger with the gleeful baa-baa sneering in her throat.

William Mills

THE COMMUTERS

The car is due any minute. I try to keep an eye out, get some coffee in me, and stuff my books and papers into a briefcase. Our trip takes an hour from my place, which is on the semi-rural outskirts of the city. It takes Simone and Staunton twenty minutes to get to me. We teach at a small bush-league college in Blackston, Louisiana. Simone is a post-war immigrant from France who teaches French. Staunton is a post-war homosexual (species, discreet) who teaches Spanish and does so because that was the easiest language he could get into. I am the youngest of the commuters, but none of us has finished our doctoral work, which is the only reason we travel to Blackston. Blackston College takes what it can get.

The 1962 Chevrolet swirls into my driveway at seven-thirty. We have been commuting together since last school year and are thus relieved of the necessity of making first-meeting talk. I get in the back seat and have it all to myself. Staunton is driving, but it is not his car. It is Simone's car, the car her husband had bought new before he died last year. He was Simone's second husband, a full professor at the university in Baton Rouge. I knew him only slightly, but he had seemed a quiet fellow and little match for Simone. It was not Simone that killed him, though, but a peculiar cancer—the kind where you're here today, gone tomorrow, with not much visible change or pain in the going. Simone had not seemed very saddened by his death, which was a month or so after we began traveling together.

I find Simone an interesting bird, even though she can drive you up the wall in a minute. She has fairly short, curly hair that is black as a raven's wing, and I think the color is natural even though she is in her forties. It's shiny and healthy like a citizen of the Mediterranean. Her eyes are dark brown, but the whites have just a touch of what looks like yellow (more on some days than others) which I suspect derives from her nocturnal imbibing. She brought her love of French wine with her to this side of the Atlantic. We do not socialize together, but she almost daily describes some party she has gone to. She has other features that resemble those of a raven. Her nose has a very high bridge that suggests a beak, and along with her high cheekbones it accentuates her thin, severe face. The face would fit readily in a Goya, but her generally kind and effervescent spirit keeps it from looking like any particular face I have seen in the family of Charles IV, for example. Simone is no devotee of athletics, yet she has a careful, slender figure.

Her greatest misfortune, in my opinion, is her raucous, screeching voice. I think her classes in French get a very human rendering of certain concierges, however, which must have, for her students, put to rest the cliché that all French is romantic. This is a voice that could momentarily stand against a German infantryman, which it did in 1940, before he belted Simone across her high-bridged nose, slapped her on the rear, and told her to get him something to eat. Her first husband died during the same month, June, when Herr Hitler decided he wanted France, too. One day as we narrowly missed a log truck, Simone told us that her young husband had been run over by one of his own army's trucks. This earned him a French decoration, which was given to her.

All in all, Simone strikes me as mostly depthless and harmless. One is bound to have some compassion for a woman with two husbands out from under her, in spite of her screeching voice. Staunton has confided rather sniggeringly that she now and then takes on young men in their twenties. Most of the time, this begins with renting them a very cheap room in her big house, or maybe helping them with their French. According to Staunton, they all take advantage—but I think more power to her.

Staunton and Simone are talking about last night's chamber ensemble at LSU. They really live in that academic community rather than in Blackston's. Of course, Blackston has no chamber ensemble. Most of the faculty who live in Blackston take up hobbies and stack up years toward retirement.

"Did you see how that cellist handled his bow? You would have thought he was cutting up a side of beef," Staunton remarked, keeping his eyes on the road—something Simone had never been able to do. She drove for a week, but we asked her to stop. She kept running off the highway, and this road is not one to be careless on. Two lanes with lots of log trucks.

"Out of all that crowd, half of them came to the party afterwards." This remark reflects Simone's real reason for going. She is interested in people.

A great deal of the time, Staunton is doing his bitchy best to attack whoever comes within his sights. He is mostly bald at thirty with a few strands of hair pulled over the top and given as much attention as a Medusa at her hairdresser's. He is egg shaped, but saves himself by wearing very expensive clothes with a conservative style so that he comes off more like a banker. His most distinguishing mark is his missing chin—unusual for someone his age. It is not the result of too much fat; it is just that the bones that should have cantilevered his chin were foreshortened.

"I exchanged a few words with the cellist at the party, and he was perfectly oafish. After the Budapest, all this was such a comedown." Staunton goes on like this much of the time, and he fits a type so well that after meeting him, most people react the way they do when they see another swallowtail. It's interesting, the swallowtail is behaving quite normally, and they turn their attention to something else. Staunton is just as harmless as Simone, though not as pretty as a swallowtail. And he has to keep up with a lot of names. This coloratura had ousted so-and-so at the Met, this ballet dancer hit his partner with his pump and she *certainly* deserved it, and wasn't it fatefully sad that Gregorian suffered a certain rigidity once it was universally performed in the eleventh century.

After fifteen minutes of the journey, the landscape announces a motif that it will pursue until we get to Blackston. Mostly a poor-white version of Fitzgerald's Valley of the Ashes. The land is absolutely flat and the highway closely parallels some railroad tracks. As is not unusual in many sections of the United States, little villages or towns appear with regularity every five miles—towns that had sprung up with the railroad. The first little town was larger than the rest, as it was fed by the industry of the city. Numerous families live here to "get away from it all"—"all" being the big, bad city.

As we pass through this little town today, the conversation in our car drops off. Simone fishes around in her purse for some makeup, and Staunton pushes in the car lighter and begins packing a cigarette on the horn. The reason for this nervous silence is that we normally picked up Henry Brown at this point. Even though Henry is not with us now, there is still the conditioned reflex to turn down Cloverdale Street and stop in front of his small tract house of dingy pink asbestos siding, the kind of house that looks tempting enough in an architect's rendering but never in reality. It had been run-down when Henry and his wife Audrey rented it. I think the landlord was the Federal Housing Authority because the owner had flown the coop, as Henry used to say. When we would drive up, all of his six children would still be waiting to be taken to school or nursery. His wife occasionally appeared behind the screen door, her hair still up in tight pin-curls as she prepared for work. All of their children were under nine years old.

Actually, the Browns were not out of their element in this small town. They had moved down from northern Louisiana, and the people back in the hills there looked like the same breeding that you find here. It's remotely Scotch-Irish, but the blood had been tempered in the hot Southern sun. Henry's complexion was a brown that was somehow different, though. Everything about Henry was brown, his wavy hair, his eyes, his clothes, his briefcase, as if an artist had been charged with tinting the image to go with his name and life. He was thirty-five years old, but talked like a man fifty or sixty years old in the way that many younger men in the South learn to do.

Henry's avenue to the English department was not unique but still interesting. There are failed preachers, priests, and latter-day mystics in English departments, it seems to me, because this is a refuge of last resort. Many of them had majors in English before they started toward divinity schools. But as their old ghosts deserted them and gradually the places were taken up by others, these people had drifted back into English. We even get a few of them over in history, where I am. Henry had come from a very poor, red-clay family. As I gather the story, a family in the Baptist church offered to keep him after he was in junior high school and his father had given permission. The school in the hills was not good, and Henry had demonstrated more than the neighborhood average of interest in book things. This all culminated in Henry's graduation from a Baptist seminary, and he and his wife had settled into a parsonage. I never knew why he left the ministry, but it wasn't because he ceased to have *any* faith, because he still took his family to the Baptist church right up to the end.

After finishing another degree in English, he had joined our group commuting to Blackston. Well, Henry's threshold for ornaments and fluffy art-talk was much lower than my own, and since he rode in the back seat with me, we fell to our own conversations most of the time, which bored Simone and Staunton stiff. They certainly didn't feel left out. Henry soon discovered that I was a man of no faith, and of course there is a much more fertile field for discussion between a strong believer and an atheist than between a believer and nominal believers like Simone and Staunton. Simone was Catholic, and Staunton once described himself as very High Church Anglican and one who might bolt for Rome in a fit because of "better theater." His words, not mine.

Henry's "serious conversation" was more his choice than my own. Much of the time, such conversations simply lead to flustered feelings with nobody learning anything but having his own position made more intractable. Such matters are one thing over a cup of coffee, but quite another when one is locked into the prison of a commuter's car. Even Simone and Staunton couldn't avoid Henry's talk of salvation and the like. Normally Henry didn't slip off into such cauldrons, and his own faith had eroded enough that he could consider with a renewed curiosity and honesty matters that had fallen formerly into rhythmic affirmation.

Ten or fifteen minutes would often pass with talk about his wife and children. His wife worked as a secretary in the little town and she did not like it. Henry was trying to get enough for a downpayment on a small piece of land where he could garden and have some animals. He thought this would be good for the children, especially, but he said his wife seemed to have little sympathy for this dream, small though it was. Of all places, Henry had wanted his land in the vicinity we whizzed past now, hellishly desolate in the winter. In this flat country, there were no wild mountains unchanged by the seasons, nor even any

snow to cover the dead ocherous land. What broke the dullness were
the open sores of greasy-walled filling stations cluttered with piles of
old tires and tubes and their ESSO signs that flapped in the February
wind.

A subject we had kicked about for several days in the very early fall,
I have recalled numerous times in the last two months. Where does
one find the imperative for social action if there is no God? Why is he
to feel responsible for anyone else?

As we turned the matter around and around, we naturally got no
closer to the answer, I suspect, after the conversations than before.
Henry felt (and I must admit my hunch is he was right) that Dostoy-
evsky's idea that all things were possible if there were no God was the
only logical one. It was mostly an accident when I noted one day that
one of the new French Existentialists asserted that the basis of responsibility was that one was free to leave the earth if he chose, but that if
he decided to stay, he was responsible, or that was the gist of it. Henry
pondered that, and then we moved on to other matters as the fall came
toward us in a shower of lectures and papers to grade. But Henry did
not forget the words, for every now and then when some matter at
school would come up, perhaps an absurdity that only an administrator
could dream up, he would grin one of his rare grins, his white teeth
stark against his steady brownness, and remark to me, "Well, if we
don't like it, we can leave." It was like a private joke that the two of us
shared.

Two months ago my back went out as it likes to do in the cold
months. All I have to do is twist the wrong way on a cold morning or
lift the garbage can wrong and it spasms. I called Simone very early to
tell her not to pick me up and at a more respectable time called my
department head to let him in on the good news. He is a kindly old
man, not given to irony, but on that morning he acknowledged my
reason for not coming in as if I were deceiving him. Having the
morning face me like it did, I tried to pamper my back. I filled the
bath with scalding hot water and turned the radio on, even put a
magazine close at hand. The regular five-minute newscast broke the
story about a Blackston professor, Henry Brown, who had bludgeoned

to death five of his six children, shot his wife, and then blown his own brains out.

The evening paper went into detail, and I called Simone when she returned home, to find out what she knew. Simone declared excitedly that when they got to Henry's house, there were police cars all over the place, that nobody was being let in, and that a deputy had simply blurted out, "Ma'am, Mr. Brown ain't going to school this morning. He's done killed himself. Now you'll have to move on, please ma'am." The evening paper said that Henry Brown had the day before gone to a bank in Blackston, borrowed a couple of thousand dollars on his signature and had the loan insured, which was not unusual. Bankers like to look out for themselves. In the early hours of the morning, Henry had called his brother-in-law and told him what he planned to do. The brother-in-law was to pay the funeral expenses with the money which Henry had borrowed and which would not have to be paid back. Before the brother-in-law could call the police and they could get over, Henry had taken a ball-peen hammer and clubbed his big wife first and shot her with a .22 pistol either then or later; he then clubbed all of his children with the hammer, and the ones who still moved he shot in the head. Then he killed himself with one shot. There had been some running about, the reporter wrote, because the house was very bloody. The professor had left a note, the story went on, and it said, "This is the only way all of us will get out of this rotten world together." The story concluded that one of the children had survived and was in critical condition.

We don't have far to go now to get to Blackston, and Henry's little town is long gone. Simone and Staunton have resumed their banter about the Metropolitan Opera touring group that will perform *Medea* this coming Saturday. Staunton is comparing this cast with the one he heard at La Scalla, or maybe on a record he has.

Henry's action could be understood in a lot of ways, I think. His wife kept harping on him and killing his dreams, he faced frustrating money problems with so many children, and so on. The morning he had gone to the bank he had come by my office to chat, but I was on my way to a class. All I remember was he had a gleam in his brown eyes as if he knew something I didn't know. I only interpret this in this way after the fact. I can't help wondering though, if I had been free to talk with Henry, would it have made any difference? Of course, I can't really be held responsible for something I did not know about.

The people in Blackston have treated the event like scum covering a pond after a stone is thrown in; the scum covers the hole right back over. It's as if what he did threatened them so much they had to go on the defensive right away. For a lot of the students, the explanation was a lot easier because Henry was "in English." If a professor of dairy science had done the same thing, it would have been more problematic. I understand the fact that life must go on and that people must turn their attention to the living. There was no reason for the college to stay in mourning for Henry Brown.

I'm the one with the problem, and I know it. Henry is my problem. Why did he do this thing? I remember he used to grind his teeth a lot and the muscles would knot in his jaw. This was the whole time I knew him. So, okay, there was a lot of hostility in him. That doesn't explain it away. And I won't have it, at least in Henry's case, that he was "simply" crazy and didn't know what he was doing. Not that you can't be crazy and lay elaborate plans. Of course you can. But Henry knew what he was about, I'm convinced. For those students and teachers who knew Henry, that's what put the mortal fear in them. Which brings up my idle remark about some French Existentialists and what . . . my own culpability? Henry was a grown man. But that does not entirely make his ghost go away. I must say it brought home what bloody instruments ideas are. There is also the problem of why Henry had to kill his children and his wife if he was the one who had decided to go, and this may bear on the whole question.

Henry had no sense of style, and I don't mean this in the flippant way Staunton would have said it. He just had no sense of the right moves. I believe Henry was sincere about killing all his children so that they could go with him. Why he wanted to take his wife leaves me baffled. But then he botched his grand move; he left a daughter with a damaged brain and yet a memory of what had happened. It's a ghastly thought, but he couldn't even do this right. Matters of style and large ideas should not be pursued unless one is willing to train for the complete gesture. Otherwise it is as bad as forcing a ten-year-old ballet student to do the *Ritual Fire Dance to Exorcise Evil Spirits.*

We have finished our journey to Blackston, and Simone waves at two of her students. She is well-liked. Which leads me to observe that Simone and Staunton will very likely not murder. I also note that Henry's ghost has not been explained or put to flight. As we get ready to go our separate ways, Simone gaily asks me to go to see *Medea* with her on Saturday and to a party afterwards. I surprise her by accepting.

William Peden

ABSENT THEE FROM FELICITY

"It's almost time," she called. "The rocket's supposed to go off in a few minutes." So he placed the manuscript on the walnut surface of his desk and hurried into the living room.

"This would be a good time to have a color TV, wouldn't it?" He half-closed his eyes. "They've been saying that the blast-off will be as bright as the sun. A million people down there, I read in the *Post-Dispatch*, waiting, watching. Came there from all over the country. I can't understand it, can you?"

She shrugged her shoulders and returned her gaze to the familiar bespectacled face of the announcer. "No, I wouldn't want to be there myself. Not with all that mob. But I can understand why other people might want to see it."

Then abruptly, just as he had settled into his comfortable chair, the count-down had stopped. The announcer was ad-libbing desperately, and then he was joined by a commentator with a German accent, and there was much talk and speculation about the reasons for the hold. Shaking his head in disbelief and disappointment, he rose from his chair, and started for the kitchen. "I need a drink, just a short one. How about you?"

"A short one would be nice." She raised her voice slightly as he opened the icebox door and fumbled for the ice cubes. "Oh dear, he just said it will be at least an hour before it goes off."

"*Goes* off? Hummpf! *If* it goes off. I'm inclined to think it *won't* go off. I doubt that it'll ever get off the ground."

So they drank their drinks and watched the tube, and just as they decided to give up and get ready for bed, the phone in the adjoining room rang.

"I'll get it," he grumbled. "Damn it, I wish people wouldn't call me at this hour."

i spend ten or twelve hours a week talking with the little bastards about their work and still they call me at home when i'm trying to relax they're cannibals they eat me up no matter what time i get to the office they're lined up outside the door waiting their manuscripts in their hands they lurk around the corridor like hyenas simply slavering it's beginning to get me down i'm nothing but a surrogate papa or something they don't give me time to write anything of my own i wish to god they'd leave me alone for a while

He picked up the receiver impatiently. "Hello," he said, and she smiled as the harshness slowly drained from his voice. "Who? Oh, Rufus. How are you, Rufus?"

"You *what?*"

. . . .

"Incredible!"

. . . .

"I assume you're completely sincere about all this, Rufus?"

. . . .

"You're not high, are you?"

. . . .

"That's good, that's very good."

. . . .

"That's interesting, Rufus. Very interesting indeed."

. . . .

"In a robe? You're wearing a purple robe?"

. . . .

"Do you think that's wise, Rufus? In this weather, I mean. It's bitter cold tonight; it's only five above, I heard it on the television a few minutes ago."

. . . .

"No, the damned rocket *didn't* go off."

. . . .

"Oh, you don't care? You couldn't care less?"

. . . .

"You don't feel the cold anymore?"

. . . .

"Since *what?*"

. . . .

"Look, why don't you just stay inside, sort of take things easy, think things over the rest of the night."

. . . .

"No, I can't say I have. Really, Ru. . . ."

"Yes, we *must* talk these things over. But not tonight. Just stay there tonight, Rufus. It's terribly cold, I can hear the ice crackling on the trees."

. . . .

"Yes, early, at my office. Yes, Rufus. And do be careful. Stay inside, will you?"

She heard the receiver click and then he was back in the living room, absently stroking the bridge of his nose.

"One of your writing students is in trouble again, I gather."

"Yes, that was Rufus." He glanced at the television screen. "Anything happen while I was on the phone?"

"No, not really. They think they've discovered what's wrong, though. They think everything's about to be *go* and A-O-K, and all that. But who's Rufus? What's his problem? That was an awfully long phone call."

"He had a lot to talk about." He shook his head and wiped his brow with the back of his hand. "That was Rufus Berg. He was in the short-story seminar. A year ago I think it was. He was very good, really talented. I published one of his stories in *Midlands*."

"Berg? Rufus Berg?" She frowned slightly. "I don't remember him. I can't recall that name."

"How could you forget him? You must remember him, from the time we had the class over before Christmas. Rufus was the fat one, huge really. Enormous."

fat as pontius pilate unlovely flesh bulging beneath a faded blue sweatshirt number sixty-nine soixante neuf i wonder if he realized pale of face and acne-scarred dark hair to this shoulders headband peace symbol the works i wonder

"Oh, *that* one. Of course I remember *him*, I just couldn't recall the name. So awkward but so, so sweet, in a way, in spite of . . . everything. I liked him, he really had a sweet way about him. And he brought you that little statue, didn't he?"

"That's right, he was the one. I thought he'd left school; it's been months since I'd seen or heard from him. But we ran into each other in the Commons a couple of weeks ago; we had a cup of coffee together. He's grown a beard."

"I expect he looks better with a beard, doesn't he? But what did he want? Why did he call you?'

"Yes, he did look better; I mean his face was better. But I think he's flipped. I'm afraid he's really flipped-out this time."

"Oh, that's too bad. What's his problem?"

He sank into the chair in front of the television where, on the screen, swirling vapor shrouded the enormous rocket. "To make a long story short, he told me he was the Son of God."

"The Son of God! For Heaven's sake!"

"He said that earlier today he'd been informed he was the reincarnated Christ."

"Informed! Informed by whom?"

"By God."

"By God?" Again she frowned, her fair brow furrowed in thought. "He wasn't high, was he? He must have been high. He'd been fooling around with drugs when he was one of your students, hadn't he?"

"Yes, he had, but I don't think he was high tonight. As a matter of fact, he seemed quite calm. Oh, there was a sort of suppressed excitement in his voice, you might even say a note of triumph, but he seemed completely sober. No, I don't think he was high at all."

"He couldn't have been putting you on, could he?"

"No, I honestly don't think he was putting me on. He could have been, of course, but I don't think so. He just isn't that kind of person, not at all; it wouldn't be in his nature to do anything like that."

"But if he wasn't stoned, or if he wasn't playing some kind of stupid joke, then what?"

"Who knows? Maybe he *is* the Son of God. You can't prove it by me. He. . . ."

"That's a fine remark from an Episcopalian."

"Ex-Episcopalian, please." He smiled at her tolerantly, his eyes half-closed in thought. "I remember his telling me, that night before Christmas, that either he was a priest in some God cult or was working on it—he'd always been up to his armpits in mysticism and mythology; that's one of the reasons he gave me that statue of Thoth."

ra has spoken thoth has written god of the arts and sciences patron of writers and of literature hermes trismegistus three times very very great the true universal demi-urge hatched the world-egg at hermopilis magna moon-god head of a baboon and the tiny phallus fine as a scribe's quill

"That poor boy."

"Whatever it was that he was into, it really worked. And today was the, uh, climax. He's the chosen one, he said. The perfect man—don't smile, I believe he's absolutely serious—the result of hundreds of years of evolution—no, of evolving; that's what he said."

"My goodness! That poor boy."

"Don't be too sorry for him. I think he's as happy as a lark about the whole business."

"But how? When?"

"It all happened today. He'd been having premonitions, stirrings I think he called them, so it didn't come as a complete surprise to him. Today it all exploded. In one blinding flash. Just like that. He was walking downtown, and suddenly God spoke to him. Said he was his Son. Just like that."

"Amazing. But I still think he may have been putting you on."

"No, I'm convinced that he means it."

"Then I think we should call Jimmy."

He looked at his watch before answering. "Not a bad idea but I expect Jimmy's had a hard day. I'll bet the clinic was jumping from morning till night. This awful weather, and Christmas just around the corner; you know, don't you, more men commit suicide in December than any other month of the year? Jimmy told me that himself. . . ." Absently he ran his fingers through his thinning hair. "I'd sure like to have his opinion, but I don't think we should call him tonight. Tomorrow maybe, but not tonight."

"Well, if you think so. But what about poor Rufus?"

"I hope he'll be all right." He shook his head slowly. "You know what else he said God told him? God said, Rufus, go buy yourself a white robe and dye it purple and put it on. He bought it when he was downtown, he said; he's wearing it now."

"That poor child."

"And then do you know what he said? You won't believe this. Rufus said that God told him to go to King Arthur's and get his hair washed."

"You're making that up. King Arthur's? That fancy uni-sex barber-shop on the Strollway?"

"That's right, King Arthur's. So he went there and got his hair washed. With the robe, the whole business cost him about fifty dollars."

"Fifty dollars! And I expect the poor boy's as poor as a church-mouse."

"That's right."

"And then what?"

"He wasn't really too clear about what happened next; he was getting pretty excited at that point. All I could gather was that he's fixing to go out and announce it . . . his new status, you might say."

"Going out? From where?"

"He's been living with—rooming with, I guess, would be more accurate—some babe. They live in one of those fleabags on Hitt or Paquin. I can't think of her name, but she was one of my students, too. She and Rufus were in the seminar the same year; that's when they met. I don't remember her too well. She was a pale little thing, not the sort of person you'd ever remember."

"Hmmmm. But didn't you say that he wasn't interested in women?"

"Yes, I expect I did. Most of his stories were about homosexuals. Homosexuals and mystics."

"That Rufus!"

"He was, uh, slightly manic when he told me about her. They're planning to build a pyramid or something in Missouri, or maybe in Canada. . . ."

"A pyramid? In Missouri or Canada! Good Heavens!"

"He said they'd have a little nest—those were his exact words—in the center of the pyramid where the air would always be pure and unpolluted; he was very big on ecology at one time, I recall. And then they'd float off somewhere together. He said something about taking her to nirvana with him eventually."

"Taking her to nirvana with him? You don't think he's dangerous, do you?" Half serious, half humorous, she lowered her voice. "*I love you, baby, let me take you to nirvana with me.* Maybe we'd better call up Jimmy after all."

"No, let's not call Jimmy tonight. I don't think Rufus is dangerous. He was always as gentle as a lamb in my class." Rubbing his forehead with thumb and fingers, he walked across the room and peered at the icy branches beyond the frost-swirled window. "I don't know, maybe you're right," he said after a long silence. "You never can tell. Those big gentle ones are the ones who can really blow up." Again he studied the silvery darkness. "Eliot's all wrong, you know," he said suddenly, more to himself than to her. "He's all wrong about April being the cruelest month. It's December. Christ! What a month, what a season, it's been. Nixon reelected, the war still going on, all those plane crashes! And now the damned rocket not going off!" Shaking his shoulders angrily, he switched off the television set.

"And Christmas just around the corner. I used to love Christmas but, you know, I'm beginning to dread it. I suppose those damned carolers with the canned music will be around soon. I'm not going to give them a penny this year. It's an invasion of privacy."

He glared at her, and she smiled undestandingly but remained silent. "Besides, I've already sent a check to the Episcopal Church."

She nodded.

"Sure, I guess Rufus could be dangerous. In this weather, anybody could be dangerous. Everything's freezing! All that ice and sleet! When I came home from the office this afternoon, the trees were sighing. I've never heard them like that, sighing and rustling; it's unnatural. No wonder that poor bluejay flew into the dining-room window yesterday; he'd lost his whole sense of balance, his gyroscope was all fouled up." He shook his head sadly at the recollection. "No wonder Rufus thinks he's the Son of God. No wonder he wants to creep into his pyramid and take that poor woman to nirvana. But I don't think he's dangerous. I don't think Rufus would hurt *anybody*."

"I just wish he wouldn't go wandering around the University in the outfit. Someone could beat him up; you've said yourself they're still a lot of hoods at the University."

"No one's going to beat Rufus up. He's as strong as an ox."

"Well, he might get his feelings hurt, or something. I'd hate for him to have his feelings hurt. Or he could catch pneumonia. Walking around the University in a purple gown on a night like this!"

Again he shook his head and turned on the television. For a long moment he gazed at the announcer. "I doubt that the thing will fly," he said sadly. "I expect it won't get off the ground this time. Let's go to bed."

She rose slowly, reluctantly. "Don't you think maybe you should call him? You could *tell* him to stay inside. He likes you; he respects your advice. You could tell him *not* to go around announcing it till he's talked with you tomorrow."

"God, honey, I've got to get to bed. I've got two classes tomorrow. And half a dozen conferences with the cannibals." He undressed slowly, his forehead wrinkling. "Besides, I don't know his number. It'd probably be in that woman's name, and I can't remember her name. I've been trying to remember it but I can't. But I don't think you need worry about him." He rubbed his jaw thoughtfully. "I'll call Jimmy tomorrow, though. I'll get him to see Rufus. So let's not worry about Rufus any more. Not tonight, anyhow."

He leaned over and kissed her good-night, and turned off the light; they lay together, silent, not touching. "Rufus is really pretty lucky, come to think of it."

"Lucky? How do you mean, lucky?"

"Well, he's got a lot going for him, all things considered. In a way."

"I'm glad you think so."

"Look," he said, upset at the dryness of her voice. "I'm as concerned about Rufus as you are. But I can't run all over town looking for him. He's probably snug in bed with that poor woman, in or out of his goddamn robe."

"All right, all right," she said, and lightly patted his shoulder. "I don't want you to do anything. Let's go to sleep."

She turned on her side and in a few moments was breathing gently. But sleep did not come to him that easily. He lay beside her stiffly, uncomfortable, wanting to turn over, to stretch his legs, but fearing to wake her up. He lay there for a long time, uncomfortable, listening to the wind in the icy branches.

Clay Reynolds

MEXICO

Curly Hughs sat on the tailgate of his GMC pickup, smoked a
cigarette, sipped a luke-warm beer, and watched Elwood Hays use a
fwo-foot length of telephone cable to beat the absolute living shit out
of Charlie Donahue. Since the two combatants were lodge brothers
and very close friends, Curly had promised Charlie he would stop the
fight before Elwood got seriously hurt, but things had been going on
for nearly ten minutes now, and it didn't look like Charlie was going
to get in another lick. He'd thrown the first punch, of course, but that
was the last time he'd touched Elwood at all. Elwood had touched him,
though. He kept right on touching him, too, and every time that piece
of phone cable came down on Charlie's back and side, Curly thought
it might be the last time Charlie would get up.

Elwood needed a good licking, Curly thought. It was a shame that
he wasn't getting it.

"Are you goin' to come over here an' *help* me or not?" Charlie called
between blows from the phone cable. "You're supposed to be my
friend."

Curly took another sip of beer and thought the matter over. Elwood
had been screwing Charlie's wife while he worked the swing out at the
gyp mill for about six months. Rumor was that Charlie's newest kid—
his third—was Elwood's, too, but word around the lodge was that the
kid might belong to any number of good old boys who had paid Louise
a visit while he was earning double-time during the past several years.

Louise was a lot younger than Charlie and still a looker, even if she did have three kids. Curly had thought about her quite a bit lately himself.

Elwood didn't say anything, but he was huffing and puffing and swinging at Charlie with wide arches that showed the sweat stains under his arms, even though they were just getting over a norther and it was chilly. They were both forty pounds overweight, and they had both been drinking for several hours. It should have been an even match, except Elwood had the cable on him when they got started.

He started working the cable on Charlie's head, and Curly tossed the beer bottle into a cardboard box in the pickup's bed and slid down. He found an axe-handle under the tool box and pulled it out. It was muddy in J. D.'s parking lot, and the joint's neon sign's lights reflected prettily in the puddles. He stepped carefully to keep from getting his boots messed up.

"Elwood, you 'bout had enough?" Curly asked. He rolled up his sleeves and walked around a big puddle over by the two men. Charlie was down in the mud and whimpering, trying to keep the cable from hitting him in the face again.

Elwood paused and looked at Curly for a minute. "What?" he asked.

Curly stepped up, squared off, and swung the handle around from the right. Elwood received the blow solidly on the back of his head and dropped like a box of rocks. He didn't get up.

"Why in hell didn't you do that a while ago?" Charlie demanded. He climbed to his feet and began trying to wipe the mud off his jeans. Blood streamed from his nose and also from two or three mean cuts on his face and hands. "That son of a bitch damn near beat me to death."

"You looked like you might of got him on the run any minute there," Curly said. He glanced down at Elwood, who was still out cold. "I told you to hit him on the jaw. He's got a glass jaw."

"Well," Charlie found his cap and began slapping wet gravel off of it, "I didn't get much of a chance. Where'n hell he get that pipe?"

"Guess he had it in his truck," Curly said. "An' it wasn't a pipe. It was a telephone cable. He works for the telephone company."

"Yeah, well, it felt like a pipe. But his truck's way over yonder." Charlie pointed out vaguely toward the end of the parking lot where Elwood's green Ford Supercab was parked in the fog. "He didn't have time to go get it. Had it with him. Like to knocked my teeth out." He stuck two fingers into his mouth and worked them around. When he spit, it was bloody in the neon reflections. "Man don't walk around with a pipe in his pants."

"Well, you were in there telling God an' half the world what you were going to do when you saw him. Guess somebody warned him, an' he was just drunk enough to go get it."

Charlie inspected Elwood's form. He was still out cold. "He screwed Louise. We had a fight last night, an' she told me."

Curly didn't respond. He went back to the pickup's cab and found two more beers. "We going to go to Mexico or not?" he asked.

"I don't know," Charlie limped over. He fingered his torso in search of broken bones. Curly opened his beer and handed the other to Charlie. "I might be all busted up. I'm hurtin' too much to tell."

"Goddamnit, you said we were goin'," Curly said. "You said you had the money. I sure don't. You got two days off. 'Sides, we promised Jackpot."

Jackpot was also a close friend, and a lodge brother. He used to ride bulls on the international circuit, but he got too old and too busted up. He was now retired, but he didn't have any pension.

"Why can't he get laid 'round here like everybody else does? Why we got to go all the way to Mexico?"

" 'Cause he stutters. An' he's so ugly, there's not a whore in Dallas or Fort Worth that'd touch him. Not one he can afford, anyhow."

Charlie looked down at his ruined clothes. "I got to go home an' change. That son of a bitch broke my nose."

"Well, then, let's do it."

Charlie stood still for a moment, bent one leg up from the knee to see if it still worked, and nodded. Curly lit a cigarette and started around to the other side of the cab. "Say, you want to take him with us?" Charlie pointed at Elwood.

"We're already taking Jackpot," Curly said. "Can't get more'n three in the cab. Goddamn Highway Patrol's sure to pull us over we get four in there."

"Yeah, but Elwood was plannin' to go," Charlie argued. "If we hadn't got into a fight, we'd already be halfway there. He was wantin' to go."

Curly stepped gingerly over to Elwood's slumped form. "We could throw him in the back, I guess," he said. "But you take him. I don't want to mess up my shirt."

Charlie limped over and hefted Elwood's dead weight. Curly finally had to help, but he kept Elwood's muddy boots out at arm's length while they dumped him into the bed and slammed the tailgate shut.

"Think he'll be all right?" Charlie wondered when they pulled out into the highway lane.

"Get him a blanket from your place," Curly suggested. "That'll keep him warm."

"Listen, you fat, no 'count son of a bitch, you think you're goin' to go runnin' all over the goddamn country an' leavin' me here with the kids again, you got 'nother think comin'," Louise screeched at Charlie when he stomped past her into their twelve-by-forty mobile home. He ignored her and started peeling the wet, muddy and bloody clothes from his body, leaving them where they fell. "You're s'posed to fix the dispose-all this weekend. Toilets is stopped up, too. That'un of the kids won't quit runnin'. You ain't goin' nowhere."

She suddenly realized he was not alone, shaded her eyes, although it was pitch beyond the spill of light from the doorway, and sweetened her tone. "Oh, hi, Curly, Jackpot. Y'all come on in here. Watch them steps. They're rotten."

She turned and yelled back toward the hallway, "That's somethin' *else* his highness was supposed to take care of this weekend."

"Hi, L-L-Louise," Jackpot said, removing his hat and twisting it in his hands. Curly just nodded and lit a cigarette as he came into the room and sat down on a barstool at the counter. Two kids were taking apart a stuffed animal in front of a country-rock video that blared out of a console color TV in the corner. In the back, where Charlie was banging around, the baby squalled.

"Why don't you pick that baby up?" Louise yelled. She moved behind the counter and picked up a cigarette she had left burning in an ashtray, took a drag, and blew a stray lock of hair away from her eyes with the smoke. "He needs changin'," she sighed. "Charlie'd rather have a tooth pulled'n change a dirty diaper."

She had on a white blouse tied in a knot beneath small, firm breasts. She wore no bra, and her nipples were tiny, pink buttons beneath the cloth. Long, dark hair spun down both sides of her face and draped across her shoulders. Her exposed tummy was flat, tight, in spite of her having an eight-month-old baby and two other children besides. Curly remembered that she had the biggest collection of home-workout video tapes in town, or so Charlie bragged. Her jeans were tight around firm tubes of thigh.

"Where the hell's my good shirt?" Charlie bellowed over the baby's crying. "The one with the purple flowers on it?"

"Up yours," Louise yelled back. Then she turned a warm smile on her guests. "Y'all want some coffee or a beer or somethin'?" Curly remembered that she had been a waitress at a truckstop out on 287.

"D-D-D-Don't go to no t-t-trouble," Jackpot said. He flopped his long form down on the floor and started tickling the kids, who melted into a squirming mass of squeals and screams.

"I could use a beer," Curly said. He always like to watch Louise bend over into the refrigerator while she fished around for the bottles, which really wasn't necessary since the whole bottom two shelves were solidly stocked with beer. She had a nice rear end, he thought. It was her best feature.

He was enjoying the show when Charlie stormed into the room. He had put on clean jeans, but he hadn't found the shirt. His huge white belly flopped out over the belt buckle. His navel looked like a hairy badger hole, and bruises from Elwood's cable were already purpling across his back and sides.

"Goddamnit, Louise," he yelled. "Seems like the least you could do is keep my shirts clean." He started digging through a plastic laundry basket in the corner.

"Clean you own goddamn shirts," she squawked back at him. "I got better things to do." Then she set the beer bottle on the counter in front of Curly. Sweat rolled down it when it hit the humidity of the room. Her nails were long and bright red. "I ain't your slave," she finished softly and with a new smile for Curly. "You sure you don't want a beer, Jackpot?" Her blue eyes never left Curly's.

"Well, l-l-long's you're servin'," Jackpot said painfully. One of the children had him down on the floor and was trying to bite his hand. The other was jumping up and down on his skinny stomach. "These k-k-kids get b-b-bigger every time I see 'em. They're h-h-h-harder to handle'n a gr-gr-green Brahma."

"Yeah, well, they're a handful," Louise called from inside the refrigerator. Curly was sure she gave her bottom an extra wiggle or two just for his benefit. "But I got me a new day-care center," she said as she turned and produced another bottle. "They'll be over there every afternoon from two to six," she said. Her voice softened, and her smile was directed again at Curly. "Two to six," she repeated when she twisted off the top.

Jackpot kicked the kids off of him just as one landed a deep kick to his groin. He had a sick grin on his face when he limped over and took the beer with no comment. His face was bright red.

"Give her more goddamn time to watch soap operas an' paint her goddamn toenails," Charlie grumbled. He pulled a ball of wrinkles from the basket, sniffed it, and nodded. When he pulled it on and stretched it over his stomach, the creases magically smoothed out into a bright western shirt with huge purple roses above the yoke. "Spends more time on the floor stretched out in front of the TV'n she does in the kitchen. Ain't had nothin' to eat 'round here that wasn't froze or boiled in a year."

"Charlie," she said, her blue eyes growing large as she studied him. "What in God's name happened to your face? It looks like you took on a whole bale of bobbed-wire."

"That son of a bitch Elwood Hays come at me with a pipe," Charlie explained over his shoulder. He disappeared down the hall again.

"That right?" Louise asked Curly. Her face showed a confusion of shock and satisfaction.

He nodded. " 'Cept it wasn't a pipe. It was a phone cable."

She looked doubtfully at the plastic line running from the telephone to the jack in the wall. "Phone cable?"

"It's r-r-rubber-lined glass. T-T-T-Two inches thick," Jackpot explained. "I got hit up 'side the h-h-head with one of them once. N-N-Nigger boy du-done it over in Hou-Houston at the r-r-r-rodeo. Put my d-d-d-dick in the du-dirt, I can tell you. Got my wallet an' my c-car ke-ke-keys 'fore I could see straight. I can't see how ol' Ch-Ch-Ch-Charlie's walkin' 'round."

"How's Elwood?" Louise asked both of them. "Is he okay?" There was concern in her voice, but not much.

"I guess he's okay," Charlie said. He came around the counter and went to the refrigerator. He had a pink afghan in his hands. "Curly here dropped him with a pole axe just as he was 'bout to put my lights out for good. Ain't that right, Curly?"

Curly said nothing and sipped his beer.

"You had a fight with Elwood, too?" she asked, her eyes now narrowing. "What'd y'all do, gang up on him?"

"Hell, no," Charlie said. He dragged a cooler out from beside the refrigerator and started emptying ice trays into it. "I walked up and asked him if he'd been over here sniffin' your crotch, like you said he had, an' he just come up an' hit me with that pipe."

"I never said any such a thing!"

"Did, too. Standin' right over there. You said he'd took you 'to the limits of satisfaction.' Don't that beat all?" Charlie looked at Curly and Jackpot for sympathy. "Man's wife talkin' to him like that. It's them goddamn TV talk-shows that does it."

Jackpot nodded wisely.

"Well, I was mad," Louise said. "I might of said anything."

"Well, he didn't deny it," Charlie said. He tossed the empty trays into the sink, then dumped the remains of the ice maker's bucket into the cooler as well. "An' I was just gettin' a mudhole stomped in my butt when Curly here jumped up an' knocked him down. That was all. We were defending your honor."

She looked from Curly to Jackpot to Charlie. "That right?" A grin cornered her mouth up at one end.

She was so cute, Curly couldn't stand it. He looked at his bottle and read the label.

"You still drivin' for Woodrow's Wholesale Gas?" she asked Curly.

He shook his head. "Quit this mornin'."

She licked her lips. "You need to come by for a cup of coffee sometime."

Curly felt suddenly too warm and re-read the label. Two to six, he thought.

"I wa-wa-wasn't there," Jackpot said. "They co-come for me after it was over. Get me 'nother bu-beer, Ch-Ch-Charlie."

Charlie obliged and then began shoving the better part of a case of bottles into the cooler.

"So where's he at, now?" Louise asked. Her painted fingertips bracketed her bare midriff and she cocked a hip.

"Back of my truck," Curly said. "He's still out."

She flew out the door.

"Kids, y'all be good for your mama," Charlie ordered absently as he closed the cooler and hefted it up onto the counter. One of them was urinating into a large pot with a dead plant in it. The other was back to work on the stuffed animal. Clouds of cotton swirled around the room in front of the TV while he worked. "Here," Charlie handed the afghan to Jackpot. "We can cover him up with this."

"He's sleepin' like a baby," Louise said as she pushed past them on her way back inside. "He's got him a goose egg on the back of his noggin, but I guess you didn't hurt him none. Where you goin' with my afghan?"

Charlie had the cooler and was already outside. "Mexico. We got to cover him up so he don't freeze," he said. "Grab some tater chips, Curly."

"Not with Aunt Harriet's afghan you don't," Louise yelled. "It was the last thing she did for me was make that afghan." She disappeared inside as Curly followed Jackpot outside.

Curly found two jumbo bags on top of the refrigerator. A bottle of hot sauce was on the shelf next to the sink. He took that, too.

Charlie opened Curly's pickup and put the cooler in the floorboard. Jackpot stood uncertainly next to the truck bed with the afghan in his hands.

"Let's go," Charlie yelled. "Shotgun!"

"I already cu-cu-called 'shotgun,' g-goddamnit," Jackpot yelled. Then he offered, "Let's tr-tr-tr-trade off."

"All I know is I'm drivin'," Curly said.

"Here," Louise emerged with a ragged yellow comforter in her hands. "Use this. We got it when we had to bring that sideboard home from Mama's."

"Goddamn sideboard gave me a hernia," Charlie said, holding open the door. "Throw it on him, an' get in. It's startin' to rain."

Jackpot made the exchange and dumped the comforter over Elwood, then he climbed in the middle.

"You *ain't* goin', Charlie," Louise yelled. "I told you that you ain't runnin' off an' leavin' me every time you get a weekend."

"We'll be back on Sunday," Charlie hollered back and shut the door. "If you get a chance, why don't you take the Chevy in for a tune-up. It's runnin' ragged."

"Goddamnit, Charlie, I'm tellin' you, you better not go!"

"Well, you can just stand there an' tell it to the tail lights of this here truck," he said lightly. " 'Cause I'm goin'. I work goddamn hard, an' I need my rest an' relaxation."

"You're just goin' down there to consort with Mescan whores," she accused.

"Well, least they give me peace," he said softly. "One way or another," he chuckled. "Be back on Sunday," he called louder. "Tell the kids I'll bring 'em a pretty."

"Well, I won't be here," she threatened. "I mean it! I'm goin' to Mama's."

"That'll last 'til the water boils," he grumbled and opened a beer. "Sunday," he called as Curly started the truck and began to back out. "An' don't forget 'bout the Chevy."

"I mean it!" she called angrily. "If you go, you can just as well stay gone." Then she dropped her tone to a lower, sweeter pitch. "Good to see you again, Curly," she said. "You don't be a stranger, hear?" One hand escaped the afghan and curled a strand of hair around a red nail.

They were at a rest-stop a hundred twenty-five miles south of town before Charlie realized he had left his wallet in his other pants.

"You re-re-reckon Elwood's got any mu-mu-mu-money on him?" Jackpot asked. It was seven in the morning, and they sat at the International Bridge in Laredo and contemplated the border. Jackpot looked older and uglier than ever, Curly thought. His graying red hair stuck out in five directions at once, and he was so thin, it was a wonder he could keep his trousers up.

Curly lit a cigarette and looked through the rear glass. Elwood's dark form was humped under the comforter. "It'd be the first time," he admitted.

Charlie slumped against the door, sound asleep. They had finished off all the beer they had, and they couldn't buy any more before eight o'clock in the states or until they crossed the border into Mexico.

"Well, ju-ju-ju-just how in hell we goin' to get our horns c-c-c-clipped, if we don't have the pr-pr-price?" Jackpot moaned.

"We ain't here to get *our* horns clipped," Curly pointed out. "We're here to get *your* horns clipped, an' it don't look like we got the price of more'n a trim."

The trips to Mexico had originally been Jackpot's idea, Curly remembered. He was so ugly, so skinny, that he couldn't even get one of the honkeytonk retreads over to Oklahoma to dance with him, let alone give him a tumble, even if he had the courage to talk to one of them, which he didn't. His stutter accentuated his natural shyness to the point where it was an aggravation. The infrequent trips to Mexico were his only chance to satisfy what he called his "nu-nu-natural urges," and since he had been picked up for DWI five or six times, he couldn't drive anymore and relied on Curly or some other friend to provide transportation. He didn't have enough money to buy a car anyway.

"Ch-Ch-Charlie owes me a hundred dollars," Jackpot whined. "For puttin' that gr-gravel down in this du-du-driveway. He said he'd p-p-p-pay me when we got here to keep me from bu-bu-bu-blowin' it back home."

"Well, Charlie's money's still 'back home,' so I guess you won't be 'bu-bu-bu-blowin' it' here either." Curly was angry.

"Ain't you g-g-got any mu-money?"

"I got eighteen dollars, an' you got twelve," Curly said. "We're out of beer, an' we ain't ate nothin' but chips all night."

"You got a cr-cr-credit c-c-c-card," Jackpot accused.

"That'll do for food an' gas," Curly sighed, "but it won't buy what you want."

"Thought you wanted it, too," Jackpot said.

Curly didn't answer. He normally did indulge himself on these trips. It was harmless fun, he usually thought. Besides, he had come to like Mexico. It was warm, sunny, relaxed, homey. He could really kick back there and be somebody he never could be back home. Propane

truck drivers don't get much respect, he knew, which was why he had
quit.

This time, though, he couldn't get his mind off Louise, off her blue
eyes and perky little tits and flat little belly, off her cute little bottom
swishing from side to side while she found the beers in the refrigerator.
Somehow the prospect of a Mexican girl didn't grab him right at the
moment. And he was suddenly tired.

"I'd be glad to chip in my money," he said. "I can live without it.
But we still ain't got enough."

"Well, shit," Jackpot said. "Shit, shit, shit." He was almost crying.

"I know a place," Charlie muttered. He was waking up and stretched
as best he could inside the cab. "Two dollars'll do. You may come home
with the blisterin' drips, but it'll do the job."

"Well, let's gu-gu-go," Jackpot said. "Let's j-just go."

Curly dropped the shifter and eased the truck into the bridge lane.

"What 'bout ol' Elwood?" Charlie looked behind them into the bed.

"Let him sleep," Curly said. "Mescans won't care, an' I know I
don't."

The row of buildings on Nuevo Laredo's southwest side toward which
Charlie directed them looked as if they hadn't changed since the
Revolution of 1824. The streets were dusty chugholes, and there were
no lights. Some buildings still had hitching posts in front of them.
Crumbling Spanish Imperial architecture fronted the dirtiest series of
shops, houses, bars and brothels Curly had ever seen. He parked the
pickup in an alley, and they piled out. Charlie pissed on the side of a
building while a scrawny dog barked at them and two doe-eyed children
looked on, and Curly and Jackpot inspected Elwood.

"You 'wake?" Curly asked Elwood, but he only groaned and rolled
over.

"Lemme 'lone," he grumbled when Jackpot also prodded him. "Got
me a headache. Just take me home. I'm cold."

"He don't nu-nu-know where he is," Jackpot said. "R-R-R-Reckon
we ought to haul him out? Get a du-du-drink or two in him?"

"Let him be," Charlie offered. "He's not hurtin' nobody." He pulled
the comforter up to cover Elwood's head and then tucked it under his

feet. "Looks like a load of manure," he said. "Not even Mescans'll steal shit."

They sauntered around the corner and drifted into the first door marked "Cantina" they found.

Even though it was now bright daylight outside, the inside of the cantina was dark and smoky. A few swarthy men sat around tables or rested their heads on folded arms behind piles of bottles and glasses. Two women dressed in see-through black lace nightgowns and spiked heels lounged next to the bar. They looked sleepy and tired. The bartender glowered at the newcomers as they took a table.

"*Servesas. Tres,*" Curly yelled, and the publican's frown melted to a disinterested look as he pulled three Carta Blancas from a cooler and handed them to the girls. They shrugged off their weariness and brought over the beers. Curly paid them three dollars and tipped them another.

"You from *Tejas?*" one of them asked. "College boys?"

"No, we're not no goddamn college boys," Charlie said in an outrush of a belch. "We're just horny gringos. How much?"

They looked from one to the other and then back down to Charlie. "Twenty bucks, American," the one who spoke first said. "That's for straight up. Anything fancy costs you more."

"Twenty bucks!" Charlie boomed. "*Chica,* you didn't get twenty bucks when you was a virgin in the donkey show. Two dollars is the price, 'less y'all are sellin' something' you're not showin'." He put one finger on a nostril of his battered nose and made a loud sniffing noise.

Curly looked at the two girls while they tried to decide how to accept the fat American's insult and proposition. One was about sixteen and so thin she almost didn't have breasts. Acne scars ran down both cheeks, and her eyes were too close together. The one who was doing the talking was meatier and had big tits, and her complexion was clear, but she wasn't much older, he didn't think. Neither was particularly appealing.

"You're kiddin' me," she said. "Two dollars went out with black-and-white TV. You want me to be nice, you pay the whole damn price," she rhymed. "Fifteen, straight up. Bottomline. And no nose candy."

"Must of been some ol' boys from south Dallas down here," Charlie jabbed Jackpot in the ribs. "We'll think 'bout it," he said. "Get us three more beers."

They stalked off, and Curly studied their naked hips undulating beneath the thin fabric. All he could think about was Louise, and it made him surly. Normally they were in better joints than this one. "We'll go find someplace else," he promised. He wanted to go to another cantina he knew, a place where the morning sun was warming on a bright patio and the beer was colder. The girls were prettier there, too.

"They're all ru-ru-right," Jackpot urged. "If we can g-g-get them to cu-come down, then they're f-f-f-fine. Either of them."

"You got the taste of a mongrel dog," Charlie said. "We can do better than that."

"Not for f-fifteen d-d-dollars, we can't," Jackpot whined. "An' for tu-tu-tu-two times, that's all we g-g-got."

"Less the beers," Curly added. "I don't think they take Master Card here."

The girls came back with new bottles. Curly peeled off four more dollars. The beer was extra expensive here, like the girls.

Charlie got up and hefted his crotch. "I'm goin' to scout 'round," he said, "see what else there is 'round here." He took the bottle and left.

"Give me your cash," Curly said. Jackpot obliged.

With Charlie gone, the girls came back. One sat on each of their laps and began kissing their necks and feeling of their crotches. Curly took over the negotiations while Jackpot grinned and blushed.

"Ten dollars, straight up, two times," he said to the girl on Jackpot's lap. She was the fat one, and she was doing a good job on the lanky cowboy. His narrow, ugly face contorted in pleasure as she ran her hands down into his shirt. She seemed to like him.

The girl looked into Curly's face, then nodded, rose, accepted the bills, and led Jackpot off to the back room where the cribs were. The other girl continued to work on Curly until he asked her to bring him another beer.

"What's matter?" she asked when he paid her. "You don' like girls?" She squeezed his crotch and found nothing doing there.

He couldn't help it. All he could think of was Louise and her tight little body. "War wound," he said, his mind clouded with thoughts of her long red nails running across his back. "I can't."

She looked sympathetic. "I fin' away," she said. "Fi' bucks. No bullshit."

"It's all right," he said, handing her an extra dollar for a tip. "I'm drivin'."

That seemed to satisfy her, although she left with a pout when she sauntered back to lean on the bar and resume her bored, tired posture.

After two more beers, Curly felt the need to piss, so he rose and went to the john. It was padlocked, and a sign that said "Out of Order" in both English and Spanish was nailed across it. Judging from the rust on the nails, it had been there a while. Four or five "Gig 'Em's" had been scrawled across the lettering, and they had been, in turn, marked out and "Hook 'Em's" had been painted across them.

He left the cantina and went out onto the street. It had been deserted when they arrived, but now, it was full of people moving here and there. Kids bugged him to pay for a shoe-shine or to buy chewing gum, a woman, or almost anything else he might want. He found a café with a working toilet three doors down, and after he came out, he wandered off toward another "Cantina" sign four blocks away. Women now were everywhere. They leaned out of windows of the old adobe buildings and spoke suggestively to him in Spanish when he passed.

This was one of the things he liked best about Mexico, he thought. The people came out into the streets and moved around without worrying about cars and work. He had never been deeper into the country than the border towns, but he suspected that the whole country was like this. Bright, warm, a lazy place, where there was no pressure. Sex was open and aboveboard, and if he couldn't find it for love, he could always find it for money. The prices, in fact, fell with every offer. Twenty dollars dropped to fifteen, then ten, and finally he found the two-dollar bargains Charlie had promised offered from the mouth of a scabby urchin of about twelve. She kept pointing toward an alley and saying "Dos bucks Estadas Unidas?" in between making jerking motions with her hand.

He wasn't interested in any of the offers and kept shaking his head. Try as he might, he couldn't get Louise off his mind, and he now felt bad for being here when he might have sent Charlie and Jackpot down here on their own and stayed there with her. The thoughts bothered him, and he started actively looking for Charlie to try to put things back into perspective. This trip was threatening to put him right off Mexico.

He found him in the fourth place he tried. Charlie was drunk. He had two girls on his lap and a half-dozen empty bottles on the table in front of him. The marks on his face from the beating the night before were bright red, and huge sweat rings descended from his armpits. His hands wandered from swollen breast to naked hip to exposed crotch and back again as he fondled the women, who were laughing and drinking right along with him. Unlike the other bars, this one seemed full of Mexican men, and most of them were scowling at the big loud American in the center of the room.

"They don't speak *no* English here, *amigo*," Charlie yelled when he saw Curly coming up. "An' they take credit cards for poontang. Glad you found me. I must have a forty-dollar tab. I already nailed Lolinda here," he pinched one of the girls on the bottom and made her start up and playfully slap out at him. "Soon's I get the tank refilled, I'm goin' for Maria. You might give one of 'em a try. She's a pistol." He pinched her, too, and she slapped him a little harder than her friend did.

The girls were prettier than the pair at the other place, Curly noticed. For a moment, he felt sorry for Jackpot. He started to sit down and waved at the bartender for another round of beers. "*Dos*," he said. "*Quatro*," he amended in answer to the man's frown and gesture toward the girls.

The pinching-slapping game did not stop with one round and was now escalating. Every time one of the girls slapped, Charlie would pinch her again. Then when he picked up his beer, the one he pinched last would slap him again. The girls, Curly realized, weren't just prettier, they were older, too. This was more like the Mexico he liked, and his thoughts of Louise began to fade.

The bartender sent a different girl with the round of beers. There were five bottles on her tray. Like the others, she was just barely wearing anything at all. But she was prettier, better built, softer, somehow.

"Hee robnin' a tab," she smiled, then she started to sit down on Curly's lap. "*Me llama Madonna. Como cinema* star, big time. *Verdad?*"

A barking slap like the shot of a pistol rang out, and Lolinda jumped up and started rubbing her buttock. Charlie had his hand to his cheek, which was growing more red than it already was.

"Son of a bitch!" he said.

"*Cabrone!*" she said.

"*Puta!*" Charlie replied and she slapped him again, hard. This time his head snapped to one side, and before he could look around, Maria, who was still on his lap, opened her hand and hit him on the other cheek and flashed his face around the opposite way. She giggled and looked at her friend for approval.

Curly stood up and pushed Madonna away from him. He heard other chairs squeaking back in the bar.

"Shit," Charlie yelled. "That hurt!"

"C'mon," Curly said, glancing at the door. The bartender vaulted over the bar, a baseball bat in his hand.

When he looked back, Charlie had picked up the full beer and dumped it on top of Maria's head. She screamed and raced to Lolinda and the other girl. Charlie grabbed up two full bottles, one in each hand, gave them a quick shake, and sprayed all three of them.

"Hose down these bitches," he laughed. "Cool 'em off."

The girls backed off. Their doused negligees were clinging to their bodies, rendering them completely naked, and they looked around the room in embarrassment. It suddenly seemed very quiet. Curly looked around the room. Two dozen angry faces stared. All of them were male. The bartender stood where he was, bat at the ready, a dark threat in his eyes.

"Let's get the hell out of here," Curly said, and he turned and ran out the door. Charlie was right behind him.

It was Curly's intention to run back to the first bar, pick up Jackpot, and then hightail it back to the U.S. That might have worked, he thought, but when they swung by the pickup and looked inside, Elwood was gone.

"Think he went inside?" Charlie was breathing heavily, and went over and watered the side of the building in the same place he had before. The dog was gone also, but the same two kids stared wide-eyed at him.

"Maybe," Curly said. "But we weren't there. Jackpot's in the back with a girl."

They split up and started looked up and down the streets, but Elwood was nowhere to be seen. Curly noticed that the formerly friendly and solicitous faces had now turned angry. No children swarmed around him trying to sell him anything. He kept asking for "*gringo largo,*" which was the only way he could think of to describe Elwood, but his question and hand-signaled descriptions were met with hostile blank looks and indifferent shrugs. Charlie had also disappeared.

"Hey, Gringo," a kid of about ten said when Curly passed him. "I know somethin' you don'."

Curly approached him. The kid looked at him evenly and stuck out his hand. "Ten bucks. American."

"Here's two," Curly pulled the bills from his pocket.

"I want five."

"People in hell want ice water."

The kid shrugged. "It's valuable shit, Man."

The kid took the folded bills, but Curly kept his fingers firmly on them. "What?"

"The *federales* is looking for you."

"Who?"

"The cops, Man. They is looking for you an' your frien'. The fat one. They know where your trucks is, an' you better get the hell out of Dodge."

"Elwood?" Then Curly remembered. He and Curly had run out of that bar without paying, to say nothing of leaving behind three beer-soaked women.

"*Gracias,*" he said, and he let go of the bills.

"Hey, no sweat, Man," the kid said and ran off. Probably gone to tell them where I am, Curly thought.

He looked up and down two side streets and finally gave up and went back to the first cantina. He was surprised to find Elwood sitting next to Jackpot, drinking a beer. His clothes were splotched with dried mud.

"We're low on cash," Curly warned when he walked up.

"It's my first round," Elwood said.

"You have any money?"

"Nope."

"Well, go easy," Curly sat down and waved at one of the girls to bring him one as well. "And we need to shake a leg. Soon as Charlie gets back, we need to split." He accepted the beer and paid their tab with the last of their money. "What I want to know," he said as he wiped his face with a hankerchief, "is how it can be so goddamn cold up at home and so goddamn warm down here."

"I got a th-th-theory on that," Jackpot said. "It's them ch-ch-ch-chili peppers all these Mu-Mescans eat. They m-m-make the air hot when they br-br-br-breathe an' f-fart."

Curly couldn't tell if he was serious and sneered at him.

"I'm su-su-serious," Jackpot insisted. "I read that in a m-m-magazine. It's tu-tu-true in India, too, on account of all the ch-ch-cheyenne p-p-p-peppers."

"Cayenne," Curly said.

"*Ch-ch-eyenne.*" Jackpot put his long legs out on a chair in front of him. There was hole in the toe of one of his boots. He was a different man now. Full of himself. "I r-r-rodeoed over there. I know somethin' 'b-b-b-bout it. That c-c-curry j-j-j-junk is f-full of ch-cheyenne p-p-p-pepper."

"You don't know shit," Curly said. He looked at the door. He wished Charlie would show up.

"What *I* want to know," Elwood said, moving his hand up to the obvious knot on his head, "is what the hell I'm doin' in Mexico. I got me a headache."

"We told you we was g-g-g-goin' to Mexico," Jackpot said. "Du-Du-Don't you remember?"

Curly looked at the round lump on the back of Elwood's head and braced himself for an outburst. He had hit him harder than he should have. He was now thinking he should have hit Charlie instead.

"I don't remember much of nothin', " Elwood said. "All I know is that I wake up with a headache the size of Dallas, 'bout a hundred Mescan kids lookin' at me in the back of Curly's pickup, an' when I get out I'm in Mexico."

"Du-Du-Don't you r-r-remember beatin' h-h-h-hell out of Ch-Ch-Charlie last night?" Jackpot asked. Curly looked away.

"Me? Why'd I do that? I like ol' Charlie. We're lodge brothers."

"On account of L-Louise."

"Louise," Elwood moved his hand down and rubbed his chin. "Oh, yeah."

The door to the cantina suddenly burst open, and Charlie barreled through the room, upsetting tables and knocking over several of the sleeping men.

"Goddamn cops is right behind me," he yelled. "Run for it!" He disappeared through the back hallway.

"What?" Elwood stood. "What's he talkin' 'bout?" He took a step over toward the door to look out and was immediately confronted by a short, fat Mexican in khakis and a white shirt and small, straw hat. He had a tiny badge pinned to his shirt pocket, and he carried a steel automatic in his hand. He seemed as shocked to find Elwood's massive frame in front of him as Elwood was to see the pistol rising toward him.

"Now, hold on," Elwood said. "Just a second, *amigo.*"

The Mexican didn't hear or understand him. He jammed the pistol into Elwood's generous belly and pulled the trigger.

No one could move. Curly saw the whole thing as if in slow motion. He saw the fabric of Elwood's mud-stained shirt pressed inward from the pressure of the pistol's barrel, he saw the Mexican's brown finger tighten on the trigger, and he saw the hammer falling a millimeter at a time toward the back of the slide. He wanted to yell, but he didn't have time. Aside from the heavy breathing of the Mexican policeman, the only sound that was audible in the room was the flat click of the hammer striking an empty chamber and the sudden outrush of air from Elwood's lungs.

Elwood's eyes rolled back into his head, and he fell like he was cut off at the ankles. There was a loud thud when his head hit the floor.

"Landed right on the same place where you hit him at," Jackpot said.

It was after dawn, Sunday, when they got back home. They had talked it nearly to death before they reached San Antonio, and Curly was so tired of thinking about it that he had let his fantasies about Louise take over and run wild just to keep himself awake. Elwood was in the middle of the cab, asleep and leaning alternately on him and

Jackpot. Charlie was huddled under the comforter in the pickup's bed, his body swathed in ace bandages. A new norther had blown in overnight, and the temperature seemed to drop five degrees with every mile they covered. All Charlie had for help from the cold was the remains of a twelve-pack Curly bought for him at a liquor store in Laredo.

"I don't r-r-reckon I'll g-g-g-go down to Mu-Mu-Mexico no more," Jackpot said. His words startled Curly, who had just finished a drawn-out fantasy about taking a bath with Louise in a huge tub filled with bubbles. He wondered what her legs looked like. He'd never seen her in anything but tight jeans. He had forgotten all about Jackpot, about why they went to Mexico in the first place.

"Why not?"

"Too du-du-dangerous," Jackpot said. " 'S-S-Sides, I think I already g-got somethin'. When we st-st-st-stopped back there to pu-pu-piss, it was already b-b-b-burnin'. Ch-Ch-Charlie said the same thing."

"You don't feel it that fast."

"Well, I p-p-probably got somethin' anyway. Cr-Cr-Crabs or some-thin'. You n-n-know my luck. I c-can't see su-su-su-spendin' any time in a Mu-Mescan jail, n-n-either," he said. "That's g-g-g-good enough reason."

Curly had to agree. It had cost him over five hundred dollars to keep them all from being locked up and to get them out of the country. He had to go to the market, where the *jefe* arranged with one of the merchants to ring up a phoney charge for merchandise on his Master Card, then to hand over the cash, for a nice gratuity, of course.

They rode in silence for a while longer, and then Elwood woke up. The lights of town were apparent on the horizon. The sun would be up in a while. Elwood picked up the conversation where he had dropped it somewhere south of Waco when he fell asleep.

"Son of a bitch like to got me killed. A lodge brother. Don't that beat all?" He asked them again. It was about the four-hundredth time he'd put the question to them since they left the Valley behind them.

Curly and Jackpot didn't say anything. There was nothing to say. Curly never was sure whether the Mexican cop's gun misfired or if he knew it wasn't loaded and was only planning to use it to scare Charlie. It didn't matter, though. It had scared the piss out of Elwood. No sooner had he hit the floor than he was grabbed up by the two women and hauled to the back. When they brought him to the jail several hours later, he had a huge swath of bandages wrapped around his head like a turban and a silly grin on his face that disappeared the second he saw Charlie.

Charlie was in bad shape. Five or six of the guys from the other bar were waiting at the cantina's back door with baseball bats when he ran on through and tried to get away. They cracked two of his ribs and knocked out a couple of teeth before the cop got around to breaking it up and arresting him, Curly, and Jackpot and hauling them in. They took him to a doctor, who put ace bandages around Charlie and charged Curly another fifty dollars. The Master Card felt heavy in his wallet.

"I could of died, you know that?" Elwood asked them when the silence continued. "Died in Mexico. Did he ever think of that? What'd Estelle-Lee say? She thinks I'm at a church retreat up at Lake Lugert this weekend. I'd of been in the doghouse forever if I'd got killed, an' it'd all been that son of a bitch's fault."

Curly and Jackpot stayed quiet, and Elwood became more awake and fumed. "Prob'ly got the clap, too," he muttered. "Them girls wouldn't let me 'lone." They let him off at J. D.'s parking lot where his pickup still waited on him.

"Next time you go to Mexico," he said, "wish you'd count me out. Man can get hurt down there."

"We'll l-l-leave you home n-n-next time," Jackpot promised. "It's no p-p-p-place for men lu-like us."

Curly saw the telephone cable lying in the parking lot where Elwood had dropped it on Friday night.

"I don't think there'll be a next time," he said.

Elwood nodded and glanced into the back of the pickup. "I'm not due home 'til tonight," he wondered aloud. "What'll I tell my Estelle-Lee?"

"Tell her it br-br-br-broke up early. There's wu-wu-weather comin'," Jackpot offered with a glance up at the sky.

There was, too, Curly thought. The air felt like snow.

Elwood nodded and looked back toward Charlie, who hadn't moved. "You goin' to take him to the hospital?"

"It's up to him," Curly said. He hadn't thought about it.

"Well, you ought to. Twenty-four-hour observation," he said wisely. "The lodge'll pay for it. I'm treasurer. I'll see to it."

"He's got bu-bu-benefits out the ass," Jackpot said.

"I know that," Elwood said. "You ought to take him to the doctor, anyhow. That man belongs in a hospital. Promise me you'll do that. I mean it." His brow furrowed in sincerity.

Curly nodded and touched his cap's brim in a salute of acknowledgement. Elwood straightened the bandages which were threatening to fall off and staggered toward his truck. "Get him inside," Curly said. "Colder'n a witch's *tit* out there."

Jackpot helped Charlie into the cab, out of the cold, and they took off toward Jackpot's camper-trailer on the northwest side.

"Dont r-r-rreckon I'll be g-goin' back down to Mu-Mu-Mexico," Jackpot repeated when he shut the pickup's door and Charlie rolled down the window to hear what he wanted to say. "R-R-Reckon I had enough of that for a s-s-spell."

"I'll remember that," Curly said. The countryside seemed gray, cold, dead. In his mind, even with all that happened, Mexico seemed golden, warm, and lively. The wind was whipping dust all around Jackpot, and he had to hold his cap on his head. Low gray clouds pushed toward the south in a panic of frosty air. " 'Though I'd have to say, I preferred the weather."

"Eat more ch-ch-cheyenne p-p-p-peppers," Jackpot advised. His teeth were chattering. "I'm gu-gu-glad I don't live d-d-down there. Place stinks."

"You can say that again," Charlie muttered. It was the first thing he'd said since they left the night before.

"See ya," Jackpot said, and he turned and started away toward his trailer.

They turned around on the highway and headed toward the east side of town. The pickup rocked in the wind. Freezing rain pecked at the glass.

"Reckon you can let me out here," Charlie said all of a sudden. They were approaching the blinking light that marked the place where the bypass skirted the town.

"What?"

"Said, let me out anywhere you want along here."

"This is the middle of the goddamn highway. It's freezin' out there."

"That's right."

"You'll get run over."

Charlie looked at him and grinned. "Naw. Just let me out."

"Don't you want to go to a hospital?"

"Hell, I been hurt worse'n this wrestlin' with my kids. Pull over."

"Ain't you goin' home?" Curly steered the pickup off to one side and started slowing down.

"Nope," Charlie said. "I been doin' some thinkin', an' I decided I ain't goin' home."

"What about Louise?" Curly asked. He felt something dropping inside him, like an elevator falling from the top of a building. He saw her bottom sticking out of the refrigerator once more.

"She'll be all right," Charlie said. He lit a cigarette. "She never liked me much in the first place. Only married me 'cause she was knocked up an' I had a job. An' there's Elwood." He sighed heavily and winced with pain. "She's got lots of friends. More'n I ever had. An' then, there's you."

"Me?"

"Better'n Elwood," Charlie said, scooting over a bit and putting his hands out of the comforter and into the stream of hot air from the heater. "That dumb-ass son of a bitch. This was all his fault."

"You sayin' I ain't your friend?" Curly felt hurt, but not much. He just needed to ask the question.

"You are today," Charlie said. "But sooner or later, it'd be you an' me goin' at it just like me an' Elwood was. An' Louise'd probably just be standing there rootin' you on. She always liked you. Like as not, one of us'd kill the other. Just stop the truck. I'll get out here."

Curly stopped, and Charlie looked down between his legs. "Any beer left?"

Curly helped him look and came up with one can. "It's hot. It was wedged up against the cooler an' the heater vent."

Charlie took it, opened the door, and stepped out. "It'll cool down out here," he said. He pulled the comforter out behind him and threw it over his shoulders. "Take that cooler back to Louise. It's her mama's. Make her pay you back for all the shit you run up on your card down there. An' tell her to get a tune-up on the goddamn Chevy." He grinned. "Tell her I'll write sometime. An' give her a kiss for me." He winked and stood back from the truck. "Kids, too," he yelled, "but be careful. They bite."

"Where you goin' to go?"

"Anywhere but Mexico," Charlie hollered over the wind. He was grinning.

Curly pulled back onto the highway. The last time he saw Charlie, he was bundled under the ragged comforter and drinking down the beer.

It had started to sleet by the time Curly pulled into the muddy gravel driveway that led up to Charlie and Louise's mobile home. He jumped out and cursed the wind while he dragged the cooler out of the cab and pulled it up onto the rotten wood of the porch. He could hear the TV blaring through the glass louvers of the door when he knocked. He banged twice more before the door swung open. He couldn't say exactly what he was feeling. But he wished his heart would quit pounding.

Heat from the inside washed over him when the door opened, and one of the kids stood before him, naked except for a pair of ragged, dirty underwear. Cartoons jumped on the TV. The other child was torturing a hamster in the middle of the room, and several boxes of cereal were ripped open and scattered everywhere.

"Your mama home?" Curly asked. He wondered how Louise would act. The kid didn't answer but jammed a filthy thumb into his mouth. His underwear, Curly could see, was sopping wet. His face was covered with chocolate.

He started to go on in, to holler for Louise, but then his eyes fell on the counter where he had sat and enjoyed watching her rear-end display two nights before. A bundle of bandages, like a turban, was piled next to a coffee cup and two empty beer bottles. Charlie's wallet lay next to them. He stepped back. A chill deeper than that caused by any north wind shocked through him.

"She got company?" he asked the kid. No answer. The child's whole hand joined his thumb in his mouth. Urine ran down his leg.

Curly stepped inside and cast his eyes back toward the hall that led to the rear of the home. He heard the baby yowling over loud country music.

"Well, you tell her her cooler's here," he said to the kid. He opened Charlie's wallet and counted out three hundred dollars in twenties. He didn't take it all. "An' tell her . . . never mind."

He pushed the door to, got in his pickup and backed out. When he used a bandana to wipe the fog off the windshield, he saw Elwood's green Ford Supercab parked by a hedgerow three lots down.

There was still over a thousand dollars credit left on his charge card, he remembered. "Mexico," he said to his reflection in the rearview mirror.

He pushed the truck back onto the highway, out into the wind, shivered once, then he pointed it south.

Mary Lee Settle

DOGS

Mrs. Webster says that she remembers when only large Southern families who belonged there lived on Chatham, Dunmore, and North Streets. In 1900, it was a new subdivision, carved out of the last farm left within the city limits of Norfolk, Virginia. The streets were all named for members of the House of Lords. The front lawns were all alike, and everyone kept servants who were underpaid.

In old photographs it still looks like raw and naked farmland with spindly trees defining the new roads. Now the trees almost meet over the streets. The huge solid houses have aged into brick and stone monuments to a past when everyone was "well-off" and life was supposed to be more stable. I don't believe it was, because a residue of the times remains and can be read like books about Southern stereo-types, when relatives lived together and got on each other's nerves, old women developed strange habits, men committed suicide when they lost their money or their minds, and plain people were no kin. The whole district is now on the Historic Register, and nobody can put up a fence or a garage without the approval of a committee appointed by the city council. This makes Mrs. Webster absolutely furious.

Some of the facades have Sir Walter Scott towers, some are Banker's Edwardian. There are Swiss chalet porches, Mansard roofs, and orna-mental chimneys, but all the details are different icing on the same basic cake.

Inside, under twelve-foot ceilings, behind fourteen-inch-thick walls, you can read the changes in the neighborhood by the colors. In the houses that the young parents have bought, there are dark green or red or lemon yellow rooms with bright white woodwork and ceilings. The walls are splashed with modern paintings. The parents play catch with their children in the front yards. In the early evening the games spill out into the street, and there is the sound of Mrs. Webster's window being slammed shut, mingled with the bird-calls of children in the twilight. Mrs. Webster is eighty-four and she rules a kingdom that no longer exists, except in echoes and hints.

Her house, like the houses of the few old people who are left, still has cream ceilings and woodwork that has turned the color of dust. The living room and the dining room are the same dull cream and green gone sad, history in a color scheme. Cream and green were the colors of harmony in the early Twenties when, as soon as their parents died, the then-young reacted to the dark damask walls of the older generation and brought Ricketts and Shannon into fashion thirty years after they had revolutionized the dark interiors of London and painted Oscar Wilde's house in Tite Street. Now, in England, cream and green are Ministry of Works, Scheme E, used for prison walls. On Chatham, Dunmore, and North Streets, it is the faded symbol of polite revolt a long time ago. The wall sconces have bulbs shaped like candles and opaque parchment shades that clamp onto them like angry jaws.

Outside the houses that have not changed hands, the shrubs are thick with flat, oily leaves, and the holly is mean and prickly to keep children away. The heavy planting has long since become a thieves' shelter, but the old don't recognize this. Mrs. Webster talks about a time when there were no robberies. She says nobody would have dared.

Mrs. Webster, whose father was an Episcopal clergyman and whose mother was a Carver, still lives in the house where she was born on Dunmore Street. She says she was the first child born there, with her voice a little hushed, as if she were as historic as Virginia Dare.

She remembers every change, every marriage, every scandal. There were never very many on Dunmore Street, but she makes of them what she can. She once led the German, which was the ball where every girl (she says "gel") on the Three Streets came out at the Yacht Club. Then she adds, "Well, almost every gel." There is a yellowed picture of her when she was seventeen in a white beaded dress. She is holding flowers and crinkling her eyes and smiling. The frame is silver and it sits on a Duncan Phyffe table that belongs in the family. It is a charming picture. She still smiles like that, crinkling her eyes. She says she was told once by a beau that her smile was devastating. Then she adds, "It's a crying shame the boys don't pay compliments anymore. The gels don't know what they miss."

You can see her on sunny days in spring, her behind tilted up in the air, worrying her cerise azaleas, which are like small trees. She wears a man's shirt leftover from Mr. Webster, and gardening gloves, and one of those wrap-around denim skirts she sends away for to the same mail-order house she has always used. On late afternoons in summer, when a breeze has finally risen from the surface of the ornamental water that nearly surrounds the oasis of the Three Streets, she wears a sweet, frilly blouse and a flowered skirt, and makes her eyes crinkle when you meet her on her daily walk.

The lawns of the young are spaced with softly colored flowering shrubs and spring bulbs. Their houses all have burglar alarms.

Everyone keeps dogs, and it is by the breeds that they choose that you know them and their politics. The cream-and-green conservatives expel onto front porches fat, aging spaniels and little barking terriers in defiance of the leash law that did not exist when they were young. Mrs. Webster's dog is an insane mongrel bitch she says is part terrier, called Bounce.

"Our dogs," she says, as if there have always been a pack of hounds instead of the one inevitable dog that has looked like its predecessors for years, "are always called Bounce."

In the liberal houses there are large purebread poodles, Golden Retrievers, Dalmations, and English Setters. In two of the houses, there are more ominous German shephards and Dobermans that their owners refuse to put on leashes, as if they needed their animal power to control the streets.

One man, Mr. Tripp, has both. He patrols with them in the early afternoon as if he expected an invasion of Dunmore Street. He hollers, "Huyh, Beau," and "Hyuh, Stu," in the voice of the upwardly mobile South. He is seventy-three and he once worked for the CIA. He is still mysterious about this.

Mrs. Webster pretends he doesn't exist. So does Bounce, the only dog that doesn't bark to get into the house when it hears him coming.

There is one house on Dunmore Street where there are no dogs, but the house is alive with them, day in, day out. Mrs. MacArthur lives there. Mrs. Webster says that she and her husband, "a jumped-up rear admiral, the war, you know," bought the house in 1950. She says Mrs. MacArthur was forty then if she was a day, but she still tried to look like June Allyson. "Her husband," she says, "was simply years older," and then adds, "I don't know what they expected."

"They were from New Jersey," she almost whispers this, and then, "she wore slacks with high-heeled shoes."

Admiral MacArthur retired a few years later. They had a daughter who grew up on Dunmore Street. "But of course," Mrs. Webster says, "they never really took part." That remark, translated, means that their daughter did not come out at the German, and that the Mac-Arthurs, like Mr. Tripp, were treated as if they did not exist. "After all," Mrs. Webster says, "there were always so many Navy people.

"When the daughter married for the first time—but always into the Navy, I'll say that for her," Mrs. Webster tells the story, doing her devastating crinkle, "they asked everybody in the neighborhood to the wedding. It was quite embarrassing. We discussed it. We honestly didn't know what to do about it. I suppose they do that kind of thing in New Jersey. They had the reception at *home*. Can you imagine? I mean, not even the Navy mess or whatever they call it.

"The morning of the wedding I was out teaching Bounce to stay out of the street. She was only two then and just the dearest little thing. The van from the bakery stopped in front of the MacArthurs' house, and Bounce saw the delivery man. He was carrying a huge wedding cake in a box. Bounce ran across the road and bit him in the leg. I felt terrible about that part, he had to have those shots, but of course the insurance paid. But then, Bounce was so funny I couldn't help laughing. When the box flew open and the wedding cake dropped right into the middle of the road, she ate the groom before I could grab her. After that, I really thought I ought to go to the wedding and take a little present by the house, but of course I didn't stay. Mrs. MacArthur was very cool to me even after I apologized profusely."

Now Mrs. MacArthur's daughter lives with her third husband in California. When the admiral was still alive, they sent her son by her first husband back to live on Dunmore Street because they were at the end of their rope. The admiral died eight years ago. Mrs. Webster thought she ought to go to the funeral at All Saints, although she did

point out that they were never very active there. She was the only
person who wore white gloves and carried her own 1928 Prayer Book.
All through the new service, she slipped the pages, annoyed. Afterward
she said she just didn't know. "Until the day he died, he never let her
write a check or drive a car. He waited on her hand and foot. She
didn't even wear black."

Now only Mrs. MacArthur and her grandson live in the house on
Dunmore Street, still marooned there among strangers. He is twenty-
three and unemployed. He is building a boat in the driveway which he
plans to sail across the Atlantic the other way. At night the arc welder
he uses lights the trees with a weird white glare.

They imitate the Southerners they think surround them, as victims
imitate their oppressors for camouflage. Their shrubs are oily and
prickly, their walls are cream and green, and at night their shades are
drawn tight, not against the new paranoid fear of rapists, but the old
one of neighbors and, most of all, their dogs.

Outside of the arc welder, Mrs. MacArthur's major concession to
modern life is the telephone. "She has one in nearly every room," Mrs.
Webster says. At the briefest bark from any dog in the neighborhood,
the telephone inside the owner's house rings. When it is answered,
there is one of those silences, fraught not with heavy breathing but
with electric fury.

When it all began, the neighbors thought that it was burglars
checking to see if they were at home, so every month or so a new dog
was added until Mrs. MacArthur succeeded in surrounding herself with
a canine siege. The dogs seem to know something. They pull at their
leashes until they get to her shrubs. Their owners have let them turn
the leaves brown.

All of the neighbors know what she is doing, and since they are
easy-going people they leave her alone, except for the brown bushes.
But her ears have become so acute that even a bark inside the house
brings the inevitable telephone call, as regular as clockwork, as well-
timed as a television commercial. Once, in fact, a commercial for dog
food triggered five calls in rapid succession to neighbors watching a
"M.A.S.H." rerun.

"Children bark now as they walk past her house on their way home
from school," Mrs. Webster says. Mrs. MacArthur's calls follow them

all over the neighborhood. Five years ago she bought a pale yellow cat and had it neutered. It has grown huge. It sits on her doorstep in the sun and attracts dog barks. Methodically she lets it out and then goes and sits by the telephone, waiting. In the daytime you can see her through the organdy curtains.

Her hair is a bird's nest. She wears tennis shoes without stockings and a wrap-around denim skirt like Mrs. Webster's winter and summer, day and night. She speaks to nobody. If she were poor and in a large city, she would be accosting people in the street, shouting obscenities. On Dunmore Street, the phones ring. Around her the neighbors are amused, and as cruel as only indifference can be. They are tolerant, which means nobody knows what to do about her or cares.

Eve Shelnutt

DISTANCE

Already someone will have put him on the train in northern Iowa—
the boy who will remember to buy the flowers.

And, there, it didn't rain unexpectedly, drops falling as fast as wishes
from a gray-painted sky. Someone would have fed him something
warm, a person old enough to have a vision of his narrow face pasted
to the window, and miles of grass bent flat by wind. Dry wind almost
silver through grasses never reflecting the sky.

The note pinned to his shirt pocket gives him away, not because he
is not beautiful or bright enough—all boys of that age are beautiful
from pride and the urge to run away. It brightens their eyes, even when
they keep them calm and hooded.

Simply, in a scrawl on blue: "You can have him. He was not really
mine anyway."

But what does that mean?

And who instructed him carefully about the flowers, fixed the
oatmeal so that he would travel on its warmth, let him pet the cats a
final time, and did not want him to cry?

From the platform, she must have seen the thin, pale stalk of his
neck jutting just above the train's window. Maybe only that, the shade
half-drawn. Saw the muscles of the neck push his head back against,
almost into, the seat, his eyes (unseen?) looking straight ahead as if he
imagined he would die and, like a bird or a flower, didn't know to ask
for mercy.

Then the train moved once, held back, moved. A jerking, accumulating—a connotation for the word *train*, as her smell would have connoted for him *mother* or *woman* or whatever she was to him.

He should have gotten off then. But his pride was of the opposite sort, not to have her face grow wild when it was now set. She must have seemed fragile, something showing on her without precedent in his life that held him back. Or everything he had seen, being around her, coalescing at once.

And a boy's body does not call what it does a revelation; it moves or it stays put, implicated in some unnameable embrace, feral. He must think that he leaves *for* her, her sake, for some mysterious life that had only been suggested—a raggedness of movement.

It wasn't there now; he looked once.

Suppose he relaxed, alone but for a small, tinted flame, interior.

Or maybe the note in his pocket was more normal; whatever that may mean in the context of sending a boy to live with strangers. He had lost the note or letter by the time he got to Kalamazoo—read it and thrown it away; read it and held it in one hand—not for the words' comfort but for being simply something of her; held it until it crumpled from his sweat.

Maybe, even then, when he was eight, she was partially educated, reader, say, of William Blake, by some accident, and was propelled to explain as evenly as possible.

"He's mine, but you know that. And because he, at least, has done nothing disgraceful, I trust you will take him in before I taint him in some way, like teaching him my fears."

Sitting at the kitchen table—the only table—where she wrote the note, a single bulb hanging over it, creating (if she could have known, standing back observing) a lovely picture, she might have listed to herself what seemed like a plethora of fears, and shivered. Well, they included almost everything in the modern world, did they not?

He slept, then, in the next room, blissfully unaware. She was certain that his intelligence, what she thought it indicated of his potential, was far greater than hers.

"His father was much older than I, and died soon after the birth. He has been around a few men, but how, still going to school as I am, would I meet men like your husbands to bring home?"

In fact, her men were usually musicians, or at least young men who played musical instruments—Spanish guitar, flute, mandolin, music a kind of promontory leading to her; it *got* to her in some way she was ashamed of. They were like artist-princes, drifting, pretending. "He's almost old enough to see it all."

See what?

If this is what the boy read, what would he understand of the phrases? It was comprehensive, what she said. Reading it, he may have felt exhilarated by its opacity: something to discover, later. For seconds, even for minutes, he would have felt older, more capable, and sat up straighter in the seat, noticing the nubby brown of the train's seat covers, how faded the sun had made the green window shade.

During the first day of his travel, after driving home alone, she would have arranged the cans on the kitchen shelves to keep herself from running outside in a frenzy of panic which, having imagined it hundreds of times when she had thought he was in danger, her body had memorized as proper response. To let go voluntarily the boy for whom she would have killed: "I have thought it through many times, and I have decided that I want him to have what all of you can offer him. Now, before it's too late."

And they knew he was on the train—the conductors, both decent-looking men, and an older woman whose job it was to rent pillows until 9:15, when the train pulled up next to a closed depot and let her out to meet a man in a beige truck that was parked near the tracks.

Asking for special treatment, since he was so young, she had lied, saying she herself had no money for a ticket (that much was true), only enough for the boy, whose father, much older than she (it *had* been true), lay dying in a veterans' hospital in Kalamazoo, Michigan (where there was such a hospital), and he was asking to see the boy a final time.

Did the boy hear this lie about his father and ride, then, with an image of him under sheets, waiting? Faceless, inert?

And what could they say but, disapprovingly, yes? And the boy's father *had* seen the boy, then, soon after, fallen, breaking bones in his rib cage and hips, and died soon after, when she had convinced herself that he was invincible, because he had wanted to be.

But he had been in no war; there was no pension—the tiny house was rented. She had the car, she had her health, and she had a confidence in fate, now.

Sometimes, when he was still very small, she had looked at the boy puzzled, as if trying to remember how she had come to have him, the new unnaturalness of a child with no family.

"And that is my point: *I* am not, by myself, a family. I see that now, or I've seen it all along and am now acting on it."

He, the husband, would have stopped her. And that, for all of the boy's seventh year, had been the stupefying part: her husband's voice seeming to say, "But we can work this out. We're not incapable people, you know." It ran—his voice—like a tape recorder through her head, and only lately had she begun to argue back. You aren't *here.* Or softly: *You aren't here.* Simply, seriously, each time more quietly, which meant that, daily, the boy was in more danger of being sent away.

The cat slept in his room, on a wool blanket in a corner—*his* cat, the other one being hers, now both hers, he may have thought to himself, but skeptically since he did not believe an animal could be so simply handed over. If he had the thought, it was a prophecy, except that someone must voice a prophecy or it remains dormant, simply a fate whose time is coming.

She, his mother (had he known, would a shared thought, however differently worded, have drawn them more together, cemented them?) had thought, whenever she read, that all words were prophecy, announcements that kept fate tamed, quiet, coming softly on thin, yellow legs.

How many times before he died had Blake said his own death, how many ways?

On the afternoon of the day the boy departed, it began to rain, the serious rain of fall, with its promise of cold (but not nearly, there, the kind of cold the boy was headed towards—Michigan's snow, sleet, wind, blueness of a sky brittle with cold).

Then, she had gone out, driving around aimlessly until parking to watch a bike race, the racers, one of whom she knew, going over a hill, disappearing, then reappearing so quickly that it made nothing of the road she and he often walked.

Watching him fly past four times, she knew she was through with him. Or she imagined she was, until that night when she let him in. Whimpering, almost, as soon as he had closed the door. . . .

The boy had, on getting on the train, put his off-white canvas bag on the seat beside him. It contained his food as well as the clothes, a few books. She thought he would be calm enough to read. His *body* appeared calm—it was a trait he had learned while watching her: she stopped, shook her shoulders, looked around slowly, breathed in, and opened wide the fingers of each hand, even if he happened to be holding her right hand. His would fall, her fingers spreading.

With her, was anything natural? Opening the door that evening (he was still in his biking clothes, the ones that seemed to shrink him, making him look too young, too small to make love to anyone), she felt she was in two places at once, inside herself needing him before she broke from the pain kept slightly aside all day like something parallel and too familiar to need looking at, but also she seemed to stand back observing herself opening the door and, as the whimper bubbled up, throwing herself at him. A traveling back and forth of herself. Even a third position: herself coolly thinking, considering it pathetic—her gestures of remorse that had to take into account his arrival, the open door, the rain on his jacket, the wind blowing her blue stationery from the table where two cans she hadn't known where to place in the cabinets were sitting.

She wished, now, he hadn't come, a wish she was free to have now that he had. A promise, in fact, extracted from him two days before when she had begun to imagine the scene at the train, not her feelings, only the picture of the boy in one place, herself in another, and a white, blank space behind her, a precipice, unless she filled it imaginatively with her house and some activity in it.

Well, he would stay—why not, whatever transpired between them beside the point. She knew now: activity would have this edge, to be gone through only as if to get to the other side, each action accompanied by a sensation of restlessness of real life to begin again.

Ah, so this was the difference between what death ended and choice ended. The boy and she still had volition, still occupied space pushing forward with them encased in little envelopes of time. Her son might reappear at any moment: the possibility had a kind of logic despite her quite clear instructions. "He should be raised as if all four of you are his parents. He will grow up feeling doubly lucky, and he will forget, eventually, since he's so young."

So, obviously, given the contradictions of her thoughts, she hadn't considered everything. Her biker took off his windbreaker and shook it while she sat on the edge of a chair.

"You should have gone with me to the train station."

"But I was in training all day," which she pictured—a blur, a smear of bike and person while, it seemed, they, she and the boy, stood motionless.

"Still, it would have made a difference. In what he saw. Since you encouraged it: 'Are you sure he's sleeping?' and 'Shush, he'll hear you.' "

"I didn't 'encourage' it."

"It was when I felt the most dangerous, you know. When you said something and I agreed in some way, even when I didn't say anything."

How true, she thought, but she was aware, too, of what they said filling the room in the way she had anticipated its being filled when she had made him promise to come regardless of how tired the afternoon race had made him.

So she had gotten what she had asked for.

And, later, after whatever explosion of feeling was gotten through between now and then—something building in her indictment and in how casually he answered her, in the disjunction between their two states—they would make love because, so late, there would be little else to do or because, so late, for her to refuse would incite another panic, distracting her.

Left uninstructed, the boy would have eaten all of the food in the brown paper bag inside the canvas one, an activity since the books inside the canvas bag seemed to have no relationship to him, simply there on one side of his clothes. Unrecognizable, almost.

But she had stopped in front of him, twice, once in the kitchen before leaving and again after she had locked the car doors at the station. Both times she had taken his narrow face between her hands and recited the rules for the trip (and far beyond into the limitlessness of his entrustment to someone other than herself), waiting between each for it to enter his head, wedded to the steadiness of her eyes looking directly into his.

She had learned this gesture from her husband, his hands taking hers over the white sheet, his eyes uncommonly clear: "Promise me you'll *do* something with yourself," whatever it had meant; the tone and substance: a gravity meant to impart a kind of serene will that could function as a benediction. And much later she would compare the occasions—his, hers with the boy—to what she had learned of the way children, especially children, were given no similar opportunity to receive instructions at Buchenwald, Auschwitz, or, for that matter, anywhere events disallowed calm, final instructions, even if the words themselves were not applicable.

The boy drank the orange juice, and then two bottles of the apple juice, afterwards carefully zipping the bag closed with the bottles restored to the space he had taken them from, in a slowness of order uncommon for him.

Now the grass in the moving field outside the window was almost invisible, then, suddenly, gone as light above each window of the compartment came on. He saw that his face and the face of the old woman across the aisle were reflected in the glass, unless he leaned forward and put his face flat against the window. Then, in the distance, farmhouses came and went, with their barns, and the lights shining from tall poles making visible the fences and the moving shapes of penned animals.

He slept, or his legs, hanging unsupported halfway to the floor, numbed and drew the rest of him into a semi-sleep, his clean hands opening to form a shallow cup on his navy cotton pants.

This may have been the picture of him she had had, beyond mentioning since it was for herself and not for him—a steady moving forward.

Already, one having driven with her husband across town to be with the other, the two aunts were inspecting a final time the room that was

to be his. Not his mother's sisters but *her* mother's—the one who had
died leaving this mess, which their capabilities (she *must* have counted
on it) would fix.

The room was anything anyone could want, put together with the
dredged-up impulses and images from the long-past era of their fertility,
when *they*, not, for heaven's sakes, the niece at age sixteen, should
have had their children.

And now these rays of love: directed so long in the controlled ways
of women who loved without children having cemented them to their
husbands, seeing to the upkeep of their bodies and the small rituals of
couples, with enough money to back them up, to support these
thousand acts of maintenance.

They switched off the light and joined the men for whom so much
had been considered and inserted into time so that it would pass well.

All four would go, of course, to meet the boy, although anything
could have happened on the way, which the aunts kepts unspoken.
Possibly a fear leaked out in their movements, too bustling, but their
movement would not be a betrayal of fear unless the other one, or one
of their husbands, mentioned it. And they were careful people; it was
what, in her mind, had recommended them to the mother, having
been in their homes once, briefly, when she was fifteen.

The fathers—both the boy's mother's and the boy's: well, one
disaster led straight to another, did it not? Unless someone with will
intervened, providing order and space for thought—an atmosphere
conducive to thought. Possibly the aunts considered climate a factor,
and here the pristine days of winter were coming, to be deliberately
arranged into seasons' rituals, colors, even something so simple as
giving the boy hot chocolate after he came in from sledding with his
friends.

"My trouble," the mother may have written in the note that would
disappear during the trip, "is a feeling of not experiencing his childhood, and I think it must feel the same to him, as if he's living simply
adjacent to me when I'm unable to spend what must be the necessary
time—time slowed down—to look into *his* life, not only mine, happening now.

"I can't seem to *inhabit* him, and keep seeing him as both mine and not-mine. If he isn't standing next to me, I think about what I should do, should be doing, have done and haven't done to recognize his life. Every thought seems self-conscious, almost unnatural, as if the *way* I go about thinking prevents any possibility of what the thought is for ever coming to fruition. And this awkwardness only disappears when he's with me, next to me in the car or on a walk, for instance."

But maybe these were only sentences she had thought; possibly other words framed her thoughts, words that, in daily exchanges with the boy, would have been communicated to him somehow, to make his rights as a child seem paramount to her, even if she were, day-by-day, accruing reasons to give him away.

Either these words in a letter or similar statements conveyed as they did things together—the effect of them would have been to give him something while simultaneously drawing it away, into her, the giver. A tension, not a strain of feeling but an irresoluteness. Possibly it made him feel careful, almost as if he had been sick, sometime earlier.

At 9:00, the woman with the pillows had passed through what was the train's last occupied car and, making no sale, had gone again through the vacuum-operated door, turning back to look at its two passengers, wondering why the boy had been put there, away from the others. But maybe the old woman was the boy's grandmother—too old to be trusted—on a separate seat to give them sleeping room.

Having had the three bottles of juice, now he had to find the bathroom, and he walked, holding on tightly each time he moved forward, to the next car, half-full, and through it to the next, where men sat drinking and playing cards.

Making love that night, what she had felt was the racer-musician's insubstantiality, although he was as he always was, exactly the same, no more or less attentive, considerate, the same in every way.

Only now, in bed with him for the first time when he would not need to leave at dawn so as not to give a wrong impression to the boy— now she felt as if her back, her spine, were exposed to the door, to the possibility of its being opened by some thief or murderer or bum when, never once, while the boy slept in the next room, had she imagined the possibility after locking the door for the night.

The pile of clothes on the floor seemed insubstantial, hers dwarfing his not because she was larger but because he wore so little, as if he never looked at them to find them ridiculous.

It could be that, then, she closed off from him, no matter that she rested her head on his shoulder, with one hand between her legs made wet by him. Not separated from him in such a way as to see him through some thin sheath of protection—like a frozen lake—until another desire, another nature in herself asserted itself like a warming. Simply, because she wouldn't give him up easily, she felt older than he, although, chronogically, at age twenty-seven, he was three years beyond her.

Her sudden dislike startled her, his *name*: "Gene." She would rather have said "Eugene" as a way to give him weight, if that were possible. And all of this too was a distraction, a way or reinserting herself into some racket of ordinariness by which the radical nature of the morning would subside through noise.

The train's bathroom was nothing like her description; she had said it would be similar to those on Greyhound buses, which they rode every year when going to put flowers on the grave of the man who had been, she said, his father.

This was a small room separated from the card players by two doors and a small hallway with a red light inside a dome fixed above the second door. Inside were seats in a row under the window. A man sat on one, sleeping, snoring with his mouth open, his hands over his stomach, partially exposed because his pants were unzipped and his shirt partially pulled out.

When he finished, had zipped his pants inside the cubicle, and was washing his hands as she had reminded him to, the man woke up or had been awake. He noticed it and almost jumped back when he reached up for the paper towels. The man wasn't moving, only winking at him, first one eye, then the other, a game.

His mother had been wrong about the room and had also said nothing about a car with tables and a set of machines for crackers, or men drinking in the car from paper cups.

He had to step around the man's feet to put the wet towel in the bin. And now, when he stepped around them again and began pushing the door open, it slammed open, seeming to fly from his hands as if, accidentally, he had pushed it too hard, when it had seemed heavy.

Then he was being lifted up by one arm, lifted and twisted around in one motion, to the man's face.

"Is *this* what we've got?"—slamming the boy back against the wall opposite the open door. "Well *keep* it." He put his fingers on the boy's cheeks, pressing until his lips formed a pucker. "God! A runt!" dropping the boy and slamming the second door behind him.

So now, having waited and then walked with his head down through the roomful of tables to his own car, he sat breathing steadily, one short breath deliberately followed by another until his chest began to feel normal.

He knew, now, that he would not eat or drink more of what she had packed, would not leave his seat unless he had arrived.

She had been wrong about the bathroom; she hadn't known about the car with tables. . . . And he couldn't fall asleep since the woman was asleep and too old to help him if she were awake. Help him how, against what? It was what he didn't know, what *she* hadn't imagined, except that he was not to talk to strangers, and he had obeyed.

When he was asleep, he cried to himself, except he saw when he brought his shirttail out to wipe his face and then stuffed it back in that he hadn't been asleep, had been pretending with his eyes *almost* closed, because he couldn't sleep now. Now it wasn't allowed.

She said, upon waking, that he was almost there and soon she would be able to call. Not to talk to him—as she had explained, now it would not be good to talk since he would make a new life there, going, oh, to drawing lessons at the art center (a brochure had advertised them, their work with young children a speciality of the museum) and of course to school and to the park across from the museum and all the other things boys did—whatever, too, the aunts' husbands thought to take him to, having to do with sports, "which I've neglected for you."

But the aunts, or one of them, would say he had arrived: "He's right here beside me."

And then life would begin again; she would be in her classes in order to resume removing what had been her husband's superiority in knowledge that had made her envy him, had given her the sense that it was the one thing to possess now that he was gone, some guarantee against anything whole being wholly ruined again. A corner to turn. In class she approached it slowly, hopefully, full of a kind of faith that was inexplicable except in how she had absorbed his final words, when he had been cold and nevertheless caressive, and had caused an ache between her legs. And memories not much changed but driven inward.

It was the aunts who noticed the beauty of the morning, its light made more brilliant by the clearness of the sky seemingly purified by a sudden drop overnight in temperature. Light pouring into the windows in what was to be the boy's room, which the aunt in whose house the room was located described to the one across town, also restless until the train was met.

But none of them was free to see the day apart from its meaning to them, the weather's pragmatic registering on them, except possibly the boy.

Not the mother, since "Gene" or "Eugene" was still there, a new event requiring accommodation around her inward focus, but seamlessly because she felt or thought she should feel some gratitude, and because it would be only later that she sent him away, got rid of him, extracted her life from his, to whatever extent the two had meshed.

He had watched all night what light there was and, early, when it was still pale, had moved slowly, pulling one leg up, to take off his left sock and remove the money she had given him for flowers. He put it in his shirt pocket, where the note had been, and he sat still again, waiting while the scenery changed to include towns and all that went with them, the train slowing, sometimes coming to a full stop, then picking up speed again as the sky lightened.

She must have asked about the flower-seller, called and known and told him what was true even now. The woman came through after one of the train's stops, so he was able to buy the carnations, six of them, three for each aunt, as she had said, since she had not wanted him to know that, without them, how would the aunts know who he was?

He tore the thin green paper wrapped around them into half and wrapped both sets of three into separate squares of paper—his own decision—and held them together in one hand.

When she called, it was from a pay phone, because she didn't have a phone in the house. She chose the one inside the drugstore, with its door and little fan, which she cut off in order to hear better.

"He's here," the aunt said, flatly. And she waited for more, listening to her aunt's breathing, then: "What more do you want? We agreed. 'He's *here*.'"

So she had promised, in her note or by telephone when making the arrangements. And to herself, a sub-vocalization within a litany of promises: she wasn't to talk to him. What did she want now—a description?

And so she wasn't to hear that the boy, standing on the metal steps of the train and while climbing down with his canvas bag in one hand, the carnations in the other, a porter waiting at the foot of the steps, had begun to wet himself, and that it streamed down the inside of his pants.

That he had begun to cry when he felt it, and that he hadn't been able to stop himself from crying even when the aunts rushed up, crying, "Baby, hush, hush, it'll be all right, everything's all right, you're fine, you'll be fine now, you did just fine, it's all right," over and over. The husbands were standing back, taking the bag, the flowers, and then taking out their cigarettes while their wives talked to the boy and smoothed his hair, got a sweater from the canvas bag, and put it on him.

And she wasn't to know that, in the red car, both aunts in one, the uncles in the other, with him in the front, one aunt behind on the back seat, that they began—between pointing out to him all there was to do in Kalamazoo—began to talk about her, the mother or whatever she was to him now.

Somehow they saw on him what the trip had been like, saw, he imagined, even the man in the bathroom, what it may have meant. And couldn't say (not to him but over him) enough about the disgrace such a trip had been for someone so young—its unthinkability in an unsafe world, its typicality as a scheme from the atypical part of the family, how anything, anything at all might have happened, when he was precious, truly beautiful and quiet and obviously intelligent to have remembered the flowers, surprising though it was that *she* had any money to give him for them. . . .

It seemed to animate them, excite them, to say what might have gone wrong, to imagine all that she had not imagined, and then to recite his state not minutes before. While he, in order to listen without their realizing he was listening, turned around in his seat to look at the town where he would live.

So straight, so soon, so fast, before his memories and hers changed?

In bed, after his hot chocolate, with a stuffed bear beside him given by one of the uncles, as he watched the light through the shade, he began to sense an unfairness. Or at least something wrong or something slipping away as if it were finished, like a train's view.

Or it was a stubbornness he had felt many times before, with her, over some small thing, rising now, here, but connected with her, greeting him not *against* her with her attached. An almost hot sensation, of pleasure, each time it came—when he turned in the covers.

It . . . it was a kind of travel, unknown to the aunts or the two uncles, or to her.

It wasn't *her* fault—the sentence that he managed and that impregnated him. A weighing against what *was* her fault (the description of the bathroom, for instance).

And over several weeks, he began to feel (because the aunts talked on the phone and went over again her crimes of ignorance and neglect and pure youth and breeding and waywardness and no-doubt sexuality and choices connected to it) a sifting through of truth from distortion, as if a drape covered one and, like a piece of clothing, encased it next to him.

She went around carefully then, moving carefully as though she had been released from a hospital and could not be sure of the sharpness of alien objects of the places wherein she moved.

"I know I will miss him," she may have included in her note, "but that will be *my* concern," which it was, but more than what may have been a blithe accounting of it in a note had prepared her for.

Dutifully, he went to the new school and brought from it a boy to play with, and he ate what the aunts provided, waiting but uncertain for what. A redress of an imbalance? And how would it come when, now, they never said her name, mentioned her at all?

She had talked about his father often, a shadow brought to the table when they ate, or went walking, or, as he grew, when similarities between them began to be apparent to her, where the memory rested.

To her teachers who asked, to the man at the meat counter where she shopped, to a neighbor, even to Gene, she brought him out, explaining where he was and why.

But how many times could she do that, sucking from a bare fact a repeated need for its repetition?

She let his room stay as it was, and this too was one of the differences: death demanded a disposing because the face came up even in objects to admonish: *You're still looking at me.* When it had been a husband: somehow sexual and thus indecent. But this. . . . Maybe his things were like ornaments.

Did he return?

Suppose, using all of his intelligence, he got back, having stolen the ticket-money from one of the uncles and, from what he remembered of the note—something he learned from it—knew how to say what a ticket-master, a conductor would require.

And, coming flowerless, found her several weeks later drinking coffee alone in a café in town, in the afternoon, between her classes.

Oh, their mutual panting, after a second of disbelief. Their locking together in a purer uniting than birth, then each explaining at once, the words colliding, how they had not been separated at all, not at all.

And then the reckless laughing—holding on—laughing because, between them, they had outmaneuvered the world this time and hence forever. My God, you can *hear* it, everyone turning to watch, how they are outshining everything. . . .

Whose business, then, would it be, when they are seen taking their walks or, much later, buying him a first suit or brown shoes or picking out a second cat to replace the one that ran away: whose business is it that, now, to anyone taking the time to watch, to evaluate, they appear uncommonly close, that in their smallest sentences and manners and inaction and silences—then, almost perceptible—some suggestion of death or its surrogate hangs about them and, for the young, the uninitiated, makes them, as a pair and sometimes individually, hard to look at, hard to love?

Darcey Steinke

ON THIS BARE ISLAND

With the sandpipers tiddling around his feet and a ridge of dusk's pink clouds balanced behind him, Michael looked containable, like a memory, and I thought of a time at the beginning of our marriage when his hips left bruises on my pelvis. But he'd gained weight long since then, and his hair had thinned considerably; he was duck-like now in the shimmering waves.

Looking at him I tried out ex-husband, stranger. But I knew that he was the frame around my affairs, as home ornaments and divides one's travels. Without him I would have moved from affair to affair, each one being, both marvelously illicit and totally doomed. It made me restless and angry that I would be an ordinary divorcée if I left him, and I imagined killing him; how he'd fall back onto the maroon rug with Persian blue birds. Though I wouldn't do it, even fantasies of murder make me feel god-like. I straightened my shoulders and walked into the dunes.

Hidden among sea oats, I took out Jason's letter. The envelope was gray and fragrant, with the address typed in earnest, hard-struck characters. When I opened one end, a handful of gardenia petals fell out. They were from a plant kept in his bathroom, and I knew because of the petals that littered the drain he occasionally floated the flowers in his bath. The way those petals sometimes stuck to the tub's edge suggested the feel of skin to skin, and I wondered if Jason meant them as an effort in subliminal seduction. But on this beach they looked as ordinary and unevocative as clam shells. It was as I reached down to gather the blossoms that I first saw the lovers clung together.

Averting my eyes, surprised into stillness, I was like a deer that hopes incomprehension and inaction will render it invisible. I thought I knew what the woman felt: there was a time with a boy on a riverbank when car lights flashed from across the water and illuminated my body; it was a familiar female equation . . . abandon changed quickly to shame.

I wanted to make it easy for her, give her a chance to cover up, see if she was the kind to want an awkward hello. So without moving, I pushed my eyes to the edge of vision and saw that the valley was large and whale-shaped, deep enough that the sound of wind and waves was blocked. Still, I heard no murmur or scramble for clothing. I looked closer and was startled to see that the lovers were huge and still. The woman was on the man so that her back faced the stars and they were part of the sand that had blown like snowdrifts. She seemed melded to the man and the man to the sandy valley. Grains on her back scintillated in light from Venus, and because neither lover was tan, they glowed a little as light colors will on a darkening beach.

My foot slid forward several steps in an avalanche of sand. They were quiet, and I realized then that they were dead. The air darkened and the waves seemed far away like the ocean heard in a hand-held shell. I thought: *this is where it has taken me.* It was like I had entered some final and illicit room. The moment stretched. I watched a ghost-crab skid into its hole and waited for some sensation. I'd always expected to find a dead body, and now there was that click, not heard but sensed, when something you've dreaded is suddenly and undeniably in the works. I was terrified of the lovers' clarity but drawn by them as I have been to altars.

Her body seemed swollen whereas the man's was long and thin like a figure in an El Greco. His one arm and palm were drowned with sand, so his fingers seemed to stand independently. Leaning close, I moved her hair and saw her eyes were obsidian and her lips bluish and pellucid like a shell. The woman mesmerized me; it was like gazing at my own image in water. She was not my double but seemed instead to hold some sense of my face as photographs of dead relatives do.

The man's head, wedged under hers, showed only his cheekbone and chin. No bullet holes marked their faces, but there was a fairy circle of dried blood mixed with sand around their heads and the gun nearby that looked like a fish, a very deep-sea one.

I guessed I knew how it had happened. She had decided days earlier that she could not live with the choices she'd made. In killing the alternative—leaving a husband, children maybe—she'd hollowed herself out. So there was this second decision to die with her lover, long before the gnawing atavism for others would sting her into doubt. So in the motel bed, in the deep part of the night, she'd whispered her crazy plan to make love in the dunes. He'd followed her like a sleepwalker, thinking of the pleasures of her body. He'd been puzzled by her preoccupation, by the way she'd loitered under the sky, her body shadowed with sea oats. She was waiting, the gun cool against her stomach, for something that would convince her to stay in this world.

It never occured to me to run back and tell Michael. To say I've seen the lovers, even now, seems like admitting insanity. Whom could I tell that they were giants, so big that her arm was full as a tree limb and his height that of a man on stilts? It seemed impossible that they could have had names, worked jobs, knew God. They were captured like models, alive but lifeless in the confines of a painting.

Their silence made me conscious of the blood moving through me and the geometry of my bones. It was darker now and chilly. Where the sun had set, there was a band of burgundy. I knew the lovers were a presage, a black charm that showed me that the secret to fidelity was really just an ordinary kind of fear and that all physical actions were not without their whisps of morality. The woman's hair blew and for a crazy second I thought she'd lift her head. The thought made me flush. I felt as if I were standing too close to a fire and there was a burning in my stomach that darted and pulled. First came the loss of stars and sky and then of darkness too. I saw that what I was now was what I would always be, that I had not taught myself the things one must and had based my life on some obscure idea that I was different, special, allowed. I had a sensation that terrified me: it was thick and dull like running warm water on your freezing hands or being caught in a lie.

Myriad noisy gulls came then and hovered. Kneeling down, I turned the woman's huge blank face and realized I could touch her anywhere, even kiss her, push my tongue into her cavernous mouth. I took my jacket and swung it over their heads. The material rattled and fell to the shape of a face cast with longing. I stood, wondering how long it would be before the sand devoured them.

Dabney Stuart

WITNESS

"Forget it," Mercy Layton said. She hauled herself up from the couch
and smoothed a confusion of wrinkles from her dress. She made her
habitual trek across the living room to the picture window, turning her
back on Reston. Because of her position she could see her reflection,
but not his. The rolls of fat that seemed gradually to be usurping her
face bothered her no more than usual, but she had a strange sense that
one day she would recede into herself and disappear. She said again,
biting off the words as if they were palpable objects, "Just forget it."

She knew how much Reston hated that phrase, how dear a weapon
it had become for her in the last few months. She had developed a
sense of exactly what places to use it in their arguments. It almost
saddened her to notice again how predictable and frequent those
arguments had become.

"Forget what?" he asked. "Hell, there's nothing to forget. It's easy
to forget nothing. Words in the wind." She could hear the smile in his
voice. "What was it exactly you wanted me to forget?"

She turned her 240 pounds slowly toward him. "I was just asking
how much more of your life you're going to spend writing your bloody
play. If it weren't for your footsteps going up and down the stairs to
that cell in the basement, I wouldn't know if you were alive."

"Oh, I'm alive," he said. "There's life, and there's life."

"And yours is vile," she said, interested in the neutral tone of her
voice.

"Probably," he said. "But not all that vile. At least I keep most of it to myself." He reached into his shirt pocket and pulled out a jade-green earring shaped like a teardrop. He began toying with it.

"Putting it into words isn't keeping it to yourself, not that it matters. How can you get any pleasure out of doing that play?" It was an old question she'd never asked, but living amid disbelief and exasperation for almost three years led her to articulate it. She wished she hadn't.

"I'm glad you've abandoned your distinction between writing and doing. Because I *am* doing." In spite of the chill in the October air, he unbuttoned two buttons of his shirt with his free hand. "Writing is doing. A deed. Deeds."

"Well, I know it affects you as if it were behavior, but—"

"Not behavior, action. If it were mere behavior, I wouldn't need you."

"Okay, okay." She tried to quell the whine creeping into her voice. "Action. But why such ghastly action? A father kidnapping his own children. Stuffing their dead bodies up an old man's chimney. And how can you make *fun* of it?"

"Their grandfather's chimney. Don't forget how in Act II the old man has to face the past, his daughter's healthy betrayal, her vicious repudiation. As for the pleasure, well. . . ." He held the earring by its clip and short chain up to the sunlight flowing through the picture window. "Lachrymae rerum," he muttered to himself. He began to dangle the earring between them. "You are getting sleepy," he intoned. "Your eyes are becoming heavy, you are getting—"

"Oh, stop it!" She stepped toward him, reached over the coffee table and tried to grab the earring. He kept it just beyond her hand, smiling.

"I was just trying to answer all your nosy questions," he said. "This here earring"—his voice tilted into a down-home accent she knew was a parody of the way her kinfolk talked—"is the gen-you-wine relic of the woman I murdered in Act I, scene 1. What I'm holding here is pow'r. Pyoor pow'r." His voice leveled again. "This is the key to everything right here, before your very eyes."

"Yeah, I know," she said, turning back toward the window, weariness creeping into her tone. And she did know. It maddened her, but somehow she did. Of course there was pleasure in it. There was pleasure, complicated and rarely understandable, she thought, in making anything. Power, too.

Even a play, she grudgingly admitted to herself, though in her heavily cushioned heart she knew there had to be a crucial difference. No matter how glibly he toyed with her, words weren't equal to deeds, or even a very good substitute for them. Some trick of the mind made the sunlight seem to flash in the plate-glass window, as if to signal an agreement meant solely for her.

She remembered making mud pies, or mud cities it was, after a long rain in the so-called parking lot of a scond-rate resort hotel where her parents had brought her for a vacation, when she was six. Even then she was huge, and she sat heavily in the mud, parting and kneading mounds of it, making buildings and canals, over one of which she managed, with the help of a curved stick, to construct a rude bridge.

The pleasure of the making was inseparable from the surroundings in which it was done. The slovenly, viscous swinishness of her wallowing involved her completely, an atmosphere she almost breathed. She remembered being totally bewildered when her father, who seldom touched her at all, hoisted her by the armpits from her kingdom, shattering her oblivion, and cursed her as he carried her to the shed where maintenance equipment for the golf course was kept. He had hosed her off violently, as if her condition were a threat to him.

For some years now, she had been aware that whenever she thought, or talked, about why people would want to live in cities like New York or Chicago or Los Angeles, the image of herself hunkered in that mud, building with it, the only substance in the world, always asserted itself.

"The materials at hand," she said softly, a coda to her musings.

"Not exactly," Reston said. She didn't turn toward him, but she could hear the abominable smile in his voice. "All materials are at hand more or less. One chooses, after a fashion."

Shit, thought Mercy. He is so frigging predictable. For a moment she wondered if perhaps *that*, his predictability, was the only thing that really disconcerted her. No matter what she thought, however subtle it appeared to her at first, she could accurately anticipate his response. After a fashion, for God's sake. One minute his writing is action, the next he reduces it to a matter of taste. The vulgarity of it didn't bother her, but the illogic did. It was incoherent, a game in which the rules themselves didn't change as much as the way they were worded. He'd just as well not even be there. Half the time he wasn't, and when he was, he was usually abstracted, off in some whiz-bang, hot-shot grotto of mental profundity no one could penetrate.

Yet, she thought, I don't need to penetrate it. It's as if I know what he's going to say before he says it. All I have to do is say something first, and I could probably construct most of the conversation from that.

She was about to turn and confront him with this discovery, about to present him to himself, about to be hard and clean and terse, when she realized something else. If she said nothing, he would say nothing. In fact, in the three years they had shared this dinky ranch house in suburban Harmony, *he* had never initiated a conversation. What she could predict were his responses, the whole complicated web of them in any context, but it was always she who established the context.

So I *don't* need him, she thought. The opposite wasn't true, however, and she realized that, too. In fact, she had always known he needed her. That was why she was still here. Her discoveries led her back to a place she was intimately familiar with. She existed because he needed to be forgiven. The circularity of her interior journey satisfied her in a way her conversations with Reston never did. She felt she was a part of him. The conventional phrase didn't please her, but it bore enough truth for her to accept it.

When she finally spoke, again softly, turning toward him, the only issue of her thoughts Reston heard was the word "conventional," which fit the direction of his thoughts so perfectly that he would never have guessed what had gone on in her mind.

"Half right again," he said. "Conventions are ways to use the materials, but they are also materials themselves. They have to be molded, too."

"I see," she said. He was about to lecture and, apart from her dislike of textbooks and pedantry, she wished to forestall that because she knew what he would say. She had learned that the best way to do that was simply to agree, or passively admit she understood something, whether she did or not.

It worked. He said nothing further. He gave his attention to the earring.

She watched him. I still don't understand how that earring is the key to anything, she thought. All I've been doing is answering my own questions. Jesus. She cringed at the new considerations looming before her. Ever since he brought that damn thing home, it's been like another person in the house, she thought. Somehow he works up a meaning for it, but I can't. I can't talk to the bloody thing. He doesn't *have* to talk to it; he can invent a place for it in his play and believe that's where it belongs. The little circles of his galaxy, inaccessible to anyone else.

Except on stage? It had been over a year since she'd read his play, but she could remember the central woman wearing earrings like the one he was holding. Her ex-husband had taken one of them after he killed her early in Act I, a piece of business Reston then hoped his audience would forget until the small-town sheriff found it much later, apparently by accident. Even on stage, though, with all the audience's sense of collusion in the plot, everything was self-contained, self-referential. The earring there was dead. This one, on the other hand, was alive, here, mysterious. Before her very eyes. He could take his stage and shove it.

The distance between them which she kept uncovering didn't surprise her much anymore. Even though she found deep satisfaction in the role she had been created for, she reached points like this when she wanted to be independent of his will, his almost hypnotic manipulations. At such moments her sense of being apart from him shifted subtly until she felt she was two people, as a grown creature may intuit within herself the seed of a new being.

She lumbered past him, the inside of her thighs rubbing uncomfortably together. She went through the cramped hall into the bedroom and eased herself down onto the bed.

She shoved the copy of *Cakes and Ale* from its place on top of a small stack of comic books she kept on the bedside table. It fell to the floor, thudding dully.

She heaved herself up on an elbow and thumbed through the fifteen or so gaudy comics. She picked up one from the pile, flopped back on the pillow. A smile began to crinkle the flesh around her eyes.

Almost immediately she was immersed in the Fantastic Four's magnificently implausible efforts to save the planet from the Stone Man. As always, the blunt but affectionately ugly power of The Thing, who was plain Ben to his chums, warmed her, but in this particular episode she was most taken with the fact that lovely, lithe, slim, enticing Sue Richards was pregnant.

In the living room, Reston remained sitting on the couch, swinging the earring back and forth before him, like a pendulum. Then he stood up, placed the earring on top of the bookcase clock, and went downstairs to work on his bloody play.

It isn't very bloody, he thought, walking down the stairs to the basement. Not bloody at all, in fact, if you took the word literally. He wondered where Mercy had picked up the odd British slang. From Maugham? Couldn't be the movies, since she never went.

But nobody in his play bled. He had the ex-husband shoot his wife five times in the same hole in the temple in the opening scene. He'd been given to understand that a small-caliber bullet wound there didn't make much mess.

The murders of the two children were by suffocation, and were offstage. You couldn't get much more bloodless than that. He admitted he wasn't satisifed so far with the scene in which he'd set the deaths of the children. Having an outsider—a dim-witted detective from the big city who was overly impressed with himself—report the activity without knowing what it signified was more difficult than Reston had expected. Too static. The character himself wasn't interesting yet either.

Reston stood in the doorway to his writing room and decided to give that scene one more chance. If he couldn't make it convincing this time, he'd imply the deaths through conversation, and scrap the detective.

Too many characters frothed the moil.

He entered the room and switched on the bare 100-watt bulb that hung by a cord from the ceiling. Same old cinderblock walls with his drafts taped haphazardly here and there, same steamer trunk in the middle of the cement floor. He pushed some of the pages of his manuscript aside and sat down on a thin cushion, the one luxury he permitted himself down there.

His pencil lay tilted slightly on one of the bosses at a corner of the trunk. He looked at the blank page facing him, a rectangle of pure white against the scarred black top. He waited.

Not bloody, he thought. But vile. She's right about that.

And not the first to be, either. Since he'd started writing the play nearly three years ago, it had had two group readings. The first had occurred prematurely: he'd finished only an act and a half (of a planned three) and should have known better. But the second, less than a year ago, had been from a sixth draft of the whole play and had had a purpose beyond his own edification. A producer from Boston had agreed to come if Reston could arrange the reading in Washington. Washington was only four hours from Harmony, where he lived and wrote in small-town seclusion, and he had friends there in the theater, so it had been relatively easy to set up.

When it had become clear to the producer that the two kids were murdered by their father, he'd stopped the reading. Very courteously, very quietly. "I can't stomach *Richard III* with its flimsy excuse of abjectly perverse regal ambition as the cause of filicide. This lacks any motivation at all. Such vileness may be what the theater is coming to near the end of the century, but I won't spend my money to encourage it." Or words to that effect. It hadn't taken five minutes, but no one wanted to resume. People had muttered apologies and good will, but there wasn't much enthusiasm for the choices Reston had made. The reading had been going badly anyhow. The producer's interruption had been a relief.

It had taken Reston about two months to recover and get back to work.

In the last eight months he'd done three more drafts, but he had to admit to himself he'd made no substantial changes. Same opening-scene murder, same offstage suffocation of the boy and girl, same manic ramblings of the grandfather, though he'd shifted them from Act I to Act II. The dialogue may have been a screw or two tighter, and the character of the misleadingly slow country sheriff was surprisingly effective. But he could still hear the producer's razor-like judgment, echoed now by Mercy.

Why was he still fucking around with this play? Why had he chosen the subject? Why was he clearly obsessed with it? Why did he feel like he was waging war when he worked on it? Who was the enemy? The questions were no less familiar, or intractable, than the cement biting at his tailbone through the thin cushion. He shifted his weight to the other cheek and rested his head on the trunk. His right hand knocked the pen to the floor. It skidded about a foot and came to rest in a curl of one of the manuscript pages littering the room. In the shadow it created, it looked like a dried-up dog turd.

"My shit," Reston muttered, and refused to follow the seductive Freudian path the metaphor offered him. He'd been down it before, and regardless of its possible truth, he'd decided it was a self-reflexive dead end. Knowing that his art was a sublimation of his fascination with his feces gave him knowledge, but neither understanding nor peace, nor a way out of his obsession.

It didn't help to remember Renfro either. He hadn't wanted a dog, but his mother—who had lived in a world where only puppets and their *Good-Housekeeping* stereotyped tableaus were real—had foisted one off on him for his birthday. Somewhere between five and seven, he wasn't sure any longer, but it had to be before eight because that was the year she had walked out on his father, made way for her inordinate, repetitive successor. As usual, she had projected her image of a child's desires onto him without regard for or curiosity about what he might really want.

It was a drooling, stinky little cocker spaniel puppy, who almost immediately peed in Reston's lap. To his mother this was somehow cute, perhaps because Reston was the one who had to clean it up.

He had had to house-train the wretched dog, too. For six months or so, his mornings began with him in the basement scooping up Renfro's scattered night's business. The first night Reston had covered the entire floor with newspaper. The idea—her idea—was to reduce the acreage of newsprint weekly until Renfro learned he was supposed to shit on it and not on the gradually more spacious cement floor.

This meant, of course, that when Renfro erred he had to be punished. Perhaps the only pleasure Reston got from that animal, who lived to be eighteen, was sticking his hot little bulb of a nose in the turds he laid off the newspaper.

So was his daily obsession with his play a compensation for those eternal months? He was obviously increasing the expanse of paper on the floor of his room, covering it with his own squiggly black markings.

Take that, Renfro, he thought, looking at the pen which had stimulated these musings.

Take that, Mother.

Trouble was, neither Renfro nor his mother (nor his stepmother) were perambulating the planet anymore.

However you looked at it, here he was, leaning on this dumb trunk, surrounded by his own production, as much the victim of his imagination as any man. He might as well have been talking to himself.

Why can't I work in an air-conditioned sunlit room on a computer screen like all the other screwed-up playwrights I know? He reached up and pushed the lightbulb so it spun.

"Shit," he said, omitting the possessive this time from his favorite expletive which explained everything, and nothing. He experienced a peculiar satisfaction in the saying of that word, but only in the saying of it. There seemed to be no extension of his pleasure beyond the making of the sound itself.

He eased his butt away from the trunk and rested his torso more comfortably on its top. The edge smudged into his ribs a little, but he managed to ignore it sufficiently to relax.

Angry and bitter, he thought. Such a long time ago to be in the here and now.

Kill, kill, kill.

He started to drift toward sleep in spite of himself. I'll never write another line. I'll burn this room and all that's in it. I'll take a trip somewhere I've never been and become another man. No more words.

No more memories.

No more dreams.

He faded on those refrains into a flaccid sleep. Occasionally he twitched involuntarily, his legs making a rustle among the pages on the floor. In spite of himself and all the energy he invested in the evasion of his play, he dreamed.

In his dream he is wearing infantry fatigues and a helmet.

He lies on his back on a surface of smooth, flat stones, his head, neck and upper torso inserted in a cramped space. He looks up a long, vertical tunnel, irregular in its progression skyward, little chinks of mortar and corners of stone jutting out so he could use them for toeholds if he climbed the tunnel. If there were room for the adult human body to insert itself.

He doesn't climb it. The thought of climbing it as he stares upward at the small squares of blue at its top makes him break into a sweat; he retreats, leaving the tunnel above him behind him.

Manuevuring, he remembers with great effort his mission—to climb the hill to the big house with the chimney tunnel, the big house on the hill, and toss it into the air and catch it, as if it were this very old worn smooth lustrous earring he is now tossing into the air and catching, this lustrous memory, green and tear-shaped, tossing it gently up, two or three memories belonged to his wife, the mother of his children two—he cannot remember why the small tunnel was empty— then missing it, the earring slipping through his fingers, oh he will never climb the hill, never find it. He goes to his knees in the long grasses, scratching for it, the earring that has smoothed his slippery fingers.

He digs deeply into the grasses until he tires, is so tired. He lies on his back again, his shoulder blades digging in, inching forward, his newly acquired rifle above his head; he moves a hundred yards that way, the grass thickening, becoming marshy, until his rifle and then his head meet an obstacle. He lays the rifle across his chest, skews his head sideways, chin to shoulder, his eyes tilting upward toward the obstruction his hands do not believe: he sees two little children wearing olive uniforms and helmets.

Shocked, his whole body electrified, stiffening, he throws his arms away, the rifle spins in slow motion skyward. He relaxes. He rests his head on the children, he pillows his head on the children.

Within his dream he sleeps.

"Baby dollink," a voice bends over him. "Now baby dollink, you must not ask kveschins." A snide voice, a creeping voice, conspiratorial. "I am Herr Doktor Traumacher, at your serviss." Reston is at the mercy of this arrogant voice bending over him, condescending to him. "It iss bad for your hellth, dollink baby. Now be a good dollink and be still in your chair."

Reston feels himself turn to jelly, feels under him a dentist's chair in the hospital. The operating doctor appears spotlighted, holding a glittering syringe across his splendid white chest-smock.

"It won't hurt, liebchen." Traumacher cranks back the back of his chair, floats on his smile toward Reston semi-reclining, and one by one painlessly injects a deep green semiprecious liquid into the ends of his fingers, his now feelingless fingers.

"You cee? I am ressponcible. I vill look out for you, mein schatz. Vee haff only your best interests at harrt. Relax. Zee varr iss ofer. Zee churny iss ofer. You are gettink sleepy."

The voice soothes his ear, filling the darkness. The spotlight glides slowly, the doctor floats behind him. Relaxed, Reston is a whim, free-floating, the warm, green substance gradually dispersing through his veins. He feels transparent, a network of himself. He sees a snowstorm of white pages surround him in the air, waft and blow in the breeze, caress his airy skin, cradle him. Funny black insects lift themselves from the pages, invade his body, threaten to occupy him as if he were their fatherlode, then vanish.

Behind him the doctor draws a towel from his smock sleeve, twirls it stretching between his hands, twirls it again.

" 'F wedersehn. You arr almosst zu heimat. Not farr. Here iss a little souvenir to take mit." He puts the earring into Reston's open relaxed palm, which closes tightly upon it, a reflex.

He bends his elbow and rests his little fist on his chest.

"Zee antecetik may wear off beforr you arrive, but vee haff done our besst." Traumacher, fading, gives one more twirl to the towel and *snap* he flicks with the towel Reston's ass, and the chair puffs and chugs, chugs and puffs, whooo ooo whooo goes the whistle, gathers speed— Reston rides in the observation car, clickety-clacking, a railroaded family vacation sunlight glittering noonday over hills and plains.

Expansively Reston says to his wife and children, "We have everything we need right here: no home, no possessions, no future, no past. I'm sorry you must stand but as you see there is only one seat in the car. But here we are."

As the train stops silently, his wife removes one of her lustrous earrings, shaped like a teardrop, and places it in the palm of Reston's hand. His fingers close slowly over it.

They step away from the train into the deserted silence.

The train departs slowly.

They walk across the tracks and stand in the broad square before the station. The woman and the children gradually fade into nothingness.

Reston looks down at the smooth stones.

Inlaid there inside a circle of reddish-brown tiles is the name of the town, in white.

It is O.

It burns with clarity. Reston lays the earring in its center.

He begins to wake, in a slow panic. The receding voice of Trau-macher returns to say, "Have you no mercy?" echoing itself. The last word slips from Reston's dreaming ear to his waking lips, and he sits up to hear himself whispering it, repeating it, not as a prayer, or even a plea, but as a curse one might utter who, rejecting his future, seeks ahead of time to remove from it the quality he most fears it will afford him.

Hearing himself, he stopped in mid-syllable. He stood and brushed his pants, wiped his forehead. Rubbing his butt, he made his way back upstairs and sat again on the couch. Hardly fifteen minutes had passed since he had last stared at the picture window, but he felt heavy and old. The sun spilled over the sill like butter. He began to feel an odd queasiness in his chest.

"I don't make fun of it," he mumbled.

"What do you call it, then?" Mercy stood in the shadow of the hall entrance. She looked both radiant and bleary-eyed, but Reston didn't notice. He kept staring at the window. "Your dumb sheriff, and your dumber big-city gumshoe. Standing around, pumped up with them-selves, playing games while those two children get killed. You don't really call that serious? How is an audience of real people supposed to respond to that?"

But even as she spoke, she realized none of this mattered to her any longer. She felt neither rage nor petulance, but rather a faint hint of her attention shifting, almost imperceptibly, to another plane of regard. No so much because she had chosen anything, but because he had. It made both Reston and herself seem less physical for an instant. Maybe one day I'll simply assume him into myself, or *vice versa*, or pack my bag while he's jacking off in the basement and vanish into mid-air. She realized she didn't care much which of those alternatives occurred.

But she went on anyway, partly out of habit. She had, after all, been helping him this way—not as a sounding board but as a stimulus and environment—since she'd turned up on his doorstep three years ago. She hadn't answered an ad exactly. It was more that she had sensed a need and pinpointed it accurately, something she had a definitive talent for. It made her dependent, but she understood that as part of who she was, what she was in the world for. Hearing unspoken cries for help was no less a matter of course for her than carrying around its vestigious dewclaw was for a house cat.

In spite of the implications of her last name—which Reston had laughed at when she introduced herself—there had been no sexual experience between them. Lots of titillating innuendo—he seemed to think it should be titillating—and some incipient fondling, which always aggravated her because she knew it would lead nowhere and meant nothing to him in the way of affection. But no nakedness, no physical friction, no juicy emollients for the bruised psyche.

She knew, of course, she was unattractive to him because of her size, and the odors that accompanied it. She'd long ago learned to live with that, to be pleased with herself, in fact, as many more cosmetically inclined, leaner women seemed not to be. She could have given him pleasures that would have driven *him* up a chimney with wild delight. But it seemed irrelevant. When she arrived, he was already in the initial stages of absorption with his play. All his energy and passion had thereafter been directed to it. He wouldn't have eaten enough to stay alive if she hadn't seen to that part of the daily routine.

So in spite of, and because of, everything, she tried again to carry it on, keep the verbal reminders of his complex need flowing, continue to give him a way out of the mire into which he seemed determined to disappear. It was an effort to overcome the lassitude in her voice.

"You keep telling me about mirroring the fragmentary nature of the end of the century. I'll never understand what shit like that means. Or what it means to you to say it." She moved into the room where she could see him. His vacant eyes didn't surprise her, but the depth of the vacancy did. His expression didn't have its usual quality of temporary application. It disturbed her. She walked the rest of the way to the picture window and looked through her reflection out at the noncommittal street.

"I think you've spent all this time throwing a monstrous smoke screen between yourself and what you really need to write about. A total evasion. I take back that stuff about the audience. What does it mean to you to make up the lives in that play?"

Suddenly laughter blurted wildly into the room. She turned. If Reston hadn't rolled off the couch and begun holding his hands to his stomach, she would have wondered where the sound came from. He never laughed. But there he was, writhing about, almost sobbing with mirth.

"Are you in pain?" she asked, hearing sarcasm in her words for the first time. It was a relief.

As abruptly as he had started, he stopped. He sat up, silently, leaning against the edge of the coffee table. "Only when I laugh," he said. "Only when I make fun of it."

She stared at him a moment and then turned back to the window. When she looked at her reflection this time, it seemed briefly to have dimmed. A trick of light, she thought, but almost simultaneously she was granted an insight which made her ample constitution feel like so much lifeless lard. She understood suddenly that Reston's odd behavior wasn't a sign of his relaxing because he was nearing the end of his play, a three-year marathon of discipline and frustration and denial. No. He was wound tighter. His spurt of frivolity was a symptom of desperation, and it was neither vague nor momentary. She was sure of that. He has passed some crucial phase, she thought, and instead of feeling he's progressing from a beginning, he now moves toward an end. "I've always been a mode of his articulation," she muttered, not a new thought, but what she added in a tone of fear and tentativeness and sorrow was. "He's given up hope. He doesn't think I'm possible anymore. He's turned completely inward."

Her voice startled her, or rather reminded her that he was present and could hear, and, hearing, would undoubtedly answer. But he didn't.

"Reston?" she said. Still no answer.

She turned again and found the room empty. Her incipient surprise, fed by the indications of change he had dangled like toys before her, strengthened. I'll have to get used to a new rhythm at least, she told herself, unwilling to give up too quickly. It doesn't matter. He's gone down to the basement again. That much won't change anyway. She took no comfort from the realization.

She walked aimlessly into the kitchen and ate the last three bananas browning on top of the refrigerator. She relieved herself in the bathroom, sitting there longer than necessary, looking vacantly through the minuscule window at the breezy top of a Lombardy poplar. Swing and sway the Reston way, she thought, and the uneasiness that accompanied the phrases made her abandon her perch and go back into her bedroom.

After a minute of riffling and shuffling, she took a handful of her comic books and threw them across the room. The pulpy pages spread; the wad that left her hand singly exploded in air like fireworks. A couple made it to the wall she had aimed at, but most of them fluttered and skewed errantly, dropping every which way. She had read them all, the whole bloody lot, at least twice.

She turned again—turn, turn, turn, she thought, and then muttered, "God. Popsongplay. I must be going out of my mind, I can't get you out of my mind. God"—and stalked into the living room again.

What she couldn't get out of her mind was her faded image in the picture window, and the ideas which had complemented it. His need of her, which earlier she had been certain about, shuffled around in her mind like a dilapidated wino searching for a place to lie down. "Well, maybe I can't figure out a way for him to face me again," she asserted, but she was aware that the poor derelict could settle itself in only one place, so she said that too: "He believes that if he doesn't do it himself, it isn't done."

She shivered. She looked around to see if a window had been left open, and then realized her chill wasn't caused by any draft but was internal, caused partly by her despondency over Reston's inability to seek help where he was an obstacle to himself. Nevertheless, she felt her left wrist with her right hand. It was clammy. She was clammy. The air in the room seemed to appropriate some of the clamminess from her body. It seemed to thicken, interfering with her breathing.

She started to sit down, slowly, as if she were an egg, on the chair which faced the picture window, but she arrested her motion when the doorbell rang.

She went laboriously to the door. As she watched her hand reach out to open it, she felt her fear lump in her chest. Its shape resembled the knob she grasped. She opened the door with such apprehension and gentleness that an observer, herself for example, might have thought she was performing the last act of her life.

"It's time," a cordial voice said. The sounds came from a shape before her, but its outlines were vague and its face a hodgepodge of spots and squiggles scattered on a sloppy hunk of what could have been damp clay.

Mercy let go of the doorknob as if it were glass and might fall and break. With her other hand she unconsciously wiped away some moisture that had accumulated in her eyes and leaked onto her cheeks. She was not thorough in her gesture, however, and what she missed began to run slowly through the network of rivulets on her face. Later it would drop, glistening, from her chin.

The form solidified, the features easing into place. The line of mouth seemed to open horizontally, revealing a white shininess which itself parted. The brief words she heard seemed to issue from the coalesence in the doorway, but she had the sensation of her own vocal chords vibrating in sympathy. "We're here, as you hoped. Don't be afraid."

Mercy looked on both sides of the sparkling figure and, seeing nothing, craned her neck in order to peer behind it. She discovered no one else, and her perplexity over his use of the plural pronoun increased. She backed slowly into the living room, retracing her steps until she felt the edge of the chair press against her calves. She sat down. She sat very still.

The figure entered and looked around the room. "Not uncomfortable, where you've been living," it said. It was able to speak through its brightness without apparently disturbing it. "We hoped this would be a friendly place, at least." It spoke not by rote, but there was a peculiar distance of intonation, as if the source of the voice was both present and remote. "What an ineffable teardrop," it added, directing its eyes toward the clock on top of the bookcase. "Time should always be crowned by a teardrop."

Mercy felt a fleeting shock of familiarity in the odd phrase, as if it were a clue in a complicated charade. She wanted to ask the young man—for so the figure appeared to her—why he seemed so distant, almost an alien creature, but the hypnotic rhythms of the voice continued, and she couldn't draw words from her mouth.

"Have you found a way to help him lead himself out of the bubble? All the vibrations shimmer with sadness and regret. But don't feel as though you've failed. It's only time."

Mercy moved her mouth tentatively, but still no sound issued from it. She was not sure what to say. She was surprised he had chosen to appear this way, not according to her expectation. It forced her inward. Her attention seemed focused on some spot at the remote center of her body. She thought of the way Mr. Spock when he was wounded or injured would become absolutely self-engaged, aiming his entire consciousness at the pain in order to combat and defeat it. Yet she felt no pain, or at least under normal circumstances would not have used the word to designate the sense of dissolution that preoccupied her. She barely breathed.

A curious lightness began to possess her. The drop reached her chin, fell. It made a disproportionate stain on her lap.

"Only time," the voice echoed in the room, in Mercy's throat, "It's not all he has, but it *is* what he must find himself through." Mercy was vaguely aware that she wanted to tell Reston this, that it might be the most important thing she'd never said.

"Don't be so hard on yourself," the figure said, and Mercy willed the words through herself toward the air Reston was breathing in the basement.

There was little left of her by now. The release of the drop of moisture from her chin had acted as a signal and she began to sweat profusely, to drain, as it were. The only movement she had made since this apparition had arrived was to turn her head toward the picture window, as if hoping for some kind of confirmation of her being. She had seen only the glass and the glass and the glass, a deep blankness neither backed by green trees and blue sky nor filled with the slightest semblance of herself.

"Everything is as it should be. Don't be afraid," he told her, she told herself. "This is the assumption you have so devoutly wished for for so long."

He extended his hands. Mercy felt herself, whatever that meant, want, in a final nimbus of will, to say *But this is a mistake. It isn't myself*

I wished it for, but the words dispersed before they were spoken and she floated effortlessly to him, was received, so to speak, into him, feeling it had never mattered what shape she had expected this to take. The two of them departed as one person.

If anyone—Reston, for instance, coming up from the rec room in the basement, sighing with repletion, having arrived at the other side of his exacting and parasitic drama—had appeared at the back of the room not long after, he would have seen the remains of what seemed a very large puddle on the rug in front of an easy chair. From there a trail of stains decreasing in size traced a path to the threshold of the front door. The door itself stood open, a stunning spangle of sunlight filling the frame.

Anita Thompson

MOTHER'S WEDDING

Yesterday, I kept seeing spiders out of the corners of my eyes. As soon as I saw one crawling up the nearest wall, I twisted my eyes around to find another spinning on my shoulder. I brushed them out of my hair and into the sink while turning the left faucet. In the bedroom, I found webs. There was a web in the neck of my gown as if someone had taken needle and thread back and forth. I took the wedding dress out of the bag that hung in the hall closet. I remembered the cleaner saying he had found spiders' eggs behind the seed pearls. Zipping the bag, I asked if he had gotten rid of them. He said yes, and gave me a receipt.

Laying the dress on the yellowed-eyelet bed cover, I pricked my finger on a pin. A droplet of blood stained the cuff. My mother will stop the ceremony if she sees the blood dot. She will run to the altar and swear he is holding my hand too tight. In the evenings at the house, her eyes would slice him like the thin cloud crossing a moon. She watched him according to stars and tides. I didn't mind.

Last summer, she almost drowned. She was looking at her reflection in the brown water when a wave hit her from behind and pulled her under the surface. We sat there laughing, joking. Then he jumped in. He saw her thighs sliding on a rock and rolled her onto his lap. Lying in the grass, after three pumps, she was choking and repeating "Lord," "Lord." I think he saved her only because there wasn't anything else to do. I sat there sunbathing, watching the thin grasshoppers slip between her trembling legs.

As I licked the blood from my finger, I thought of giving birth. I let blood sit on my tongue for a minute before I pressed it into the roof of my mouth. I would never have a child. I imagined a yellow baby with its eyes sewn shut and a black scar falling down its chest. A cat would take its breath away. Zipping the bag, I sniffed only the collar of the dress. There was still a hint of Mother's perfume. It smelled dead.

Yesterday, I called the florist and asked if the flowers could be picked up. He sounded hoarse, as if he had been drinking the night before. Maybe he was at the bar with the woman down the street. I tried to remember if her light was on as I told him my name. He said he remembered me well, and described what I wore the day I ordered the flowers, even the missing pearl button from the back of my blouse. He said he sent the flowers to a funeral home on the corner across the street from the church. I forgot what I said, but he told me he would clip flowers from his garden. As I laid the receiver down, my cat walked past the doorway down the left hall. Its whiskers cut the wall. When I turned to close the door, I glanced into a portrait of Mother and Father. It was snowing.

The hall was swelling like a blister. I tried to grab the banister, but it licked my palm. Looking down its back at me, the cat vined round each spoke like poison ivy on a branch. At the foot of the stairs, there was a mirror staring at me. I pulled my skin under the eyes over the cheekbones. He had told me I had her bones. I never knew if he liked that. Mother kept her thin hair wound up on her head. When I was a child, I thought she kept her skin pulled back with a large safety pin. Wrinkles shoveled lines from her wide, dry sockets down to the backs of her ears. If she cried, I thought her face would have rivers and her ears would be oceans. I stood in the mirror, watching my breasts rise, and fall.

Last night I phoned him. He answered on the second ring. He asked me about the weather and the cat; then he said he loved me and that he couldn't stand it if I died. I giggled, and imagined him behind me with his arms around my raised waist, his lips on the bones of my shoulders. A wind stirred underneath my robe. It lightly touched the bottom of my back, wrapping around my side and up my chest slowly like a wet snake. His voice echoed through the phone as if I were at the end of a tunnel. He hung up, and I fell on my back into a corner like a dead insect.

I woke up this morning with the light from the window forming icicles on the ceiling. I feared one would fall and break into a million pieces on my forehead. I rolled over on my stomach. From the door, I heard Mother screaming for me to get up and get dressed. As I pressed my cheek against the splintered floor, I felt her feet slap me as she walked across the tile in the other room. I think she was daring me to wake up. The light tied my hair in a knot around the back of my neck. It was trying to strangle me. I raised up and looked down. Broken shells covered the pillow. As I looked down my left leg, there was a leech dragging over my thigh. I sat up and found another in the cup of my elbow. It was staring at me. More and more appeared. My head twitched right and left; the walls yanked my arms back and forth. I couldn't get them off. One twisted in my ear, and I couldn't understand what it was saying. In a mirror, there were more on my back. A mother leech had apparently made a nest under my hairline last night while I slept.

I stepped into the shower. Water puddled around my feet. As I sat naked at the back of the tub, water began to rim my neck. Ice formed on the glass faucet, and I saw a fat man in the tile on the wall.

Two hours ago, I put the dress on. As crisp as a new doll's dress, it scratched my skin when I moved. While I wrapped my hair on my head like a crown, I heard Beethoven playing downstairs. Mother brought me a glass of red wine. I licked the dust off the lip of the glass and took daisies out of the vase standing on a dresser. The stems dripped, and water split down my wrist. I moved the hands of the clock ahead seventeen minutes. It was snowing again.

The flower girl thinks her hair is growing too fast. She tells her mother she wants her nails painted, too, as her mother takes a butterfly from a purse and wipes its wing across her eyelid. Ahead, the preacher nods his head back and forth.

I walk across the withered petals scattered across the aisle. My mother's pearl necklace wraps itself tighter; I can hardly breathe. As I take a last vow, I hear them whispering about her. I don't mind. After we light a candle, I close my eyes. Mother hasn't noticed the blood. He bites me, and we leave.

We drive to a hotel. He smiles and hands the man behind the desk a wadded bill. I wonder if it is foreign. The room is small, and the bleached yellow paint is melting like wax. I am peeling pictures off the wall when he rubs past me. The mirror is on fire as he shaves my inside. His wet tongue slaps me, and he almost swallows me. I tell him my stomach hurts, and he stops. As he lies choking, I sit up and turn on the television. There is static. He can see only my black back. I imagine Mother finding spiders in her bed. It is dark outside, and it is still snowing.

Tom Whalen

SHE CAME, THEN, TO THIS SEA

And she saw in the people's faces no purpose. Why did they live in these ramshackle huts on stilts? The flotsam and debris. The corrosive salt air. Mildew. Cold.

Why did they live in these flatlands by the sea? Their nets for crabs, their boats for fishing. The marsh. Sea grass. Offshore rigs on the horizon.

Only because this is where they lived. Only this.

She taught their children how to sing in French, nothing more, and they sang or stared, their faces pasty with the cold, each class blurring into the next.

No one knew her, she had no reason to be among them.

In the café she sat alone over her plate of fish and mashed potatoes.

On the beach where she walked at dusk, light cascaded from her arms.

Came why but to shed what had gone before. The drift to here and all gone of what had been. Who had left whom. Where. Or no one, only the possibility before it could take form. But not afraid, not from fear, but from the fact of loss, of knowing this is not enough, nor this. And far from family, a mother dead, a father heart-landed and remarried.

So here in winter to see what would break, while the children fumbled through their days as did she, and at the corner grocery always the same retarded boy eating pig knuckles and a Honeybun and drinking Coke after Coke.

When she first saw him, he said, "Hey, baby, you want a date?" But Mr. Donatelli said, "Don't mind Marvin, Miss, he means no harm."

And perhaps none of them did, but their lawns were bare, their houses sagged with moisture. Too many hurricanes had sucked life from the town, as if the inhabitants and their houses were of no more value than the flotsam she found on the beach, the washed-up boards and logs, shriveled jellyfish, nylon ropes, brain coral.

"They're a mean people," her former principal had told her. "Too long by the sea. Don't go."

But she did not find them mean, only small and twisted and bitter.

Even the children, finally, as they individualized, she saw as stunted both physically and mentally. Dull creatures, fed on TV and Catholicism. Their eyes darted about the classroom as if looking for somewhere to escape to.

At night a hand passed over her face. It was her own, but felt separate, as if no part of her connected. The sounds of the cars on the highway, of the waves a hundred yards behind her garage apartment, of the gulls cawing for their last scraps of food—each sound, too, separate. Her nightlight spread shadows across her long room.

Her ex-lover visited her one Friday night. She let him stay the night—his body, memory and warmth, sweat and the familiar potatoish smell—but only the night. The whispers and sentences. The lips. Tongue. Sex.

The sea at dawn, brown and cold, slid out like a drawer.

Though the coach and his wife, whose house she lived behind, invited her to dinner, introduced her to the other faculty, gave her homemade mulberry wine.

Though the days sometimes blossomed with sun.

Though she assiduously, she thought, did her job.

Though the retarded boy for a week followed her to school and afterwards was waiting for her and she allowed him to do errands for her, collect driftwood, say, bring her milk from the store, but often as not he would forget his task and not return, and finally she asked Mr. Donatelli to stop him from following her and for days she did not see him at the store drinking his Cokes, and when she did see him again, half his face had caved in, no one knew if he had been in a fight or an accident, he sat on a stool in the corner beside a barrel of fishing rods and swung his head from side to side.

The weeks, like waves, folded one into the other.

The days. The hours. Her hands.

On the horizon clouds bloomed from the soil of the sea.

Her body thinned in the air.

The cold, she saw, attenuated everything—the abandoned jetty, the waves, trees, faces.

The sun behind clouds a pale coin.

What we are permitted to see, to trace.

Though she bit her nails, ripped skin from her dried lips.

Some days, in the late afternoon, she attended the Blue Moon at Happy Hour. At that time, only the old cronies gathered there to clack across the dark oak table their dominoes. The light crepuscular, a gray gauze. No one bothered her. She drank her twenty-cent beers in peace and watched the men shuffle the pieces, their hands like wings.

Not to stay past dusk, the dancing, the puddles of beer, the Blue Moon painted in the center of the floor buried by bodies.

Bikers then. Veterans.

Stayed once to hear one's tales up and down the Mekong. Reefers the size of her index finger, they toked up on the wharf behind the bar.

The babble around her. You from here? She's not from here. You understand what I mean?

She don't understand, my friend, she not from around here.

Politics.

Refineries.

The jeweled skeletons of dinosaurs.

You understand that? You see that?

Wide and lovely.

I'm drawing on it.

So I was out on deck toking up and a boat passed and I said, Hey, Fuselier, and he said, Hey, Castille, and we passed one another. Fucking weird, right?

Too stoned.

She's not from around here.

From where then?

Who's dancing?

They sniffed her like dogs, then turned gracefully oddly away.

Alone then.

The night sky exponential with stars.

Distance spreading and clouds backlit by the moon.

As if here, with the voices behind her, the gray water under the wharf, as if here, with stars filling the sky, all was slipping away, as if here the universe itself was slipping out of its sleeve, and her thoughts, and why.

Here or elsewhere.

Though she was still young, not yet thirty.

Though she was still young.

At the window of the café, looking out upon what once was a town square. Rain.

And the parents on Parents Night rancid with perfume and frettings and beer.

That this composes, she thought, a life. Who returns. Who stays. Bundles held together by marsh grass and the cycles of rain. Around the fumblings and vague pains and the men with their need of seducing. The children chanting from books.

The crepe-draped gym. The flag and prayer. To let it suffice where the enigma was that there was none.

That nothing held here. Only attitude, bitter and gray, remained.

To have come here alone.

This then.

To have come alone.

To see what would live, what would break.

To slip each day into her body draped in its own shadows.

A blood horizon at dawn. Her teacup warming her hands.

What nests here? Ibis. Cranes.

Tankers far out to sea.

Bird shrieks burst from mangroves.

The day's first arch.

Hours at this window.

Winter as still as her hands on the table.

Composed in this cavern.

Luminous and apprehended.

Only this she wanted.

But could not obtain.

Though she listened for the chorus on the crest of the wave.

Though she listened.

Though his letters lay unread on the floor at the foot of her bed.

Though this and this. And this.

At dusk, at dawn, lured, she walked.

Not to think of her colleagues, of the retarded boy, of the followers and shop owners, workers and adulterers in this backwater by the sea.

Only of the horizon riddled with finger-like clouds.

Hatless in the cold.

The light glinting hyphens on the waves.

The sand soft from rain.

What forms held? The offshore rigs. The abandoned jetty. Not even these in the gray upon gray. Ciphers. The earth's furniture. Cold moving through her blood, her bones, she walked east to west and west to east along the beach where few came even in summer and no one in winter, the strand too narrow, the water thick with mud and the refineries' refuse, the sand flecked with broken bottles, tires, frayed rope, whatever the sea deposited there, and the scratchings of gulls and pipers, and sand crabs scurrying sideways, blurring into sand.

At dawn, at dusk, the chaos of gulls at feed.

The beach, like a magician's cane, extending.

The smell, in the cold, of the sea.

What was left. What was waste.

Here at the cold Gulf.

The air furtive, somehow, and, somehow, globular. Her skin opened to it. Her eyes.

Opened to the mist, wanting a center, articulate, complete.

Though the waves like sheets descended.

Though the air flaked onto her hands.

Though she thought, I am here, the job will end and this season.

Though she thought more of an end that continues.

And walked out on the jetty, its planks rotted, some missing, walked out as far as she could, felt the pilings wobble with the waves, the earth.

Past the rigs, past the tankers that dotted the ocean, there was only what there was—gray water, gray sky, gray air. And wind flicked wet in her face. And beneath her the jetty moved, the earth moved, the universe.

Here, then, in the void she stood and looked out at the dark spreading.

And she stood here on the jetty, in the wind, and watched the dark spread, watched the waves rumpling in, listened to them surge and recede beneath her.

Stood and listened and watched and waited.

Until the moon broke through, the waves glistened. The air.

Until the landscape erased.

Until only the code of the sea remained.

Only this.

An emptying storm.

An immense activity, somehow, she knew, was occurring. But what was it?

What was missed?

The faces of the men weathered like old tarpaulin.

Gray dunes, black trees, and silence.

The oil and the sea.

The planet, like an eye, lolled in its socket.

And she turned, unbalanced, and walked carefully back in the dark.

The days, then, in their procession, and what preceded.

Sheets heavy with the moisture of sleep. Heavy in a glass. A kind of crib on stilts. Amidst nights of more than one moon. A night that is not night. A mist and beyond.

She found, one day on the beach, a porpoise. Washed up. Decayed. At first she didn't know what it was, was attracted by the shape, by the colors, a grayish pink and lavender and blue. But then she saw, half-buried in the sand, the remains of the tail, and then the body eaten out, ribs showed through, and between the ribs small shells.

She bent down.

Looked into the pool of the eye.

Looked in.

All gone out.

Except the white.

What trembled the air?
Winter. The beach.
Unbearable, at times, the nights and days.
Unspeakable.
A quicker end to where the eyes gazed.
Random gone to gray.
The shells crumbled beneath her fingers.
The wind bitter as stalks in her mouth.
The wharf like a finger descending into the sea.
Though now the others all nodded and some smiled.
The rhythms of her days.
The beach a cut across a neck.
Though her apartment, this little rectangular container of light, gave, somehow, lovingly in the wind.
Though she was alone and the children sang of plucking feathers and heads.
Though winter lingered at the Gulf.
Lingered and sang.
Until her job ended, and he came again.
And again, somehow, she agreed.
What was left.
What was waste.
What spoke now.

Allen Wier

BASTARD

At 2:22, the morning of September 12, the year 1944, I was born in the Medical and Surgical Memorial Hospital in San Antonio, Texas. My birth certificate lists the attending physician as C. H. Dittman, my weight as six pounds, eleven and one-half ounces. On back of the birth certificate are two tiny purple footprints beneath the declaration *Unchanging Evidence of Identity*—but I still have to accept these facts, like all history, on faith. This does not make me doubt what I believe I know about the past. That such knowledge is only educated speculation adds to the pleasure of drawing conclusions. I read what I like: geography, history, anthropology—land and lore. But I can bear witness only to what I remember.

It's a city now, but during the time I'm remembering, San Antonio was just a big town. They'd started building expressways, but for the most part my father drove us down narrow, crowded streets. Neon sombreros and cocktail glasses turned gravel parking lots lavender as the sun sank behind roofs and cast an orange glow over tourist courts shaped like the tepees used by Comanche Indians less than a century earlier. Used cars posed under strings of lightbulbs next to pink stucco gas stations and army-surplus stores. We rode past curb-service joints where girls snuggled close to soldiers in dark coupes parked beneath canopies, trays of burger baskets on the cars' windows; past honkeytonks where doors were propped open and Mexican border music and willowly shadows sashayed out onto sidewalks to mingle with boys in tight black trousers who strutted like straight razors.

In those days, San Antonio did not host the conventions and tourists it does now. Near downtown, small frame houses, close to the streets and to one another, were separated in back by alleys lined with telephone poles and garbage cans. Here and there an oleander bush, dust whitening its poisonous leaves, grew against a screened porch. A few hackberries and one or two palm trees stuck up above the rooftops. These neighborhoods gave way to brick warehouses with steel casement windows along double and triple railroad tracks: my father's territory.

His line was Industrial and Commercial Janitorial Chemical and Maintenance Supplies: mops, brooms, brushes, detergents, cleansers, waxes, polishes, retardants and sealants. He told Fuller Brush Man jokes. I figured he wasn't a great salesman, because my mother worked afternoons at a branch of the public library, and because he nearly always knocked off work around the time I got out of school. It was years before it occurred to me that he quit work early in order to be there when I got home.

Home, during the time I'm remembering, was a house we'd just moved into, in a new subdivision south of town where the hills flatten out and oaks give way to short mesquites and cactus. As soon as we moved in, we began clearing our lot of rocks. We laid out squares of carpet grass till our yard was a green and caliche-white checkerboard on which we guyed up a few live oaks.

Picture the straight streets and bare lawns, the identical rows of brick houses, to understand why my father got me up early one Wednesday morning—the beginning of April and already so hot I slept without covers, a window fan barely moving the stiff hairs of my flat-top haircut—to go with him to a building-supply house where he'd made a deal to swap three cardboard barrels of industrial cleanser for two sets of white aluminum shutters to decorate our front windows and mark the house. He was tired of driving down our street and not recognizing which driveway was his.

Worried that I would be late for school—I had a math test second period—I unlocked the door to the storeroom where my father kept the cleanser. I worked hard enough to sweat up my school shirt, wobbling barrels of the sweet-smelling red powder one at a time across the carport.

While my father finished a "quick" cup of coffee, I remembered all the times I'd waited for him, all the times he'd taken me with him to make a "quick" call. I'd grown up listening to him tell his customers what a smart boy I was, *Not like his old man, no sir, takes after his mama, got her brains and her looks to boot.*

My mother was not pretty, but she had ways that made her seem so. She spoke quietly, as if working at the library made her forget how to raise her voice, and I often whispered words to her. Freckles splattered her face the way raindrops on a windowpane splatter a face with shadows. Her hair was the color of those freckles, her eyes between hazel and green, changing with her surroundings. I remember one hot afternoon planting and watering—a scarf tied around the back of her head kept her hair up off her sweaty skin, and her cheeks were smudged with dirt—my father knelt on the hard earth working a square of sod into place. He stopped and looked up at her, and I looked too. Her eyes were gold in the sun, and when she smiled at him, her eyebrows lifted and her face opened up. I like to think that for a moment I saw her as my father did.

My father was what my mother called *a nice size*—"not so big he looked dumb, but big enough to hold you tight." He had, she said, bedroom eyes and was a good dancer. "Oh, he was wild, your daddy was, and so good-looking. Plenty of girls envied me." More than once I heard her say she'd never know what made him fall for her, but I could tell by the way she smiled into her reflection in the window over the kitchen sink that she knew more than she would tell. And fall for her he had. At his funeral, as if I had asked her, she leaned over and whispered, "Your daddy was never unfaithful to me."

With me, he was a jokester, poking and punching like an awkward adolescent, mussing the top of my head like a distant uncle. He never knew when to quit. My cheek stung with the rub of his night-time beard, my shoulder slowly gave up the red fingerprints of his pinches and squeezes; recollections of him are burned, sore places—small aches that feel better in memory.

The morning I want to tell about, my father came out the kitchen door onto the carport, a white coffee cup he held to his lips covering his nose, mouth, and chin like a surgical mask. He slipped the empty cup to my mother in the space, and the moment between the closing screened door and the jamb, it slapped.

"What're we up to here?" he said—to me, to her, to himself, to no one in particular.

In her robe, behind the screen which dimmed her like an underexposed photo, my mother looked like she had not yet thrown off the fuzziness of sleep. With both hands she held his cup and watched my father back the station wagon down the drive and into the street where he hit the brakes—the taillights red as a secretary's nail polish—and lurched forward, hit the brakes again and threw it into reverse, driving like a parking-lot attendant. The engine whined as he backed onto the carport, stopping when the bumper just touched my leg—*stop on a dime and give you change*, I'd often heard him say. I hefted the barrels into the back of the wagon.

As we eased down the driveway, our house got smaller in the mirror on my side of the car. Then we were going down the street and our house disappeared into all the anonymous others. My fingers were wrinkled from my long effort to wake up in the shower, and enough of the red cleaning powder had escaped the cardboard barrels to fill the creases in my skin. Both my hands looked lacerated.

A week earlier, I had gone with my father into one of the Gebhardt Spice Company's warehouses, chili-powder fumes burning my eyes and nose, and seen him demonstrate the cleanser—red dust, he called it. I'd watched him unbutton his sport coat and nod at Mexican workers who were pushing loaded dollies out to the truck docks. The Mexicans nodded back, smiled, spoke Spanish words to my father and to one another and kept working. My father's upraised left hand held a lid like a tambourine, his right hand disappeared into a cardboard barrel. He took a step back, dipped his head and swung his arm the way a magician bows and sweeps his arm out before a trick. Pixie dust, the red powder sprinkled through my father's fingers and spattered the concrete floor like droplets of blood. The Mexican men grew silent; they eyed a redheaded, red-faced man who had an oval patch sewn over his shirt pocket, the name *Andy* stitched there in script. Andy grinned and took his time shaking a cigarette from a pack of Luckies. The Mexican men stopped, eased their dollies upright and waited. The white pack of cigarettes with its round red label jerked and danced in Andy's hand in the dim light. Andy's match flared and he bent to his cupped hands, one eye squinted against the flame. He nodded once and breathed out smoke. The Mexican men stood silent, heads slightly bowed. Though I didn't see it then, I remember them as parishioners at mass. My father waited while Andy pinched the tip of his tongue, then held his hand down at his side and flicked his middle finger from his thumb like someone who had covertly picked his nose.

What came next embarrassed me then, though the memory of it does not. My father knelt to his sample case and took out the wide head of a sweeper broom and twirled it onto a long handle he'd leaned against a stack of boxes. He hefted the broom and smiled in pantomime just as I'd once seen a clown hold a broom and smile. He gave it a shake, popped the sweeper head flat against the handle, then folded it out again, his eyebrows moving up as if to say, "Folds flat for easy storage." Then he bent and swept, silent and solemn as Emmett Kelly. Magically, he swept a swath of concrete clean as fresh-poured. Done, he brushed his hands together and rested them on his hips.

My father clapped Andy on the shoulder. I followed them to the office, where a woman named Shirley was making a fresh pot of coffee.

"Don't suppose that red stuff'd work in here?" Andy said, and he tapped his work shoe on the stained linoleum office floor.

"Do a bear shit in the woods?" my father said. Then he said, "Pardon my French, Shirley." He and Andy grinned, and Shirley leaned close to me, laughing a minty laugh. She offered me a Coke and a stick of Juicy Fruit. She put her hands, warm, on my shoulders, her nails red, red against my shirt, and then stepped back, her arms curved bridges from her shoulders across to me, held me as if waiting for music so we could begin to dance. Standing close, breathing her powder and perfume and feeling her heat, was like standing close to a cotton-candy machine, sweet-smelling and bright, lightbulbs warming the glass box that holds the pink cloud of spun sugar. If I were rude to Shirley, I knew, I would disappoint my father and turn his praises of me into lies. Shirley sat on the edges of her desk and crossed and swung her legs. Her stockings tightened and her legs whispered, and I watched light wiggle up her shins to disappear beneath her dress. Beside Shirley's typewriter lay two work gloves—both right hands—palms up, fingers curled stiff, two rough brown hands waiting to be held.

"I guess I'll go on outside and wait in the car," I said.

"Here," he tossed me the keys. When I reached and caught them, he caught my arm, gave me a hard squeeze. "Might be something you want to listen to on the radio." He winked at me as if he had invented radio, dreamed it up and designed it to work in our car especially for me. The radio was always on. The tuning knob turned all the way in either direction but the red line stayed on the same station—news and weather on the hour and half-hour, sales pitches and hit tunes in between.

The morning we headed down our street to get shutters, it was not yet eight o'clock. On the car radio a man's voice was forecasting the weather: more of the same—hot and dry. Then the morning business report came on, talk about stocks and bonds, utilities, the commodities market, and then something called *trading in futures*.

"Hey," my father said. He stopped hard enough that I grabbed the door handle. "Want to skip school today? Play hooky, hang out with your old man?" His hand was on my thigh, thumb and fingers squeezing above my knee until he found that soft spot that gives an electric shock, your leg's funny bone.

"I've got a math test."

He nodded, but I knew he was thinking, "Better yet, skip school and get out of a test."

There was a haze over the pavement, heat waves already wiggling up. We were on the Poteet Highway. As we got closer to town, traffic got heavier, loud through our windows rolled down for air. A pickup pulled in front of us, and my father hit the brakes, pitching me against the dash. He shook his head, didn't say a word. The pickup, an old Dodge, had been hot rodded and had had a recent, do-it-yourself paint job, glossy black. The rear was jacked up and two chrome exhausts puffed blue smoke. My father leaned his head out, checking the highway ahead; he glanced at the rearview and pulled into the other lane. As we passed the truck, I saw where someone had painted a big, gold bumblebee on the side of the bed with paint that looked like the glittery gold ink my mother had used with a quill pen for signing our Christmas cards. Beneath the chubby bee was the hand-painted word: STINGER. The truck's driver turned and glared at us. A kid—he was just a kid. He couldn't have been much older than I was. I wondered if he had a license to drive.

As soon as we pulled back into the right lane, I heard a loud drone.

I looked behind us, but the Dodge wasn't there; it was passing us on the right, on the shoulder. Gravel pinged against our car and a sharp click left a tiny blue-green star on my side of the windshield.

"Goddamn," my father said, in the exact tone he'd say Yes Ma'am when my mother asked him to pick up a loaf of bread at the ice house, which is what convenience stores used to be called in San Antonio.

We went another mile, maybe less, and the road became four lanes. My father pulled alongside the truck. He turned to look at the driver but the kid stared straight ahead. His window was rolled all the way up, hot as it was, and I knew it didn't work. My father shook his head and smiled. "I hope you'll have better sense." He accelerated, and I was pressed back as the station wagon lunged ahead. The pesky black truck surged forward, too. "What're we up to here?" my father said. He slowed and the truck slowed. Then the truck began to speed up and slow down, speed up and slow down—a galloping horse, its black nose nodding as it rocked and bucked beside us. "Little bastard," my father whispered; he stared ahead with both hands on the wheel and looked as calm as a Sunday driver, except his knuckles were white.

The teen-ager driving the truck stared, his face frozen, his lips pulled back exposing his teeth. It was a face I knew from a movie, an astronaut, lift off, G-force. We were so close I saw the pearl snaps on the kid's short-sleeved cowboy shirt, so close I was sure I could reach out and wrap my fingers around his door handle, open the door a crack, reach inside and touch the smooth skin beneath his ear.

I saw a yellow warning sign; then I saw the kid see it, too. He hunched forward. More signs: Construction Ahead, Right Lane Ends. The pickup nosed ahead; then we caught up. The truck angled toward us; we didn't veer or slow up. The kid turned his head my way, his eyes wide. My father did not move. The kid opened his mouth, closed it again.

I do not know if my father saw the warnings, though I don't see how he could have missed them. The black truck strained ahead again and started to nose past us. My jaw was clinched and my right foot pressed the floorboard. I wasn't going to let him cut in. "Bastard," I said. I think the corner of my father's mouth twitched with the faintest hint of a smile. "Bastard," I said, louder; the word felt good coming out of my mouth. Then we were speeding up, too. The kid looked right at me, looked at me as if he knew me.

I have no idea how long all this took. People often describe split seconds of crisis in terms of slow motion or stop action. This was not that slow. This seemed like regular life at regular speed with me seeing and thinking a notch or two faster. I believe nothing was lost on me that morning. On our left was a Mobil station, the winged horse flying slow revolutions above the roof; on our right a Brahma bull (everyone I knew said Bray-mer) the color of caliche stood alone behind three strands of barbed wire. The bull raised his head, high as the hump between his shoulders, his pendulous dewlap swaying. Behind him, the field turned white where it met the horizon.

Ahead, the pavement went over a dry wash, and there was a new concrete abutment—the reason the lane was closed. All the kid had to do was slow down. He had time to pull onto the shoulder, to pull over and wait for a safe opening.

The black truck swerved off the highway the way one of the fighter planes that buzzed our house from Lackland or Kelly Air Force Base would tip a wing and veer out of formation. The truck's front fender struck four fence posts, one after the other, *ack-ack-ack-ack*—a fighter plane, mowing them down, snapping them off close to the ground. Steel whips, long strands of barbed wire coiled and uncoiled, popped like anti-aircraft guns.

The pickup bounced sideways and almost stalled—rear wheels spinning dust and smoke—then roared, wheels digging in, and shot back onto pavement. It smashed through a wooden barricade, and my anger congealed into fear, cold and hard as a block of ice. The truck bore down in a way that looked intentional and butted into concrete. The engine stopped, and I realized how loud it had been. By then we had gone past, over the wash. My father pulled onto the shoulder and we got out. We stepped across new concrete. Neither of us ran.

Other cars had stopped. The truck's engine snapped and clicked, hot metal cooling. Steam came out from under the hood, and something red spilled onto the pavement—blood, I thought, until I smelled antifreeze. The window glass was cracked—a 10,000-piece puzzle. A man ran up from an old Studebaker Champion, his plaid sport coat open, his red tie lolling like a tongue in the heat. The man jerked the door open, and glass pieces fell onto the seat and floorboard where they reflected the sun like diamonds. The door panel was missing and there was no window crank. A woman in a white sundress and sandals ran up, running slewfoot the way some women do, holding a quilt against her chest. She spread the quilt out beside the truck and helped the man lift the boy and ease him onto the quilt. In the field behind the boy's truck, the Brahma bull bucked up white clouds of dust and barbed wire twanged like a pedal steel guitar. Above the boy's head, the sun shone brightly on the painted bee, on the bright gold word STINGER. The sun also shone on the kids' dark hair that stuck up in points, fine as a baby's hair. Below his left shirtsleeve, above his elbow, two gashes looked deep, almost black blood oozing steadily out. The woman brushed small triangles and rectangles of glass off his arms and finger-painted him red from his elbows to his hands.

"Where do you hurt, son?" the man in the tie asked.

The kid's mouth twitched; his boy's eyes fluttered but didn't open. I already knew they were brown, like mine. I ran my eyes over him; there was no damage I could see but the cuts on his arm and a purple dent like a cleft in his chin. He was breathing hard, and pink, foamy spit came out onto his lips.

"They wouldn't let me in," he said, blowing bloody spit. "Damnit," his shoulders shook and tears streaked his cheeks, "they wouldn't let me in."

I don't think I've ever been as scared. I tried to bring my anger back, to force the fear away. You were wrong, I thought. My father was right. My father was in his lane; he obeyed the signs. Why didn't you slow down? I ached with hatred for that boy, and I ached with fear that he might die.

My father hadn't spoken. On the balls of his feet he leaned over the kneeling woman, who held the quilt against the boy's heaving chest. The boy's eyes jerked open as a doll's do when you snatch it up.

"They wouldn't let me in," he yelled. His injuries hadn't weakened his voice or his anger.

My father leaned his face out over the boy's open eyes, as if he were showing himself, seeing whether the boy knew him, whether the boy could pick him from a police line-up.

And then the police were there, the flashing red light of their squad car barely visible in the brightness of the morning. One policeman, a nameplate over his pocket read "R. Gonzales," squatted and told the boy an ambulance was on the way, while the other, "A. Hooks," used a long flashlight like a whisk broom and motioned people away. "Go on, folks, this isn't your business. Go on where you got to go. Clear the area."

My father nodded. I followed him to our car. We got in and he started the engine and we sat there listening to the steady clatter of what I knew must be a valve lifter sticking. He looked in his mirror and eased down the shoulder onto the road. Then he slowed and pulled off again. He turned off the engine. We'd gone about half a mile farther from the wreck, but he didn't back up. He opened the door and got out and started walking back. I caught up and we matched steps, our shoes slapping the pavement. An ambulance had arrived, and while we kept walking, it drove past us headed into town, siren wailing.

"It's me—I'm the one," my father told the policeman, A. Hooks, who'd shooed people away. "I'm the one he was talking about."

Hooks was writing on a clipboard. He didn't look up. "A one-vehicle accident. That's what we got here. Failure to observe warning signs. I've got all the witnesses I need."

The sun was bright behind my father's head, and his face was just a dark shape.

"Do you know where they took him?" he asked.

"Beats me. It was Suburban Ambulance Service. Ask them."

"Was he dead?" I asked.

Hooks lowered his clipboard and gave me a hard look. "I'm writing up one fatality on this report," he said. I looked at my father, whose face seemed to have gone white, though it may have been the sun. "That bull over yonder." The policeman pointed with his pencil. There, behind the downed fence posts, lay the Brahma bull, like an outcropping of limestone. "Barbed wire wrapped tighter'n hell around his neck, he went crazy trying to pull free. Tore himself up so bad he's lying there bleeding to death. Bastard'll be dead, time I find out who owns him."

The dying bull wasn't moving or making a sound. He looked like part of the natural landscape. My father and I turned and walked back to our station wagon. The only sounds were our steps on the gravel shoulder and two or three cars that blew past. Later, I thought I should have touched my father, squeezed his arm or punched it or put my hand in the small of his back or patted his shoulder the way I'd seen him pat the shoulder of a customer. If I'd thought about it at the time, I don't know if I would have done it, and if I had, I don't know if it would have made a difference. But I didn't think about it. I thought about the Brahma bull bleeding to death on the sun-bleached ground and tried to remember where I'd read that Brahmas had been brought to Texas from India because they could stand the heat. *If you can't stand the heat,* my father often said, *get out of the kitchen.*

What did we do next? We went on into town and picked up two sets of house shutters. While we were at the builder's supply, my father bought a three-eighths-inch power drill and a masonry bit, screws, and lead anchors. I missed homeroom and first period but got to school in time for my math test. My best stuff was history, literature, geography—classes like that. The test was plane geometry. I wrote a proof my teacher later read to the class and said he was going to save. I remember, I made an A.

When I got home from school, my father wasn't there. By four-thirty, when my mother got home from the library, he still wasn't home. She'd brought me four new books: *The Voice of the Coyote,* by J. Frank Dobie; *The Rise and Fall of Jessie James,* by Robertus Love; *All About the Weather,* by Ivan Ray Tannehill; and *Profiles in Courage,* by John F. Kennedy. I helped her cook supper and we talked. She asked me about my test and I said I thought I did fine. Then I told her we'd seen a wreck that morning. I said the boy in the pickup was driving too fast and went out of control.

"Was he hurt?" she asked.

"No. A little maybe. The police took care of everything. They took him off in an ambulance, but he wasn't hurt bad." I hoped I was telling the truth.

"An ambulance." She shook her head. "God grant strength to his mother," she said so softly I wasn't sure if she was speaking to me or whispering a prayer.

The station wagon pulled into the carport just as I was putting a bowl of black-eyed peas on the table. My father came into the kitchen and squeezed the back of my neck and kissed my mother's cheek.

When we sat down to eat, she asked him about the accident. He'd just put a bite of meat into his mouth. He sat still a moment and looked at me over his fork. For the first time all afternoon, I heard the steady motor of the refrigerator. He shook his head and chewed. Then he took a drink of iced tea.

"Told you about that, did he?" He smiled at me, not a good smile.

"He said the driver was about his age. He said you all saw it happen, saw them take him away in an ambulance."

"Ambulance," my father repeated. The refrigerator shuddered and stopped, the motor cycling. The kitchen was so quiet I heard an ice cube settle in my glass of tea.

"He wasn't really hurt," I said.

"He knocked down a fence and drove into a *concrete* bridge," she said, whispering the word concrete.

"Well," my father put a forkful of peas into his mouth and chewed, "there's not much more to report." He looked at me, but spoke to my mother. "I wouldn't worry about it."

She hunched her shoulders up as if she were chilled. "It's just the sort of thing I do worry about," she said. She touched my arm and looked me in the eyes, "I worry about something happening to *you*. I guess I'll worry till I die."

"I guess you will," my father said, and none of us talked the rest of the meal.

The following Sunday was Easter, and we all went to early worship. After Sunday school, my mother wanted to ride up into the hill country to see the wildflowers in bloom. We took Highway 281 north toward Blanco and turned off onto winding Ranch Road and saw bluebonnets and Indian paintbrush. We got back to town in time for a late lunch at Luby's Cafeteria. When we got home, my father and I put the shutters up. It was an easy job. My father said the new drill was *a real beaut*. He whistled while he worked, his song silenced by the whine of the drill, his lips pursed as if patiently offering a kiss. When we finished, we walked down to the street and looked back at the house, and he said, "You'll never miss this house, now, Son. Spot it a mile away. Find it in the dark."

The rest of the day, he holed up at the kitchen table figuring income taxes. My mother and I watched the Sunday afternoon TV movie, *The*

Man in the Iron Mask with Joan Bennett and Louis Hayward, who plays Louis XIV's twin brother, kept in an iron mask so no one will see his face. Then we read until dark. I started *The Rise and Fall of Jessie James*; she was reading a book by Ring Lardner called *The Love Nest and Other Stories*.

My mother and I ate supper on TV trays in the den so my father wouldn't have to move his stacks of bills and receipts. After supper she took him a cup of coffee and asked how it was going and he said not too good. The audience on Ed Sullivan laughed, and then my father said, "None of this adds up right." My mother said something back, though I couldn't make out her words. "Damned if I will," he said.

I went to the kitchen and got an apple, and he glared at me. His face was red and he shook his head. My mother twisted a cup towel between her hands. I bit into my apple and tried to think of something to say, some way to shift their attention, but he said they had things to discuss and would I please go back into the den. I closed the door behind me and stood there a minute, holding my apple up in the air, listening.

"Our income," my mother said, "doesn't live up to your ideas."

"For Christ's sake, Alice," he yelled, "the drill was marked-down. I got the shutters for nothing."

It was not the first time money talk had led to a fight between them and wouldn't be the last. I sat in front of the television and tried not to listen. My father got louder, then something banged—his fist against the table or my mother slamming a cabinet door. She came out of the kitchen and hurried through the den. She closed their bedroom door behind her, and the house was so quiet I turned down the TV. An hour later, my father came out of the kitchen and went back to the bedroom. Soon, my mother appeared in the gray light of the television, clutching sheets and a quilt.

She took the back cushions off the couch, and I helped her tuck a sheet over the seat cushions. The quilt was one my grandmother—my father's mother—made before she died. I have wondered since whether my mother was thinking about the quilt's pattern, a design of interlocking circles called "wedding ring." It was soft and clean and smelled of the cedar chest where my mother stored keepsakes.

A bed on a couch may be a discomfort to some, but is always inviting to me—a holiday night and out-of-town company, awake in the den with only the glowing light of the TV, the rest of the house quiet with sleep—cozy and special (like a secret, somehow). I think my mother felt that way, too, because she fixed hot chocolate, and we sat there on the bed we'd made so she could lie down in anger, and she smiled.

"I'm just cutting off my nose to spite my face," she said. "This is no punishment for your father. He's probably already sawing logs, spread out across our bed." She moved her hand over the quilt, palm down, around and around, following the tracks of stitches. She sipped from her cup, her eyes shiny from tears or from the heat coming up off the milk.

I drank my hot chocolate, hiding behind the cup.

"Nothing bothers him," she said. "As soon as his head hits the pillow, he's asleep. Clear conscience, I guess, but sometimes it makes me so mad." Her teeth bright blue in the television light, she smiled while she complained—as if my father's ability to sleep regardless of calamity were secretly prideful to her. "I wish I were more like him," she said. "I wish you were," she whispered.

She waited for me to say something, but I only nodded.

"I've already forgiven him," she said. "You want to sleep here tonight?"

"Sure," I said.

I lay there in the dark and watched the ten-o'clock news, watching as I had each evening since it happened, for a report of the wreck. There had been a shooting, a wife had discovered her husband with another woman. The wife stared at me from the television screen, shaking her head back and forth, *no, no,* and when two Bexar county deputies took her by the arms, her body went stiff and they had to carry her. Her husband, who was expected to recover, was shown lying on a stretcher, his body a white mound. As they slid him into an ambulance, he smiled and waved. After the weather report—continued heat and drought, no relief in sight—I turned the television off.

I'd searched the pages of the San Antonio *Light,* read all the stories printed since the accident. A smallish headline, EASTER MIRACLE, had caught my eye that morning: the music minister and the choir director of the Trinity Baptist Church, returning from a conference in Houston, had walked away with only scratches when their single-engine Cessna hit a power line and came down in a field of maize east of San Antonio.

The day the wreck happened, during lunch period at school I'd gone to the pay phone by the Coke machine and called the Suburban Ambulance Service; then, starting with the Medical and Surgical Memorial where I was born, phoned every hospital in the yellow pages. There was no record of an accident on the Poteet Highway. No news had to mean that the boy had not been seriously injured and that the death of one Brahma bull, even in unusual circumstances, did not warrant public notice.

For a while, I saw the cop in his dark uniform as a priest hearing my father's confession and absolving him with the sacrificial Brahma bull. Later, I realized I was seeking my own absolution. It seems to me, God gives us rules to keep, then sets us up to break them. I've wondered why: so we'll feel guilty? so we'll ask forgiveness? so we'll need Him? I've wondered if that boy did die but, somehow, it never got reported. I've wondered if he ever forgot the singing barbed wire and the impact of concrete and if he still drives recklessly. I've wondered how often, in the past thirty years, he's met a station wagon in traffic and looked for my father's face, for my face, behind the windshield.

I picture a man, old as I am, beside me at a light, both our engines idling. He's in a dented black pickup, a painted-gold bumblebee and STINGER no longer bright-shining but still visible on the truck's side. He turns, and the boy's face stares at me from behind a mask of middle-age.

I've wondered if the face of Louis XIV's twin brother, the face behind the iron mask, mirrored the slow, daily changes in the king's face. I recall looking down at my father's face in his casket. That face—fixed smile, tiny veins like cracks in a fleshy nose, hair gray where a stranger had brushed it back from the temples—is the face I now see staring back at me from my medicine-cabinet mirror. I've wondered about the sins of the father being visited upon the son, wondered what those sins might include.

What I finally decided is this: that moment in the bright sun on the side of the highway was not my father's moment—it was mine. Whatever would have made my father stay awake at night, as unable to sleep as I was lying under my grandmother's wedding-ring quilt, had happened to him long ago, if at all. I don't know whether he ever stared into a face with blood on its lips and hurt in its eyes and saw himself staring back. I know what losses I recognized when I looked into the wounded face of a boy still innocent enough not to slow down, still guiltless enough to be angry, not scared. What I saw was my own defiant face, the way I used to be, without shame, before that moment happened to me.

AFTERWORD

Time and the Tide in the Southern Short Story
Madison Smartt Bell

Perhaps since the War Between the States itself, and certainly since the literary Southern Renascence became conscious of itself in the thirties and forties, educated Southerners, and Southern writers especially, have taken their sense of history as a point of pride. Now, as the end of the century approaches, one may be tempted to wonder whether this pride has degenerated into mere vanity—declining from the deadliest of sins to a mere venal one. That special Southern historical sense may have become no more than a conventional piety of a style of Southern literary criticism which, as the novelist Madison Jones was heard to mutter in the audience of a critical panel five years ago, has long since passed "beyond refinement."

In any event, the deep sense of history is less likely to be associated with short Southern stories than with big Southern novels: Faulkner's Yoknapatawpha opus, Robert Penn Warren's excursions into the regional past, *Roots* even, or George Garrett's Elizabethan trilogy; those last two works carry a sharpened awareness of history into other regions altogether. Short stories, on the other hand, are not expected to express the long continuum from past into present, although they very well can, and sometimes still do.

The two surviving elders of the Southern short story, Eudora Welty and Peter Taylor, have moved in quite drastically different directions in their use of time in their work. In this narrow sense, Welty's stories appear to be more conventional, by contemporary standards. The span of time they typically seek to portray is brief: the day, the hour, the moment. Their effect is an immediate effect. Although there are powerful historical currents running through many of Welty's stories, their channels are mostly subterranean.

So it is with "The Hitch-Hikers," one of her best (each of her stories is one of her best). The traveling salesman Harris is a desperately dislocated man who can recognize his condition only by contrast to the two tramps he picks up in his car, whose language itself reflects a certainty of identity which Harris can in no way match: "I come down from the hills. . . . We had us owls for chickens and fox for yard dogs but we sung true."[1] After Harris stops for the night in a hotel, the two tramps quarrel over a scheme to make off with his car, and one of them kills the other by clubbing him with a bottle. What could it mean to a man like Harris? "In his room, Harris lay down on the bed without undressing or turning out the light. He was too tired to sleep. Half blinded by the unshaded bulb he stared at the bare plaster walls and the equally white surface of the mirror above the empty dresser. Presently he got up and turned on the ceiling fan, to create some motion and sound in the room. It was a defective fan which clicked with each revolution, on and on. He lay perfectly still beneath it, with his clothes on, unconsciously breathing in a rhythm related to the beat of the fan."[2]

One would hardly wish to be any nearer a moment than this. Of course it is a distinctly null moment. It is frozen, except for the clock-like sound and moment of the fan, which insists on the story's oppressive proximity to real time:

> He could forgive nothing in this evening. But it was too like other evenings, this town was too like other towns, for him to move out of this lying still clothed on the bed, even into comfort or despair. Even the rain—there was often rain, there was often a party, and there had been other violence not of his doing—other fights, not quite so pointless, but fights in his car; fights, unheralded confessions, sudden lovemaking—

---

1. Eudora Welty, *Collected Stories* (New York: Harcourt Brace Jovanovich, 1980) 64.

2. Ibid, 71.

none of any of this his, not his to keep, but belonging to the people of these towns he passed through, coming out of their rooted pasts and their mock rambles, coming out of their time. He himself had no time. He was free; helpless.[3]

This may be Welty's clearest image of a future which she foresaw a long time ago, and which we have now inherited. Once the man of the future (like Tate's George Posy), the deracinated Harris is now very much the man of the present. It is noteworthy that the eternal present which he inhabits is in the story's scheme of things a sort of hell on earth. In its very unity of effect, the story conveys a wholesale loss of history. Not all Welty's stories are about this kind of loss. But most of them do work within a very compact temporal period. This history which struggles so energetically to force itself upward into the present moment is implied more than it is stated, even in a story so rich with history as, for example, "Clytie."

The majority of Southern story writers have and still do follow a similar technical pattern—working very tightly to packets of real time. Flannery O'Connor certainly did so, for reasons probably more religious than aesthetic. Her stories reside in a perpetual state of eschatological apprehension—each moment is potentially that when the soul will be summoned to judgment. O'Connor's work is ahistorical, then, from the moment of its conception. Another, less dogmatic moral fabulist, George Garrett, also sticks close to clock and calendar in his short fiction, which is often complicated, however, by the presence of a ghostly voice which floats above the action and ranges more freely through larger chronologies than the action details. A younger generation of short-story writers has adopted these methods of managing time within strict limits, probably without question, for the most part.

In increasingly dramatic contrast to this general tendency is the work of Peter Taylor, who by moving in a different direction has discovered very different possibilities. Peter Taylor is quintessentially a story writer: his recent novel, A Summons to Memphis, is simply a longer and more detailed version of his old story "Dean of Men." As a story writer he has certain important abilities that scarcely anyone else

---

3. Ibid, 71.

in the South or anywhere else in America appears to possess or even desire.

Each of Taylor's stories has the potential of a novel. Many cover the amount of real time that a novel would address—a long novel too, a "saga." Taylor's gift is for engaging, convincing, compelling summary. He is able to make his stories account for the whole lives of their characters—and not through the flashbacks or the short bursts of background exposition that real-time stories conventionally employ. In reading a Taylor story, one seems to pass through the lives of the characters alongside them, so that when the present moment is reached, it is all the more potent with meaning. The short story is Taylor's ideal form because of his extraordinary ability to fuse a long chronology with some particularly revealing instant, as in his master-piece (one of them) "A Wife of Nashville":

> Helen Ruth put her hands on the handlebar of the teacart. She pushed the cart a little way over the tile floor but stopped when he repeated his question. It wasn't to answer the question that she stopped, however. "Oh, my dears!" she said, addressing her whole family. Then it was a long time before she said anything more. John R. and the three boys remained seated at the table, and while Helen Ruth gazed past them and toward the front window of the sun parlor, they sat silent and still, as though they were in a picture. What could she say to them, she kept asking herself. And each time she asked the question, she received for answer some different memory of seeming unrelated things out of the past twenty years of her life. These things presented themselves as answers to her question and each of them seemed satisfactory to her. But how little sense it would make to her husband and her grown sons, she reflected, if she should suddenly begin telling them about the long hours she had spent waiting in that apartment at the Vaux Hall while John R. was on the road for the Standard Candy Company, and in the same breath should tell them about how plainly she used to talk to Jane Blakemore and how Jane pretended the baby made her nervous and went back to Thornton. Or suppose she should abruptly remind John R. of how ill at ease the wives of his hunting friends used to make her feel and how she had later driven Sarah's worthless husband out of the yard, threatening to call a bluecoat. What if she should suddenly say that because a woman's husband hunts, there is no reason for *her* to hunt, any more than because a man's wife sews, there is reason for him to sew. She felt that she would be willing to say anything at all, no matter how cruel or absurd it was, if it would make them understand that everything that

happened in life only demonstrated in some way the lonesomeness that people felt. She was ready to tell them about sitting in the old nursery at Thornton and waiting for Carrie and Jane Blackemore to come out of the cabin in the yard. If it would make them see what she had been so long in learning to see, she would even talk about the "so much else" that had been missing from her life and that she had not been able to name, and about the foolish mysteries she had so nobly accepted upon her reconciliation with John R. To her, these things were all one now; they were her loneliness, the loneliness from which everybody, knowingly or unknowingly, suffered. But she knew that her husband and her sons did not recognize her loneliness or Jess McGehee's or their own.[4]

There could be no more convincing illustration of the old Southern literary touchstone—that the past inhabits the present and is alive within it. There is also almost no other Southern story writer capable of achieving such an effect, except for Elizabeth Spencer. Her latest collection, *Jack of Diamonds*, shows her adept at bringing twenty- or thirty-year blocks of familial history within the borders of a single story, like the extraordinary "Cousins"; however short such a story may be, the reader must feel that it has come a long, long way through time to reach its present.

Why this quality is now so rare among younger and newer Southern story writers is a mystery whose solution may be suggested by the probablity that the Southern writer's education now takes place not in splendidly romantic isolation but in some writers' workshop somewhere. Creative-writing instruction has been too carelessly demonized of late; good workshops do more good than harm, bad ones the reverse, but all workshops do tend to function as behavioral-training modules, where apprentice writers are in one way or another rewarded for success and punished for failure. The most basic success expected of them is verisimilitude, which is more easily gained by the novice through action and dialogue than through summary. Thus the trainee writer is apt to be discouraged from ever attempting to write the sort of brilliant summary at which Taylor and Elizabeth Spencer excel, although, as Andrew Lytle has observed, "fiction *is* a summary—summary of scenes leading up the the scene which you need."[5] The specifically scenic

4. Peter Taylor, *Collected Stories* (New York: Viking Penguin, 1986), 280.
5. *Chronicles*, September 1988.

quality of fiction, its real-time component, Lytle regards as a borrowing from theater. Nothing wrong with that method—Welty, O'Connor, and Garrett have written their finest stories in this mode—except that its limits are arbitrary.

There are still exceptions to this rule to be found—a few Southern story writers who have found some highly unusual ways of breaking the constraint of real time. R.H.W. Dillard, in long stories like "The Bog," "The Road," "The Death-eater," and "Omniphobia," has pretty well managed to smash the clock altogether with his signature blend of truly comic and truly frightening surrealism. In a somewhat similar vein, Cathryn Hankla and Fred Chappell have in their different ways used highly unusual techniques to encapsulate personal history. The title story of Hankla's first collection, *Learning the Mother Tongue*, ties the history of a childhood to the acquisition of language; in another, the narrator's life story is cunningly summarized by a parrot. In Chappell's *I Am One of You Forever*, stories that seem firmly grounded in a verisimilar here-and-now can suddenly, vastly enlarge their temporal scope by dextrous shifts into the fantastic:

> The tear on my mother's cheek got larger and larger. It detached from her face and became a shiny globe, widening outward like an inflating balloon. At first the tear floated in air between them, but as it expanded took my mother and father into itself. I saw them suspended, separate but beginning to drift slowly toward one another. Then my mother looked past my father's shoulder, looked through the bright skin of the tear, at me. The tear enlarged until at last it took me in too. It was warm and salt. As soon as I got used to the strange light inside the tear, I began to swim clumsily toward my parents.[6]

Dillard, Hankla, and Chappell are mavericks, uniquely innovative stylists who seem to come out of nowhere, but if any younger writer can write the profoundly historical story in the grand old manner, it is Richard Bausch in his latest collection, *The Fireman's Wife*. "Letter to the Lady of the House," which elegantly evokes the sweet and the sour of a five-decade-long marriage, might in its technique and its tone almost be a deliberate homage to Peter Taylor. In stories of a more contemporary feeling, "The Brace," "Equity," and the title story,

---

6. Fred Chappell, *I Am One of You Forever* (Baton Rouge: LSU Press, 1985), 6.

Bausch displays the different ways he's discovered for bringing a long history forward to the moment where it matters most.

And in that skill he is almost alone, at least in his generation. If the Southern short story is by and large losing its peculiar historical sense, then what is it that makes it peculiarly Southern? That question, academic or not, tends to come up in quarters where the old touchstones are fondled—asked by younger writers and critics like David Madden and Marc Stengel who seem to feel that the literature promoted under the Southern label is becoming increasingly remote from the realities of present-day Southern life. It's a subject that can hardly help but arise at a time when the South, demographically and culturally, is losing a great deal of its separateness. "Personally," says Richard Ford, "I think there is no such thing as Southern writing or Southern literature or Southern ethos. . . . What 'Southern writing' has always alibied for, of course, is *regional* writing—writing with an asterisk. The minor leagues."[7]

Ford, whose collection *Rock Springs* was certainly one of the most critically successful volumes of the last decade, seems to have largely succeeded in his effort to disassociate himself from what he conceives as the curse of regionalism. His wish to do so is roughly congruent with the nature of his work: to tell and retell the story of a drifter who begins in a state of total moral isolation. For the typical Ford protagonist, the deracination of Welty's Harris is carried to the nth degree, though the Ford character will make a more strenuous effort to invent his own rules for honorable living within that condition.

"And by Southern literature, what would we mean, anyway?" Ford asks. "Writing just by Southerners? Or just writing about the South? Could we also mean writing by people born in the South but living elsewhere? Or writing by people not born in the South but living there? . . . Would writing by Southerners on nonSouthern subjects also qualify?"[8] One need not share Ford's disparaging attitude toward "*regional* writing" to think these are all very good questions.

It's not only Southerners, now or ever, who know how to do the regional. But the new popularity of regional fiction, all over, provides

---

7. "A Stubborn Sense of Place," *Harper's*, August 1986.
8. Ibid.

a salutary counterbalance to the powerful waves of homogenization which keep sweeping the country again and again. There are always temptations for Southern writers to indulge in "mainstreaming," after the fashion of Bobbie Ann Mason's schooling herself to write rule-book *New Yorker* stories with a Southern flavoring. On the other hand, there are several other young women writers whose stories are authentically, intransigently rooted in their places. "Bypass" is a lovely example from Lisa Koger's first collection, *Farlanburg Stories*, a volume which braids the relentless modernization of Southern life with much of the old agrarian ethic. That's a trick also brought off by Alyson Hagy in *Madonna on Her Back*, though her toughest, strongest stories are those in the most traditional cast, like the classic "Mister Makes." That same admirable and dangerous stubbornness can be found in any story from Mary Hood's two collections, *And Venus Is Blue* and *How Far She Went*; indeed, there's something almost atavistic in her stories, heard sometimes as a spooky echo of the voice of Flannery O'Connor.

There are ironies too, which lie close to the surface of this renewed regionalism. The funny thing is that anyone can do it now, or anyone can try. Mary Hood, whose work is so unmistakably Southern, makes a point of mentioning she's half from the North: "I am like Laurie Lee's fabulous two-headed sheep, which could 'sing harmoniously in a double voice and cross-question itself for hours.' "[9] Native New Jerseyite Alan Cheuse shows what handy turns he can do on the Southern theme in his new colletion, *The Tennessee Waltz*. Moving in the opposite direction, Kelly Cherry shows in her recent "novel-in-stories" (*My Life and Doctor Joyce Brothers*) what ordinary Middle-American angst feels like when a transplanted Southern woman experiences it. Then there are new kinds of stories in the works based on new and extraordinary circumstances of Southern living—like Robert Olin Butler's story cycle about the Vietnamese communities of Louisiana.

Generally speaking, a certain sort of story of rural or small-town life is no longer exclusively Southern, if it ever was. Some of the themes once claimed as traditionally Southern have been reclaimed in recent work by Carolyn Chute and Robert Olmstead. And by John Dufresne, whose first collection, *The Way That Water Enters Stone*, is in spite of

---

9. Ibid.

the unfortunate title one of the finest of the year. Dufresne, wherever he is from, can do Southern and New England voices with equal conviction. It becomes less place than issue that matters, and all over the new regional story writing appear the survivors who have washed up into backwaters of the cultural mainstream which would smother them with its bland indifference. They have their common characteristics, Southern or not: an anger, a stubbornness, an indomitable individualism, and (how one comes back to it) a tragically gorgeous weakness for the sin of pride.

One of the truisms of Southern literature is that its power comes from a radical sense of displacement—the state of being in the nation, but not of it. Because they are not shareholders in the American dream, this argument goes, Southern writers are better able to distinguish the ideal from the reality—a situation which has always been shared (uneasily) by American black and Jewish writers. If the lines of regional and ethnic writing are less clearly drawn than previously, the reason may be that American political life is now able to offer a strong dose of disillusionment, disenfranchisement even, to *all* Americans. It's funny, in a bitter way, how what is so bad for a nation can often be so good for its art.

CONTRIBUTORS

Richard Bausch is author of five novels, most recently *Violence* (1992), and two collections of short stories—*Spirits* (1987) and *The Fireman's Wife* (1990). He has twice been nominated for the PEN/Faulkner Award and has received the Hillsdale Prize for Fiction from the Fellowship of Southern Writers. He teaches at George Mason University.

Madison Smartt Bell comes from a farm near Nashville. He studied at Princeton and Hollins College, lived and worked (for a time) in New York City as a security guard for Unique Clothing Warehouse and as a sound technician for *Radio-Televisione Italiana*. At age thirty-five he has already published six novels and two collections of stories. Forthcoming is a novel—*Save Me, Joe Louis*. He is married to the poet Elizabeth Spires, and they both teach at Goucher College.

Robert Brickhouse is a graduate of Washington and Lee University and earned his M.F.A. at Virginia. He has published in a variety of literary magazines and has won Artemis Awards in both poetry and fiction. Formerly proprietor of a country general store, he now works for the Information Office of the University of Virginia.

Larry Brown, a native of Oxford, Mississippi, and a former fireman who now writes full-time, is the author of two novels, *Dirty Work* and *Joe*, and two collections of stories, *Facing the Music* and *Big Bad Love*, all published by Algonquin. He lives with his family at Yocona, Mississippi.

Fred Chappell is the author of more than twenty books—novels, poetry, collections of stories. His latest is *More Shapes Than One* (St. Martin's Press). He has taught for many years at the University of North Carolina at Greensboro.

Kelly Cherry, a former student of Fred Chappell at Greensboro, has published widely with her fiction, poetry, and non-fiction. She is author of nine books, including, most recently, *The Exiled Heart* (LSU Press). She is Professor of English at the University of Wisconsin.

Alan Cheuse is the author of three novels—*The Bohemians, The Grandmother's Club,* and, published in 1990, *The Light Possessed.* His most recent collection of stories is *The Tennessee Waltz.* He has also published a memoir, *Fall Out of Heaven.* Cheuse has taught at Tennessee, Sewanee, and the University of Houston, and is now on the faculty of George Mason University. He is really an honorary Southerner.

R. H. W. Dillard has taught for more than twenty years at Hollins College and has directed its celebrated writing program since 1971. He has published critical works and edited several anthologies. His novels are *The Book of Changes* and *The First Man on the Sun.* His short fiction has been widely published and has won a number of awards. He was co-author of the screenplay for *Frankenstein Meets the Space Monster.*

Ellen Douglas is a native Mississippian and now teaches at the University of Mississippi. She is a member of the Fellowship of Southern Writers and has written several novels, the most recent of which is *Can't Quit You, Baby.*

Lolis Eric Elie comes from New Orleans and is a professional musician as well as a writer. He received his M.F.A. from the University of Virginia, where he served on the staff of *Callaloo* magazine. Most recently he has been on tour in Europe with fellow New Orleans musician Wynton Marsalis.

Percival Everett comes from South Carolina and teaches at Notre Dame. He is the author of six books, including, recently, the novels *Zulus* and *For Her Dark Skin.*

Ben Greer, a native up-country South Carolinian, teaches at the University of South Carolina. He is a graduate of that institution and of the Hollins College Creative Writing Program. He is the author of four well-received novels, most recently *Loss of Heaven.*

Alyson Hagy comes from Rocky Mount in southwest Virginia. A graduate of Williams College with an M.F.A. from the University of Michigan, she has taught at the Universities of Virginia and Michigan and now lives in Ann Arbor. She is the author of two collections of stories, *Madonna on Her Back* and *Hardware River.*

Cathryn Hankla, who teaches at Hollins College, is author of a novel, *Blue Moon at Poor Water;* a collection of short stories, *Learning the Mothern Tongue;* and two books of poetry, *Phenomena* and *Afterimages.* She is also a photographer and filmmaker.

William Harrison comes from Texas and teaches at the University of Arkansas. He has written several novels—*The Theologian, In a Wild Sanctuary, Lessons in Paradise, Africana, Savannah Blue,* and *Burton and Speke*—as well as the screenplays for a number of feature films. His collection of short stories is *Rollerball Murder.*

Madison Jones enjoys an earned reputation as one of the major figures in modern Southern letters. He has published eight books—most recently, *Last Things* (1988). Retired to his Alabama farm now, he taught at Auburn University, beginning in 1956.

Beverly Lowry is the author of five novels, two of which—*Daddy's Girl* and *The Perfect Sonya*—have received the Texas Institute of Letters Award. Her stories have appeared in, among other places, *Playgirl, Redbook, Southwest Review,* and *The Texas Humanist.* A native of Memphis, she now lives in San Marcos, Texas.

David Madden is the author of seven novels and a number of textbooks, as well as the editor of several anthologies. His most recent collection of short fiction is *The New Orleans of Possibilities.* He has long been on the faculty of Louisiana State University.

Jill McCorkle comes from Lumberton, North Carolina, and now lives with her family in Durham and teaches at the University of North Carolina at Chapel Hill. She has published four novels with Algonquin Books. Her latest work is a collection of stories, *Crash Diet* (1992).

Bobbie Ann Mason began her literary career with two critical works— *Nabokov's Garden* (1971) and *The Girl Sleuth* (1976). Since the appearance of *Shiloh and Other Stories* (1982), she has published novels and story collections, including, most recently, *Love Life* (1989). She was winner of the PEN/ Hemingway Award for First Fiction in 1982.

Heather Ross Miller of North Carolina is both poet and fiction writer. She has taught at the University of Arkansas and at Washington and Lee University. Her most recent book is *Hard Evidence* (University of Missouri Press).

William Mills is author of three collections of poetry—*Watch for the Fox, Stained Glass,* and *The Meaning of Coyotes*—and a book of short stories, *I Know* *a Place.* He has also published a critical study of the poet Howard Nemerov, *The Stillness of Moving Things.* A native of Mississippi, Mills lives near Columbia, Missouri.

William Peden has served as an editor, critic, scholar, and defender and protector of the American short story for more than half a century. In addition to important critical studies, he has published a novel, *Twilight at Monticello,* and a number of story collections, the latest being *Fragments & Fictions* (1990).

Clay Reynolds teaches at the University of North Texas in Denton. His novels include *The Vigil, Agatite,* and *Franklin's Crossing.* His short stories have appeared widely in the literary magazines.

Mary Lee Settle produced the first of her twelve (so far) novels, *The Love Eaters,* in 1954. She is also author of five books of non-fiction and many newspaper and magazine pieces. She received the National Book Award for *Blood Tie* (1977).

Eve Shelnutt, who teaches at Ohio University, was born in Spartanburg, South Carolina. *The Musician* (1987) was her third collection of short fiction. She has published highly regarded work on creative writing and has edited a number of anthologies, the newest of which is *The Confidence Woman: 26 Women Writers at Work* (1991).

Darcey Steinke was a student of Madison Smartt Bell at Goucher College and later studied in the Creative Writing Program at the University of Virginia. Her two novels are *Up Through the Water* (chosen by the editors of the *New York Times Book Review* as one of the "Notable Books" of 1989) and *Suicide Blonde* (1992).

Dabney Stuart is editor of *Shenandoah* magazine and teaches at Washington and Lee University. He is the author of nine books of poems; a collection of short stories, *Sweet Lucy Wine* (1992); and a critical study, *Nabokov* (1978).

Anita Thompson studied with R. H. W. Dillard (and others) at Hollins College. Her fiction and poetry have appeared in literary magazines as well as anthologies, including *Contemporary Southern Short Fiction* and *Elvis in Oz.*

Tom Whalen has published poems, stories, translations, book reviews, and criticism. His most recent collection of stories is *Elongated Figures* (1991). He lives in New Orleans and teaches at Loyola University and at the New Orleans Center for the Creative Arts.

Allen Wier was born in Blanco, Texas; educated at Baylor, L.S.U., and Bowling Green; and now lives in Tuscaloosa, where he directs the Creative Writing Program at the University of Alabama. He is the author of three novels and a collection of stories, *Things About To Disappear*.